KERRY WILKINSON

NOTHING BUT TROUBLE

PAN BOOKS

First published 2017 by Pan Books
an imprint of Pan Macmillan
20 New Wharf Road, London N1 9RR
Associated companies throughout the world
www.panmacmillan.com

ISBN 978-1-4472-8544-1

1 3 5 7 9 8 6 4 2

A CIP catalogue record for this book is available from the British Library.

Typeset by Ellipsis Digital Limited, Glasgow
Printed and bound by CPI Group (UK) Ltd, Croydon, CR0 4YY

PROLOGUE

Spencer O'Brien was fighting a losing battle with the duvet. His bed was built into an alcove of the wall, the covers tightly tucked underneath the mattress on either side. He kicked his legs and flapped his elbows in a vicious battle of good versus evil, light versus darkness, man versus cotton blend. Man was ultimately victorious, wrenching out the covers and spinning into a sitting position.

He checked his phone for the time – ten past midnight – then sat unmoving, listening, sure he'd heard something outside. It wasn't unusual: he was staying in his dad's house on the end of a terrace not far from Manchester city centre. There was usually a low hum of traffic and frequently the early-morning cackle of someone on their way home after a night on the lash. It hadn't sounded like that, though, it was more like a scraping . . . as if someone was trying to get in.

Spencer reached underneath the bed and put on his slippers. There had been three apparent break-ins at his father's house in the past month. Nothing had been taken but his dad was scared, turning the fear into anger that the police were seemingly 'doing nothing'. Spencer was a twenty-five-year-old man who had – temporarily – moved back in with his dad, sleeping in his childhood bedroom, all because he couldn't bear the thought of his father being frightened and alone. His dad might be a Falklands veteran but that didn't stop him being petrified, even if he never said it.

Whatever Spencer had heard was no longer there, replaced by the rattle of the window and banging of the ancient pipes running across the attic. That was the problem with an old place like this: an intruder could have smashed the windows and stolen everything as everyone upstairs slept peacefully, completely accustomed to the house's natural clanks and clangs.

Spencer thought about wedging himself back under the covers but had never been good at getting back to sleep once he'd woken up. He also still had the headache that he'd gone to bed early with, a steady throb that felt like it was trying to push his eyes out. It crossed his mind that it could be carbon monoxide poisoning, but then he was paranoid about the state of the house. It was falling apart in all senses – which was why developers wanted to knock it down and start again.

He'd just lifted his feet out of his slippers when . . . Spencer heard another thump. His bedroom was directly above the rear door, through which the intruders seemed to be entering. He slipped across to the window, wrestling the curtain and peering into the dark mess of a back yard. He squinted towards the shadows but the moon was shrouded by cloud, making it almost impossible to see anything other than a sliver of light from the back door, creeping into a triangle across the uneven paving slabs.

Why would the light be on? And why would the back door be slightly open? It would almost be inviting someone to break in . . .

BANG!

Spencer jumped as the booming thunder of a shotgun rocked the house. He froze for a moment, knowing exactly what had happened but not wanting to believe it. His dad had been threatening this for days. If the police weren't going to do something about the wave of intruders, the invaders, the burglars that so scared him, then he would. Surely he couldn't have done it? Not this . . .

He took the stairs two at a time, hurdling the lower banister until he reached the kitchen, barely able to take in the sight that greeted him. The back door was open, the handle attached to a thin length of rope that looped over the door and across the ceiling until it dropped down, where it had been wound around the trigger of a shotgun that was tied to a dining chair. His father must have rigged the trap after Spencer went to bed early.

There was a thick spray of crimson across the back of the kitchen, blood clinging to the work surfaces and cupboard doors.

Oh, no. No, no, no, no.

Spencer crept forward, stepping around the chair and the gun until he could see the body. It was a woman who'd been blasted backwards, a bloody circular shape in the centre of her chest. Her head was resting to the side, long dark blonde hair curving around her cheeks and already matting with blood. He didn't need to check to know that she was dead. Nobody got up from this, not even in the movies.

He turned at the sound of a cry, seeing his father in the kitchen doorway. His father was in his seventies, wiry white hair darting off in all directions, stripy white and red pyjamas pure Marks and Sparks. He'd once been a proud man but his mind was slipping.

'Dad . . . what did you do?'

Niall O'Brien stared from his son to the dead woman, mouth wide. 'I . . . didn't mean . . .'

'Where'd the gun come from?'

'Is she . . . ?'

'Of course she's dead!'

Spencer's raised voice made his father shrink away, stepping back into the hallway, covering his eyes and starting to cry. His footsteps disappeared up the stairs, with Spencer wanting to follow but knowing he had to do something else first.

When the 999 call handler answered, Spencer momentarily thought about asking for the ambulance before the horror hit him once more. He didn't want to look at the body but he couldn't avoid it. He'd never seen a dead person before, let alone someone like this, blown to bits. The poor woman. Was she really a burglar? Or just someone intrigued by the open back door and the light? This was so, so bad . . . his father hadn't just rigged a lethal trap, he'd left the door open and invited intruders.

It felt as if he was on autopilot as Spencer gave his name and the address before the call handler asked for specifics. He turned back to the body, voice quivering.

'There's a woman at our house . . . she's been shot,' he said.

'Is there any immediate danger?'

'No, it's . . . complicated.'

'Can you see if she's breathing?'

'She's definitely not.'

'Is she someone known to you?'

Spencer stared at the body, about to say 'no' when it dawned on him that she seemed horribly familiar. She'd been wearing a suit when he saw her before but now she was in jeans and a jacket.

He gasped a reply, crumpling to his knees. 'Oh, no.'

'Spencer?'

'She's a police officer,' he stumbled. 'She was here the other week.'

There was a short pause before the handler replied. She sounded unsteady herself. Shocked. 'To confirm, you're saying that a police officer has been shot at your house?'

'She's some sort of detective . . . she came round because there's been a bunch of break-ins at my dad's house. There's something that's come out of her pocket, an ID card – it's right here.'

'Mr O'Brien, you shouldn't—'

'I can see it from where I am. There's blood all over it but her name's clear. It's Detective Inspector Jessica Daniel.'

1

THREE WEEKS PREVIOUSLY

Phoebe drummed her fingers on the steering wheel, enjoying the sunshine on the back of her knuckles. It was officially summer. Well, not *officially*, but the sun was out and Manchester was bathing in its wondrous glow. That was as good as declaring it was summer, even if it only lasted for the morning.

She squinted into the distance, wondering why nobody ever did anything about the state of the traffic heading into the city every morning. There were traffic lights everywhere, as if the council were paid according to how many times the damned things blinked red. Somewhere ahead, a car horn beeped, then another and another, vehicles communicating via the medium of a high-pitched bleating.

It wasn't doing Phoebe's dull headache any good.

She pulled down the sun visor, shielding her gaze from the glare off the car ahead and closed her eyes. On the radio, the track changed to something upbeat: something that brought back memories of dancing on Friday night. It was by someone who had a single letter as one of their names – like Jay Z but not as good. Dave G, or something? There was definitely a G in there. Gav P? No, that was ridiculous.

Phoebe's eyes jumped open, the seatbelt clamping against

her breastbone as the ringtone blared through the Blue-tooth headset welded to her ear. Instinctively, she touched the earpiece, expecting somebody to start moaning about the delivery of a printer or something similar. It was a Monday, for crying out loud, why couldn't people leave her alone?

'Phoebe Davies,' she said, trying to sound upbeat, 'how can I help you?'

There was a snigger and then a female voice replied: 'Is that how you always answer your phone?'

Phoebe laughed, easing the car into first and creeping along a few vehicle lengths until she reached a halt again.

'I didn't think you'd make it out of bed today,' she said. The last time she'd seen her friend Imogen was the previous day, passed out on another mate's sofa. The combination of the sun, barbecue and booze hadn't done any of them any good.

'Uggggghhhhh . . . me neither,' Imogen replied. 'How's your head?'

'Not happy – plus it's sunny and I've got to work. There's an audit today.'

'Yuck.'

'I thought there were laws about this sort of thing? What's the point in the European convention on human rights if it doesn't include having a day off when the sun's out?'

Imogen wasn't listening. She smacked her lips together and Phoebe could tell she was grinning. 'You'll never guess who Nicola went home with after you left yesterday.'

'Who?'

7

'Guess.'

'Not Leo . . . ?'

'Aww, yuck. Course not. No one's ever gone home with him. It was Dylan.'

Phoebe was about to reply when the car behind beeped its horn. She realised the traffic was moving, though she wasn't.

'Hang on.'

She yanked the gearstick into first and bunny-hopped forward, engine growling in protest. All too soon, the lights flickered back to red as she came to a halt at a four-way junction. She glanced in her rear-view mirror to see the man in the red van behind waving his arms around, calling her a list of names that she didn't need to be a lip-reading expert to understand.

BEEEEEEEEEEEEP!

'All right, piss off.'

Imogen's voice echoed from the tinny speaker. 'Me?'

'Not you, some bloke behind me is having a heart attack. Anyway, *Nicola* went home with *Dylan?*'

The traffic started to filter across the junction, weaving around as cars turned onto the main road, heading into, or away from, the city centre. Phoebe glanced in her mirror again, where red van man was still fuming. She could see a vein bulging around his eye.

'Yeah, so Dylan was, like, totally trying it on with her. You know what he's like – top button undone and those really tight shorts. Anyway, Nicola'd had four Bacardi Breezers and you could tell she was up for it. One minute, she was sitting on the lounger in the garden, the next she'd disappeared. Ollie reckoned he heard noises coming from the spare bedroom but he's always exaggerating. Next thing you know, Nicola's saying goodbye, then Dylan's offering her a lift home – as if none of us knew what was going on! You'll never guess what happened next.'

Phoebe opened her mouth to reply but the words never came out. There was a squeal of wheels from in front. A prison van was waiting in the yellow criss-cross area of the junction, indicating towards the city centre. As it inched forward, a grubby white van accelerated from the opposite direction, lurching one way and then wheel-spinning side-ways at the last moment.

BOOOOOOOOOOOOOOOOOM!

The front of the white van slammed into the cabin of the prison van, making it slide, wobble as if it was going to topple over, and then settle back onto all four wheels.

Phoebe yelped, not realising the sound was her until she heard Imogen in her ear, asking what was wrong.

There was a rush of grey from the front seats of the white van – airbags – and then the doors sprung open. There were two men in jeans and trainers with hooded tops and bala-clavas. One was in black, the other blue. Each had a sawn-off shotgun pointed at the cabin of the prison van. The person in black angled the weapon to the sky and pulled the trig-ger. The bang was so loud that Phoebe jumped, unclipping her seatbelt and diving sideways so she was spread across the passenger seat, out of sight. The gearstick dug into her ribs as she heard a man's voice.

'*Out!*'

She peeped over the dashboard, where a man in a uni-form was climbing out of the prison van, arms in the air.

'Phoebes?'

Phoebe tapped her ear, ending the call and then plucked off the headset, dropping it on the driver's seat. She was trying to watch what was going on, while remaining unseen.

The first man getting out of the prison van had been joined by a second. Black hoody was aiming his shotgun towards the pair, as blue hoody grabbed something shiny from them and hurried to the back of the van. There was more shouting and then another bang. Phoebe could see other drivers in their cars, watching, not daring to intervene. She risked a quick glance behind, where the man in the red van was on his mobile. As she wondered if she should've called the police, sirens sounded in the distance. Black hoody heard them too, glancing towards the city centre and raising himself onto tiptoes. He shouted something towards his mate, who was edging sideways to peer around the two officers. They were on their knees, hands on heads, staring at the tarmac.

BANG!

Another gunshot and then black hoody ran to the back of the prison van, shouting something Phoebe couldn't make out. Moments later, the two hoodies dashed across the junction with two men in suits a little behind. The four of them disappeared behind a hedgerow at full pelt, not looking back as the blare of the sirens melded into a deafening chorus.

2

The tea machine in the canteen of Longsight Police Station snapped, crackled and popped its greeting, showing a flagrant disregard for a certain breakfast cereal company's copyright on those particular noises. That done, it croaked, wheezed, made a grinding noise, and then launched into something that sounded like someone with laryngitis trying to blow their nose. Eventually, when it had finished angling for attention, it spat out a tan plastic cup that was foaming with what was hopefully milk. Detective Inspector Jessica Daniel plucked it from the holder, sniffed the liquid, grimaced, and then crossed to the table. She leant back into the cold plastic chair and fought a brave, though ultimately losing, battle against a yawn.

'Aren't you going to get me one?' Detective Constable Dave Rowlands asked.

Jessica nodded towards the machine. 'Don't your legs work?'

'But you were already there.'

'When was the last time you bought me something?'

'Friday – that Dairy Milk in the offy, then a glass of wine in the Wounded Duck.'

Jessica rolled her eyes back into her head. What day was it again? She vaguely remembered the Friday – sitting in the hallway of the magistrates' court, only for the defendant to plead guilty at the last minute. She mooched around the shops afterwards, blamed the buses for taking her time to get back to the station, and then met her colleagues and mates, Dave Rowlands, Izzy Diamond and Archie Davey, around the corner for a swift few halves before nicking home.

On Saturday, she'd hammered through the midget-sized pile of paperwork she'd not managed to palm off onto someone else, then accidentally got stuck in the traffic from a football friendly on the way home. Schoolgirl error. Basics.

On Sunday, she'd . . . hmm . . . think . . . gone to the city centre with Bex, and then they'd spent the day in the park reading and marvelling at the blue skies and hazy ball of warmth. A rare day off when it hadn't lashed it down. Summer was here!

That meant today must be Monday. Whew, on the wrong side of thirty-five, it was a relief knowing which day of the week it was without checking.

Jessica dug into her jacket pocket, spilling a metallic clatter of coins onto the table. 'Knock yourself out,' she said, nodding at the machine.

Rowlands hunted through the shrapnel, clearing out the rest of the coppers Jessica had been trying to get rid of since the mardy cow in the post office had dumped it on her the previous week.

'You're too generous for your own good,' he said.

He scuttled past her towards the machine, smelling of the same hair gel as when she'd first met him too many years previously. Any man over the age of thirty-five with spiky hair had some serious questions to ask of himself. For the most part, Rowlands had calmed down in recent years, but those bloody spikes remained, like a baby hedgehog welded to the top of his head.

More yawning.

The tea tasted as bad as ever, most likely made with the kind of browny-grey sludge water that was usually stuck to the nation's draining boards.

Dave flopped back into the chair opposite, sipping what the machine laughably called a 'latte'.

He nodded towards the main doors. 'Aren't you supposed to be interviewing that lad from this morning?'

Jessica shrugged. 'He's not going anywhere. Besides, his solicitor's that flash twat with the BMW. The air-con downstairs is on the blink again and it's steaming in the solicitor's room. I've heard he loves the odd trip to those "saunas" out Eccles way' – bunny ears – 'so I'm sure he won't mind waiting.'

'You just don't like BMW drivers, do you?'

'Who does?'

Rowlands paused to think. 'Good point.'

More tea, another yawn.

'You off to see Niall O'Brien today?' Rowlands asked.

'I'm supposed to be but with everything else, it might end up being tomorrow. I've already been out once.'

'Doesn't he live on his own? What's he like? Nutter?'

Jessica thought of the old man living on the abandoned terrace, unwilling to sell to the housing developers. 'I dunno . . .' she replied. 'I feel sorry for the bloke.'

The smell of soggy fried potatoes was drifting invitingly from the canteen counter, a cholesterol-spreading siren luring its prey with the promise of a satisfying encounter, only to leave its victims with dysentery.

'I might get something to eat,' Rowlands said, turning.

'You're not still on the salads, are you?'

He patted his stomach. 'I'm a picture of health and fitness.'

'Maybe a Picasso.'

Rowlands turned back. 'I don't understand what your problem is.'

'Think of every story you've ever been told – anecdotes, encounters – anything remotely funny. Has any great tale in the history of mankind ever started with, "We went out for salad and . . ."?'

'What's your point?'

'That you've been a right boring sod since you started on whatever diet it is that you're on. I don't want to know how many calories are in a glass of wine – only a fun-hating bastard would even bother to add it up.'

Rowlands pointed a thumb towards the door, where Detective Chief Inspector Lewis Topper was standing with a hand on his hip. He looked suspiciously young for a DCI: all dark hair and athletic, no hints of grey. No Ordnance Survey map of wrinkles. It was sickening. His nervous breakdown was at least a decade away.

Jessica downed her tea, fighting the gag reflex. Time to get to work.

Walking from one area of Longsight Police Station to another was like moving from the Arctic to the tropics. In the cells and the solicitors' area in the basement, they were in the midst of a sultry Amazonian summer, with treacle-like humidity and sweltering temperatures. On the upper floor, where DCI Topper's office was, it was a cool, comfortable Spanish autumn: fit for shirt sleeves, linen pants, sangria in the evenings, and an afternoon siesta. On the central floor, on which lay Jessica's office, the canteen, the entrance and the interview rooms, the air-conditioning was turned up to the maximum, sending a glacial blast of Russian winter along the corridors. Someone had rigged up a heater in the corner of the interview room, which was paddling a gentle warming breeze that wasn't making much difference.

BMW-man had something green between his teeth. It was definitely something leafy, the sort of psychotic breakfast only a solicitor could eat. He'd probably blended some sort of super-veg protein shake before clambering into his too-clean German car and racing across the city when he'd heard the news. Jessica eyed him with as much disdain as she could muster, which wasn't much nowadays. Age was mellowing her. The bastard.

The client of BMW-man looked as if he'd never seen anything leafy in his life: a scrawny, runty waste of existence, whose name Jessica knew only too well. She shifted her attention to him, taking in the speckled growth on his chin that could loosely be described as stubble. His hair was a greying mess, eyes darting from one side of the interview room to the other.

'You all right, Carl?' Jessica asked.

Carl Frosham nodded quickly, swallowing and reaching for the glass of water on the table. Jessica wondered if the constable had fetched it from a toilet bowl in the men's, or if he'd gone to the water fountain. She hoped the former. Frosham's hand shook as he sipped the liquid, sloshing a little onto the floor.

'Just a bit jumpy,' he replied.

'Probably not as jumpy as that newsagent when you held a knife to his neck and threatened to rape his twelve-year-old son in front of him.'

Frosham sputtered a spray of water down his chin onto the table.

'Inspect—'

Jessica cut off the solicitor with a wave of her hand. She could feel DCI Topper watching her through the video feed, telling her telepathically that was the one he'd let go. The only one.

She held Frosham's eye: 'So . . . why didn't you run?'

He continued to shuffle nervously, inspecting his grubby fingernails to go alongside his grubbier mind. He scratched his chin, staring past Jessica towards the door and potential freedom beyond. Well, if he could get past the team of crack police officers who worked at Longsight. And Fat Pat on the front desk. Jessica could sense him thinking that he should have made a break for it after all.

His voice was high-pitched and squirrelly, as if one of his testicles were in a gradually tightening vice. It was the type of thing he'd probably enjoy.

'I'm in enough trouble, ain't I?' Frosham said.

'You've got that right. What happened?'

Frosham peered sideways at his solicitor, who remained unmoved. 'Am I gonna . . . ?'

Jessica glanced between the men, knowing the prisoner would've already been told this. 'You're not going to get credit for staying in a prison van when it's been rammed by another vehicle. The fact you're incarcerated in the first place should give you a clue that you're going to be punished. That said, if you're *really* helpful, I might be able to rustle up a Yorkie before we send you back – but I'm not promising. It depends what mood the vending machine's in.'

'Right . . .'

Jessica looked at the solicitor, wondering if he was going to help. The answer was a clear, uninterested, wordless 'no'.

'I'm not asking for a kidney,' Jessica added. 'You were in the van, on the way to court for sentencing, when another vehicle crashed into it. What happened?'

Frosham glanced at the camera again, then his solicitor, and then, finally, Jessica.

'There was a big bang,' he said, presumably referring to the incident, not starting a debate over evolution versus the Bible.

'Go on . . .'

'That's pretty much it. One minute we're bumping along – those vans are bloody uncomfortable. You should do something about it.'

Jessica underlined the words 'toilet water' on her pad. 'I'll get right on it.'

Frosham nodded. 'The next minute, everything's spinning and some bloke's outside, shouting for us to get away from the door—'

'What did he sound like? Local?'

'I dunno. Kinda normal. Anyway, there's another bang and then the doors fly open. There's this guy in a baklava and he's got the keys for the cages. He opened them all and then the other two ran for it.'

Jessica presumed the attackers weren't wearing pastry-related desserts, so let the slip go.

'Did he say anything?' she asked.

'Only "stand back" when the doors were closed, but we were in cages anyway.'

'What about the other prisoners?'

'Nobody was saying anything.'

Jessica opened the file in front of her, held up a photograph. 'Owen Priestley – a friendly chap, though you probably wouldn't introduce him to your daughter. He robbed an off-licence with a sawn-off. When the till got stuck, he used the butt to beat the owner into intensive care. Despite a splash of his blood being at the scene, he pleaded not guilty.'

She looked up, catching Frosham's eye – he was another not-guilty merchant. Some people couldn't help themselves, enjoying the farce of the trial, hearing the details repeated over and over. They were going down anyway, so might as well get some sport from it. Frosham didn't take the bait.

'Nine months back,' she continued, 'Priestley slashed someone across the face while in prison. No one knows where he got the knife. He was on his way back to court today to have his sentence increased. Do you know him?'

Frosham shook his head.

'Sure?'

'I've read about him, like. We're on different wings.'

Jessica nodded. Of course they were – people like Frosham weren't allowed to mix with the rest of the prisoners, else they'd get more than a knife slash across the face.

'What about our second guy?' she asked. 'Kevin Jones has a long string of minor-ish crimes, ending with a robbery last year.' She glanced up again. 'He's what we call "a little shite". He was on his way to court to hopefully be sent down for four or five years. Know him?'

A shake of the head.

'And you're sure that neither of them said anything to you while in the van?'

'The first guy, Priestley, said something about the weather – "Nice day for it", that sort of thing. I ignored him.'

'Did you recognise anything about the attacker?'

Frosham shook his head. 'He was wearing a baklava.'

'What about his build? Tall? Short? Fat? Thin? White? Black? Asian? Arms? Legs?'

'Just kinda normal.'

'Did he specifically go for Priestley or Jones?'

'I dunno – he unlocked all of our cages.'

'But who did he unlock first?'

'Ummm . . .'

Jessica waited. She was assuming it wasn't Frosham, so he had only two choices. It wasn't *University Challenge*.

'. . . Priestley, I think.'

'You think, or you know?'

'I don't know.'

Great.

Jessica turned and checked the clock above the door.

Although she'd told Rowlands she wanted to make her BMW-driving friend wait, it was time to get moving. The Scene of Crime lot would be finishing with the prison van, and uniform would have had a whole bunch of front doors slammed in their faces by now. The grown-ups were ready to get involved.

'Is there anything else you can think of?' Jessica asked.

Frosham squirmed. 'I dunno . . . just . . .'

'What?'

'After the cages were open and the other two jumped onto the road, the other guy with the gun ran round to the back. He and his mate didn't seem to know what they were doing.'

Jessica sat up straighter. Useful information for once. 'How do you mean?'

'With the guns. They were waving the sawn-offs around like they were toys. I flinched when my cage was opened because I thought it might go off. They could've shot anyone.'

Frosham might be a nasty piece of work and it wasn't much comfort that he knew how people were supposed to handle weapons. In the short time since the prison van had been intercepted, the talk had been that it was a professional job. Jessica wasn't convinced when she first heard about it and she certainly wasn't now. If a person was going to attack a prison van, why do it close to the city centre on a main road? There would be witnesses everywhere and police swarming within minutes. The prison van had already travelled along a set of country roads where it was far more vulnerable. There was also something unsubtle about the attack. She'd heard stories from other forces where people had used stingers to burst a prison van's tyres. Ramming it with another car created too many unknowns in which the attackers could have been injured. One frayed seatbelt or damaged airbag, and the attackers would be in intensive care themselves. The fact they were flapping the shotguns around like water pistols only added to her unease. She'd seen criminals brandish guns and they never waved them around like actors in movies. They gripped the weapon as if it was their first-born, eyes steely and determined. Only amateurs or idiots wafted them around. That was how accidents happened.

Jessica could feel Topper's eyes on her through the video camera again, giving her the wind-up.

'I'm not sure if they're going to take you back to court, or if you're going back to prison,' Jessica told Frosham. 'For now, we're going to send you back to the cells downstairs. If you can behave yourself, someone will rustle you up a brew and that Yorkie. All right?'

Frosham answered before his solicitor could. 'I'd prefer a Turkish Delight.'

She presumed he was talking about chocolate.

In the corridor, Topper gave Jessica one of his disapproving eyebrow raises, a silent warning about her opening statement. She knew the drill. She'd seen enough of those looks.

He had his hands in his pockets but was half-turned towards the main exit. Since he'd replaced Jack Cole as the station's DCI, the main change was how hands-on he was. Cole worked from his office, Topper had a habit of sticking his oar in. Jessica preferred it when others kept their oars firmly out of her way.

'How's everything going?' she asked.

'If it *is* a pair of amateurs, they've created havoc. Sky News have a helicopter in the air; the super's on one because someone from the *Herald* called his home number; and even the BBC are covering it. Someone must have woken up the newsdesk at Salford.'

Always thinking of the media – typical of any officers with more than a pair of initials in front of their name.

'I meant have we found Priestley or Jones?'

Topper sighed and smiled at the same time, another trick straight out of the DCI handbook. It was why Jessica wouldn't be cut out for the job: she didn't do sugar-coating.

'What do you think?' he replied, setting off for the car park.

3

Topper was going through the full range of clichés – it was 'all hands on deck' and time to 'shape up or ship out'. He wanted to 'see which way the wind blows', although he'd been 'talking until I'm blue in the face' and now it was time for all the local divisions to 'pull together in a time of crisis'. He pointed out that they could have been first on the scene but 'too many cooks and all that'.

He'd joined Greater Manchester Police from a force in Scotland barely six months previously but Jessica didn't know where he was from. Sometimes he sounded Scottish, other times Irish. Even when he was being nice, he sounded annoyed.

Jessica felt like telling him that she wasn't the press officer and he didn't need to give her the official party line. Basically, they were in the shite and could very much do with finding Owen Priestley and Kevin Jones, not to mention the pair who'd broken them out of the prison van.

Manchester traffic was riddled with more chaos than usual. With one of the main four-way junctions into and out of the city closed, nobody was going anywhere fast. Well, except for them. Topper had the blue lights flashing, siren blaring, as he weaved through the glorified car park that was technically Mancunian Way.

The sun blared down on the pair of battered vans that

were still in the centre of the junction, glass and metal glittering across the tarmac. There were people in white overalls checking the scene, uniformed officers talking to witnesses and sending others on their way, and a cordon of police vehicles blocking off most of the immediate area. Above, the rotor blades of the Sky News helicopter *chikka-chikka-chikka*-ed annoyingly. There were satellite trucks parked beyond a police barrier off to one side of the junction, with a row of microphone-wielding reporters doing pieces to camera. There was also a crowd of people lined up behind another barrier, armed with mobile phones, access to You-Tube, and, presumably, nothing better to do on a Monday morning.

A superintendent from Manchester's North division – DSI Deacon – was lapping it up. He was giving a briefing to a couple of officers, half-turned so that the wall of cameras could see him, pointing towards a row of grubby brown-brick houses beyond a hedgerow. Technically, the escapees were nothing to do with him, but he'd been stuck in traffic close to the scene and got there first. In non-policing terms, he'd called shotgun. Jessica's Metropolitan district was also represented: DSI Jenkinson trussed up, ready for an impromptu-looking, though heavily orchestrated, press conference that would be occurring any minute. He was vying with his opposite number for attention. The fact there were two superintendents in one place with no golf course in sight was a miracle in itself.

If there was one thing officers in the Metropolitan division hated, it was working alongside anyone from the North, South, East or West districts. That said, any of the

Manchester areas were preferable to collaborating with police from Merseyside, the north east or Bloody Yorkshire, as they were officially known. Still, any of those were better than cooperating with any of the pricks who worked for the Met in London, although liaising with them was narrowly better than having to talk to anyone from Scotland. And it was best not to mention Wales. The British police force was separated into a collection of districts united by the fact that they couldn't stand one another.

Deacon continued pointing, showing his authority to any cameras that were trained upon him. Jessica and Topper stood listening, along with a couple of other CID members who were unlucky enough to be on shift.

'. . . Priestley, Jones and the attackers disappeared into that estate,' Deacon said, still pointing. That must be day one of the training course: how to look authoritative while pointing. 'We've got as many officers as we could get our hands on going door to door.'

'We've not found them yet,' Jenkinson interjected, talking over the other DSI. 'We've got Jones on CCTV heading towards a tower block, which we've sealed off. He lives in the area, so could be hiding anywhere.'

'Have you tried his actual flat?' Deacon asked.

Jenkinson frowned at him. 'I'm not sure how you do things up north, but that's the first thing we tried down here.'

A hint of a smile crept across Deacon's face: '*We* tend to keep *our* prisoners locked up, so don't have that problem.'

'Can't keep hold of your laptops though, can you? How many did you lose last year?'

'Sorry, were you talking to me, or going massively over budget?'

The two DSIs stared at each other, on the brink of debating who had the biggest dad.

Jessica ditched protocol and politeness, speaking over the pair of them. 'Surely Priestley's the priority?'

The pair of superintendents – superintendi?, superintendo? – turned to face her.

'It's just that Jones is a bit of an idiot,' Jessica continued quickly. 'He's been done for all sorts over the years and always gets caught. This is where he comes from, so he'll be in a mate's flat. Sooner or later, he'll nip out for a packet of Hobnobs and we'll get him. Priestley's a nasty piece of work.'

Jenkinson was nodding slowly, though he might have been trying to remember her name. 'I was about to say precisely that,' he replied.

Deacon was nodding too, not wanting to cede control that he didn't have in the first place. 'I was coming to that, too. A witness saw three men getting into a silver Volkswagen. With Jones spotted heading towards the tower block, it's likely the hijackers were there for Priestley. We got a call five minutes ago from someone out Eccles way, saying there was a silver vehicle on fire on the industrial estate that backs onto the M602.'

Jessica stopped herself from sighing – that was the single piece of information they needed. She didn't need to say anything because Topper had already taken a step back to the car.

'We'll go,' he said.

*

It was always the way when the neighbouring forces came together. The higher-ups would argue over stupid things, fuss over who got to go on TV, and then, eventually, the rest of the team would get to work. Topper didn't say it but his silence showed his relief that the DSIs were staying out of the way. As Topper and Jessica headed to Eccles, the super-intendents would be talking to the media, appealing for witnesses, and chucking in the odd long word to make themselves seem more on the ball than they were. The former DSI in the Metropolitan district – Aylesbury – once got the words 'idiosyncratic' and 'dichotomy' into a confer-ence, which impressed even Jessica. Still, only clever dicks used long words when a short one would do.

If Priestley and the pair who'd broken him out were going for ostentatious, then they'd certainly achieved it. The silver Volkswagen had been dumped at the side of a disused warehouse and then set on fire. Unfortunately for them, it had been left a little too close to a wheelie bin filled with something flammable. Balls of black smoke were bil-lowing into the air, threatening a nearby factory. Workers in dark blue overalls were filming the scene on mobile phones as fire officers doused the vehicle, bin, and surrounding area with jets of water.

Jessica and Topper were barely out of the car when they were back in it. Someone working on the industrial estate had seen three men racing away in a black Astra, which had since been spotted driving erratically a couple of miles away in the streets, zigzagging along the back of the Trafford Park train station. Topper had stopped spouting clichés but the journey was riddled with silent resignation that they might be following a trail all day and there were more productive things that could be done from the station.

Topper pulled up behind a pool car on the maze of tight streets packed with red-brick houses and low walls. An apron-clad woman was outside one of the houses, talking to a uniformed officer, pointing towards the abandoned black Astra at the front of the house.

'. . . so who's going to move it?' she asked.

The officer was scribbling in his notebook as Jessica and Topper arrived, ID cards at the ready.

'More of you,' she added, throwing her hands into the air. She was in her late forties, the curtain-twitching, gossipy sort that police officers loved. She checked her watch, shaking her head. 'I can't talk long, I've got a cake in the oven. It's my Anthony's birthday.'

Ooh, cake.

Jessica's stomach grumbled.

With the crash scene, the fire on the industrial estate and now this, the Scene of Crime team were going to be busy. The uniformed officer would have to waste the rest of his morning waiting next to the Astra, ensuring no one went near it, as they waited for one of the flatbeds to pick it up.

Jessica nodded towards the vehicle. 'Did you see anyone getting out?' she asked.

The homeowner was pointing a finger, still flapping her arms. 'See 'em? I gave 'em a piece of my mind.' She pointed at her house and the handwritten sign taped to the inside of the living-room window:

'People are always trying to leave their cars 'ere, then get a train into the city. Saves on parking. Soon as I saw 'em pull in, I was out of the house telling 'em to do one.'

'How many were there?' Jessica asked.

'Three – then I went inside and saw that one on the news and called you straight away.' She wiped her hands on the apron, proud of herself. If there was one thing that got people riled up, it was other people parking – perfectly legally – in front of their houses. When in uniform, Jessica had been to two fights and an attempted murder arising from disputes over where neighbours parked their cars.

'Who did you see?' Jessica asked.

'Somebody Priestley.'

'Did you get a good look at the other people who were in the car with him?'

She shook her head, wafting a hand in the vague direction of the crossroads at the end of the road. 'Oh, they were off and away with their hoods up.'

'But you said you gave them a piece of your mind . . .'

'Oh, I did. I told that fella to move his car. Didn't realise who it was at the time.'

'What did he say?'

The woman snorted, peering over her shoulder conspiratorially. 'I won't repeat the exact language, but he told me to . . .' She lowered her voice so much that Jessica missed the first word. The second was definitely 'off'.

'What did he do then?' Jessica asked.

She pointed towards the junction again. 'He ran off too.'

'Did you see where they went?'

'I think they dropped down onto the train tracks.' She pointed to her left, away from the city centre. 'Heading that way . . . now, if you'll excuse me, I've got one cake to get out of the oven, and another to ice.' Her eyebrows arched towards the Astra. 'You going to move that, or what?'

Jessica smiled at the uniformed officer. 'Our colleague here's the man to ask . . .'

Stitch-up complete, Jessica and Topper headed towards the four-way junction. Three of the roads led further into the estate, with the final side a small two-house cul-de-sac with a brick wall at the end. It was high enough to be tough to climb by one lone person but not too much of a challenge with two or three helping each another. The pylons on the other side signalled the train lines.

'She must've followed them down the road if she saw them going over the top of the wall onto the train tracks,' Jessica said.

Topper was nodding, glancing from house to house. More PCs would eventually be on their way but there was so much going on, neither of them knew when that might be.

'I'll knock on a few doors,' he said, 'you call in.'

There was one person at the station who always knew what was going on. Detective Sergeant Isobel Diamond answered on the second ring. She was perhaps Jessica's best friend, certainly the colleague she trusted the most. Izzy had recently been promoted but still found time to do a lot of the groundwork for whatever Jessica was working on. If Jessica had her way, Izzy would work solely for her: the two of them against the world. With Izzy's talent, good grace, and social skills alongside Jessica's natural ability to piss people off, they made a good team.

In the background, Jessica could hear the rush of officers racing around, though Izzy sounded calm.

'Having fun?' Izzy asked.

'I'm at Trafford Park staring at a brick wall,' Jessica replied.

'You always did know how to enjoy yourself.'

'Can you check the transport police logs and see if anyone reported men on the tracks around Trafford Park, heading away from the city.'

'Humphrey Park's the next stop on that line,' Izzy replied.

'Did you know that off the top of your head?'

'Yep.'

'And you were laughing at me for being sad.'

There was the tip-tapping of a keyboard and a low humming. 'I'm not sure about the transport police but we did get a match for that Astra,' Izzy said. 'It was nicked from the Morrisons car park in Eccles last week. Someone's checking ANPR at the moment – not that it matters if it's been abandoned. Hang on . . .'

Jessica was strolling back and forth along the length of the wall as the line went muffled. Topper had already knocked on the doors of both houses in the cul-de-sac, without reply, so he crossed the junction and was trying another.

Izzy's voice was suddenly back. 'You'll get it on your radio in a moment,' she said. 'Someone just called 999 to say that three men were acting suspiciously close to an abandoned pub by Humphrey Park. Tactical firearms are already on their way.'

It was only a five-minute drive and as Jessica and Topper arrived, two dark blue police vans pulled in, followed by more marked cars. The pub was a square, detached building within a javelin-throw of the park. Huge boulders had been placed to deter travellers at the entrance of a rubbish-strewn, moss-ridden, crumbling car park, but there was a smart black car parked in front. Metal plates were bolted to each of the pub windows, with a large **PLOT TO LET OR SELL** sign pinned high above the main door. The pub sat on a corner, with a set of double doors opening onto each of the streets. There were criss-crossed planks across the doors, though, even from across the road, Jessica could see the wood was rotting.

More police cars arrived, blocking the roads, as officers decked out in helmets and thick pads emerged from the vans, MP5s in hand. Thankfully, no one had tipped off Sky News, with the helicopter nowhere in sight. The last thing they needed was an armed siege in full view of the media.

The remaining officers were dashing along the surrounding pavements, urging people back into their houses, but one woman was arguing with a uniformed officer, pointing towards the pub. As Jessica and Topper arrived, she turned to them, hoping for support.

'I'm Mrs Briggs,' she insisted. 'I'm the one who called you.'

She was older than the cake-baker down the road, but

still had the excited air of someone who made it her job to know everyone else's business. In fairness, it wasn't every day a bunch of people turned up with machine guns to surround a pub. Drinking after hours wasn't usually treated so harshly.

'You still need to go back into your house,' Topper said, putting on his kindly talk-to-the-public voice. It was an octave higher than his usual tone. He smiled too much when he used it, like a used-car salesman about to sell a punter the front half of one car welded to the back half of something else. Smiling didn't suit him.

Mrs Briggs shifted from foot to foot, trying to peer around them towards the pub, where the tactical firearms team were getting into position. There wasn't time to argue and, short of frogmarching her inside or arresting her, they didn't have too many options. Topper nodded towards the police car. 'You can sit in the back, just don't . . . touch any-thing.'

The three of them retreated to their vehicle, parked across the junction from the pub with a wall of officers and parked cars between them and the action. With the angle at which they were parked, they had a ringside seat.

Jessica was in the passenger seat, Topper behind the wheel, Mrs Briggs fidgeting for a better view behind.

'What exactly did you see?' Jessica asked, not turning.

Mrs Briggs was pressed against the window. 'I told the woman on the phone – three men were ripping away the planks covering the doors, then they headed inside.'

'How long ago?'

'Twenty minutes or so?'

Talk about rapid response time – they'd excelled themselves. Funny what GMP *could* do when there was a news helicopter nearby.

'Are you sure no one left?' Jessica asked.

'The woman on the phone kept me on the line, so I talked her through it. They could've sneaked out the back windows, but no one came out the doors.'

The firearms team were almost in place, a handful around the back, most at the front.

'What did they look like?' Jessica asked.

'Dunno really – they were all in dark clothes, plus my eyes aren't what they were. When I said there were three of them, the woman on the line got a bit excited and told me to stay on the line. I didn't expect all this.'

As soon as the call came in, the handler had elevated it. Because of the seriousness of the break-out, someone had alerted tactical firearms straight away. It wasn't exactly standard procedure, but then prison vans weren't rammed every day of the week. Something didn't feel right, though. There had been a degree of planning to the break, with at least three vehicles involved, so why end up in an abandoned pub? They could have gone anywhere.

Jessica's thoughts were interrupted by the crunch and smash of the firearms team pouring through both sets of the pub's front doors. They could hear the action on the radio, a series of shouts, people saying 'clear', then a louder 'show me your hands' and 'get on the ground'. Mrs Briggs was shuffling anxiously behind Jessica, waiting for the big moment when the gunshots began. There was nothing like a good police shooting on a Monday morning to raise the quality of local gossip.

Instead, a man's terrified voice whimpered through the radio: 'I'm just an estate agent – you can call my office.'

Topper reached forward and switched the radio off, sighing.

There was silence. A long, punctuated silence. When she spoke, Mrs Briggs's voice was a whisper. 'Sorry.'

'Better safe than sorry,' Topper replied diplomatically.

'They were skulking around and it looked like they were breaking in. It was all very suspicious.'

'You did fine,' he said, which was a nice way of glossing over that reporting an estate agent for looking shifty was like reporting a doctor for having bad handwriting. It was a mistake anyone could make.

At least no one had been shot.

Jessica rolled over, slapping a hand towards the nightstand, where her phone was chirping, wanting attention. It was dark, too early for this . . . and her bloody phone wasn't there anyway. She fumbled in the gloom, before realising there was someone next to her. This wasn't her house, wasn't her bed.

Light was flashing from her phone's screen, sending a spiral of annoyance into the air from the floor as she finally grabbed it, fumbling with the screen and mumbling something that might've been a 'hello'.

The covers were twisted in a tight knot around her lower half but Jessica kicked and fought until she was free, disturbing the man next to her, who rolled over and started to groan. She put a hand over his mouth as she listened to the caller. She'd seen and heard so much over the years that she didn't think she could be shocked any further, yet the news left her stunned. She sat upright, removing her hand from the man's mouth. He'd got the message and gone quiet.

'I'll be right there,' Jessica said, hanging up.

There was no light on her side of the bed, so she stood, fumbling along the wall, around the corner and towards the door.

'What are you doing?' the man asked.

'Getting up.'

'Why . . . ? It's, like, stupid o'clock.'

Jessica snapped the light switch, filling the room with a dim orange glow. The man shrieked, grabbing at the duvet and covering his head.

'You're not a vampire, are you?' she grumbled, finding yesterday's clothes on the floor, before opening his wardrobe to find one of the shirts she'd left. The fact she kept anything at his flat made her annoyed with herself. She shouldn't be here, she should be at home, yet she couldn't stop coming back. He wanted her, which was more important than whether she wanted him.

Jessica started getting dressed as he slowly emerged from under the covers, squinting, but eyeing her up and down at the same time.

'No,' Jessica said.

'What?'

'I'm on my way out.'

'I didn't say anything!' he replied with a smile.

'You were thinking it.'

He smirked, running a hand through his slightly curly hair, which sprung back into its usual position. 'What's going on?'

Jessica sighed, sitting on the edge of the bed and trying to put on her ankle boots. She didn't want to look at him.

'Well, Detective Constable Davey, you remember our escaped prisoners? Owen Priestley's been found.'

'Oh . . . where?' A pause. 'Can't someone else deal with it?'

Jessica finally wrestled the first boot over her ankle. 'Perhaps – but the fact somebody's put him in a noose and hanged him from a bridge over the M60 means there's probably something dodgy going on.'

4

Jessica clicked closed the door of Archie's flat and headed down the stairs, trying to make as little noise as possible. Leaving in the early hours always felt a little . . . stop-out-ish. She emerged onto the hall directly below Archie's as a door opened, revealing a yawning woman in a dressing gown and slippers. She was in her thirties, with brown hair, and looked thoroughly exhausted, waving a hand in front of her mouth apologetically.

'Oh, hi . . .' she said.

Jessica really didn't want to get into a conversation but the other woman was quickly out of her flat, half-blocking the stairs.

She stuck out her hand. 'I'm Paige.'

Jessica reluctantly shook the hand. 'Jessica, but I, er . . . have to go.'

'Are you friends with Arch upstairs?'

'Um, yeah . . .'

'Are you a police officer too?' Paige stepped back, taking in Jessica's crumpled suit. 'Oh, is that where you're going now? You on a case, or something?'

'Something like that.'

Paige looked her up and down again in a wordless bitchy stare. It left Jessica with the distinct impression that Archie and Paige had been 'friends' at one point, too . . . which was just wonderful. One more person who knew about Jessica's late-night visits.

'I really have to go,' Jessica said. 'Nice meeting you.'

'You too.'

The best thing about the motorway at five in the morning was that there was hardly anyone else on it. Jessica bombed around the ring road from Archie's Stretford flat to the nightmare junction where the M60 met the M602 link road. It was the main way into the city from the north, a few junctions along from the Trafford Centre and its 11,000 parking spaces. If that wasn't bad enough, it intersected the M62, with Liverpool to the west and Yorkshire to the east. Between half six and half nine in the morning, plus half three to seven in the evening – not to mention the weekends leading up to Christmas – it was one, big, barely moving gateway to hell.

The matrix signs read **MOTORWAY CLOSED AHEAD** but Jessica continued driving until she reached a pair of police cars parked across the lanes. A yawning uniformed officer beckoned her towards the exit ramp, but Jessica fumbled the ID from her pocket and just about remembered she was a DI, not a DS. It was too early in the morning for tough questions like, 'Who are you?'

Considering the amount of times she'd been stuck in unmoving traffic on this stretch of road, there was something unerringly satisfying about parking in the centre lane of the motorway. There was nothing satisfying about the sight ahead as Jessica pulled her suit jacket tight and started to walk towards the bridge. With the longest day and her birthday recently gone, the summer sunshine was out in force, despite the early hour. It wasn't yet warm, but the morning lustre was casting the shadow of Owen Priestley's dangling body across the tarmac in front of her. Jessica stepped around the pool of darkness, shivering, as she continued towards the bridge. There was a handful of officers on the ground, but more leaning against the railing of the crossing above, peering down at her. DCI Topper was there, nodding in acknowledgement.

Jessica angled up, staring at the man's body, his neck still tied within the noose. His body was limp, eyes closed, unmistakeably dead as the breeze bobbed him gently back and forth. Her throat was dry, skin tingling. The sight was intoxicating: utterly grim, yet so out of the ordinary that it was hard to turn away from.

She scrambled up the bank to find more police officers at both ends of the pedestrian bridge. The air smelled of summer: blossoming plants and cut grass, accentuated by the early-morning warmth. As the road met the horizon, there was an orange haze booming, melding into the endless indigo sky. If it wasn't for the sight below, it would be a beautiful morning.

Topper waved her across, yawning, before his features settled in the resigned state of a man who knew his week had gone from pretty poor to appalling.

'Isn't someone going to get him down?' Jessica asked.

The don't-be-a-moron alert blazed in her mind as Topper tilted his head sideways, eyebrows pulled down. 'What would you suggest? We get a couple of people in to haul him back over the bridge, or we cut through the rope and let him splat onto the carriageway?'

'Yeah, sorry, too early.'

Topper nodded, not annoyed. She guessed it wasn't the first time that morning someone had asked the obvious. 'We're not entirely sure how to get him down,' he said. 'It's too tall for a forklift, so we're getting one of those flatbed up-and-down platform lorry things that they use in factories to stack pallets. We're going to park it under him, then try to untie the rope after the Scene of Crime lot have had a look. Even if it works, we're going to be here for hours.'

'Wonderful.'

Topper nodded back to the bridge. 'The rope's been looped around the railing and then tied.'

Jessica's mind was slowly waking up. 'So he was probably dead before he was hanged?'

'Perhaps. His body would have been quite the weight for one or two people to hold while the rope was being tied. I guess we'll find out.' Topper yawned, hand in front of his mouth, blinking away the tears, voice slightly quieter. 'I should've stayed in Scotland.'

'Why'd you come down? All the heroin and Proclaimers songs finally get to you?'

Jessica grinned, biting her bottom lip, unsure if they had that sort of relationship yet. She'd started off by hating him but there was now mutual respect. Topper didn't laugh, but then he rarely did. He didn't tell her off, which was, in her mind, an endorsement.

'My wife's one of you,' he replied, the first time Jessica had known him to mention his family.

'*Female?*' she replied.

His lips cracked into something close to a smile. 'English. She'd been talking about coming back for a while and when the notice came around saying GMP were looking for a new DCI, I figured why not apply.'

Jessica remained quiet, wondering what he was going to follow it with. Instead, the sound of a man's voice at the far end of the walkway made Topper blink back to where they were. They watched a pair of uniformed officers send the dog-walker back the way he'd come. There'd be a lot of that happening through the morning.

'This should be a busy area depending on the time of day,' Topper said, pointing to the far side of the road. 'There's Eccles Rugby Club, an athletics track, Winton Park and a primary school that way, then a housing estate on the other side. One of the officers says the only pub is on the main road, so there'd be no need to cross here in the early hours. When everyone wakes up, we can ask for witnesses but, if anyone had seen anything, you'd have thought they'd have already called us.'

'CCTV?' Jessica asked, turning in a circle but not seeing a camera.

'Someone's checking the motorway cameras just in case but it's likely whoever left Priestley parked at one end of the bridge and carried him up. It doesn't look like there are many local cameras.'

'Who called us?'

'A motorist called 101, saying there was something dangling from a motorway bridge. He thought it was a bag of rubbish, or an out-of-season Guy Fawkes. The motorway police didn't prioritise it because they were dealing with an incident near Stockport – and it was three in the morning. When they came along, they were expecting it to be a shop dummy or something similar. They had quite the shock.'

'So Priestley's been here for at least three hours?'

'The motorist's call came through at half two, so around that.' Topper stifled another yawn, running a hand through his hair, even though he didn't seem as if he'd rushed out of bed. He was in a clean suit and shirt, shoes shiny, eyes alert, if a little watery from the yawning. 'I didn't know if I should call you,' he said.

Jessica shrugged – it wasn't the first time she'd had the early-morning call and almost certainly wouldn't be the last. 'I assume this means Priestley's ours to deal with.'

'Sort of,' he said. 'Superintendent Jenkinson's the face of the investigation but since those Robin Hood robberies were tidied up, we've – and by proxy I mean *you've* – been in the chief constable's good books. He called me at home. Everything's going to be run from Longsight. We're trying to find out who attacked the prison van and, now, who killed Owen Priestley.'

'I'm guessing someone had a score to settle after the robbery he was sent down for . . .' She tailed off, the train of thought ebbing away. 'Does this mean we're getting extra officers?'

A raised eyebrow. 'What do you think?'

'I'd settle for air-conditioning that works and a vending machine that doesn't keep stealing pound coins.'

He turned slightly, Jessica following his lead, until they were both gazing towards the edge of the bridge, where

Priestley was still hanging. She hoped the lorry turned up soon, before people on the adjoining estates got out of bed and started to wonder why the roads around them were closed. Regardless of who Priestley was, it'd be awful if someone got a photo of his body swaying as it dangled from the bridge.

'I'll talk to the labs and see what we can get and how quickly,' Topper added. 'But they were already backed up before the prison van crash yesterday. Hopefully, we'll get a post mortem on Priestley by the end of the day to tell us if he was already dead before he was hanged but we shouldn't rely on that happening in time. We're going to have to dig properly into his background.'

'Do you think this could be payback for the off-licence robbery?'

Topper's features remained unmoved as he gazed towards the body. Another police car was pulling up underneath the bridge, a pair of officers climbing out and peering up towards the horror above.

'How are you fixed for today?' Topper asked.

'I've got to get to Niall O'Brien's house.'

'Ah, yes . . . Mr O'Brien.'

'He's not as nutty as everyone thinks. He's just scared.'

Topper chewed his lip. 'Is anyone actually breaking into his house?'

'I don't know. Our Scene of Crime lot found nothing – no fingerprints, no DNA. Even *he* says nothing's been stolen.'

'So what's going on?'

'Niall's an old man . . . confused, perhaps. I don't know. He says he finds his back door open and things moved.'

'Like what?'

'When I was there last, he said somebody did the washing up while he was asleep.'

Topper squeezed the bridge of his nose. 'How did this end up on your desk?'

'He was threatening to call the papers and say we weren't doing anything. Somehow it wound up with Funtime—'

'DI Franks.'

Jessica stifled a smile – Funtime was the kindest of the nicknames. 'Right. Either way, the paperwork wound up with me.'

Which was a polite way of saying that, in her – correct – opinion, there was no way DI Franks should be allowed to interact with any sentient, semi-sensible life forms, let alone speak to frightened pensioners. He was an accident waiting to happen. If it was down to her, she wouldn't let him speak to pot plants, for fear of them withering and dying in order to avoid any future communications.

'There's something else,' Topper said. 'I've not been here long enough, but does the name Richard Hyde mean anything to you?'

It was early and Jessica's mind still wasn't functioning properly, the fuzzy greyness misting across her thoughts. 'I've definitely heard it before,' she said.

'He's not strictly on our patch. He runs a casino around Oldham but the Serious Crime Division have been interested in him for a while. I should've told you yesterday but things were busy after we left the pub, then I had to debrief the super, then there was paperwork . . .' He tailed off, waving a weary hand in the air. 'I was called over to Newton Heath, where there was a guy from the SCD waiting to talk to me.'

Jessica hated visiting the main police headquarters, and *really* disliked working with Serious Crime. They'd once taken a case from her and, from her experience, their in-volvement only ever brought more trouble – and work – for her and her colleagues. They investigated larger patterns of crime that were too much for the regular CID, mainly gangs, drugs and anything weapon-related. It meant there was crossover with what Jessica did but when lines were drawn, the SCD almost always got their way.

Topper continued: 'He said that, although Hyde runs the casino, he's suspected of, if not implicated in, involvement in all sorts of gang activity around the city. They've been trying to pin something on him for years, without any luck.'

'What sort of things do they think he's up to?'

'The usual: drugs, money-laundering, girls—'

'Squeezing from the middle of the toothpaste tube; eating all the Quality Street, then putting the empty wrappers back in the tin . . .'

Topper was even closer to grinning this time, lips twitch-ing before settling back into place. 'Priestley used to be one of Hyde's men,' he said. 'Before the off-licence robbery, he worked as one of the managers at Hyde's casino.'

It took a moment for it to click with Jessica. 'If Priestley managed a casino, why was he robbing off-licences?'

Topper nodded shortly. 'Which was exactly what I asked

the Serious Crime officer – but he couldn't answer. In the file, Priestley never admitted anything to do with the robbery and nobody found a motive, other than money. He had a clean record before the off-licence, then he slashed the other prisoner while inside and here we are.'

'If they're saying there's more to Hyde than just his casino, does that mean they think he had something to do with the break-out?'

'I guess that's what we're here to find out.'

Jessica stopped, feeling an extra tickle of warmth on her face. She shifted back to stare at the body, a tingle creeping along her back, telling her to look away.

The thought came to her with a gasp – it should have been obvious in the first place but it was too early. 'What if Priestley was broken out so he could be killed?' she asked.

Another taut nod, as if Topper had spent the entire conversation wondering when she'd catch on. 'Precisely.'

5

Jessica was dawdling along at barely thirty on the motor-way, heading east. The traffic heading towards Priestley's hanging body had been turned around, so everyone was travelling in the same direction.

Izzy's voice poured from the tinny speaker of Jessica's phone, which was rattling precariously on the dashboard of her red Corsa. Her previous vehicle had blown up in a mys-tery of apparently failed parts followed by an inquest that would never give her closure. That car had built-in Blue-tooth, fancy seats, a port to connect and charge her phone, plus more buttons than she could be bothered to figure out. It started first time all the time and had no character to it, like the contents of a celebrity magazine: all style, little sub-stance. Jessica felt far more at home in the rattling Vauxhall. Dependably British in the sense that it might fall apart at any moment.

Like her.

'The journey to the station was a sodding nightmare,' Izzy said.

'That's 'cos some bastards have closed the motorway in both directions.'

'It's no wonder everyone hates us. Where are you off to?'

'Oldham.'

There was a small pause, a moment of judgement. '*Oldham?* Does anyone go there voluntarily?'

'Hang on.'

Jessica leant forward, pushing her phone back towards the windscreen as she tried to change lane. A lorry was looming behind, completely obscuring her view, far too close to her bumper, driver no doubt annoyed that he didn't have a cyclist to run over. Jessica kept an eye on her inside mirror, hoping for a gap as her indicator continued to blink. No one let her in.

'Not quite Oldham,' Jessica added, 'Middleton.'

'Wow, you know how to let your hair down.'

'I'm off to talk to Richard Hyde. Did you get my message?'

'The one about pinning Dave down and shaving his head?'

'No . . . that was just me thinking out loud last night. The one from this morning.'

'Yeah, give me a mo.'

The car in the inside lane flashed its lights and Jessica swerved left, wincing as the lorry stormed past her, sending a spray of grit across her window, only to jam on the brakes as the driver reached the car in front.

'Right . . .' Izzy said, 'there's not a lot in the system about Owen Priestley and Richard Hyde together. Priestley worked in Hyde's casino in Oldham. I found a court report where the prosecution said they'd known each other for more than twenty years.'

'How old was Priestley?'

'Forty-six. Hyde's fifty-eight.'

'What are their records like?'

'Hyde has a drink-driving from years ago but that's it.'

Jessica heard a tapping of keys from the other end of the line. If Hyde really was the gangster the Serious Crime lot thought he was – and they wouldn't be wrong – then it was no wonder they were desperate to pin something on him. He wouldn't have even gone to prison for the drink-driving. They'd probably been looking to build a case for years, which perhaps made it all the stranger that Topper had told her to go and have a word. Usually, the SCD didn't want officers lower down the chain trampling over their potential cases.

Izzy was making a humming noise before she returned. 'Priestley has an attempted murder charge from last year after using a smuggled knife to slash a fellow inmate in prison. There's the armed robbery and GBH charges from the year before that, but nothing previous.'

That was exactly as Jessica remembered from checking herself. She'd wondered if she skim-read too quickly, missing something obvious. It was all a bit strange – why would a casino manager in his forties with a clean criminal record suddenly decide to rob an off-licence?

'You still there?' Izzy asked.

'Just coming up to the motorway exit.'

'I've got something else for you if you want.'

'I'm only interested if it's a vicious rumour about someone we work with.'

'It's to do with Richard Hyde.'

'Oh . . . go on.'

'When I got your message, I spoke to one of my contacts at HQ.'

'You have *other* friends?'

Izzy giggled. 'That's what happens when you smile at people and say hello.'

'I've never smiled at anyone from HQ.'

Another laugh: 'I thought you were going to stop at the word "anyone".'

'Give me a sec.' Jessica took the motorway exit and waited for the sat nav to sort itself out. She turned left, heading towards Alkrington Woods, the place where an anarchist, devil-worshipping cult had somehow operated without anyone from GMP noticing. The day after it all came out had been one of those times where officers went out of their way to find things to do away from the station. Jessica felt even worse when she realised a private investigator she knew had been at the centre of it all. They had an 'exchange of views' about the fact she found out what happened from the chief inspector, rather than from him.

Jessica rolled up to a set of traffic lights, nudged her phone away from the edge of the dashboard again, apologised to Izzy, and then asked her to continue.

'My source reckons Hyde's recently retired and that his daughter, Natalie, now runs the family empire,' Izzy said.

'Hmmm . . .'

If that was true, Jessica wondered if that meant Hyde's daughter was controlling the rest of his enterprises. The 'drugs, money-laundering and girls' as Topper had put it.

'What else is in Hyde's empire?' Jessica asked.

'There's the casino in Oldham, plus pubs and clubs

around the area, mainly north Manchester. I can probably get you a list . . . well, get Archie to do it . . .'

The pause had a breathy, suspicious-sounding air. Izzy was seemingly aware of everything going on at the station and, though she couldn't discern the nature of Jessica and Archie's relationship for sure, she gave the impression of knowing exactly what was going on. As all good officers could.

'Do that,' Jessica replied firmly, before realising she didn't actually need the information. She'd been so keen to show she wasn't soft on Archie that she'd answered without thinking.

'I've got another name for you,' Izzy said, 'Harry Irwell.'

'Didn't he die a couple of years back?'

'Pretty much – one month after Nicholas Long.'

Memories flooded through her. Jessica had lost nearly a year of her life, haunted by things she'd rather not think about. Long and Irwell were 'people of interest' to the police – crime bosses in every way other than that which mattered: there was little evidence to prove it. After they died within a few weeks of one another, the city went through a land grab, which, presumably, led back to Richard Hyde, among others. Jessica had missed the months in which that had happened, but it was no wonder Serious Crime were interested in Hyde.

'Irwell and Hyde were rivals,' Izzy added.

'I remember an incident in a pizza shop years ago, just after I became a DC. It was around the corner from the station and this guy had his hand held inside a burning oven. Neighbours called, thinking there'd been a robbery, but when I got there, the skin was dripping off the poor sod. The smell was awful. A couple of others had been beaten up but none of them would say anything. This bloke almost lost his hand but kept repeating "accident, accident". The inspector I was with at the time said it was tit for tat, Irwell versus Hyde, that it had been going on for years.'

Jessica shuddered at the thought – DI Thomas, another ghost she'd rather forget. Her career was full of them.

'We've not had things like that for a while, have we . . . ?' For once, Izzy didn't sound sure.

'I don't know . . .' Jessica replied. 'It'll have been rumbling on somewhere in the city, probably away from the centre. There's always a demand for drugs and girls.' Jessica paused, tracking the sat nav as she continued along the main road, wondering when she'd have to turn off. Not quite yet. 'Who's Natalie Hyde?' she asked.

'No idea,' Izzy replied. 'She doesn't have a record that I can see and the name doesn't match anything on the databases. There's a son too – Richie Hyde, though we have very little on him either.'

The sat nav started flashing, wanting Jessica to turn left and then banging on about bearing right, whatever that meant.

'I've gotta go,' Jessica said, thanking Izzy for the help and then listening as the line went quiet. She followed the sat nav's instructions, passing through a housing estate and emerging onto a road flanked by tall hedges and wide green fields that glistened in the sunshine. After half a mile, the smug-sounding woman's voice told her she'd reached her destination – a large house with imposing gates at the front and towering hedges around the side. Through the gates, Jessica could see a spread of trimmed lush grass, bowling-green perfect. There was wealth, given the expanse of land, but nothing too showy: no soaring fountains, built-in stables, or topiary.

Jessica pressed the buzzer next to the gate and waited. When nobody replied, she squinted through the gate, taking in the clear driveway and not spotting any move-ment from the house itself. When Topper had sent her off to speak to Richard Hyde, it hadn't crossed either of their minds that he might be out. She could head back to the station, but seeing as the traffic into the centre was barely moving, that'd take at least an hour. Instead, she checked the address of Hyde's casino, and then made her way back to Middleton, before following the road to Oldham.

The road quickly became a shambolic mess of lanes, with arrows stupidly painted on the same surface where cars had stopped on top. The sat nav was being unhelpful but Jessica eventually spotted a sign and then followed the road to an out-of-town retail park. At least half of the units had the shutters down, out of business, giving the area a run-down, desolate look. There was a massive expanse of tarmac given over to the almost empty car park, with only a smat-tering of vehicles dripped around the area. Jessica continued following the signs, around the stores, past a cinema and row of restaurants, until she saw the Crown Casino. It was still morning, not time to open, yet the neon strip of blind-ing, blinking lights still burned into the blue sky.

Not quite Vegas. Viva Las Chadderton.

If somebody had no idea what gambling was, then the

boards around the walls of the casino offered little clue. It advertised 'over one hundred screens showing sports', 'two-for-one pizzas', 'cocktail specials', 'pool and snooker' and 'free WiFi'. No mention of the table or card games; the one-armed bandits; the fruit machines; and definitely not the shattered marriages and wasted lives.

The sign on the front door read *CLOSED* but there was a smaller note telling delivery drivers to go around the back. Jessica peered up at the security cameras, wondering if she was being watched, before following the edge of the building, out of the shadow and into the warmth. As she walked, she realised the surprising thing was what she wasn't seeing. Usually, vast expanses of car park around these types of places meant young people hanging around, skid marks from handbrake turns and doughnutting cars, crushed, empty cans of Red Bull tossed to the kerb, smashed alcopop bottles, and a general sense of shabbiness. In this area around the casino, it was spotless.

At the rear of the casino, there was a sleek, shiny grey Jaguar, and a sporty-looking red Audi. A tall metal fence stretched along the edge of the tarmac, separating it from a grass bank and the road. Jessica stood underneath a pair of security cameras and pressed the button next to the door marked 'deliveries only'.

Moments later, a female voice answered: 'Who are you looking for?'

'Is that Natalie?'

There was an awkward pause. 'Who's asking?'

Jessica fumbled in her pocket, holding up her ID to the camera and introducing herself.

'What do you want?' the voice asked.

Jessica repocketed the ID and took out her wallet. 'I've got a hundred quid to waste and figured I could either flush it down the toilet, or come here and do the same thing.'

Unsurprisingly, there was no amusement. 'We're not open.'

'Perhaps I can come in for a word, then? It's about Owen Priestley.'

There was a click, silence, and then: 'Wait there.'

Natalie Hyde was far from the person Jessica had pictured. She had expected a tough, battle-scarred matriarch, not someone younger than her. Natalie was thirty at the most, with long, dark, slightly wavy hair as if she was off out for cocktails. There was a steely determination in Natalie's brown eyes and a definite hostility towards Jessica, probably the police in general. She was wearing a smart business suit, holding herself tall and authoritatively. Jessica had the sense that, if they weren't in polar opposite jobs, they'd likely get on well. Either that or hate one another.

After the briefest of introductions, Natalie led Jessica along an echoing, concrete corridor. The air-conditioning billowed through the passage, goosebumps tickling Jessica's arms. They kept moving until Natalie opened a heavy door, heading into an office with a bank of CCTV monitors on one wall that showed picture-perfect images of the empty gaming floor and the car park. Filing cabinets lined the other wall, with a plain canteen-style table and a pair of twisty-turny leather office chairs in the centre.

'I was looking for your dad,' Jessica said, as they sat.

'He's away.'

'Where?'

'Holiday.' Natalie peered at a clock on the wall over the monitors. 'He gets back this afternoon. I can pass on a message – he's always delighted to cooperate with the police . . .' She smiled with her lips, not her eyes, focusing back on Jessica. Game on.

Considering what had happened to Priestley that morning, Jessica wondered if it was a convenient absence.

'Perhaps you can help?' Jessica said, as sweetly as she could. Two could play this game. 'I gather Owen Priestley worked here until around two years ago, when he committed an armed robbery. He was broken out of a prison van yesterday. I'm looking for a bit of background.'

Natalie shook her head, pursing her lips. 'Sorry, I lived abroad until two and a half years ago. I don't know many of Dad's old guard.'

'I gather you run this place now . . .'

Fish, fish, fish.

Natalie barely reacted. 'That's why I came back – Dad was looking to retire. Can't blame him really.'

'I suppose it must be tough, being in charge of . . . everything he has.'

Still no reaction: 'It's hard work here.'

'Where did you live when you were overseas?'

Natalie maintained the steely eye contact. 'Here and there – Spain mainly.'

'But your father lived here . . . ?'

'Right.'

'Any particular reason you were abroad?'

Natalie smiled sweetly again. 'You'd have to ask my father.'

'I'm asking you.'

She shrugged. 'I really don't know.'

'Nothing to do with any enemies your father may have made . . . ?'

Natalie remained cool, not taking the bait. 'You're asking the wrong person, Inspector.'

Jessica wondered if it was a coincidence that Natalie had returned at more or less the same time that Harry Irwell had died. It seemed unlikely.

Natalie's eyes flickered towards the monitor as she finally showed some emotion, a scowl flickering across her features and remaining. 'For God's sake . . .'

She stood quickly, heading for the door, hissing 'I'll be back' as she stomped into the corridor.

Jessica spun to face the monitors. The only movement was from a man she didn't recognise holding a glass underneath one of the optics behind the bar. She peered into the corridor, where Natalie was rapidly racing away.

She hadn't *specifically* been told to wait, so . . .

Jessica hurried after the other woman, following a corridor past a host of closed doors, up a ramp, and around a corner until she reached a set of double doors with a numbered keypad at the side. Natalie was just inputting the final digit as Jessica arrived. The scowl was still blanketed across her face, but she said nothing as Jessica followed her onto the main floor of the casino. They whizzed across the soft carpet, past empty gaming tables and unused machines until they reached a bar not too far from the entrance. The man from the monitor turned to face the pair of them as Natalie reached the counter, poking a finger towards him.

'What have I told you about free samples?' she said harshly.

The man eyed Jessica and then focused back on Natalie. He had dark hair, with thick-rimmed glasses and a gaze that Jessica had seen very recently . . .

'Oh, piss off,' he said.

'You're supposed to be checking the float,' Natalie replied.

'I've done that. You're not the boss of me.'

'We're not still on this, are we? Dad couldn't have been much clearer.'

Richie Hyde shared his sister's brown eyes but his had none of the danger. He was wearing a suit with an open-necked shirt but, though it looked expensive, he seemed uncomfortable in it, as if he was between two sizes. The way he glared at his sister told a lengthy story – he was the *man*, yet his sister was running things. He'd always been second-best: a son in a daddy's-girl world.

Richie nodded over his sister's shoulder. 'Who's she?'

Natalie started to answer but Jessica spoke over her, introducing herself, full title and all, getting the reaction she expected.

'You got a warrant?' he snarled.

'Why? Is there something to hide?'

Richie opened his mouth but Natalie flashed him a dangerous look. '*She's* here for a chat. There's no problem.'

The siblings glared at each other, before Jessica decided to see how far she could push it. Topper had specifically sent her here. She wasn't the attack dog she might have once been, but she still had a natural talent for getting on others' nerves.

'How does it feel to be bossed around by your sister?' she asked, keeping her tone as innocently inquisitive as she could manage.

Richie's gaze shifted in an instant, switching dangerously towards Jessica. 'What did you say?'

'It's just a question.'

Natalie stepped between them but Richie pushed himself up on the bar. 'How would it feel if I slipped something in your drink and took you out back for a bit of fun?'

'Richie!' Natalie spun, furious. 'Jesus, keep your trap shut.'

'What are you going to do? Tell Dad, like always?'

They glared at each other again but Jessica had seen what she wanted. She'd been threatened by bigger and better people than Richie Hyde and didn't believe for a moment that he had it in him. The jibe about his sister running to their father was hitting Natalie where it hurt.

Natalie was biting her lip, eyebrows twitching. If Jessica hadn't been there, there could've been a full-on physical fight – Jessica's money would have been on the sister.

Natalie turned back to Jessica, lips pressed together. 'Sorry about my brother – he was joking but he's nowhere near as funny as he thinks.' She took a breath. 'As I was saying, you need to talk to my father but he doesn't get back from holiday until this afternoon. I can leave a message, or . . .'

Jessica handed a card across to the other woman. 'Just tell him we were hoping to talk to him.'

Natalie angled towards the front door. 'I will.'

Jessica got back into her car but didn't start the engine. She watched the locked doors at the front of the casino and phoned Izzy.

'Is Topper back yet?' Jessica asked.

'Nope, I think he's still around the motorway bridge. Franks is swanning around like he owns the place.'

Detective Inspector Franks was equal to Jessica in rank and, with DCI Topper and Jessica away from the station, he was the highest-ranked CID officer on site. That meant next to nothing considering he had his own cases to deal with, but it wouldn't be the first time he'd gone on a power trip.

'What's he up to?'

'Ordering the constables around, plus he came to the sergeant station and asked what we were all up to.'

'Did you tell him to piss off back to the public toilets he came from?'

'I didn't exactly put it like that . . .'

'I'm just letting you know that Richard Hyde's on holiday,' Jessica said. 'He gets back this afternoon. His daughter's pretty good at trying to be nice but his son's an accident waiting to happen.'

Izzy was unmoved: 'You on your way back?'

'If I can get through the traffic.'

'We've got a picture of one of the pair who rammed the prison van yesterday.'

'Where'd that come from?'

'Someone took a picture on his phone.'

'Why didn't we know this yesterday?'

'No idea – the guy was wearing a balaclava but he lifted it as they ran off. We know who it is.'

'Already?'

'There's a birthmark on his cheek – he's one of our regulars. Our friendly neighbourhood breaker and enterer.'

Jessica knew exactly who Izzy meant – a serial offender, who seemed to have a permanent problem recognising what belonged to him and what didn't.

'Seriously?' Jessica replied. 'Irfan Nabil broke two people out of a prison van? He's going up in the world.'

'People are out looking for him now. Franks jumped on it.'

'What's it got to do with him?'

'Who knows – but no one was around to say any differently. He told us not to bother the guv with it.'

'The glory-hunting bastard.' Jessica checked the clock on her dashboard. 'All right, sod it, I'm on my way. Unlike Wanky Frankie, I've got an idea where Irfan might be.'

6

The neon sign at the front of the nail bar was advertising all-over tans and a 'Vegas Strip – the new Brazilian'. Ick, sod that. It was wedged almost in the middle of a small row of shops, with a Londis next to a Chinese at one end; then a pizza shop, hairdressers and pet store at the other.

DC Archie Davey crouched and then climbed into the passenger seat of Jessica's car. He smelled of the shower.

'Y'a'ight,' he said. Three words in one, Manc-style.

'Did you get away from the station all right?' Jessica asked.

'I had to go out the back way 'cos Funtime's patrolling the corridors, not doing any work himself.'

'This happens every bloody time Lewis leaves the station.'

'Oh aye, "Lewis". On first-name terms with the guv, are we?'

'Get lost, Arch.'

He shuffled in the seat. 'All right, I didn't mean anything by it, like.' He nodded at the nail bar. 'What are we doing here anyway? Everyone else is searching for Irfan on the estate where he lives.'

'That's because Franks is a glory-hunting moron who should stick to his own cases.'

'Why am I here?'

'To nick round the back, just in case. If no one's popped out in five minutes, come back here.'

'Do you think Irfan's inside?'

'What? Getting a manicure? If I thought that, it wouldn't just be me and you.'

'Who is inside?'

'His sister. Let's go.'

Jessica waited for Archie to sidle around the side of the Londis, heading to the passage at the rear of the shops. He was strutting in the way he always did, knees slightly bent, the lad about town. Sometimes she thought she couldn't stand him, other times she wasn't sure what she felt. He was good at his job but the pair of them had crossed a line from which they couldn't retreat.

When he had disappeared, Jessica entered the nail bar, checking from side to side until she spotted Falak Nabil sitting behind a screen, out of sight from the front window, sipping something green and steaming from a cup. The woman behind the counter asked if she could help but Jessica ignored her, angling in the other direction.

'Hey, Falak,' she said.

Irfan Nabil's sister was in her early twenties, long, straight black hair stretching down her back. She was wearing skinny jeans and a black top, with a beautifully embroidered satin scarf that wrapped across the top of her head and looped under her chin. She smiled, before the recognition set in. She sank in her seat, sighing silently.

'Can I borrow you for five minutes?' Jessica asked.

There was an awkward glance between Falak and her boss, with Jessica not wanting to reveal she was police.

Jessica looked between them, before Falak spoke. 'I'll only be five minutes.' The other woman took in Jessica, before nodding tersely.

Out front, Jessica leant on her car, smiling thinly. 'Sorry,' she said.

Falak had her arms crossed, back to the shop. 'What's *he* done now?'

'I can't say but I do need to find him.'

The younger woman was grinding her teeth before she reached into a pocket and took out an e-cigarette. She gripped it between her teeth, puffing a spiral of something that smelled fruity into the air.

She held the device in between her fingers at her side. 'I don't have anything to do with Irfan, neither does the rest of my family.'

'Why not?'

Her voice was low, furious. 'Why do you think? He brings shame on us all.'

'That's why I've come to you, rather than your mum and dad. At the moment, my colleagues are searching in the area where we last knew he was living. If they can't find him, they'll go to your parents' house.'

Her eyes widened. 'They can't! Not again.'

'They won't have any choice.'

'I don't know where he is.'

'But you'll know more than your mum and dad. If your brother's not at home, where is he?'

Falak drew deeply on the e-cigarette. There was a browny-purple scrawl of henna along the length of her fingers, stretching into a swirl on her wrist. Her long, rounded nails were painted in intricate rainbow stripes, the tips a spiky silver. She watched Jessica with deep brown pupils, before taking a second suck from the tube.

'He's got a girlfriend,' she said.

Jessica scrambled into her pocket for a pad. 'What's her name?'

'I don't know . . . Sharon? Sonia? Sophie? Something with an "S". A white girl.'

'Where does she live?'

Falak glanced sideways, to where Archie was edging towards them. Jessica waved him away, watching him acknowledge and head into the Londis.

'He's a colleague,' Jessica said, nodding at Archie's back.

Falak took another breath from the e-cigarette, then fiddled with the end, before pocketing it. 'What's Irfan done?' she whispered.

'Something stupid.'

She shook her head, sucking on her bottom lip. 'If I tell you where she lives, will you make sure he's safe?'

'How do you mean?'

'Last time he was arrested, he broke two ribs. He said it was one of you, you said he was trying to escape.' She shrugged, wanting to believe her brother, but not quite able.

'There are procedures . . .'

'That didn't stop him getting his ribs broken.'

'I could take you to the station and ask you in an interview room.'

Falak smiled thinly, dismissing the implied threat. 'He could have gone by then . . . all I'm asking is that he doesn't get hurt. You're the police, isn't that the minimum we should expect?'

'I'll pick him up myself,' Jessica said.

Falak nodded, reaching for Jessica's pad and pen and scribbling a note, before handing it back. Jessica made sure she could read the handwriting and then pocketed it all.

'Thanks,' she said.

Falak gulped away a mix of annoyance and upset, half-turning to the nail bar, before replying. 'If he gets hurt, it's on you.'

Jessica was still annoyed by the time she pulled up outside the address Falak had given her. 'You're so selfish,' she told Archie, who was slouched in the passenger seat.

'What? I left the station in a rush. I only had a quid.'

'So buy two things that cost 50p. I've had to drive all the way here, listening to you slurping on a Calippo.'

'You could have had a suck.'

He sniggered childishly, not needing to add the punch-line.

Jessica tutted as she checked Falak's note to make sure they were at the right place. It was a run-down semi-detached, with grubby double-glazed windows, a soil-streaked front yard, and a battered tumble dryer left on its side at the edge of the pavement. It sat at the centre of a row of simi-larly tattered properties.

Archie was clucking his teeth, nodding at the house. He'd wedged his empty ice-lolly tube on her dashboard and was making no effort to remove it. If she'd done that, it wouldn't have been a problem – she was hardly a clean freak – but the fact he'd assumed he could dump stuff in her car was infuriating. She wanted to tell him off but if he used the word 'nagging', there was every chance she'd lose it.

'You reckon he's inside?' Archie spoke with a click as he used his tongue to try to free something from between his teeth. He was *so* annoying.

'Maybe.'

'Why haven't you called anyone?'

'It's complicated.'

'*Right.*' He spoke in the annoying way that made it clear he knew it wasn't.

'Can you do me a favour, Arch?'

He pushed forward in the seat. 'What?'

'If anyone asks, we received urgent, time-sensitive information. Because of the state of the traffic, there was no time to report that to anyone, else we'd risk losing the suspect.'

She could feel him turning sideways to watch her. 'Of course – that's what happened, innit. Time-sensitive. Traffic. Got it.'

He might be annoying but at least she could trust him.

'It's only Irfan Nabil,' Jessica continued. 'I've arrested him before, most of the officers at the station have. Not a big deal. If he is there, we go in, grab him, out, you keep him quiet in the back seat, then we go back to the station. Easy peasy.'

'Gotcha.'

Jessica wasn't convincing even herself. Irfan had once been caught riffling through the magazines inside a newsagent at three in the morning. He wasn't *University Challenge* material – but then this wasn't a robbery, this was a break from a prison van. Still, it was that or risk breaking her promise to Falak and Jessica didn't want to do that.

'How are we going to do this?' Archie asked.

'Same as the nail bar. You pop round the back, I go through the front. If he runs, nab him. Just don't bloody hurt him.'

'What if he runs at you?'

Jessica turned to face him, eyebrows raised. 'What if he does?'

'I just mean . . .'

'What?'

He hesitated, not wanting to add: *'You're a girl.'*

She didn't force him to finish the sentence and dig himself a deeper hole. 'What are you waiting for?' she said. 'Get round the back.'

Archie did as he was told, climbing out of the car and heading to the end of the row of houses, before disappearing into the alley. Jessica took a deep breath, a little out of her depth for the first time in a while. Usually, she wouldn't give herself time to think before doing something stupid . . .

Out of the car, she first searched for a bell, before knocking hard on the glass of the double-glazed door. There was a shuffling, a clunk, and then a man's voice: 'Who is it?'

Jessica stepped away from the rippled glass, narrowly out of sight of the nearby window. 'I've got a parcel.'

There was a short pause and then: 'Leave it on the doorstep.'

'I need a signature.'

The shuffling became louder and then a shadow loomed

on the other side of the dappled glass. It moved from side to side, then there was a clicking before the door opened a sliver.

BANG!

Jessica threw her shoulder into the door, forcing it inwards but bouncing as the person inside shoved back. A man yelped but Jessica had the momentum, heaving forward until the resistance disappeared and she stumbled onto the doormat. She peered up to see Irfan's mop of black hair disappearing through the open door ahead. There was a jangle of pans and a clatter of china as Jessica heaved herself up, racing after him into a kitchen. Irfan's top half was out of the window, his trainers scrambling on the back of the tiles as the contents of the draining board scattered across the floor. Jessica lunged for him, but only managed to hold onto his shoe as he fell through the other side, landing with an 'oof'.

She kicked her way past the clutter on the floor, scrambling for the back door, which, luckily, had the key in the lock. As she dashed into the back garden, Jessica relaxed, peering up to see Archie sitting on the flapping, wriggling figure of Irfan Nabil.

'Let me go, I—' Irfan's eyes widened as he spotted Jessica, the game firmly up. 'I didn't do it,' he added desperately. Archie shifted his position, allowing Irfan to roll and then stand before the handcuffs were clipped around his wrists.

'Didn't do what?' Jessica asked.

'Whatever it is.'

'Aye, pal,' Archie replied on her behalf. 'That's what they all say.'

7

The heater in the corner of the interview room was fighting a losing battle against the power of the air-conditioning. Somewhere, an iceberg was melting, seals were dying, and Greenpeace would be going mental if they realised how much electricity was being wasted on a building that was simultaneously being cooled and heated.

Archie was restless at Jessica's side, shuffling in his seat, wanting to get involved as Jessica remained calm and spoke slowly and deliberately. Irfan Nabil was on the other side of the table sweating, which was nothing to do with the heat, or lack of. The duty solicitor had her fingers interlocked, knees crossed, generally waiting for the same thing as Jessica: Irfan to say something stupid. Sooner or later it would happen, they both knew it.

'Did you kill Owen Priestley?' Jessica asked.

Irfan couldn't sit still. 'What? No.'

'But you did break him out of the prison van?'

'No!'

He'd done well so far, the most basic of questions failing to trip him up. He'd got his own name right, too.

Jessica slid an enlarged photo that showed Irfan next to the prison van across the desk. 'That's your scar, isn't it?' she said.

She peered from the pictured scar to the actual one, a

purple moon-shaped ripple across the curve of Irfan's right cheek.

He touched his skin, no doubt wondering if he could get away with denying it.

'Er . . . maybe.'

'It *is* your scar, isn't it, Irfan?'

'Um . . .'

She passed across a second photo, the same as the first but not such a close-up. It showed Owen Priestley and a balaclava-clad figure heading across a road, then Irfan slightly behind, his balaclava two-thirds removed, glancing backwards towards the picture-taker.

'Was the balaclava itchy?' Jessica asked. 'Or hot? I bet it was warm under that in the heat yesterday. You lifted it up for a quick scratch, then kept running.'

'Um . . . no comment.'

Jessica nodded, wanting to elbow Archie to stop him wriggling. The constable was dying for a crack. She slid across a third photo – Owen Priestley's limp, lifeless body dangling from the motorway bridge. 'So, you broke him out yesterday, murdered him overnight and then left him hanging for us to find.'

Irfan's eyes widened, a small gulp giving way to a truthful cry of surprise. 'He's dead?'

'Don't you watch the news?'

'I didn't do it.'

'You broke him out and that was the last time he was seen. Seems clear-cut to me.'

'But, I . . .'

'You what?'

Irfan's neck shrank into his top, a tortoise taking shelter in its shell. 'It wasn't me.'

'Which bit wasn't you? The breaking out, or the killing?'

The solicitor spoke without turning. 'You don't have to answer that. One incident isn't necessarily linked to the other.'

'Do you believe that, Irfan?' Jessica asked. 'Is that how you think a jury will see it when they see the photo of you with Priestley?'

He shook his head.

'What does that mean?' Jessica asked.

Another shake.

'Let's say I believe you – you're not a murderer, you're a shoplifter and a thief. A pretty shoddy one at that.' She opened a cardboard folder and started to read. 'We've got possession of cannabis, possession with intent to supply cannabis, a dozen shoplifting offences, an attempted burglary, disturbing the peace, drunk and disorderly, blah, blah, blah.' Jessica looked up. 'How do you graduate from that lot to smashing someone out of a prison van?'

'It weren't my idea.'

Archie snorted, unable to control himself any longer. 'Believe me, pal, of everything we reckon you've been up to, being the brains behind the operation is not on the list.'

Jessica let it go, before again taking control. 'Which bit wasn't your idea? The break-out or the murder?'

He shrugged. 'I dunno.'

'Okay, let's go backwards. First of all, who was the other person under the balaclava?'

'When?'

'When you broke Owen Priestley out of the prison van.'

Irfan shook his head.

'What does that mean?' Jessica asked.

'No comment.'

'Are you *really* going to do this? You're looking at conspiring to assist an offender's escape from lawful custody – you can do ten years for that alone, and that's before we talk about Owen Priestley being murdered.'

'No comment.'

'If you're not going to say who you were with, then who was the person that hired you?'

'No comment.'

Jessica tried to stay calm. 'Come on, Irfan. Think of Falak, think of your mum and dad and your brothers. Ten years is a long time. If you work with us, I'll see what I can do.'

'No comment.'

Shite.

Jessica nudged Archie with her knee. Time to throw off the leash.

Archie leant forward, top lip curled. 'I know who your mates are,' Archie said, taking the file from Jessica. 'There's Scroaty McScroat, Jermaine Hipkiss, Ali Tambe, Dante Jacobs.' He paused, shaking his head, peering up at Irfan. 'Is he *really* named Dante? Seriously? *Dante?*'

Irfan was unmoved, gazing at a spot on the wall behind them.

'Then there's Jamar Sarwan – he's your best mate, isn't he? If you don't give us the name of who you were with when you broke out Priestley, we're going to pick this lot up

. . . well, not Scroaty McScroat, but the rest of 'em. Every time they ask why they're being nicked, I'll make sure I'm there, telling 'em you've been talking. They'll think you grassed.'

Irfan shook his head rapidly from side to side. 'It's nothing to do with them.'

Jessica cut in: 'So who is it to do with?'

Another headshake.

Jessica slipped her chair backwards and put a hand on Archie's shoulder, offering a quick glance to the camera in the corner above them. 'I haven't got time for this. Charge him and stick him back downstairs. We'll have him in front of the mags tomorrow and they'll refuse bail on the basis of the scar photo alone. He's going to sit in a prison cell for the next six months as he waits for trial.' She turned back to Irfan, raising her eyebrows. Last chance.

He shook his head, locking his fingers into one another, eyes fixed on the table, looking like a very frightened young man. She wondered if he was scared of prison, or worried about what might happen if he actually gave up the names.

8

There was a buzz and a crackle, then the words 'thirty seconds' fizzed through their radios. Archie leant forward in the passenger seat of Jessica's car, a kid on Christmas morning.

'This should be fun,' he said.

'More like a waste of time,' Jessica replied.

They'd been bluffing when Archie listed the names of Irfan's friends; she hadn't expected Topper to turn around and tell them to pick up all his mates. Still, it wasn't as if she, or anyone else, had a better idea. Irfan was one of the duo who had broken Owen Priestley and Kevin Jones out of the prison van. No one thought he'd murdered Priestley, but it could have been his accomplice, or whoever hired them. With Irfan unwilling to give them any details, it was desperate times – and everyone knew what desperate times called for: stupid ideas.

The flats in front were three storeys high, the once-red bricks giving way to dirty, dark stains along the height and width. Of the thirty flats, Jessica could see broken or boarded-up windows in at least six, with another half-dozen up for letting. Pity the poor bastards that ended up here. If you couldn't abide the radioactive toxins of winter in Chernobyl, there was always this dump on the border between Salford and Eccles.

Dark vans had parked around the corner, with the tactical entry team massing at the edge of the building, battering ram, pepper sprays, batons and sodding big boots at the ready. This lot and the tactical firearms squad had already picked up some serious overtime this week – and it was only Tuesday.

'Why's it a waste of time?' Archie said, not sounding particularly interested. He was waiting for the crash, bang, wallop.

'Irfan's mates are thieves, scroats and shitbags. They couldn't mastermind a chip run between them, let alone a prison-van break and hanging some guy from a bridge.'

'Irfan did.'

'No he bloody didn't – he stood around a prison van with a gun. His accomplice wasn't any of this lot.'

'What else can we do . . . well, aside from give Irfan a booting.'

Jessica turned to face him.

'What?' Archie said.

'Don't even joke.'

'I was only—'

'Well don't.'

They continued watching through the front window as the officers got into position in the middle row. Jessica didn't think Archie had meant it but it was that kind of immaturity that got people, got *them*, into trouble. Besides, if there was one thing not to joke about after the recent Pratley report into practices in the Greater Manchester Police, it was beating up suspects.

'This is a long thirty seconds,' Archie said, unable to

listen to silence any longer. Jessica was spending too much time with him, in and out of work. She liked the occasional bit of peace and harmony but there was precious little when he was around, with every moment of silence broken by his minute attention span.

Jessica didn't reply, wondering if he'd take the hint.

He didn't. He was tugging on his ear, showing a tiny glimmer of nerves.

'I was thinking about something we could do one week-end when we're both off . . .'

Jessica tried not to react. It wasn't the first time he'd sug-gested doing things away from work, away from his flat. She'd told him more than once that they weren't in any sort of relationship but he wasn't the type to take a blunt force let-down, let alone a hint.

'United are playing a pre-season friendly next month, and—'

'I'm not interested in football, Arch.'

'My parents live up Bolton way and my dad's coming down to Old Trafford for the match, while me mam's going to the Trafford Centre . . .'

Oh, no . . .

'. . . After that, we're all going out for tea and I was won-dering if . . .'

Jessica had never been so grateful to hear her radio snap into life. The male voice was short and to the point. 'All in position. On my call. Three . . . two . . . one. Go.'

Above them, the black-clad figures smashed through the flat door in a thunderous boom of splintering plastic. Jessica climbed out of her car, leaning on the bonnet and watching as a gangly-looking black lad in jeans, bright white trainers and a vest was dragged out, his legs flapping as he tried to kick the nearest officer. There was a splash of dark tattoos up and down his arms, his hair sliced into cornrows.

'I ain't done nowt,' he shouted as the officers tried to lead him down the stairs. People were emerging from nearby flats, pointing, gawking and, predictably, filming. Jessica clicked her radio. 'We've got Dante Jacobs,' she said, waiting for the replies and then giving Archie the thumbs-up: all four of Irfan's friends were in custody.

Because of the lack of cells at Longsight Police Station and the fact Irfan was currently residing there, Jessica had been set up in one of the interview 'suites' at the main Bootle Street Police Station in the centre of Manchester. It was the only twenty-four-hour PC station in the city and dealt with the vast majority of the weekend drunken buffoons who caused trouble.

The word 'suite' evoked thoughts of luxury: spacious beds, comfortable settees, plush carpets and brews that didn't taste like they'd been pissed out. Bootle Street's interview 'suite' had none of those things. What it lacked in lavishness, it more than made up for in Eastern Bloc chic. It had a table bolted to the floor, uncomfortable plastic chairs and the faint whiff of BO. Still, at least the heating worked, which was more than could be said for the ones at Longsight.

Archie was still at Jessica's side, a neglected puppy that kept coming back for more. She sipped the tea, which reminded her of something she couldn't quite place. Armpits

– something like that. It was seemingly impossible to get a decent brew at any police station in the city.

There was a knock at the door and then a PC entered with arrestee number one.

Interview one – Dante Jacobs, 22; theft from a shop x2, driving without a licence, driving without insurance, driving without due care and attention, theft from a motor vehicle x5, section 39 assault. Vest, bare tattooed arms with half-finished wonky bits that looked like he'd scrawled them himself.

'How long am I gonna be here? I've got stuff to do.'

Jessica deliberately paused to take a sip of her tea, the taste of which hadn't improved. Dante was shuffling in his seat, annoyed.

'What have you got to do later?' Jessica asked.

'Stuff.'

'Like what?'

'I'm getting me 'air sorted.'

Jessica peered at the weave of cornrows curling over his ears, dropping into a short ponytail. 'That is a *really* good idea.'

'What do you mean by that?'

'You should get that sorted. It looks like you did it yourself in the dark, with your left hand.'

He smoothed his hair down, scowling. She'd touched a nerve. He flapped a hand towards Archie. 'Least I'm not a midget.'

If they'd been anywhere else, Jessica might have chuckled. The one thing guaranteed to wind Archie up was jibes about his height. He leant across, finger jabbing at the other side of the table, about to reply, before Jessica tugged him backwards.

'What do you know about Owen Priestley?' Jessica asked.

Dante shrugged. 'Who?'

Jessica held her hand out flat in the air. 'Dead guy, 'bout yay high. Broken out of a prison van yesterday, found hanging from a motorway bridge this morning.'

'Never heard of him.'

'Your mate Irfan has – he helped break him out.'

Dante snorted. '*Irf?*'

'We've got a photo of him.'

'Nah . . . must be someone else.'

'The person in the picture has the exact same scar on his face that Irfan does.'

Dante's brow furrowed. '*Irf?* He broke someone out of a prison van?'

'There were two of them – who was the other guy?'

Dante started laughing. 'You think I know?'

'You're one of his friends and somebody knows what happened.'

He rolled his eyes, turning and glancing up to the clock. 'You must be desperate.'

Interview two – Ali Tambe, 24; possession of a Class B drug x3, possession with intent to supply a Class B drug. A rat-like wastrel of a man, dark hoody two sizes too big, joke of a moustache that even a thirteen-year-old could outgrow.

'How's business?' Jessica asked.

'What business?'

'The cannabis-growing one you keep getting caught for. Where are the plants this time – obviously not in your house, so have you got a mate growing them? Or some dingy flat somewhere?' Jessica clicked her fingers. 'Or an allotment! I can just picture you in wellies and a flat cap plodding around a patch of mud.'

Ali squirmed in his chair, eyes darting in both directions as he stroked the pathetic excuse for facial hair on his top lip. It was like a baby caterpillar. 'I dunno what you're talking about.'

'Course you don't – but you can tell me the last time you saw Irfan Nabil.'

'Irf?'

'Do you need to see a photo?'

'No, er . . . I was round his girlfriend's house on the PlayStation last Thursday but I've not seen him since.'

'What was he like?' Jessica asked.

Ali shrugged. 'How d'ya mean?'

'Was he excited? Nervous? Did he seem like he had something on his mind?'

'I dunno . . . we were playing *FIFA*, not really talking.'

Archie was nodding along – his perfect night in: the lads, few beers, ten giant bags of Walkers Sensations, *FIFA*. Job done.

'Did Irfan talk about anything he had coming up?' Jessica asked.

'Like what?'

'That's what I'm asking you.'

'Dunno . . . he was wondering when the new *Call of Duty*'s out.'

Interview three – Jamar Sarwan, 23; clean record. 800m champion, Greater Manchester Schools Championships, under 16s. Miami Dolphins shirt, small hooped earring.

'Do you remember me?' Jessica asked.

Jamar nodded, maintaining eye contact. 'You came to my house after Irf was done for robbing that offy.'

'Right,' Jessica replied, 'so we know each other. I know you're the sensible one out of this sorry lot. Dante's a thug, Ali's a weed-smoking dickhead, Jermaine does whatever he's told and Irfan has some sort of self-destruct button that he can't resist pressing. Despite having them as friends, you're the one with a job, a girlfriend, a baby, a proper life. You're a credit to society.'

Jamar shrugged, smiling narrowly, a little embarrassed. 'They're still me mates.'

'Right, and that's why I want you to do Irfan a favour. He's got himself into something serious and the stupid sod's in so deep that he doesn't want to dig himself out.'

'What?'

'He's one of the pair that knocked over that prison van yesterday.'

Jamar rocked back in the seat, head cocked disbelievingly at an angle. '*Irf?*'

'Believe me, I'm as surprised as you are.'

'Didn't those blokes have shotguns?'

'Exactly – who was the other guy?'

Jamar opened his arms, holding his hands palms-up,

looking from Archie to Jessica, entirely believably. 'I dunno, Stahh. That was Irf?'

Jessica had no idea what 'Stahh' meant. It didn't sound insulting, which was one thing.

'I can show you the photo,' she said.

'A'ight.'

Jessica passed him across the picture of Irfan: balaclava half-removed, running away from the scene of the break-out, Owen Priestley a few metres in front of him. Jamar's eyebrows shot up, worry lines appearing across his head, eyes widening. 'That's him, Stahh.'

'We know. Who's the other guy?'

He peered up, making eye contact again. 'I swear on my motha's life, I dunno.'

Archie tapped the pad in front of him: two words in capital letters: *SISTER/SISTAHH*. This is what it had come to – he was her translator. She nodded and he scribbled away the note.

'Honestly, Stahh, if I knew, I'd tell you. I got me baby at home, I don't need none of this grief.'

Jessica believed him.

Interview four – Jermaine Hipkiss, 22; possession of a Class B drug x7. A frightened boy in the body of a hulk; huge shoulders, thick neck, high-pitched voice.

'I'm not trying to catch you out here, Jermaine,' Jessica said. 'These are very simple questions, okay?'

He turned to the overworked duty solicitor, who nodded, so he nodded too.

Jessica showed him the photo of Irfan Nabil escaping

with Owen Priestley. 'Your friend helped break a man out of a prison van yesterday morning. Today, that man was found dead.' She pointed at the other man in the balaclava. 'I want you to tell me who this person is.'

'Dunno.'

'When was the last time you saw Irfan?'

Jermaine scratched his head, screwing his bottom lip into his mouth and biting it with yellow teeth. Jessica had spoken to Jermaine before but always hated it. His brutish, enormous physique housed the personality of a young teen-ager, if not medically then in her opinion. He had a string of drug offences on his record, almost certainly carrying goods for Ali Tambe.

'We played *FIFA*.'

'When was that?'

'Last week.'

'Did Irfan say anything to you about jobs he might have on?'

Jermaine's gaze flickered towards the door, unable to mask the lie. 'No.'

'I know he did.'

He shook his head vigorously, crossing his arms. 'No.'

Jessica let him stew for a few seconds, nudging Archie with her knee and hoping he knew what she wanted.

He did: 'Who won?' Archie asked.

Jermaine pouted out his bottom lip, confused. 'Huh?'

Archie relaxed into his seat: 'I had the lads round the weekend before last for a *FIFA* tournament. The five of us played round robin, then semi-finals and finals. My mate, Bod, beat me in the final. Bastard.'

Jermaine sat up straighter, uncrossing his arms and breaking into a small smile. 'I won.'

'Aah, you're good then. Who'd you play as?'

'Munich.'

'Nice . . . bit of German efficiency.' Archie rolled up his sleeve to show the Manchester United badge tattooed on his left forearm. 'I'm United. Can't bring myself to play as anyone else. Who'd you support?'

The grin was creeping further across Jermaine's face. 'Chelsea.'

'*Chelsea?* You like that London mob? I was there when we turned 'em over at Old Trafford a few months back. Belting atmosphere. Why'd you support Chelsea?'

Jermaine shrugged. 'Me dad.'

'Fair enough – my old man's been United since he was born. His old man before that. Kinda runs in the family. I've got a season ticket.'

As much as he annoyed her, Jessica knew there was no one better than Archie in the station for doing the arm-round-the-shoulder act. It wasn't even a performance – this was his life. If he wasn't a police officer, he'd have been the go-to guy for dodgy goods on his Stretford estate.

'The reason you're here today,' Archie continued, 'isn't because we're trying to catch you out, it's because Irfan's got himself in a lot of trouble. I've got mates – my pal, Bod, was caught fiddling his DSS. He told them he was living on his own but he was at his missus' house. He asked me what he should do and I told him to be honest – they were going to catch him out anyway and it'd be a lot less hassle all round if he got it over with. We know what Irfan did – all we're trying to do is make sure he doesn't get himself in more bother. D'ya get me?'

Jermaine nodded slowly.

Archie pointed at the photo. 'Do you know the other guy in the balaclava?'

He shook his head.

'But you know something, don't you?'

Jermaine said nothing at first, staring at the table, bottom lip pouting again. 'No . . .'

Jessica wrote the word *HYDE* on the pad in front of them.

'Who's Natalie Hyde?' Archie asked after the merest of glances.

Jermaine's head bolted up, head shaking, eyes all over the place. 'Dunno.'

'What about Richard Hyde?'

'Dunno.'

'Are they names that Irfan told you about?'

'No.'

'He did, didn't he?'

'No.'

'He told you someone had asked him to do a job for the Hyde family and that he was worried about how it was going to go.'

'No.'

'Who asked him to do the job?'

'Dunno.'

'But you know something.' Archie waited for Jermaine to peer up from the table again. 'Come on, Jermaine, Irfan's your mate and needs your help. If you don't know the name, then what do you know?'

There was a long pause, Archie staring at Jermaine, Jermaine staring back. Jessica and the duty solicitor were superfluous.

Jermaine's voice had dropped in pitch and volume. He looked close to tears. 'I saw him on Saturday.'

'Where?'

'Me ma lives by the Morrisons near the park.'

'Ordsall?'

Jermaine nodded. 'Irf was in the park with someone.'

'A man?' Archie asked. There was another nod and then: 'Do you know him?'

He bobbed his head from side to side.

'Would you recognise him?'

Jermaine shrugged.

The Big Book of Bastardly Shites, © Greater Manchester Police, was neither available for purchase in high-street stores, nor online. It was so rare, so one-of-a-kind, that even Amazon didn't list it – and they sold books written by any old nobody. There was no single author; instead a collection of GMP police officers had added to it over an extended period of time, creating a Bible of local pains-in-the-arse. It was a *Who's Who* of nuisances, with page after page of mugshots. What was even better was that some plucky constable, who would no doubt go far, had recently digitised the entire thing. Instead of a thick, toe-breaking compendium, every-thing was now neatly stored on the station's iPads. They were kept, along with laptops and numerous other nickable things, in a secure cabinet, for which Fat Pat kept the key.

Fat Pat worked on reception at the front of the station, a mix of desk sergeant, receptionist, staff organiser, busybody, gossip, and food critic all rolled into one. Not that his standards of culinary analysis were high; a Greggs steak bake and a Michelin-starred meal were all the same to him, and he certainly got through his fair share of steak bakes. He guarded the equipment cupboard key almost as tightly as he shielded his food, making sure items were signed out in triplicate, along with a precise time when they were due back. Anyone would've thought police officers were likely to nick stuff . . .

After arguing with him over the exact reasons for needing an iPad, then signing away her life and the lives of any future children she may have, plus the very existence of her soul, Pat finally allowed Jessica to borrow one of the tablets.

Back in the interview room, she flipped through the images one at a time as Jermaine offered a steady stream of 'nope', 'nope', 'no', 'nah', 'nope', 'no', 'hang on', 'no', 'no', and 'nope' responses.

It was a sorry affair that Jessica recognised more than half of the book's inhabitants: thieves, kiddy-fiddlers, fences, muggers, burglars, drunks, pickpockets. Every now and then, Jermaine would squint at the screen before shaking his head. *The Big Book of Bastardly Shites*, e-book edition, © Greater Manchester Police, contained more than a thousand faces.

Almost half an hour had passed when Jermaine's eyes narrowed and he started to nod slowly. Jessica had been up and working for eleven hours and was beginning to feel it.

9

'You're not even on shift,' Jessica said, although she already knew Archie's reply.

'Neither are you.'

'Yeah but I'm too important to go home.'

'You just like the sound of doors being smashed in.'

Jessica didn't know if she actually found it funny, or if the tiredness was kicking in. She laughed anyway. Who didn't like the sound of splintering wood, shattering plastic and big, burly blokes bellowing? Well, as long as it wasn't your front door they were putting through.

Ahead, the tactical entry team was pooling outside a ground-floor flat that sat in the centre of three identical apartment rows. The hexagon-shaped clothes line loaded with slightly soiled underwear was getting in the way but at least offered a tiny amount of camouflage. Tiny being the optimum word. Jessica and Archie were around the corner, out of harm's way but with a perfect view of Eric Maudsley's front door. The gorgeous summer's morning had elongated into the rest of the day, with an early evening haze of warmth coating the city in a summery spectacle. There was nothing Brits liked more than barbecue weather. The moment the mercury hit the steady height of fifteen Celsius, people were out in their gardens, gas canisters fired up, burning sausages and burgers, local A&E unit on standby. If

Jessica was normal, that's what she'd be doing. Instead, she was yet again waiting to speak to some local shite.

The call came through the radio that everyone was in position, then 'three-two-one-go'.

Boom!

Heavy boots thundered through Maudsley's front door in a satisfying cacophony. Jessica expected to hear the quick call to say Maudsley was in custody; instead there was a silence. A too-long silence.

'Ma'am . . .'

Jessica hated being called that. It made her sound like an old-time schoolmistress, cane at the ready, all set to beat the shite out of some kid who'd turned up late for a maths lesson. She headed across the crumbling patio, ducked under the thongs and bras, stepped over the remains of Eric Maudsley's front door, and entered his flat.

The smell of cannabis was so strong that she felt slightly light-headed stepping across the threshold. The hallway walls were covered with posters of cannabis leaves with red, yellow and green stripes, and a framed portrait of Bob Marley, with the word RESPECT emblazoned beneath.

Jessica headed through, entering a kitchen and then looping in a U-shape until she was in the living room. Five tactical entry officers were standing close to the door, staring towards the sofa where a man was sitting defiantly, glaring at them. Usually, if someone resisted arrest, he'd have been dragged out – but Eric Maudsley knew the drill. He was grasping a small boy to his chest, using him as a shield. There were toys dotted around the edges of the room – a soft SpongeBob SquarePants, a dinosaur poking out from a red plastic racing car, Duplo bricks, a squishy penguin. Next to the window was a television, showing a cartoon, something that looked like it could induce epilepsy at any moment, with a series of quick flashes sparking on and off. When Jessica looked back at Maudsley, she realised why the officers had stopped – it wasn't just because of the child he was holding, it was the sharp scissors in his other hand.

Maudsley was angled on the sofa, the child peering over his shoulder towards the television.

'Daddy,' the boy said.

'Watch the telly,' Maudsley snapped. He had patchy, gingery hair, with a small ring pierced through his left eyebrow. The word **CHAMPION** was tattooed on his left arm, along with some spiky symbols. There were more tattoos on his other arm but Jessica couldn't make them out.

She tapped the biggest tactical entry officer on the shoulder, speaking loud enough for everyone to hear. 'I'll deal.' She indicated the radio on her shoulder, saying for Maudsley's benefit that it was two-way and that everyone else could listen outside. The officer didn't seem convinced but he started to shuffle out regardless, leaving Jessica and Archie. Archie was watching her and Maudsley from the doorway, glancing between them.

'You too,' Jessica added.

'Are you—?'

'We're going to have a chat.'

She could feel Archie watching her as he reluctantly slipped into the kitchen. His footsteps echoed along the hallway, until there was only a solemn silence remaining, the peace punctuated by the flashing silent images on the television.

'Daddy . . .'

'Shut the fuck up,' Maudsley hissed, not moving from the sofa. His fingers tightened on the boy's back, eyes glaring through Jessica. His son had fair hair but she couldn't see much other than the back of his head.

Jessica rested on the back of an armchair, matching the man's gaze. 'What's his name?'

'What's it to you?'

'I'm Jessica and I'd really like it if you could put your son down and we can have an amicable chat.'

'Why are you here?'

'You know why.'

Maudsley shuffled slightly, shifting the position of the child. The youngster wasn't a baby, but was perhaps two or three. He was sucking on his thumb, still watching the television.

'Irfan told us everything,' Jessica said.

Maudsley's eyes blazed, fingers tightening on his son's back. 'That Paki bastard – I *knew* he was a liability. He always—' He stopped, remembering Jessica's radio was broadcasting. Irfan or no Irfan, he'd blown it.

'You're even wearing the same trainers,' Jessica added, nodding at his feet. He peered down at the white Nikes that were in the photos. 'We've got a shoe print next to the car you burnt out. What's the betting it'll match the ones you're wearing?'

Maudsley sighed but didn't reply, didn't move.

'Come on, Eric – you're small-time. Weed, imported fags,

stuff that falls off lorries. How do you go from that to breaking someone out of a prison van?'

The boy started wriggling. 'Daddy . . .'

Maudsley's other hand gripped the scissors more tightly, gaze flaring towards Jessica as he clung onto his son. 'Stop fidgeting! Watch the TV.'

The boy didn't stop squirming, turning to look at Jessica. Reluctantly, Maudsley let him, though he continued to hold the scissors in his other hand.

'What's your name?' Jessica asked.

'Theo.'

'Shut up,' Maudsley said, shunting the child off his lap onto the sofa next to him. Out of his son's eye line, he raised the scissors, holding them a little behind the boy's head, making sure Jessica could see them. A glimmer of sunlight reflected from the pointy, dangerous-looking tips.

'What do you think's going to happen here?' Jessica asked.

'I'm going to get into my car and drive away.'

'You know we can't let that happen.'

He tilted the scissors, angling the tips towards Jessica. 'It'd be awful if something happened to the kid.'

'*Theo*,' Jessica reminded him.

The boy peered up at her. 'It's finished,' he said.

'What's finished?' his father growled.

'Jason.'

The television was now showing an advert for some sort of cheese-based snack. Maudsley looked from side to side. 'Bloody remote.' The hand with the scissors didn't move but his head flipped back and forth, glancing down the back of the sofa. A remote control was on the floor next to the armchair. As soon as he turned away, Jessica angled forward and knocked it underneath the chair.

'Can you see it?' Maudsley hissed.

Jessica nodded towards a different remote next to the television. 'Is that it?'

'That's for the stereo.'

'I can't see it.'

Theo was fidgeting again. 'Daddy . . .'

Maudsley spun around, gripped his son's head with his free hand and turned him back to the television. 'Shut. Up.' He stared up at Jessica. 'Turn it over.'

'How?'

'There are buttons on the side.'

'Right.'

Jessica edged around the room, passing the window until she was standing next to the television. She crouched, peering at the buttons. 'I can't see them.'

'They're right in front of you. You've only got to shift up a channel or two.'

Jessica slid her fingers along the dimpled buttons, but didn't press down. 'There's nothing here.'

'Other side then.'

Jessica stepped to the other side and did the same. 'It's clear on this side.' For good measure, she ran her fingers along the underside. 'There are no buttons.'

'There bloody are.'

Jessica stood up straight, arms outstretched. 'I don't know what to tell you.'

He nodded towards the armchair. 'Sit there.'

Jessica did as she was told. Maudsley scooped Theo up onto his shoulder, holding the scissors in his other hand as he slowly stood, eyes not leaving Jessica.

'Don't try anything,' he growled.

'I'm not going to.'

He twisted so that he could continue to watch her as he backed towards the television. Jessica held out her hands to show she was no threat. Maudsley hoiked Theo up further, grimacing. He continued backing towards the television . . .

Jessica wasn't sure if she heard the *thwick* first, or saw him lurch forward. There was a tinkle of glass as a bullet-shaped hole appeared in the window, followed by a splash of red from Maudsley's shoulder that wasn't holding Theo. The bullet thumped into the wall opposite, passing straight through his shoulder as Jessica darted in, grabbing Theo and pulling him from Maudsley's arms as the man collapsed to the ground, shrieking in pain, reaching for the wound.

'BITCH!' he yelled, trying to get to his feet as Jessica headed for the kitchen. There was a thunderous clump of boots as officers stormed inside, pounding past her. Maudsley yelped in pain as someone pinned his arms behind his back. Jessica ignored him, continuing through the house, holding Theo in her arms. He was scrambling to peer over her shoulder but that was something no youngster should see.

They arrived outside as more officers pounded in. Three more riot vans had arrived while she'd been inside, complementing the tactical entry and firearms teams already on site.

Jessica settled Theo on the ground and knelt so they were at the same level. His eyes were wide with fear, which was no bloody wonder.

'Are you okay, pal?' Jessica asked, one hand on his shoulder.

Theo nodded slowly, a small smile creeping across his angelic face. He certainly didn't get his looks from his father. As she returned his grin, he showed exactly what he had inherited, twisting his head sideways, opening his mouth wide, and sinking his teeth deep into Jessica's flesh.

10

Bex peered at Jessica's hand, wincing. 'Ouch – did you have to get a tetanus jab for that?'

'It was a child, not a dog.'

'Same difference.'

Bex and Jessica didn't have an awkward relationship, but it was difficult to describe its nature to others. They lived in Jessica's house but weren't related. Bex was seventeen and had been homeless before moving in. Jessica was slightly more than double her age, so it wasn't quite true to say they were friends, but neither did they have a mother-daughter relationship. Whatever it was, it worked for them both. Jessica liked the company; Bex needed something, *someone*, in her life. In many ways, she was still a kid, despite everything she'd seen and done while living on the streets of Manchester.

Jessica went back to stirring the contents of the saucepan. The kitchen smelled of her childhood: sausages and baked beans. It was hard to think of a better meal.

Bex was leaning against the freezer, twiddling a strand of her long black hair, before straightening her nose ring. 'Did you go to the doctor?' she asked.

'Someone at the station looked at it.'

'Don't they put down dogs who bite?'

'I don't think the same applies with kids.'

'Yeah . . . probably fair enough.'

Jessica opened the oven door to check the sausages. She took out the tray, turned them over and then put it back in again. Sausage and beans on toast was her speciality, her forte, her . . . something else that sounded foreign and good.

'How have you been?' Bex asked. 'I saw all that stuff on the TV with the prison van and that guy on the bridge . . .'

It was a perfectly reasonable question but Jessica sensed what remained unspoken. This was the first time she'd been home in two days, having stayed at Archie's the previous evening. Bex knew Jessica was seeing someone, but not who. Jessica's fiancé, Adam, was still in a coma, the doctors unsure if he'd ever wake up. She should be spending evenings at his side, not with another man, but . . . it wasn't that simple.

Or was it?

How long could a person spend next to someone who didn't respond, didn't move, before it was impossible to take any longer? She'd spent weeks, months, at his side and now . . . she wasn't sure. There was no manual for life, no one to say how a person was supposed to act. As long as she kept moving, kept working, she could live with herself.

'Jess . . . ?'

Jessica blinked back into the kitchen, heart pumping like a piston. 'Sorry, I was miles away. Um, yeah, I'm fine. It's just busy. We got the guys who broke him out of the van, that's why I was late.' She'd blurted out the words without thinking. 'Anyway, I'm the one who should be asking you that. How long till your course starts?'

She turned to see Bex twisting on one foot, a nervous, excited bundle of energy. Not many teenagers relished studying but Bex had never had the encouragement to immerse herself in education before. After getting through a part-time winter to spring introductory course, she was now ready to go full-time. For the first time, she had self-set goals, a future that wasn't living day-to-day on the street.

'About two months,' Bex replied.

'Did you get your letter back with the confirmation?'

'Yesterday morning – history, economics and sociology. Eighteen months at college, then, hopefully, university. I would've texted but figured you were busy.'

'You can always message.' Jessica flipped off the cooker's dials and lifted up the pan. 'Right, sausage and beans on toast, *à la* Jessica.'

'I'll clear my textbooks away – they're all over the table.'

'*Textbooks?* It's a summer's day. It's sunny! You're nearly eighteen, you should be out doing stuff.'

The steam from the oven and subsequent overly sensitive smoke alarm meant she didn't get a reply.

A few minutes later, they were sitting on the sofa, plates on laps, dots of bean juice on the carpet – oops – watching a quiz show in which the combined display of knowledge wouldn't have troubled a below-average primary school student.

'What are you doing for your birthday?' Jessica asked, eyes not leaving her plate. Trying to balance, talk and think was proving harder than it should.

'Dunno.'

'Aren't you excited about turning eighteen? I was, mainly because I could use a real ID to get served.'

'It's just a number.'

Jessica finished her mouthful, watching as the show went to adverts. 'Have you ever had a birthday party?'

Bex shrugged. 'When I was six or seven, a few kids from school came round our house. One of the girls gave me this bracelet, only something cheap and sparkly, but I didn't know that at the time. I thought it was real gold. I wore it all afternoon and then put it on the stool next to my bed that night. The next morning, it was gone. I checked under the bed, under the carpet, in my drawers, my pockets, everywhere. I was crying and really upset, then I asked Mum and she said she hadn't seen it. Now I know she took it, thinking it was valuable. She probably sold it for a few quid. It took me five or six years to realise I'd not lost it.'

She finished by forking a chunk of sausage into her mouth, so matter-of-fact that she could have been talking about eating ice cream at the beach. They sat in silence for a few moments, watching a moron in a suit with a fake moustache flap his hands in an attempt to sell insurance. This was communication in the twenty-first century.

Jessica didn't want to dwell on it. 'How's the community centre?'

'Kathy from the council said she's happy to give me a reference for my CV off the back of the month I've been volunteering but I'll probably hang around and do some work through the summer.' She stuck her tongue out with a smile, waggling the stud between her teeth. 'Some of the older guys seem obsessed with my piercings. One of them was telling me how they didn't have anything like it in his day but they must've done.'

'He's probably just trying it on.'

'That's what Kathy said – she reckons a few are right flirts.'

'What do you actually do there?'

'Generally set the place up for various meetings and clubs, plus no one knows how to use the booking system on the computer, so I've taken that on. Bits and pieces.'

Volunteering at council establishments was a far cry from what Jessica had done as a seventeen-year-old. She'd got through school and then gone backpacking around south-east Asia with her friend Caroline. It was hard to compare herself to Bex: Jessica's upbringing had almost been too comfortable, she'd wanted to get away, to rough it and do something for herself. For Bex, stability and normality was something she'd never had.

Bex stood, licking her lips and reaching for Jessica's empty plate. 'I'll do it,' Jessica replied.

They went through to the kitchen together, with Jessica noticing the Post-it note stuck to the fridge, underneath a ceramic magnet.

ALF

Jessica plopped her plate in the sink and turned back to the fridge. 'Why's that there?'

Bex was trying to free something from between her teeth. 'I saw him outside earlier. He seemed a bit upset. I asked if he was okay but he didn't say much. I figured I'd mention it.'

They'd both been keeping a closer eye out for their next-door neighbour since an ambulance had come for him a couple of months previously. He wasn't a doddery old man, but was in his seventies and didn't seem to realise it. He'd still walk to the shop every morning for a paper, plus mow the lawn, vacuum, cook and clean, determined to show he could look after himself. For the most part, he could – but he'd pushed himself too far and collapsed. He'd been cleaning the house ahead of his daughter, Charlotte, visiting from London but, when she arrived, she found him collapsed in the hall. He'd been fine in the end – something to do with blood pressure – but Jessica felt guilty that she hadn't paid greater attention.

She took the note from the fridge and balled it. 'I'll knock on his door tomorrow.'

11

Alf's morning routine was clear to anyone who lived around him: he'd leave his house at exactly five to seven, off to the local shop to get a paper. Jessica waited by her front door and then left at the exact time she knew she'd see him. Despite the warmth of the morning, Alf was bundled up in a coat over a dark suit. Rain, shine; summer, winter; celebration, commiseration, Alf would always be immaculately dressed. The only time Jessica saw him wearing anything different was when he was mowing the lawn. He was always clean-shaven, with a white crew cut, the style he'd probably had all his life.

As he opened his door and spotted her over the low wall, he jumped slightly, breaking into a grin. 'Oh . . . morning, love.'

'Morning.'

'I've been meaning to ask how you are, what with Adam, and everything. Is he still . . . ?'

Jessica nodded.

'Any news?'

'Nothing's changed.' She gulped, needing to change the subject. 'Bex says she saw you yesterday but it looked like you were having a problem.'

The chirpy smile shrunk to nothing, his brow rippling with seventy years of life. His skin was tough, naturally tanned and leathery. A face that had seen things and been places. 'No, it's, um . . . a misunderstanding.'

'What is?'

'Nothing, just me being silly. You get yourself off to work.'

'If you've got a problem, that *is* my work.'

He shook his head. 'No, no, no . . . you head off.'

Jessica pressed herself against the low wall between their houses. 'The sun's out and I'll happily wait here all day.'

He sighed and nodded towards the house. 'You better come in.'

The layout of Alf's house was a mirror image of Jessica's. The carpets, wallpaper and framed photos were older but everything was infinitely cleaner. Jessica felt like she was bringing down the value simply by being there.

Alf led her into the kitchen, where there was a small dining table, a place for one already laid. The sight of the single set of cutlery and lone chair made something twinge within Jessica. She spent her days running around, trying to track people down, yet here was a lonely bloke a few metres away and she hardly ever said hello.

On the counter, a small steak was defrosting on a plate, with a potato, two carrots and a tub of gravy granules nearby: everything needed to cook his tea. A plate and butter knife rested on the draining board, small pools of water underneath, his breakfast already cleaned away. She wondered how much of his day was pre-planned, a neat routine to keep himself busy.

Jessica hovered close to the kitchen door, letting Alf fuss.

He seemed excited at having someone there, filling the kettle and hunting through his cupboards for a second mug.

He pottered to the fridge, taking out a glass milk bottle. 'Full-fat, okay?'

'Whatever you have.'

'Are you sure you don't want something to eat?'

Jessica didn't but it was hard to say no. She ended up sitting on the solitary chair at the table, two slices of toast and a milky tea in front of her. She'd told him no sugar but he'd forgotten and put some in anyway. With nowhere else to sit, having insisted she take the chair, he rested against the counter, watching her eat.

'What happened yesterday?' Jessica asked.

She felt bad as the enthusiasm seeped from him again. He shrunk, as if his polished shoes were sucking him into them. 'Lottie would be so annoyed if she knew . . .'

'Knew what?'

He took a deep breath. 'There was this woman around on Monday, knocking on doors. Really thin, dark hair, looked like she needed a good meal. She said she was looking for work but no one would give her a job. You know what it's like nowadays, everyone's struggling. She said she had a young daughter and she didn't want to claim benefits and be a burden. She was well-dressed, not like someone off the street, said her name was Anne.'

'What happened?'

Alf shrugged. 'I don't know . . . I felt sorry for her. She seemed like my Lottie. In my day, you'd go from school to work and you were set. Now, everyone's after the same jobs.

You see 'em on the news. I thought I'd help her out.' He pointed towards the living room. 'I've got years' worth of bills in there. Been meaning to go through them but never quite got to it. I thought that if she could sort them, I could have a bit of a clear-out. I didn't really have anything for her to do.'

'What did she do?'

He sighed again, shaking his head, looking away from Jessica. He didn't want sympathy. 'It's different for you now. You're brought up to trust banks but I learned from my dad. He used to get paid in cash, he'd buy his ciggies, then come home and stuff the rest in the mattress.'

'Oh . . .'

'I'm not like that, love, I have a bank account – you need one, but I still . . .'

'How much did she take?'

'She must've sneaked into the bedroom while I was in the toilet. It was under the mattress. Years' worth . . .'

'How much?'

'Course, it's my own fault. Lottie's always telling me not to be so trusting.'

Jessica waited, an uncomfortable silence filling the kitchen.

'About six thousand,' Alf whispered. 'Perhaps more. I don't really count it.'

With that, he burst into tears, chest bobbing up and down as Jessica held him on her shoulder, wondering what on earth she could possibly say.

12

Jessica sat at her desk, using her computer to search through the logs from the previous few weeks, wondering if anyone else had come forward with reports of a woman knocking on doors, looking for work. The biggest problem was the embarrassment factor. Alf hadn't spoken to her because she was a police officer, he'd told her because she lived next door and he knew her. Others might not be like that, they'd feel duped and humiliated.

The closest she could find was a similar report from almost four months previously. A few streets away from her Swinton house, an older woman had jewellery stolen by a young female who'd knocked on her door, asking for cleaning work. There was a description in the file but no one had been arrested and the case was cold, buried under a mound of other things that were simpler to crack and would get the solved statistics up.

Alf insisted he didn't want to make a fuss, not wanting an officer to visit and take a full statement, but Jessica couldn't let it lie there. The e-fit impressions of suspects were handled by trained PCs, using software from a private company. Because of the expense of sending people on the course to learn how to use the equipment, too few officers were capable and the ones who were had additional duties. Jessica spent half an hour tracking down one of the trained constables and persuaded him to pay Alf a visit unofficially. Everything was supposed to have paperwork but sometimes, when people like Alf wanted help but refused to be a burden, there were other ways.

That done, Jessica headed to the newly redesigned incident room. Over the past few years, the 'ongoing area' had been in the basement, then the ground floor, then a box room when the heating failed, then back downstairs where the constables worked. They'd not been there long when someone had knocked the radiator off the wall, flooding the entire room. That's what happened when half the recruits were six-foot-something rugby players.

Now there was a dedicated space for an incident room along the hall from DCI Topper's office. Storage files had been cleared out and there was a row of four offices where officers could hold briefings and arrange their evidence on the wall. It was so up to date, they were almost in the twenty-first century. Luckily, it was also in the temperate area of the station's eco-climate.

Photographs of Irfan Nabil and Eric Maudsley were on the left side of a whiteboard, with Owen Priestley in the centre and Kevin Jones on the right. Pictures from the scene of the van break-out were on the walls, alongside a list of names and a map.

Jessica stood next to the board, with Izzy sitting at the front, pad on her knee, a smattering of constables between her and Archie at the back. He was grinning and chatting to one of the new recruits, DC Ruth Evesham, a pretty blonde in her twenties, who'd barely touched uniform before moving sideways into CID. A bit like Jessica.

The usual crowd were in: the one who nicked pens, Andy Somethingoranother whose name Jessica couldn't remember, and Joy Bag Jane, as she didn't like to be called. Rowlands was in front of Archie, next to DI Franks, to whom he had been assigned, the poor sod. Jessica wouldn't wish that on the people she didn't like, let alone those she did. She wouldn't be surprised if Franks held his team briefings in the women's toilets.

'All right,' Jessica called, receiving something close to quiet, though Archie was still chuckling from his conversation with DC Evesham. 'The guv's been called off to Newton Heath to show the assistant chief constable how to tie his shoelaces, so you've got to put up with me.'

Joy Bag sighed, before realising she was the only one. She tried – and failed – to turn it into a yawn, avoiding Jessica's gaze. If there were any bins to be hunted through, she'd metaphorically just volunteered.

'It's been a busy forty-eight hours, so thanks for keeping up,' Jessica added. 'First thing – was Owen Priestley broken out of the prison van in order to be killed?'

It wasn't a question she expected an answer to, but Izzy piped up anyway. 'If someone wanted to get him, they could've arranged for it to happen *in* prison. He slashed another inmate while he was inside, so they could've done it back.'

Jessica nodded. 'Maybe – but the hanging is public. Someone from the estate got a picture and it's all over the Internet. If Priestley was attacked inside, it'd have barely been reported. This was humiliation. Sergeant Diamond's going to grab one of you at the end to help look beyond

Priestley's record. There are years where we don't know anything about him. Who is he? Who was he close to? Girlfriends? Boyfriends? Kids? What's he done that would require such a public death? That brings me to point two.'

She turned back to the board, only now noticing that someone had drawn a miniature phallus in the bottom right corner. What was it with men, pens, and open white spaces? It was as if they had an instinct to draw cocks on anything in front of them. Was it like this in all professions? The Chancellor stood up to read out the budget, only to see someone had drawn a mini dick in the top corner of the page?

'. . . point two,' she repeated, trying to remember where she was. 'Owen Priestley worked for Richard Hyde for at least twenty years in various capacities, most recently as a manager at a casino in Oldham. Our friends at SCD have a hard-on for Hyde, implicating him in all sorts of naughty goings-on. I can't emphasise this enough – any dealings with, or questions about, Richard Hyde and his family have to come through me or, better yet, the guv. No exceptions and no pissing about. That said, we don't want to rely on the SCD files because they're too close to it. I want a full background on Richard Hyde and his daughter, Natalie. What does he own? Where did he make his money? Who are his friends? What pies does he have fingers in? Hyde's been on holiday, so I'm part of the welcoming committee later. I might even take balloons.'

No one laughed, the bastards. She'd even rehearsed that in the ladies.

'Next up, our new number one scumbag, Eric Maudsley.'

Jessica peered down at the bite marks on her hand. 'We've got a shoe print placing him at the scene of the burnt-out Volkswagen, plus he all but admitted he was one of the people who broke out Priestley when I mentioned Irfan Nabil's name. I'm going to the hospital to have a word when I'm done here but this is where we have a problem.'

She pointed to the board, where a line had been drawn between Nabil and Maudsley. 'These two are clowns, nuisances. They're into low-level drugs and thefts. Why have they suddenly shifted from that to holding up prison vans? Where did the shotguns come from? Irfan's not speaking and I don't expect Maudsley to. I don't think anyone really believes they killed Priestley, so we need to know who hired them to break him out. This wasn't a pro job, so whoever it was didn't care if Nabil and Maudsley were caught. More importantly, they knew the pair of them wouldn't talk. Were they paid to do it? If so, where's the money? Let's bang on doors and talk to their girlfriends, neighbours, family, whoever. Have they bought anything fancy recently? Who from? How much? Phone records, Internet records, bills, you know the drill.'

Jessica paused for a drink of water, glancing towards Archie, who was trying to get DC Evesham's attention.

'The final thing is the break-out itself. We're still waiting on results to say how Priestley died – whether it was the hanging, or if he was already dead – but Kevin Jones is still out there. Is he a target? Whether or not he is, we need him back in custody.'

She sighed, ready to give the bad news.

'Detective Inspector Franks is going to head that search.'

Franks stood as the word 'Fanny' was coughed and then muffled from someone Jessica didn't spot, though it came from Archie's direction. Franks didn't seem to notice, straightening his jacket as he stood, nodding, as if he was waiting for applause, like the self-important tosser he was. For the higher-ups, he was perfect: a well-groomed corporate type, with sharp suits, a side parting, an obsession with numbers, and a 'yes, Sir' mentality that always went down well with anyone he didn't have to work with. For those alongside him, he was a toilet-sniffing weirdo, although nobody actually had evidence to back that up.

'Thank you, DI Daniel,' Franks said pompously, turning in a circle so he could face everyone, though not at the same time. 'There was a potential sighting of Kevin Jones close to the public toilets in Birchfields Park last night.'

Jessica caught Izzy's gaze and struggled not to laugh. Everything Franks got involved with somehow ended up with him and toilets. There was a snigger from someone else too, though Franks was so certain of his own importance that he never seemed to notice the contempt in which he was held.

He continued, oblivious. 'The park is close to Jones's girlfriend's house, so we're now focusing on the area around Longsight, Levenshulme, Fallowfield and Rusholme, specifically Birchfields Park. Jones's girlfriend insists she's not seen him, so we've let her loose, though we've not been able to approve any sort of surveillance yet.'

He brushed a fleck of dust from his jacket and sat, nodding at Jessica as if she needed his permission to continue. The dick.

Jessica went on: 'It's going to be particularly embarrassing if we discover Kevin Jones has been hiding across the road from here, so let's find him. DI Franks has his team, Izzy will grab one of you to help her. Everyone else should know what they're doing.' She paused, waiting for Archie to drag his gaze away from DC Evesham. 'DC Davey, you're with me. Let's go.'

13

The road on which Niall O'Brien lived was quite the sight. There had once been parallel rows of red-brick terraced houses but one side of the street had been flattened, leaving mounds of rubble surrounded by chain-link metal fences that looked pretty climbable if anyone could be bothered. The houses on Niall's side were still standing . . . just about. Every property was covered either with boards or metal panels, with numerous signs declaring them unsafe and reminding everyone that it was a criminal offence to enter.

Well, almost every property.

Archie peered at the glorified bombsite through the window of Jessica's car. 'So, let me get this straight. This dude's the only person refusing to sell and, because of that, he lives on a street with rubble on one side and a row of empty houses on the other.'

'Exactly. The developers are offering him five times what the house is worth so they can get on with it. They're looking to redo the entire area – park, houses, pond, one of those mini Tescos. Perhaps a Morrisons? I'm not sure. Either way, they've got all sorts of plans.'

'And this one bloke's holding all of that up.'

'Yep.'

Archie took a deep breath, peering from the deserted deathtrap homes to the mound of concrete. '*Why?*'

'Because he's lived here all his life and he doesn't think he should have to go. They're trying to force through one of those compulsory purchase things but it's not happened yet. For now, it's just him alone on an empty street.'

'What a nutter.'

Jessica opened her door and climbed out, walking along the centre of the deserted road. Archie had to run to catch her up.

'What's up with you?' he asked.

'He's not a nutter, Arch. He's just a man who doesn't like change.'

'Suit yourself.'

Niall was understandably not happy as Jessica and Archie knocked on his door. He was dressed in a suit, with manic white hair that had a life of its own. At one point he'd have been dapper and probably quite the catch. Now he just looked angry. As soon as he opened the door, he was jabbing a finger towards them.

'Oh, so *now* you turn up? I thought you were coming two days ago?'

Jessica could barely get her words out: 'Mr O'Brien, I—'

'And then you were coming yesterday. What is it? I'm too old to interest you?' He prodded his temples. 'You think I'm a crazy old man, so sent round some pair in uniforms who wanted to make me tea? They didn't do anything, now you're back. Is this how you work?'

'Mr O'Brien, if we could just come in . . .'

He stared between Jessica and Archie before standing to the side and waving his hand towards the room on their immediate right. Jessica had already gone through this the previous week but was surprised to see a new face in the living room. A man with longish dark hair was smiling awkwardly as they entered. He climbed up from the sofa and offered his hand. 'Hi, I'm Spencer O'Brien.' He nodded towards the front door, which was currently being slammed. 'That's my, er, dad.'

Jessica sat in the armchair, with Archie perching awkwardly on the arm and Niall joining his son on the sofa. There was a definite similarity between them facially, though Spencer practically shrunk under his father's angry onslaught. The moment the old man sat, he was leaning forward, pointing again.

'I'm not selling my house, why should I?'

Jessica held her arms apart, trying to be conciliatory. She had explained all this before. 'I'm not here to say you should sell, Mr O'Brien. It's none of my business. I'm here because you've called our station asking directly for me for five days in a row.'

'Is five the magic number? That's how many it takes to get you out?'

'I'm afraid things are very busy at the moment, I—'

'Forgotten me already, have you? Not bothered about gippos breaking into my house?'

Spencer rolled his eyes, then continued to stare at Jessica, apologising silently.

'Are you saying gypsies came into your house, Mr O'Brien?' Jessica asked. 'Last time I was here, you told me it was kids. You've also called 999 to allege the housing developer was behind the break-ins . . .'

'You calling me a liar?'

'No, I'm simply asking if there's anything to back those claims. As you know, we've checked for fingerprints and DNA, plus it's hard to do much if, as you say, nothing's *actually* been stolen.'

'They drank my milk!' He turned to Spencer, before jabbing another finger at Jessica. 'You tell 'em. There was milk in my fridge, then it was gone. Where did it go?'

Spencer cleared his throat. 'Well, er, there was milk but, er . . .'

'See – gippos breaking in here drinking my milk.'

'Right, um . . .'

Niall jumped up, clutching his crotch. 'Oh, you talk it out among yourselves. Talk, talk, talk.' He shuffled into the hallway and then disappeared up the stairs.

With his father gone, Spencer exhaled loudly. 'I'm *really* sorry. I know you're busy. I don't want you wasting your time.'

Jessica felt like sighing herself. She didn't like throwing around terms like 'Alzheimer's' or 'mental illness' but there was something not quite right. 'We *are* looking to see if there's anything in what your father's been saying,' she said. 'We've had full teams out twice to check for fingerprints and the like. As far as we can tell, your dad's simply left the back door open and then called us the next day. There's nothing around here, no witnesses, no CCTV. We've looked at nearby traffic cameras but even your dad says nothing's been stolen.'

Spencer took another breath, ruffling a hand through his hair. 'I know, I know. I'm coming to stay with him for a few weeks, hopefully to calm him down. Mum died a year ago and it's a bad time.' He glanced over his shoulder, making sure his father was still absent. 'He's not usually like this. I know the milk thing's a bit mad but I locked the back door myself when I stopped round last week. It was open in the morning.'

'Could your father have done it himself?'

Spencer shrugged. 'I don't know. He says it wasn't him.' He lowered his voice: 'I've been trying to persuade him to sell. He'd be better off in a home where they can look after him but he won't even talk about it. Says I'm trying to hide him away. I'm not, but—'

'My mum's in a home.' Jessica blurted a response without thinking. This was a situation with no winners. 'She loves it. From the way she speaks, you'd think she ran the place.'

Spencer was about to reply when Niall's footsteps started to thunder down the stairs again, voice booming through the house. 'And another thing . . .'

14

Archie had his hands in his pockets, huffing and puffing, no house to blow down. 'Everyone's moving so bloody slowly.'

'It's a hospital, Arch.'

They continued through the corridors of Salford Royal, trailing the taped yellow line on the floor they'd been told to follow.

'Yeah but everyone's limping, or they're in a wheelchair. How does anything get done around here?'

'It's a hospital! What do you expect?'

Archie sighed again. 'I dunno, a bit of enthusiasm, or at least a fast and slow lane for walking.'

'You want them to paint lanes on the floor, one for the sick people, one for everyone else?'

'Maybe . . .'

Jessica wasn't sure if it was actually what he thought, or if he was trying to wind her up. He was definitely achieving the second. They shuffled past a surprisingly young man – thirty-odd – with a Zimmer frame, with Archie somehow resisting the urge to tut.

'So . . . about my parents . . .' he said.

'You could ask DC Evesham if she's free.'

Jessica winced. The words had snapped out without any conscious thought. She had no right to be jealous, not that she was. Instead, she was . . . something else.

'I hate hospitals,' she added quickly, hoping it somehow made up for the idiocy.

Archie rambled on regardless: 'The match is in two weeks' time. It's United's first friendly of the season, then we're looking at somewhere to eat in the city centre. My mum loves this Spanish place just off Deansgate.'

'What have you told them?'

'About what?'

'About you and me.'

'Nothing.'

They stopped at a T-junction, the criss-cross of red, black and blue floor tapes heading left; yellow and green right.

'This way,' Jessica said, nodding right.

They continued towards the far side of the hospital, Archie's lip-smacking a clear sign that he had something to say but wasn't sure how. She knew she should make it easier for him, tell him what she was thinking, but that conversation felt a long way off.

Deep in the reaches of the hospital, a pair of uniformed officers were sitting outside a partially open door at the far end of the corridor. The bustle of the wards and shuffling of patients had disappeared, leaving crusty brown radiators, echoing cracked floor tiles, and a smattering of posters with an old-fashioned NHS logo and photos of needles with spattered blood. This was obviously the VIP suite.

Jessica and Archie showed their IDs to the officers, who'd been expecting them. One of them warned her off the canteen, saying the food was worse than what was served at the police station, though that seemed unlikely.

Eric Maudsley was propped up by three pillows, thick

padding across the shoulder where he'd been shot. The bullet had ripped straight through, which was the best outcome. Well, the best outcome if not being shot in the first place was discounted. He had the windowless, soulless room to himself, a small television on the table next to the bed showing a property programme.

Jessica switched off the TV and sat in front of it. 'No grapes?' she said.

The ring had been removed from Maudsley's eyebrow, leaving a saggy flap of skin hanging across his left eye. It waggled as he frowned. 'I was watching that.'

'I don't think you're going to be doing up many houses when you get sent down for ramming a prison van. As soon as the doctor signs you out, you're going to be carted off to court, then they'll remand you.'

'Where's Theo?'

'You mean they didn't leave your son in your care after you held a pair of scissors to his neck?'

'Piss off.'

'He's with social services.'

'Bastards.'

'That's a bit harsh,' Jessica replied, 'they're very complimentary about you. Well, they're not but you know what I mean.'

'You think you're so 'kin smart.'

Jessica nodded. 'I suppose it depends how you define "smart". It's not trying to set a car on fire on the edge of an industrial estate and then stepping in a patch of mud on your way to the next vehicle. It's definitely not *keeping* the trainers.'

'They cost a hundred quid!'

'Which I'm sure will be worth a few years inside. Anyway, we've got your trainers, we've got eyewitnesses, we've got another witness who saw you talking to Irfan Nabil, we've got you calling Irfan a naughty word yesterday. We'll eventually have DNA from one of the cars because there's no way you're intelligent enough to have cleaned them properly. Do you want me to go on?'

Maudsley rolled over, grunting as he turned to face the wall. 'Get lost.'

'Who killed Owen Priestley?'

He didn't move, talking to the wall. 'No idea what you're on about.'

'If you don't tell us, we'll have to assume it was you.'

'I was with Theo at my flat all of yesterday afternoon and overnight.'

'He'll testify to that, will he? How old is he? Three? Four? It's not much of an alibi.'

'Ask his mother – she'll tell you I 'ad him.'

'Who hired you?' Jessica asked.

'Go fuck yourself.'

Jessica stood, giving Archie The Look. The constable didn't hesitate, grabbing the edge of the bed and sliding it away from the wall.

'Oi!' Maudsley protested. 'Hey!'

Archie moved in between the bed and the wall, at eye level with Maudsley. 'Look, pal, we both know you were set up. You're useless and Irfan's even worse. You couldn't pinch a Mars bar between you without getting nicked. If whoever hired you wanted a job doing properly, they'd get a pro, not a pair of useless bastards. So who set you up?'

'I'll call for a nurse,' Maudsley squealed.

'You do that, pal. Not many medical professionals down this end, just two nasty uniformed bastards outside the door.'

He was snarling, sounding as if he meant it. Maudsley shook his head, wincing and reaching for his shoulder with a grimace, more scared of whoever hired him than Archie.

'Big man in a little man's body, eh?' Maudsley said.

Archie raised himself onto tiptoes, buttons firmly pressed, but Jessica cut things off before they went any further. 'Arch.'

He nodded at her, stepping away but still wanting the final word: 'You're stupider than I thought, pal.'

Maudsley rolled onto his back, wincing as he pointed a finger towards them. 'Keep walking, dwarf-man.'

'I will – I'll keep walking right into the pub tonight and have a pint, thinking of you alone in prison. Prick.'

Jessica dragged Archie out of the door, past the smirking uniformed officers, who said nothing. She turned back to them, still bundling Archie away. 'When Group Four turn up to take him to court, can you give them a message from me?'

One of the officers shrugged. 'What?'

'Tell them not to sodding lose him.'

They both laughed, which was pretty much all the police could do when it came to the private company who ran security for large parts of the court and prison service. If, or, more to the point, *when* they ballsed something up, it was the police who had to come to the rescue.

Archie was stomping through the corridors as Jessica rushed to catch him. 'Oi,' she said.

'What?'

'You've got to calm down and stop letting stuff like that get under your skin. If you're going to wind them up, they're going to fire back.'

'Whatever.'

Jessica was about to tell him to slow down when her phone started ringing.

'Where are you?' Izzy asked.

'Just leaving Salford, on my way to visit Richard Hyde, so I probably need to go via a balloon shop.'

There wasn't even a snigger. 'You might need to reconsider that.'

'Why?'

'His wife's dead.'

15

The death wasn't Jessica's only problem. She'd heard it in Izzy's voice the moment the sergeant had started speaking: her next destination was an issue too. She and Archie had left Salford and were on their way to the city centre, creeping between the lanes as they edged from red traffic light to red traffic light, sun hammering down from the perfect blue sky.

'Where are we going?' Archie asked.

'Oxford Road.'

'Why?'

'That's where the Royal Infirmary is.'

There was a pause, and then 'oh'.

Archie knew what that meant the same as Izzy did. It was the hospital where Adam lay in a room far away from the entrance, eyes closed, machine breathing for him. Jessica had spent more time there than she cared to remember. She knew the layout better than she knew the police station's. She knew the first names of some of the staff members, as they greeted her with that tilted-head 'are-you-okay?' expression.

It was another few minutes before Archie spoke again: 'Why are we going there?'

'Lisa Hyde was found floating in the River Irwell this morning. They fished her out but no one knew who she was until she arrived at the mortuary. There was a purse in her pocket full of bank cards. Her husband's already there, identifying the body.'

'Did she drown?'

'Shot in the head.'

A pause. 'Oh . . . that's worse.'

'You reckon?!'

There was more silence: not awkwardness, more confusion. Serious Crime had Richard Hyde pegged as a major player behind the scenes of Manchester's crime world, and now one of his right-hand men and his wife had been bumped off barely a day apart, all on the back of a prison van break. It felt big, probably too big for them, yet Topper wanted Jessica to visit the hospital anyway. Not only that, Izzy said Superintendent Jenkinson was at the station, so it would have gone through him. Something was happening that she couldn't figure out. Something like this would usually be bumped across to Serious Crime, yet here she was on the way to the hospital of her nightmares.

Jessica parked on the single yellow line outside the hospital, not wanting to fight for a spot in the car park, nor wanting to get stuck trying to get onto the main road on her way out again. Something else she'd had far too much of. She was about to head through the main entrance when she spotted a man dressed far too smartly for his surroundings. He was wearing a pinstripe suit with a pink tie, face tanned a mahogany brown, flicking cigarette ash towards the already full hollow on top of the bin. As Jessica approached, he peered over the top of rimless glasses, eyes distant.

'Mr Hyde?' Jessica asked.

His accent was local, half-growl, half-whisper. 'They said someone would be coming.'

She started to show him her ID but he waved a hand dismissively. 'What's your name?' he asked.

'DI Daniel.'

'Your actual name.'

'Jessica.'

He nodded. 'Someone was coming to see me before any of this and now . . .'

'I'm not necessarily here to interview you, more—'

'Because the local police want me to have a babysitter. I get it.'

'I understand it's—'

'A tough time,' he interrupted. 'Do you *really* understand?'

Usually it was a statement Jessica couldn't justify but she knew the pain of being at this hospital more than most.

Hyde continued, not waiting for Jessica. 'I already identified the body as that of my wife.'

'Right . . .'

'Why else did you want to see me?'

Jessica stumbled, not ready for the conversation. 'It doesn't matter at the moment, we can—'

'Why were you coming to see me before this?'

'We really don't have to—'

He snapped loudly, tossing the remains of the cigarette on top of the bin and nodding towards a green on the other side of the road. 'Let's just get this over with.'

Jessica watched Hyde for a few moments, trying to read

him. He sounded annoyed but his features were stern, unmoving, probably in shock. People took things in different ways. If he was angry, he wasn't showing it.

She told Archie to go for a walk, which he took a little too literally by shoving his hands in his pockets and sauntering towards the city centre, scuffing his feet like a chastened child. Which, in some ways, he was.

Jessica and Hyde sat on the bench closest to the pavement. On the other side of the grass, a group of teenagers were playing football, shirts v skins, abandoned tops for goalposts. It looked competitive, one lad sprawling towards the pavement on the far side after a shoulder charge that was followed by howls of derision.

Hyde nodded towards Archie's shuffling frame. 'Your mate doesn't look much like a cop.'

'Looks can be deceptive. I know people who seem like legitimate businessmen when, really, they have their fingers in all sorts of undesirable pies.'

Hyde said nothing, turning to watch the football.

'I wanted to talk to you about Owen Priestley,' Jessica added.

'Go on then.'

'Perhaps we should talk about your wife first? I'm assuming she was on holiday with you.'

'We flew in yesterday.'

'What happened?'

'When we landed, I got a taxi home, she took the car because she was supposed to be visiting her sister in Carlisle. We said goodbye and that was the last I saw of her.'

He spoke mechanically – this happened, that happened

– barely showing emotion, which wasn't uncommon after something horrific.

'Did you hear from her at all?'

Hyde shook his head. 'She would have messaged me at some point but she often mislaid her phone, especially in the car. I was at my casino until two in the morning. If you're worried, everything will be on camera, except for twenty minutes or so at the end of the night when I was in the car park, waiting for my daughter to drive me home.' He tapped his forehead. 'Always good to clear the mind with some fresh air after a long day.' Another pause. '*Jessica* . . . I gather you're acquainted with my daughter already.'

'We've met.'

He breathed deeply, leaning forward and resting on his knees, fingertips pressed together into a triangle. They watched the football for a few moments, the game getting rougher as one of the lads without a shirt pulled back a player with one. They pushed one another before others got in the middle, shoving them apart.

'*Boys*,' Hyde muttered.

'Do you know who killed your wife?'

Jessica's question hung between them, not something she would usually ask but a marker that she knew who he was. She wondered if he was already plotting a response, something that would make the situation infinitely worse.

He rubbed his forehead, sending flakes of crispy, slightly burnt skin into his lap. 'I suppose I always knew it would come down to this.'

'To what?'

'Someone clearly has it in for me and my family, Inspector. One of my former employees, a man close to me, was hanged from a bridge, my wife was shot in the head.'

'We can offer protection—'

Hyde snorted before she could finish the sentence. 'Aah, the police, riding to my rescue, hip-hip-hooray. Just what I've always wanted.'

'We're investigating two murders—'

'And I've given you my statement. I was on a plane when Owen was killed and I haven't seen my wife since we left the airport separately. Now do your job and find out who killed them.'

'We can only do that with your help, Mr Hyde. If there are grudges—'

He laughed, interrupting her again before settling down. When he spoke, his voice was quieter. 'I met Owen Priestley more than twenty years ago. He was a street kid, with no respect. Tried to nick my wallet while I was in one of my own pubs. I felt his hand as it slipped away but he and his mates were so practised, they had five of them around me and I didn't know which one it was. With anyone else, they'd've been away – but as soon as I called, the door was slammed shut. They thought I was some mug but it was one of my joints. I'd have waited there all weekend until someone admitted it but, eventually, Owen put his hand up. I could've given him a hiding in front of his mates but . . .'

He tailed off as someone in a shirt scored – or thought he did. The group stood around arguing about whether the ball had gone over the scattered tops, with one of them shouting that it had hit 'the woodwork'.

'. . . he started working for me the next day,' Hyde continued. 'He used to do the deliveries between my pubs and clubs, then worked his way up. He'd drive me places, plus do odd jobs at my house: gardening, DIY – he built my extension. Eventually, he ended up managing part of my casino.'

'Then he tried to rob an off-licence and nearly killed the guy behind the counter.'

Hyde sighed, pinching the top of his nose. 'According to you.'

'And the jury.'

They fell quiet again as the footballers finally agreed to continue the match. The person who'd scored/'hit the woodwork' was taking a penalty to decide if it was a goal. Jessica didn't know much about football but she was pretty sure these weren't the official rules.

'Owen Priestley was a loyal lieutenant, then?' she asked.

Hyde shrugged. 'If you say so.'

'There must be a lot of people out there jealous of your success: the pubs, the clubs, the casino, the property.'

'Success comes and goes.'

'As people like Harry Irwell and Nicholas Long know only too well.'

She could feel the bristling atmosphere as Hyde shuffled on the bench, no doubt remembering the pair who used to run areas of the city. He must be hot, wearing a full suit in the middle of another sunny day, but it didn't feel like that was why he was uncomfortable.

'What's your point?' he asked.

'That your business shares certain aspects in common

with people like Irwell and Long. They died a couple of years ago, so is this a continuation of that?'

'You tell me – you're the inspector. As far as I'm aware, Irwell's death was suspicious but no one was ever charged with it.'

Jessica wasn't sure if that was true – it hadn't been her case and she'd not read the file. 'You were married to your wife for almost thirty years, you knew Owen Priestley for more than twenty. These are two of the people closest to you, yet you're taking their deaths remarkably well.'

Jessica wondered if she'd gone too far but Hyde didn't react. Shock could do strange things to people and he seemed the measured type.

Hyde sucked his lips together, scratching his chin. 'I hope my wife's funeral is going to be properly policed.'

'I'm sure it will.'

He stood abruptly, turning back towards the hospital. 'Good – if you can't trust the police, who can you trust? Now, please leave me to grieve.'

Jessica stood, offering him a card that he ignored. 'Mr Hyde . . .'

'What?'

'If you do know who did this, you need to tell us. There can't be a retaliation, no one wants a war.'

He nodded. 'Whatever you say.'

16

Considering how jam-packed officers were at the Longsight station, it was something close to a miracle that Jessica still had an office to herself. Either that, or no one wanted to share a space with her.

Given what great company she was, it couldn't be that.

As a sergeant, she'd shared it with various officers who had since left, then her promotion had happened at the same time as a logistical reshuffle. All the sergeants had been moved to their own 'sergeant station' – surely something dreamed up by a moron with a press release in mind – and the constables had been thrown together in one giant room. DI Franks – aka Franks the Fanny, Funtime Frankie, Wanky Frankie, or something even more offensive – had opted to work in the same area as the DCs, probably so he could order them around, leaving Jessica with an office to herself. In the same way that a fish apparently grew to match its surroundings, Jessica's pile of clutter had expanded to fill the area. The desk that wasn't hers was covered by various papers, with more boxes of stuff rammed against the far wall. She didn't know what most of it was. Her own desk was plastered with notes, only some of which related to work. One day, the time would come to clear it all out – and that day would be one where she phoned in sick.

Izzy was spinning and sighing in the spare chair.

'That bad?' Jessica asked.

'I've had to put up with Funtime all morning, marching around wanting to know what everyone's up to.'

'Has he found Kevin Jones yet?'

'He checked his office and the toilets, and Kevin wasn't there, so no. He nipped out for an hour at lunch, like always. Christ knows where he goes.'

'He's probably offering free hand jobs in the park.'

'It wouldn't surprise me. Anyway, Lisa Hyde's sister confirms she never arrived in Carlisle. Lisa's car was found abandoned on a housing estate on the edge of Eccles, so she probably never made it away from Manchester.'

'Did anyone see anything?'

Izzy shook her head. 'No – but people tend to keep their heads down in that area. We're doing the usual with the traffic cameras but nothing yet.'

'Any idea how she ended up in the river?'

'Nope – she was fished out close to the centre but could've drifted. Forensics are on the case but the water damage won't be helping. The post mortem's due.'

'Is there a time of death?'

'Not yet.'

Jessica wasn't surprised. At least once a year, a body was fished out of the canal and it took them weeks to identify who it was. 'It probably doesn't matter,' she said. 'Richard Hyde says he was at the casino until two in the morning. We can request the CCTV but it'll check out. He's not the sort to give fake alibis.'

'Do you think his wife's death was something to do with him?'

Jessica took a long breath. 'Not really . . .'

'There was one report of gunshots being fired last night but it was in Stockport – kids with an air rifle shooting at traffic.'

Jessica tapped on her keyboard, waiting for her emails to load. 'Priestley died of asphyxiation,' she said, reading the summary of findings. 'He had neck injuries too, so they reckon he was beaten but alive when he was hanged from the bridge.'

Neither of them spoke, the truth too grim to think about. Priestley was no angel but it was a particularly horrible way to go. He must have really pissed someone off, either that or Richard Hyde had, and this was a message for him.

Jessica stifled a yawn with her hand, trying to blink away the moment of tiredness. As she was composing herself, Izzy launched into a yawn of her own, which set Jessica off again. Soon, they were giggling like a pair of teenagers on the back row of a bus.

Through the years, Izzy had tried red hair, then purple, but she was now back to her natural long brown. She was younger than Jessica, married, with a daughter who had turned three that spring. She balanced that with being one of the most assertive officers Jessica knew.

Izzy was smirking: 'How was Niall O'Brien?'

'Don't even ask. I don't know what to do about it.' Jessica held up a pair of notepad sheets. 'Two more phone messages. Fat Pat's threatening to get his number blocked. There's nothing else we can do. He says someone's breaking into his house but there's no sign of anyone – plus nothing's been taken.'

'So he's a nutter?'

'According to Dave and Arch . . . I've just got a bad feeling about it all. His son's staying with him for the time being. Hopefully that'll calm him down.'

Izzy nodded. 'How's everything else?'

'Okay.'

'I didn't know if it'd be awkward with the guv wanting you to go to the Infirmary . . .'

'I didn't even get inside.'

'Do you want to talk about it?'

Jessica paused, thinking, before finally whispering the name: 'Adam?'

Izzy stared at her, not needing to confirm it. There was another pause.

A long pause.

In the corridor, a pair of officers walked past, talking too loudly about which of the new recruits was likely to be the biggest 'goer'. There was the usual bustle from the nearby canteen and the hum of the overhead heating/cooling unit. Jessica stared at her computer screen, not taking in the words.

'I think I've made a huge mistake,' Jessica whispered.

From nowhere, she felt close to tears, a lump forming in her throat, eyes tingling. She bunched her sleeve and dabbed underneath her eyes, struggling to find the words. Izzy leant forward and rubbed Jessica's arm.

'Do many people know about Archie and me?' Jessica asked.

Izzy shook her head. 'No one's talking about it, so I don't think so.'

'How did you know?'

'The way he looks at you sometimes. Nothing serious – just the odd glance here or there. He'd be terrible at poker.'

Jessica did her best to compose herself. 'It happened the night after we got back from London a few months ago. We'd had a few beers and then . . . I don't know . . . it kept happening.'

'What does Archie say about Adam?'

Jessica shrugged. 'We never talk about it.'

'And why do you think it's a mistake?'

Jessica stared at her friend, wondering why she had to ask. 'Isn't it obvious?'

Izzy waited for a moment as someone walked past Jessica's office, footsteps echoing towards the canteen. 'You thought you were going to marry, have kids and grow old. Suddenly, Adam's in a coma. Everything about your life changed in an instant. That's, what, eight months ago?'

'More or less.'

'Have they given you an idea when he might wake up?'

'*If* he wakes up. They have no idea.' Jessica gulped, blinking away more tears. 'Sometimes I feel like I'm waiting for the day when someone says he should be switched off. I still visit but people don't know what it's like to talk to someone who never speaks back. He'd hate me if he knew about Archie.'

'Maybe . . .'

'You don't think he would?'

'Perhaps – he struck me as the kind of bloke who always

tried to see things from someone else's point of view. I don't think he'd hate you. He'd understand you were lonely.'

Jessica shook her head, gulping, turning away. 'It's not an excuse.'

'You've never been one to stay still.'

At first Jessica felt a ripple of anger, thinking it was a dig, but, when she turned back, Izzy's eyes told her it wasn't. She didn't mean stay *with the same man*, she meant stay *still in life*.

'What does that make me?' Jessica breathed.

'Human.'

Jessica tried to swallow the lump in her throat but it still wasn't moving. 'I'm being a cow to Archie as well,' she said. 'To everyone else, he's a Jack the Lad, but, deep down, he wants stability and a girlfriend. I'm never going to be that to him, I just want . . . I don't know . . . Adam.'

'You want to be wanted.'

Jessica peered up, confused by Izzy's bluntness. 'Huh?'

'Adam adored you and it must be hard not to have that.'

A tingle of self-awareness tickled Jessica's back. It was one thing to think it herself, another to have it pointed out. It wasn't fun to think too much about herself. Was it true? She wanted to feel needed by someone else, which was why she'd fallen into the relationship she had with Archie?

The ringing of the desk phone saved her from having to reply: her presence had been requested.

DCI Topper's office was filled with a Top Trumps of Greater Manchester Police. In terms of rank, Assistant Chief Constable William Aylesbury was unbeatable. DCI Topper had ten out of ten for best chair, given he was behind his own desk, with the visitors massed in front of him, sitting on anything they could find, or, in Jessica's case, standing next to the door. Topper would score highly in accent, too. Creepiest was DI Franks, who was sitting with his legs splayed far too wide. DSI Jenkinson had the most bored-looking category in the bag, as he fiddled with his phone, probably annoyed there was neither a golf course in sight, nor a television camera for him to get in front of. Jessica would have scored poorly in all of those categories, but romped home in the 'funniest' and 'grumpiest' classes. She'd have lost out on 'best hair' or 'best looking' to a face that was familiar, although nobody else in the room realised they knew one another.

Topper stood, pointing to the newcomer as Jessica squeezed the office door closed behind her.

'DI Daniel, this is DCI Saggers from Serious Crime.'

The officer stood, turning to shake her hand. 'Josh,' he said, winking almost imperceptibly. As if he could ever forget their first meeting: Jessica had locked him in a car that smelled of vomit. It was a long story.

'Jessica,' she replied.

Josh sat, wriggling himself into a position where he could see everyone. 'I'm going to assume everyone knows why I'm here,' he said. 'The death of Lisa Hyde, coupled with that of Owen Priestley, is potentially very worrying. There's a real concern that this is a move by a rival gang on the Hydes.'

'Why now?' Topper asked.

'The Hydes could be seen as weak because Richard Hyde

recently retired, leaving his daughter, Natalie, in charge of the family business. Whether it's because she's female, or because Richard himself has gone, is something we don't know.'

'What *do* you know?' Jessica asked, not meaning to sound aggressive.

Josh smiled at her. 'In the past couple of years, there's been a big shift in Manchester's underground crime scene. Nicholas Long and Harry Irwell died within a short period of one another. Long was murdered but it was largely unrelated to the scene in which he was involved.'

Jessica knew that only too well – she'd found the killer.

'With Irwell, the circumstances were suspicious to say the least – he overdosed with no previous signs of drug use. We suspect foul play, most likely by one of his rivals, but there was no proof and the coroner ruled accidental. As well as the Hydes to the north of the city, the bigger crime "bosses", if you like' – bunny ears – 'include Christian Fraser, who's mainly into drugs; "Carter", who was one of Irwell's men and seems to be running part of his business; plus a few Eastern Europeans muscling in, who've been focusing on people trafficking and drugs.'

Jessica felt another twinge – that was something else in which she'd been involved.

'It's an uncertain time at the moment, with each of the sides eyeing one another up. If this is a move, then it's a big one.'

Jessica was pretty sure she knew what this all meant. 'Does this mean you're taking the case?' she asked.

Josh's gaze flickered to Assistant Chief Constable Aylesbury, then he peered around the room again, talking to each of them. She wondered what she was missing.

'Serious Crime *are* involved but don't want to *appear* involved. We currently have a few things on the go and would rather not play our cards yet.'

'What does that mean?' Franks asked, probably trying to make it seem like he was paying attention.

'We're building cases but I can't really say more than that,' Josh replied. 'This could blow anything we have but, for now, we're proceeding in the way we have been.'

Josh turned to Topper, who nodded towards the assistant chief constable. 'It's filtered down from the top that we're handling this at our end and keeping Serious Crime out of it – at least to any onlookers. Someone needs to talk to these men – Fraser, Carter, and so on. Nothing accusatory, no arrests, all very off the record. Just a friendly little hello to let them know that we won't sit back and let a gang war start in this city.'

He turned to Jessica. So did Josh. And Franks. Then Superintendent Jenkinson. Finally, Assistant Chief Constable Aylesbury faced her.

'*Me?*' Jessica asked.

Four people nodded. Franks scratched his crotch.

17

Jessica sat in the station's canteen, swishing the plastic cup in an attempt to make the coffee drinkable.

'I've been stitched up,' she concluded.

'You should see it as an opportunity,' Izzy replied.

'An opportunity to be stitched up.'

'If you've got the high-ups backing you, isn't that a good thing?'

There was one particular 'high-up' whose backing Jessica didn't want, Chief Constable Graham Pomeroy. That was, perhaps, another issue. She was certain she knew things about his past that he'd rather not acknowledge. Things that happened before he was promoted. They'd spoken fewer than half-a-dozen times but it was a dangerous situation in which he knew what she'd found out. After what had happened to Adam, she'd shied away from the confrontation – for now, anyway – but he was still there, in the background, most likely keeping an eye on her.

'There's no glory to be had here,' Jessica said.

Archie had been watching the pair of them in surprising silence. If he wasn't talking, he was usually eating, but, this time, he was doing neither. He couldn't keep it up for long.

'I don't see what the problem is,' he said. 'You get to go and piss off a few jumped-up bellends, everyone's a winner.'

No one replied.

Jessica nodded towards the swish of blonde near the counter at the front of the canteen. DC Evesham was by herself, peering at the menu. Jessica was never sure why someone bothered to print off a list of dishes each day – it was largely the same: some combination of an all-day English breakfast before eleven; pie, chips and mushy peas at lunchtime; and then whatever was left before they shut up shop ahead of the evening shift arriving. After that, it was vending machine only, though the fact they had a canteen at all was still more than most places.

'Do you think someone's told her?' Jessica asked, nodding towards the constable.

'Told her what?' Archie replied.

'That eating the food isn't good for a human being's digestive system.'

Neither Izzy nor Archie said anything, so Jessica leant backwards in her chair and called across the empty room: 'Ruth.'

The constable spun, a creeping smile of recognition as Jessica waved her over. DC Evesham had been hired in the latest round of long-overdue recruitment, moving from uniformed policing in the city centre – a true baptism of raging lava for a newcomer – into CID. When Jessica had made a similar move, there'd been a buddy scheme, where she was paired with someone senior to learn the ropes. Now, there weren't enough staff, time or money to make that happen. New recruits were lobbed into the deep end and left to find their own way.

'Hi,' Evesham said.

'Has anyone warned you about the canteen food?' Jessica asked.

'No . . .'

'Just don't try anything with eggs, well, unless you're trying to lose weight and you fancy a few days with severe abdominal pains.'

'Not good, then?' she laughed, gazing down at Archie's mound of chips.

'Feel free to find out for yourself.' Jessica nodded at Archie's plate. 'He's got an iron stomach.'

The constable smiled appreciatively, before turning and heading back to the counter, jangling the change in her hand. The three of them sat watching her for a few moments before Archie, predictably, filled the silence, angling towards Izzy. 'I didn't know you were a fight fan,' he said.

'Huh?' Izzy replied.

'I saw you looking at the boxing results earlier. I didn't know you were into that.'

Izzy pinched one of his chips, one of the few things in the canteen that was hard for the cooks to get wrong.

'Apparently there's a British middleweight title fight happening in Manchester this weekend.'

Archie shook his head. 'Nah . . .'

'Bare-knuckle. Apparently people have been talking about it on Internet forums. It was passed up and somehow ended up on my desk.'

'What are you supposed to do?' Jessica asked.

'Firstly, find out if it actually *is* happening. If so, get a bunch of uniforms in to stop it. There's almost nothing on the forums – it'll all be phone calls and texts. If it is happening, I don't know the venue, time or day. I've been asking around to see if anyone knows anything about it but all I get is a bunch of blank faces and people talking about gypsies.'

'Is it travellers?' Jessica asked.

'Probably.'

It was typical of the types of thing that used to end up on Jessica's desk – minimal information from a dead-end tip but the expectation that, if there was something to it, it'd be acted upon. Jessica suspected it wasn't the bare-knuckle fight itself that would concern their bosses, more the trouble it could bring if an influx of supporters and hangers-on descended on the city for a drink-filled night of violence. Manchester had its own traveller community, who, for the most part, kept itself to itself. There was obviously some tension but a specialist liaison team acted as go-betweens for the travellers, the police, and the wider community.

'Wanna know who the British middleweight champion is?' Izzy asked.

'Go on,' Jessica said.

'Liam "Nine Fingers" Flanagan from London.'

'Does he actually have nine fingers?'

'Apparently, though I couldn't find anything where it said how he lost a finger. I spoke to someone at the Met yesterday, who passed me from department to department. Eventually I ended up talking to someone from their "diversity" team who knew the name. He called me back this morning to say that Flanagan was still in London. If he is on his way up here, then it's not happened yet – not that we can monitor him anyway. I guess we'll have to wait and see.'

Jessica offered a sympathetic shrug, the best she could manage. There was no glory to be had there, either.

'I'll ask around,' Archie said, amid a mouthful of mushy chip. Both women looked at him. 'What?' he added. 'I know people who know people. If it's on, one or two of my mates would probably be going.'

'Are you into bare-knuckle boxing?' Jessica asked.

He shrugged. 'Not really. When I was younger, I went to the odd tear-up.'

Jessica slipped her chair back, not entirely surprised. She had an afternoon of briefings with Josh ahead of her visit to Manchester's crème de la crime. As she was standing, her saviour arrived: DC Evesham, half-eaten sandwich in her hand.

'I thought you'd want to know,' the constable said. 'I was on my way back to my desk when a bunch of people charged out the other way.'

'Why?'

'They reckon they've found Kevin Jones.'

18

Birchfields Park, the place where Kevin Jones had apparently been spotted the previous evening, was less than a mile from Longsight Police Station. Jessica told Josh she'd talk to him later, insisting the escaped prisoner was more of a priority. It was – but it was also DI Franks's responsibility. It was a useful diversion, though – anything that kept her out of meetings and briefings had to be a positive thing.

When she arrived at the park, there was a wide square of blue and white police tape cordoning off the ramshackle breezeblock public toilets. Overgrown trees and bushes surrounded the building, growing into the bricks, as if devouring a meal.

A handful of locals, kids off school, dog-walkers and mucky men who lurked in the city's parks, were hanging around, sitting and standing in the sun, staring towards the building as DI Franks, a dozen uniformed officers and at least three members of CID hung around, pointing and not doing much else. Jessica headed towards the group, when Franks held his hands up, trying to shoo her away.

'Oh no, I'm not having this,' he said.

'What?' Jessica replied, easing herself into the circle.

'You're not taking credit for this.'

'I don't want credit, I'm out for a lunchtime stroll in the

park.' She nodded at the building. 'Besides, you're the toilet expert.'

Franks harrumphed, pushing himself onto tiptoes, trying to intimidate her.

'What's going on?' she asked.

'I believe the building is due for demolition this month.' Franks was showing a disturbing amount of knowledge about public toilets, which wasn't in itself a surprise. He pointed towards a row of trees that lined the park. 'Kevin Jones's girlfriend, Bronwen-something, lives on that estate. I spoke to her personally on the day Jones escaped custody but she said she hadn't heard anything. Despite the delay in approving surveillance, she was spotted coming to this block with a bag of what we think were groceries. That was an hour ago. She's not emerged since, so I suspect she must know we're here.'

Franks had really gone out on a limb by suspecting that – of course she bloody knew. Rather than go in quietly with a couple of officers, Franks had turned up with the police tape and too many people, drawn the attention of the public, and, potentially, turned it into a siege. Typ-i-bloody-cal.

'Has anyone actually seen Kevin Jones?' Jessica asked.

'Well, no . . .'

'Has anyone approached the block to speak to Bron-wen?'

'Well, no . . . I didn't think it would be prudent.'

Prudent? If they weren't so busy, DCI Topper and the superintendent would be having a fit.

'What's your plan?' Jessica asked.

'We wait it out. They can't stay in there forever.'

Jessica peered from Franks's determined face to the block and back again. 'If Bronwen took in a bag of groceries, plus they have a toilet and fresh water, they could stay there for days.'

Franks shuffled uneasily. 'They won't.'

'How do you know?'

'It's, er, not so pleasant in there.'

Jessica didn't want to know how he knew that. 'Surely it's better than a prison cell? He's going back to jail anyway, and she'll be done as an accessory. This could be their last few days together in a long time.'

'Um . . .'

This was worse than she thought. Franks had been a liability ever since he'd arrived at Longsight on the back of an unlikely promotion, but at least he'd been relatively harmless. Before she could say anything else, he'd plucked the loudhailer from his feet and was marching like a sergeant major towards the building.

'Come out with your hands up!'

Franks stood, glaring at the crumbling pile of bricks, as if his will alone could force the inhabitants to do what he wanted. There was a flicker of movement – someone with long hair poking their head around the wall, before disappearing again. Franks stood, one hand on his hip, as he put the loudhailer down again, turning back towards his small band of unfortunate followers.

'Well, they're not coming out,' he said.

His eyes were darting from side to side, realisation dawning that he should have put a little more thought into things before arriving. Jessica knew exactly what had happened – the tip had come in and he'd run out of the station with a handful of officers, front-page accolades in mind. Up until now, that sort of glory-hunting would have served him well – it had got him to where he was – but he was always going to come unstuck sooner or later. Like every industry, the police force had its fair share of useless bastards who everyone knew weren't up to the job, yet, somehow, they kept getting promotions. Some people knew how to interview well, which was most of the battle.

'You're not going to get them out by shouting,' Jessica said.

Franks rounded on her, pumping himself up taller. 'What do you suggest?' he snapped.

'A woman's touch – Kevin Jones is a small-time nobody, not a gangster. He was in the right place at the right time when Priestley was sprung. It could've been anyone. Carl Frosham decided to stay put in the prison van, Kevin ran for it. He knows he's stuck, he's just holding out as long as he can.'

Jessica took a step towards the building as Franks reached forward and grabbed her shoulder. 'Oh no, you don't,' he snarled.

She stepped away. 'You want to go and talk to them?'

He spun in a circle, peering from officer to officer, embarrassing himself as his rabbit-in-the-headlights expression made it clear he didn't. He was hoping someone had a better idea but it was too late for that. Either go and have a word, or get tactical firearms involved – again – and have a Sky News helicopter swirling as officers with machine guns lined up in the park.

Jessica snatched herself away, walking carefully towards the building. It looked like it had been built for the minimum amount possible: ugly grey blocks of stone in a square, with a rippled tin roof on top. Cottaging chic. The smell of piss caught on the gentle breeze as she neared, the heat of the past few days combining with a fetid sewer system to create a toxic summer cocktail. It was no wonder the block was being bulldozed – a hole in the ground would have been more hygienic. Brambles and nettles were thigh high, creeping through the tendrils of tree branches, all fighting the expanding, uncut hedgerow and dousing the corner of the park in a dark shadow, despite the sun slicing through the rest of the area. The temperature dropped by a few degrees, making Jessica shiver as she avoided a coating of mud that was clinging to the path. Despite the lack of rain in the past week, there were still pools of filthy water in the undergrowth, a microclimate hiding in plain sight. It was the perfect place to hole up if the smell could be overcome. There was shelter and the likelihood that no one would be paying too much attention.

Jessica's footsteps crunched across the gravelly, crumbling entrance to the toilet block, as she headed into the men's. Either she'd become accustomed to the stench, or it was the sewers outside which stank, not the toilets inside. There was a row of what could barely be called windows high on the wall – more like gaps in the concrete – but no artificial light.

'Hello,' she called, her voice echoing into the darkness.

There was a rustling, the glimmer of light catching a silhouette at the far end.

'I'm not coming closer,' Jessica added, watching the shape settle until she realised there were two people sitting next to one another. She waited, allowing her eyes to adjust until she could just about make out the scene. It looked like two people were sitting on fold-up deckchairs next to a row of sinks. One had long hair, the other was thicker-set. Neither was moving.

'You can say hello,' Jessica said.

Neither of the shapes replied.

She looked around for somewhere to sit but there were only the toilets in the cubicles next to her, so standing it was.

'Look,' Jessica said, 'this is going to happen in one of three ways. First, there are a bunch of dozy bastards out there who'll hang around until you come out. When you eventually do, they'll be tired and annoyed, it'll make a big story on the news and then, when you both end up in court, the magistrates or judge will be really pissed off. Second, someone out there will decide they'd rather be home watching *Corrie* than messing around in a park on a summer's evening. They call up a bunch of big blokes with guns, who'll storm in here, scare the shite out of you both, and nick the pair of you. Third – and this is my preferred option – you come out with me now. You can hold hands, put your arms around each other, peaceful as you like, and there'll be a belting picture on the news tonight. Your solicitor will say you're a misguided couple who'll do anything for love, we'll get Wet Wet Wet in to do some backing vocals over a video montage, and you can both make a shitty situation marginally less shitty. It's up to you. Either way, I've got a meeting to get to.'

There was a shuffling and it occurred to Jessica that, if the shadows were from something else and it was just a single person taking a wee, then she was going to look pretty silly.

Moments later, thankfully, a man's voice echoed. 'D'you reckon you can give us ten minutes?'

'Why ten minutes?' Jessica asked.

'I've just opened a bag of jam doughnuts.'

Jessica almost laughed. If she'd been locked up, or trapped in the station's canteen for long – both ideas were equally bad – she'd probably be craving a few cakes too. Suddenly she had a desire for doughnuts herself: one of those big bags of ten her mum used to get from the local bakers for a quid. Covered in sugar, blackcurrant oozing from the centre. Yum yum. She used to get one for being a good girl and tidying her room.

'Tell you what,' Jessica replied, 'I'll give you *five* minutes. Eat what you can, then come out. I'll tell everyone you're surrendering, then, in the report, I'll let everyone know how cooperative you both were. Deal?'

There was a whisper and then male and female voices spoke at the same time: 'Deal.'

19

The next day, Jessica found herself in the situation of both being on her own and feeling watched. She had Archie at her side, of course, it was too much for her to go marching into a succession of lion's dens entirely by herself – but there was no Serious Crime Division to report to, no bosses wanting immediate reports. Of course, the SCD and her bosses *did* want immediate reports but not in a way that made it look like that. That left Jessica in her car, driving from place to place, trying to remember everything for when the inevitable questions came later. A lone wolf in the middle of a hunting pack.

Thomas Braithwaite didn't even live in Greater Manchester, let alone operate in it – at least not officially. He'd made his money through manufacturing, thirty miles down the road in Liverpool – yet he was on the SCD's list as a 'person of interest' who might want to target Richard Hyde and his family.

Jessica and Archie were welcomed through an imposing set of double gates by a bulldog of a man – Iwan-something – who had a thick neck, bulky shoulders and protruding forehead. The type of specimen scientists would have sliced open in the early 1900s, trying to figure out if the shape of somebody's skull dictated their personality. Jessica didn't need to do any cutting to guess Iwan's personality – he was a bully, the type of person with whom legitimate factory owners shouldn't need to surround themselves.

Iwan led them to the rear of the house into a conservatory, where Thomas Braithwaite was sitting at a small black metal table, sipping from an espresso cup, watching his garden ahead of him. There were stables, sculpted hedges and a vast expanse of green. He had black hair that was barely beginning to grey, though it left him with the look of a man who'd seen and done a lot. He was in shape, with a tidy beard and moustache, but it was his eyes that truly told his story: deep, piercing blue that momentarily made Jessica stop still as he reached to shake her hand.

Archie acknowledged Braithwaite with a nod, sitting a little away from the table as Iwan the brute disappeared into the rest of the house.

After the introduction, Braithwaite continued staring at Jessica, not letting her go. 'I must admit,' he purred, 'I wasn't expecting a visit from Greater Manchester Police. You do realise this isn't Greater Manchester.'

'Really? I wondered what that forty-minute drive was all about.'

He didn't smile. 'To what do I owe the pleasure?'

'Richard Hyde.'

Braithwaite's gaze didn't shift, eyelids unblinking. 'What of him?'

'He's run into a bit of bad luck in recent days.'

'So I've heard. Such a tragedy.'

'Sending a card, are you? "Sorry for your loss", that sort of thing?'

Braithwaite smiled tightly. 'I'm a busy man, Inspector.'

'Really? It's ten in the morning and you're sitting in your conservatory watching the garden.'

He ran his tongue along the bottom of his teeth, weighing her up, wondering what the game was. 'Are you familiar with Confucius?'

Jessica turned to Archie. 'Doesn't he play up front for United?'

Archie started to reply, missing the joke, but Braithwaite remained tight-lipped, waiting until Archie had embarrassed himself before answering. '"Our greatest glory is not in never falling, but in rising every time we fall."'

'What's your point?' Jessica asked.

'Come now, Miss Daniel, I can tell you're an intelligent person.'

'Are you moving into Manchester?' Jessica asked, figuring she may as well be direct. He was deliberately being obscure, so it'd most likely annoy him.

'Why would I want to shift my wares into such a dump a few miles down the road?'

Digs about his beloved hometown was another of Archie's weak spots. 'You live close to Liverpool, mate,' he chirped up, unable to stop himself.

'And in Liverpool I would rather stay.'

Jessica wasn't sure if she'd been sent on a fool's errand, or if Braithwaite was lying to her face. She wouldn't be surprised by either.

'The Hydes are off-limits,' Jessica said.

Braithwaite shrugged. 'Is that supposed to intimidate me?'

'I don't care but I'm passing on the warning that, if

anything does happen, you'll have the entirety of a police force looking into everything you do.'

He nodded tightly, gaze and smile not shifting. As if telepathically, Iwan reappeared in the doorway. 'Our guests are just leaving,' Braithwaite said.

One down, a bunch more to go.

Christian Fraser was a name Jessica had heard the previous time she'd had a conversation with Josh from the SCD. Fraser ran an empire of low-level clubs and pubs around the centre of Manchester that were apparently a front for dealing drugs and laundering money. She'd never had any direct dealings with him, but the name of his not-so-dearly departed right-hand man, Scott Dewhurst, still made her shiver with fear and recognition. Dewhurst had changed something within Jessica, making her cross a line from which there was no turning back. In many ways, everything that had happened in her life since stemmed from that moment – the explosion which left Adam comatose, the inherent threat she felt from Chief Constable Pomeroy, the departure of DCI Jack Cole. She either had to live with the decision she made, or be consumed by it. For her, there was no choice: life went on.

Fraser wasn't what Jessica expected. He was short with a slim-cut suit, open-necked shirt and glasses, the sort of person on a plane who had a Californian accent and banged on about investing in a technology company no one had ever heard of. He welcomed Jessica and Archie into a plush office at the back of a 'gentleman's club' in the city centre. He was wearing a chunky gold bracelet with matching rings and smelled of too much aftershave. There were leather armchairs, a thick carpet, a whisky decanter on his desk, with an enormous framed portrait of himself on the wall. It took a certain type to decorate a workspace with a giant self-portrait; a person driven by ego and the sense that it was fine for others to think of you as a complete bellend.

DI Franks would fit in well.

Also in the office was another suit-clad dick of a man. Jessica didn't need to be introduced to know he was a solicitor: he had that look about him, all pinstripes and swept-back gingery hair, conscience uncluttered by such things as working for a gangster. The solicitor checked Jessica and Archie's IDs thoroughly, making a note of the details, before they sat.

Fraser reclined in the seat behind his desk, sipping from a heavy glass filled with mineral water poured from an expensive-looking bottle. This wasn't Buxton from down the road, it was imported from somewhere far away, distilled across the thighs of a Ukrainian virgin, bottled at source and then flogged to people with too much money.

The solicitor did the speaking: 'Your superiors were unclear as to the nature of this meeting,' he said.

Jessica made a point of ignoring him, turning to Fraser. 'I wouldn't exactly call it a meeting.'

'Yet here we are,' the solicitor continued, unconcerned by such things as being ignored, or morals.

'I wanted to ask Mr Fraser about his relationship with a possible business associate named Richard Hyde.'

The solicitor continued: 'Is there something specific you have to ask, or is it a general inquiry?'

'I was talking to Mr Fraser, not the chimpanzee with a law degree.'

Fraser smiled thinly at Jessica. She wondered if he knew who she was, knew what she did about the demise of his one-time ally.

The solicitor started to reply but Fraser spoke over him. 'Mr Hyde is a business associate and I'm very sorry for his loss.' He paused. 'Losses.'

'Fair enough – as long as you know that we know.'

'Know what?' Fraser asked.

'That we're watching. Any other moves on Hyde won't be greeted with a parade and party balloons. There's not going to be a war in this city.'

Fraser sipped from his glass, smiling. 'I don't know what you're talking about.'

'Good – we'll see ourselves out.'

Nelson Carter – or simply 'Carter' to anyone who knew him – had worked as Harry Irwell's right-hand man, up until Irwell's overdose a couple of years previously. From there, he could have faded into obscurity, but the Serious Crime Division files said he now ran Irwell's casino on behalf of his widow, Barbara. The nature of Carter's other activities was unclear, though he was still a person of interest, with a long line of brutal, yet unproven, violent acts attributed to him. He was another thug of a man, bald head, thick arms, brutish shoulders, and the sense that he didn't mind using them. Jessica and Archie were shown into an office at the back of Casino 101 on Quay Street in the city centre, where Carter met them with a ruthless show of momentary strength, crushing Jessica's fingers tightly enough to make her gasp as they shook hands. She watched Archie try – and fail – to squeeze Carter's hand back, wincing with momentary pain before Carter's paw released him. In that instant, Jessica decided to throw off the leash – she'd been polite-ish all morning and it was time to piss some people off.

'How's Babs?' Jessica asked as they sat across the desk from him.

Carter squinted at her, confused. 'Who?'

'Babs Irwell, Harry's widow. I gather she's the one who orders you around.'

His eyes glowered even more narrowly, giving a glimpse of the rampaging bull sheltering within. 'Her name's Barbara,' he said.

'Babs, Barbara; potato, pot-tah-to. How is she?'

'What's it to you?'

'I just find it interesting: Harry Irwell has no children, no natural heir, and his wife's knocking on a bit. With him out of the way, it seems very convenient that you inherit everything. Some might say Harry's death is the best thing that ever happened to you. Some might also say that the nature of his death was suspicious . . .'

Carter pursed his lips, eyeing Jessica dangerously. '*Who* might say?'

'Y'know – just *some*. Anyway, it must be hard following in Mr Irwell's shoes. You must feel quite the pressure to maintain the standards he set?'

His features were unmoved. 'Not much has changed.'

'That's what I'm worried about. Mr Irwell wasn't exactly

a reputable operator, was he? Fingers in people-trafficking pies, drug-dealing pies, money-laundering pies and all that.'

'I don't know what you're talking about.'

'Course you don't – now tell me about Richard Hyde.'

'What about him?'

'There are all sorts of rumours that Hyde and Irwell had a long-running dispute over who controlled which areas of the city.'

Carter's features didn't even flicker. 'Rumours are dangerous things.'

'That they are – I'm just making sure those rumours aren't part of a truth that's ongoing.'

Carter stood, offering his mitt of a hand again, which Jessica didn't shake. 'If that's all,' he said, 'then you should leave.'

Outside the casino, Jessica was about to clamber back into her car when her eye was caught by the shiny black Rolls Royce across the road. The glass was tinted, sun gleaming from the newly washed paintwork, yet there was something about it that seemed wrong. She took a few steps backwards, craning her neck to spot the HYD3S number plate, and then crossed the road, rapping on the driver's window. As Archie slotted in behind her, the window hummed down, revealing the annoyed brown eyes of Richie Hyde. The last time she'd spoken to him had been in the casino, where he'd been shushed by his sister; now he was alone.

'Why are you here?' Jessica asked.

Richie glared at her with contempt. 'What's it to you?'

'I don't want things escalating. I know your mother's—'

'What? Murdered? Shot in the head?'

'We're looking into it,' Jessica said. 'We have people checking the ballistics, the forensics, security cameras, everything – but it takes time.'

One of his eyes was twitching, betraying his fury. 'So they sent *you*? What's wrong with a man?'

Jessica let it go. 'You should go home, Richie.'

The door clicked open slightly. 'This needs to be dealt with by a man, a proper man.' Jessica shoved the door closed with her hip.

'You're not dealing with anything,' she said. 'You're going to go home and let us sort it.'

He eyed her up and down, lips twisting into a sneer. 'How about you get in the car and we'll have a bit of fun on the way?'

Richie snatched at her wrist, squeezing and pulling before she had a chance to move. Archie lunged forward, grabbing him by the throat as Jessica pulled her arm away. 'You try it, pal,' Archie said, pushing himself further through the window. Richie's eyes bulged, smile disappearing as he realised Archie was serious. Richie was the affluent kid acting like a street punk; Archie was the real deal and they both knew it. Richie squeaked and squealed like a cornered piggy before Archie shoved him backwards.

There was a red mark on Jessica's wrist from where Richie had been too quick for her. The car window hummed until it was halfway up, though the top of Richie's head was still visible.

'He your boyfriend?' Richie sneered, straining for confidence again. 'You should keep him on a leash – perhaps he'll like that.'

Jessica stared through the window. 'If it wasn't for what happened to your mother, you'd be face-down on the tarmac with my friend's knee jammed into your bollocks. Now piss off before we nick you for assaulting an officer.'

He waggled his tongue at her provocatively before the window hummed fully closed and the engine roared to life, sending a cloud of exhaust fumes towards them as he accelerated to the junction and turned left without indicating.

'What a prick,' Archie spat.

'I don't need you to defend me, Arch.'

'I thought—'

'You thought grabbing him by the throat was a good idea? What if he complains? If I told the truth, you'd be suspended.'

'Aye, well—'

Jessica sighed, rubbing his arm. 'But thanks.'

He thrust his shoulders forward, puffing his chest out. 'What d'ya reckon?'

'That we're three down and none of them know anything. It's all a bit of amusement for them, watching us chase our tails and talk in riddles because we can't accuse them of anything outright. Serious Crime should do their own dirty work.'

'Do you reckon it's foreign gangs moving in?'

Jessica shook her head. 'I doubt it – this lot would be up in arms. Carter, Fraser, Braithwaite, Hyde and the rest will spend years arguing over a petty few clubs and pubs but the minute foreigners step on toes, they all work together. None of them have mentioned anything.'

'So who's moving on Hyde?'

Jessica bobbed from one foot to the other, wishing she had an answer. 'Who knows? Let's get the rest of this list ticked off, then we can go get some grub.'

They crossed the road back to the car, with Archie leaning on the passenger's side. 'You up to much tonight?' he asked.

She couldn't meet his eye. 'Yep, got loads on at home.'

20

After talking to the rest of the names on Josh's list of scum-bags, grabbing a burger with Archie, and then reporting everything back, Jessica was told by DCI Topper she should go home a whopping forty minutes early. It was better than the usual practice of staying late but she wasn't in the mood for sitting on the sofa watching some nonsense on television. Instead, she drove back to Swinton, weaving through the streets close to her home until she found the correct address.

Nerys Morrow seemed confused as she opened the door a few inches, taking Jessica's ID inside. 'You can phone the number if you want to check who I am,' Jessica said.

A pair of eyes appeared in the gap before the door opened further, revealing a woman in her late sixties, nursing a dodgy hip that left her leaning to one side. She had wiry, curly grey hair, appearing older than Jessica's next-door neighbour, even though she was younger.

'Sorry,' Nerys said, peering beyond Jessica to the road behind, 'I'm a bit careful nowadays.'

It wasn't a surprise considering Nerys had been scammed by a younger woman knocking at her door, much like Alf had been. She shuffled along the hallway, waiting for Jessica to lock the front door, before leading the way into a living room. The walls were covered with framed photographs of years gone by: beaches, parks, birthday cakes, Christmas crackers with party hats, thumbs-ups, hugs, smiles, smiles, smiles. A catalogue spanning a lifetime of family. Jessica turned in a circle, taking it all in, as Nerys pressed herself into a comfy-looking armchair.

'That's my Neil,' she said, not needing to point at any particular image because he was everywhere: Neil and Nerys, Nerys and Neil.

'We were married for forty-nine years,' she said, voice cracking slightly, no need to fill in the blanks.

Jessica didn't reply, feeling the twinge of the lifetime the woman had lost.

'I was hoping someone would be back,' Nerys added. 'I thought you'd forgotten.'

'Sorry?'

'After that woman came to my house, you sent police officers round and they wrote everything down, then I didn't hear anything. Have you caught her?'

Jessica shook her head. 'Sorry, Mrs Morrow, that's not exactly why I'm here.'

'Oh . . .'

'My next-door neighbour suffered an incident a little similar to the one you experienced and I'm trying to find out if the same woman was involved.'

Nerys pushed herself up from the chair, trying to stand but grimacing. She clicked her fingers, which Jessica wasn't sure she'd ever seen an older person doing. It seemed strange. 'I remembered her name – but only after your policewoman left. I wrote it down, it's on the fridge.'

'I'll go,' Jessica said.

She smiled as she entered the kitchen – the fridge was covered by a mass of Sudoku puzzle magnets, a mishmash of words from famous sayings for someone to reorder, and individual letters. At the top, 'Annie' was spelled out in a mix of purple, green and fluorescent yellow plastic characters.

Jessica had a quick look around the near-spotless kitchen but there was little to see, other than a small pile of dust and grit sitting next to the bin, ready to be scooped up. She returned to the living room, returning Nerys's smile.

'Her name was Annie?' Jessica asked.

'It came to me days after your policewoman had left. I thought about calling you again but couldn't find the number and didn't want to call 999. I figured someone would get back to me in the end.'

'Annie' hadn't been in the report Jessica had seen, but Alf said the woman who called at his door was 'Anne'. Either of them could have misheard – or the woman could have given different names. It was enough of a similarity, though.

'Did anyone ever come out and draw up a picture of the woman?' Jessica asked.

Nerys shook her head.

It was a little awkward because it sounded like the case hadn't fully been investigated. Things like that could happen for so many reasons, largely to do with workload and resources. It was too easy to judge someone else's incompetence when the circumstances weren't known, unless it was DI Franks, of course, who really was a buffoon.

Jessica fiddled with her phone, apologising as she logged

into her emails and found the e-fit Alf had given the previous day. She turned the screen around, knowing instantly from Nerys's gasp and hand over the mouth that it was the same person.

'Annie,' she whispered, tears forming in the corners of her eye. She tugged a tissue from her sleeve, waving Jessica away, not wanting sympathy. 'Neil always said I was too trusting, too soft. Sometimes I thought he was too hard on others but he was right, wasn't he?'

'Do you want to talk about what happened?' Jessica asked.

'I already told the other woman.'

'If you tell me, I promise I'll do all I can to find her.'

Nerys dabbed at her nose and eyes, then slipped the tissue back into her sleeve. 'I thought it was the window cleaner,' she said. 'He usually comes in the middle of the afternoon every couple of weeks and goes up on the ladders. We have a quick natter and I make him a brew.' She paused. 'Oh, you must think I'm so rude, I've not offered you one.'

'I'm fine, honestly.'

She nodded. 'I opened the door, thinking it was him, but it was this young woman, pretty with long dark hair but she looked a little put-upon. She said she had a daughter at school, but she was going door to door, hoping to do some work. She said she'd been laid off by this cleaning company – that they sacked all the English ones and hired a bunch of Romanians who'd do it for less. It sort of sounded right but I dunno . . . you hear these things. I just wanted to help . . .'

Jessica gave her a few moments to compose herself. The

embarrassment was clearly greater than any financial loss, which was probably why more people hadn't come forward. Jessica wondered how many others had been targeted by Annie. Preying on a person's goodwill really was one of the worst crimes, not just because of the immediate effect, but because of the lasting damage it did to people's sense of wanting to help others.

'She said she wanted work and didn't want to claim benefits,' Nerys added. 'I struggle with my back nowadays and asked if she'd do a bit of cleaning. I can't get down to the bath and the oven like I used to be able to. I sat in here, listening to her while away, and then paid her. She even did a good job. You should see what she did with the oven – it's not been that clean in years. I was telling her to come back, that there'd be more, but then, when I went upstairs . . .' Nerys gulped. 'There's this case in which I keep all my documents – cheque book, cash, paying-in slips, everything the building society sends me.'

'How much did she take?'

'A few hundred.' She smiled, though there was little humour. 'It's not the money. Neil was sensible with things like that: he made sure I was taken care of with his policies and what-not. There was all the hassle of phoning the building society, then you have to explain what happened. They cancelled everything but then you have to go into town and show them your passport.' Another sigh. 'I don't want it happening to other people – that's what I told your woman.'

Jessica unlocked her phone screen, staring at the face of Annie, hoping she'd be able to keep the promise of finding her.

21

Jessica's first of three days off in a row didn't involve much 'being off'. She called the station, talking to DCI Topper, who said the Serious Crime Division were happy with her work from the day before and that, so far, it didn't look as if there had been any other city-wide incidents. Kevin Jones was back in prison, facing additional charges for escaping lawful custody, and his girlfriend had been charged for helping him. The murder investigations into who killed Owen Priestley and Lisa Hyde wasn't going well, with a lack of forensics or witnesses. They each reeked of a professional job, with few clues other than the connection to Richard Hyde, as if the entire thing had been planned and carried out to perfection. Irfan Nabil and Eric Maudsley were still refusing to name names as to who hired them to crash into the prison van, leaving the police with little to go on.

She told Topper she'd stay in contact through her days off, even though he told her not to, and then Jessica went to do something she never thought she would.

Bex was spending a few hours volunteering at the community centre for the weekly coffee morning. Jessica pictured old people in cardigans, musing over the old days, all sipping Nescafé instant with plates of digestives, but what she actually found was an endearing mix of all ages coming together to share their weeks with one another.

As well as the older people, there were single mothers, a nervous-looking man who didn't take off his backpack, and a couple somewhere in their thirties.

After the sight of single chairs sitting at dining tables in Alf and Nerys's houses, Jessica felt slightly ashamed that she had prejudged it all. It also gave her an opportunity to see Bex as her own person. The centre was owned by the council but the event was staffed by volunteers, of which Bex was the youngest by at least twenty years. Everyone knew her name as she flitted from person to person, saying hello, bringing drinks and chit-chatting in a way that Jessica had never been able to. She'd struggle through awkward pauses, wondering what to say, but others, like Izzy and Bex, could fill those silences with small talk that was a wonder in itself. Within minutes, Bex had the room enraptured, men and women nodding appreciatively as she passed by and fetched drinks. She'd come so far from the young girl living on the streets, and wasn't even eighteen for another day.

The coffee morning was a strange mix of everything and nothing. In essence, it was a bunch of strangers in a room, sipping hot drinks and having a natter. Beyond that, it was more of an opportunity to bring people together. Jessica barely even spoke to the people who lived around her, let alone others, but the friendly atmosphere left her wondering why there weren't more events like this in communities, encouraging people to talk about their lives in a way that'd make others understand. It was harder to do bad things to one another once a person had taken a glimpse into their neighbour's life.

Jessica felt like a stranger, out of her depth, trying to

smile and say hello, but never really having the words. She could walk into the realms of criminals and know instinctively which buttons to press; when it came to normal people, she felt lost.

She introduced herself as a police officer, showing the e-fit of Annie, only to get a succession of shaken heads and concerned looks. She wondered if she was making things worse, instilling fear where she should be reassuring.

Jessica wasn't sure what she expected – Topper said they'd get the e-fit image onto the force's website, but nobody looked at that, no matter how many times the press department banged on about the number of social media likes and followers they had. Unsurprisingly, that number hadn't impacted on the number of cases solved. When it came to social media, if it wasn't short videos of people falling over, animals looking adorable, or some factually incorrect piece of nonsense banging on about foreigners, Europe, or alleged paedos, then the general public weren't interested.

As for traditional media coverage, it was hard to ask papers and broadcasters to plug two things at the same time; they did have soap-star spottings to report on, after all. With all of the focus on finding who killed Priestley and Lisa Hyde, a low-level con-woman was way down the list of priorities. Jessica wasn't even supposed to be investigating the case, it being considered something with which a constable or possibly a sergeant should deal. Still, she didn't have anything better to do on a day off, which probably said more about her than it did anyone else.

Jessica asked everyone if they'd seen Annie and was

about to say goodbye to Bex when she realised there was one person she'd missed. A woman was hovering close to the ladies' toilets, wearing a hoody that was a size or three too big for her. She was thin, spindly robin legs sticking out from a knee-length skirt, dirty blonde hair hanging to her shoulders. Jessica was about to approach when she realised the woman was staring across the room, entirely focused on one person: Bex. Jessica stopped, sitting on one of the plastic chairs as a small group chattered around her. Bex was pouring tea from a large urn into a cup for one of the older men, laughing at one of his jokes and then showing him her tongue piercing. The blonde woman continued staring, following Bex around the room as she moved to the next group, asking if anyone wanted a refill. With a shudder, the watcher suddenly became aware that she was being watched. She turned, catching Jessica's eye for the briefest of moments before dropping her gaze to the floor. She looked sideways quickly and then hurried through the exit without a word.

Jessica didn't bother mentioning the woman to Bex, not wanting to spread any more worry after what could only be described as a low-level disaster at the community centre. She'd hoped someone would recognise Annie but there was nothing.

The sun was still shining, leaving Jessica to wonder if there wasn't something better she should be doing with her free time as she drove to the motorway. She followed the M60, retracing her route from earlier in the week until she arrived at the Hydes' Oldham casino. It had been open for less than an hour when Jessica walked through the main doors, but the fruit machines were already ding-ding-dinging. Along one side, long rows of televisions were showing horse races and football matches that had to be either highlights, or from somewhere else in the world. Some of the gaming tables were empty, but not as many as Jessica might have guessed. At least half of the blackjack and roulette areas had men – always men – focusing intently, tossing dwindling piles of chips towards the centre. Jessica headed towards the bar where Richie Hyde had threatened her, taking in the room. The only women she could spot were those who worked there, serving drinks or, in a couple of cases, dealing cards. It was undoubtedly a man's world in which Natalie Hyde found herself.

After touring the floor, not exactly sure what she was looking for but giving herself a feel of the place, Jessica eventually returned to the front. She was about to tell the burly suited man who she was and ask for Natalie but there was no need. The elder of the Hyde siblings bounded through a door that was a part of the wall, horizontal slats camouflaging it from inquisitive eyes unless a person knew where to look. She was smart in a dark business suit, hand outstretched in greeting, though her steely dark eyes told a different story.

'Inspector, to what do I owe the pleasure?'

Jessica shook her hand. 'Is there somewhere we can talk?'

'Are you on duty?'

'Sort of.'

Natalie nodded back towards the door, opening it and

initially letting Jessica lead the way through a warren of corridors that lined the edges of the casino. It was like two worlds, the outer one visible to the public: bright lights and the clamour of the machines. Barely metres away, there were soulless concrete passageways linking everything else. There were odd signs for 'changing room' and 'staff area', but no doors were open. Dotted across the ceiling were intermittent dark domes, housing security cameras, with Jessica in no doubt that every step she'd taken since entering the casino had been recorded.

Jessica had no idea where she was going but Natalie soon had them outside the same office in which Jessica had been before. Inside, Jessica was transfixed by the wall of monitors. It provided a glimpse into the world of how others lived. The people gambling were from all walks of life: old, young, suits, T-shirts, shiny shoes, Converse, singles, small groups. It wasn't even the weekend, yet the floor was half-full. Oldham was on the outskirts of Manchester, an area that had boomed during the Industrial Revolution, built on the cotton trade that had dissipated to such a degree that it left the area desperately searching for a twenty-first century identity. Was this it? Endless streams of betting shops on the route in and a giant casino?

Natalie slotted in behind the desk, sitting forward assertively. 'What can I do for you?' she asked.

'I wanted to tell you in person that I've visited a select group of local businessmen, names you'd know – Fraser, Carter, Braithwaite. They're all aware that the police are taking the attack on your family seriously.'

'I should think so, too.'

'I also have to say the same thing to you – nobody wants a war. If you, your father or anyone else knows who's responsible for what's happened, you have to work with us. We can't allow things to get out of hand.'

Natalie barely acknowledged her, watching the computer monitor instead. 'I have no idea to what you're referring.'

'Funnily enough, that's what they said. Nobody knows what's going on and it's all one big coincidence. There's something else, though.'

'What?'

'Richie – he was hanging around Casino 101 when I was visiting Carter.'

Natalie sighed, rolling her eyes and scribbling something on a pad in front of her. 'Fine – I'll have a word. I'm not my brother's keeper, though.'

'Someone needs to be.'

Natalie stabbed a full stop on the pad and looked up. 'If I want your advice I'll ask.'

Jessica gave her a few seconds to calm down. 'We don't have to be enemies,' she said. 'We're a similar age, we both work in a man's world. I want to find out who killed your mother, not argue over little things.'

'Is that why you were such a bitch when you first came here?'

Jessica let Natalie have that one – she wasn't entirely wrong. Natalie was twenty-eight, Richie twenty-five. Natalie had a maturity to her looks that made her appear older but not in a bad way.

'Can I ask you something personal?' Jessica said.

'Only if you're happy not to get an answer.'

'Your father seemed devastated by your mother's death, but you . . .'

'What? You think I don't care?'

'I have no right to say that.'

Natalie breathed through her nose, mashing her lips into one another before turning away. 'My mother sent Richie and me abroad when we were kids. I know Dad didn't stop her but at least he arranged for us to come back. It's hard to feel like you have a mother when you don't know her. I'm sorry for Dad, but that's about it.'

Natalie was blinking rapidly, seemingly annoyed she'd let her hardened façade drop. Jessica knew that feeling, a moment of vulnerability that felt like a weakness. Natalie flashed a hand towards the door, standing. 'If that's all you have to tell me, then you should have just called. I'll get someone to show you the way out.'

Jessica's day off ended with her back at the station, or close to it. The Wounded Duck was a few streets away, not the pub where Jessica and co used to go after shift, instead a trendier wine bar utterly inappropriate for the area. It was Izzy who'd finally had enough of the dive in which they used to go drinking, not to mention that too many locals knew it was a police officer's pub. Apart from the moaners whingeing on about every mundane problem they had – and asking why the police weren't doing anything, there were those who'd get abusive, straying close to the line of breaking the law, but not crossing it.

Friday at the Wounded Duck was two-for-one night,

meaning it was packed with people enticed by the prices but slightly bemused at the lack of ale choice. Jessica, Izzy, Rowlands and Archie had grabbed a booth and were busy putting the world to rights or, more to the point, discussing the ways in which DI Franks was the bane of their lives. Rowlands had it the worst, fingers clamped around a lemonade and lime, diet unbroken. The boring salad-munching sod.

'I actually have to share the corner of the office with him now,' Rowlands moaned.

'I've heard he likes middle-aged men with spiky hair,' Jessica replied, winking at Izzy.

'I'm not middle-aged.'

'Close enough. You're just his type.'

'He was trying to get me to verify his timings for that Kevin Jones bodge-job, which would partly get him off the hook. He reckons he was on his lunch when the report came in, and, because he was already out, he went straight to the park.'

'What did you say?'

'I wasn't even there – he'd sent me off to deal with a break-in just off Deansgate.'

Rowlands continued moping, finishing the rest of his drink and then asking what people wanted. There was his wishy-washy, non-alcoholic, boring somethingoranother; Izzy's hangman's noose; Archie's pint of Stella; and Jessica's club foot – the drink, not the deformity. Rowlands slunk his way across to the bar, disappearing into a crowd of people trying to get served.

'I hope he doesn't hang himself,' Izzy said.

'He just needs a good sha . . .' Archie tailed off, adding: 'Wrong crowd.'

Aside from Jessica, the other three were dressed in their work clothes, a suit jacket hanging over the edge of each seat. There was a small cheer as the lights dimmed and a DJ started prattling from the back corner, raising and dimming the music in between his inane warbling.

Izzy shuffled closer to Jessica, leaning across to make sure Archie could hear her. 'Have you heard anything about tomorrow or Sunday?'

'What about it?' Archie replied.

'The boxing match.'

'It ain't this weekend.'

'We've got posts on an Internet forum saying it's Sunday night,' Izzy insisted. 'We're just trying to get the venue.'

Archie shook his head. 'Not a chance – I've got one of my mates on the case. He'd know if it was happening and he says no.'

Izzy pulled a face, not liking being out of the loop. She turned back to Jessica. 'Any plans for your days off?'

'Big food shop, cleaning, it's non-stop rock and roll round my place. I am getting my hair sorted tomorrow, though.'

Archie stared at her, biting his bottom lip.

'What?' Jessica asked.

'*You* get your hair done?'

'Are you saying it looks un . . . done – like I'm a perman-ent mess?'

Izzy sniggered. Archie had unwittingly fallen into the

trap. 'Er . . . No, like, it's just . . .' He tailed off, knowing there was no good way to get himself out of the mire.

'Where d'you go?' Izzy asked.

'This place round the corner from my house – Hair 'n' Dipity.'

Archie snorted. 'That doesn't even work!' He turned towards the bar. 'Hang about, what's going on there . . . ?' Archie nodded ahead, where, like Moses parting the Red Sea, a gap had emerged, giving them a clear view of Rowlands leaning against the counter, standing next to a woman with blonde hair. They were talking to each other. *Talking!*

'Is she actually laughing at one of his jokes?' Izzy asked, disbelievingly.

Rowlands was smiling back at the mystery woman, paying no attention to the barman, who moved onto the next customer. Jessica could only see her from the side but the flirty stranger seemed normal – two legs, two arms, hair, eyes, nose. No obvious deformities.

'Maybe she's lost something?' Izzy said. 'She dropped it around the bar area and she's wondering if he's seen it.'

'Aye, aye,' Archie interrupted. The woman was touching Rowlands's arm, not in a 'have you seen my lost purse?' way, but in a 'my, what a nice arm you have' way. She was still giggling, flicking back her hair and half-turning towards them before returning to touch Rowlands's arm.

'The lucky sod,' Archie said. 'He'll be all over her like a horny octopus.' He glanced around quickly. 'Sorry, wrong crowd.'

As he kept a steady eye on the bar, a woman passed in

front of them, before turning around. 'Arch?' She was pretty, somewhere in her thirties, in a short dress.

'Oh . . . hi . . . what you doing out here?'

Izzy elbowed Jessica gently. It was cop-off night in the Wounded Duck. The woman seemed vaguely familiar, though Jessica couldn't place her.

'Oh, y'know . . . one of my mates fancied something different . . .' She turned to Jessica. 'Oh, hi again.'

Jessica suddenly realised who she was. When they'd first met, Paige had been in a dressing gown with dark hair; now she had lighter highlights and was dressed far more provocatively. She reached forward to shake Jessica's hand, simultaneously giving Archie an eyeful of some rather impressive cleavage. Even Izzy gulped.

'Hi,' Jessica said but Paige's attention was back to Archie.

'Fancy a drink?'

'I, er . . . yeah, why not?'

Archie eased himself out from behind the table, shrugged towards Jessica and Izzy, then disappeared through the crowds.

'Who's she?' Izzy asked.

'She lives below Archie.'

'Oh . . . she gave you quite the dirty look.'

'I could barely see over her chest.'

Not wanting to get into a conversation over her late-night/early-morning departures, Jessica went quiet. The two of them continued watching as Rowlands eventually remembered why he was at the bar – it only took him ten minutes. Soon after, the barman returned with the drinks, Rowlands passing him a note and seemingly forgetting there might be change. As he turned, Izzy and Jessica quickly spun away in an attempt to make it look like they hadn't been spying on him. Rowlands and the blonde woman arrived at the table and laid down the drinks, apparently not noticing Archie had disappeared. Rowlands had the look of someone who couldn't quite believe his luck, slightly raised eyebrows screaming 'I know!'

'I'm just nicking over to Katy's table for a bit,' Rowlands said, grin so wide that he looked like a Muppet with a big flappy head. 'Katy' – assuming that was her real name and she wasn't some con-woman – smiled sweetly but, as they turned to leave, a purse fell out of her bag, landing with a plop at Jessica's feet. Jessica leant forward and plucked it from the floor, glancing at the driving licence through the transparent window on the back, before calling after them.

As soon as they had gone, Jessica turned back to Izzy. 'Hmm . . . want to know what Katy's full name is?'

'Go on,' Izzy replied.

'Katherine Franks.'

There was a pause. '*Franks*?' Izzy hissed.

'How old do you reckon she was?' Jessica asked. 'Mid-twenties?'

'*Our* Franks – Funtime Frankie – is forty-four,' Izzy replied, 'so she could be . . .'

'He's never mentioned he's got kids.'

'He never talks about anything but himself,' Izzy pointed out.

They sat watching Rowlands and Katy sitting at a table together, laughing and smiling, like they'd known each other for years.

She was blonde, pretty, apparently funny, interested in Rowlands. She couldn't be related to DI Franks . . . could she?

22

Jessica's second day off started with the result of all results – no hangover! Either the Wounded Duck was watering down the spirits, or her body was returning to its formerly youthful state, with a wonderfully helpful degree of alcohol tolerance. She preferred to believe she was getting younger but knew deep down she should probably send an email to the weights and measures people.

It was Saturday morning: another bright, sunny day, birds chirping, summer beckoning, the city her oyster . . . which meant, inevitably, she was going to work anyway. Topper called first thing for a catch-up and then Izzy phoned straight after. Jessica was in the kitchen, picking at a piece of toast as Bex showered upstairs.

'How's the hangover?' Izzy asked.

'Non-existent. You?'

'The same. Me, Mal and Amber are off to Blackpool Pleasure Beach. Have you heard about Monday?'

'The guv just called – it's Lisa Hyde's funeral. The body's been released because the post mortem's done and the forensics are sorted. Everyone's had their shifts swapped. If anyone gets murdered over the next forty-eight hours, they're pretty much going to have to investigate it them-selves.'

'Is that a direct quote for the press office?'

Jessica laughed. 'Word for word.'

'You're taking it easy today then?' Izzy replied. 'Feet up, day in the garden, reading a book . . . ?'

'What do you think?'

'That the investigation into who killed Priestley and Lisa Hyde is going nowhere.'

'You'd be right. Topper says we're going to have to crack on with "old-fashioned policing" but I think that must've come from a press release. No one's talking.'

'If that's the case then why aren't you giving yourself an actual day off?'

Jessica stood, putting her crumb-ridden plate in the sink and then walking into the hallway and up the stairs, phone to her ear. 'Irfan Nabil and Eric Maudsley must have been paid for smashing into the prison van, so where's the money?'

'Hasn't one of the DCs been on that?'

'Yeah but I'm going to knock on a few doors anyway.'

'If you're really that bored, you can come along to the Pleasure Beach with us.'

Jessica headed into her bedroom at the front of the house, skirting around a pile of unwashed clothes on the floor and wondering if she should make the bed. Was there any point? It'd only get unmade . . .

'Does standing in line all day sound like something I'd do?'

Izzy laughed. 'Good point.'

Jessica pulled back the curtains, staring out to where a milkman's cart was stopped in the middle of the street. It was the first time she'd seen a milkman in years, and what time of the morning was this? It was gone nine – he surely should have been delivering at five or six? He left a glass bottle outside a door across the road, then hurried back to his cart before heading off, leaving the street empty and silent.

'Who are you going to see?' Izzy asked.

'Carol Ficus – she's the mother of Theo, the kid whose neck Eric Maudsley held scissors against. Someone went to get her statement but she answered no comment to everything. I'm going to see if she'll say anything more to me.'

'The second word will probably be "off".'

'You don't think my charming manner will win her over?'

Izzy laughed. 'Ten quid says you get a door slammed in your face.'

'You're on. You still coming over later?'

'Of course.'

A flash of movement caught Jessica's eye as a blonde woman poked her head around a wall that led into a ginnel separating two rows of terraces halfway along the street opposite the house. The woman emerged onto the pavement, checking something in her hand and then peering along the row of houses. She was wearing skinny jeans and dark boots, but the oversized hoody was the same: the woman from the community centre who'd been watching Bex.

Jessica stepped away from the window. She wished Izzy a good time and then hung up. Even though Jessica could see the street, she was pretty sure the angle meant the woman couldn't see her. The mystery woman edged forward, not quite crouching behind the parked cars, but certainly making an effort to stay out of sight. She checked her hand again, before stopping directly across the road, staring at Jessica's house. She was probably in her forties, though it was difficult to judge an age at that distance. The woman took a phone from her pocket and typed something in, before putting it away again. After another glance, she shoved her hands in her pockets and hurried back the way she'd come, heading into the alley.

Jessica raced down the stairs, trying to force her feet into a pair of trainers and cursing herself for never untying the laces. In the same way that the bed would only get unmade again, her trainers would end up needing to be retied, so why untie them in the first place? *For reasons like this!* She finally managed to get the shoes on, heading out of the front door, gazing along the street towards the alley, where there was no movement.

After waiting for a car to pass, Jessica crossed the road, slowing as she edged along the street, eyes fixed on the entrance to the ginnel. She was three or four house-widths away from the turn when a face popped around the corner. The woman's eyes met Jessica's momentarily, widening in recognition, before she gasped, turning and running. Jessica started to follow but slipped on an empty packet of fags as she spun into the alley. The woman had a lead to start with, which was only increasing. Jessica was many things, but athlete was pushing it, especially the morning after a night on two-for-one cocktails. Jessica's ankle jarred on the cobbles but the blonde hadn't looked back, barrelling into the passage that ran parallel to the houses and then disappearing out the other end, past the corner shop, towards a row of trees. Jessica knew she had no chance of catching her and, with a stitch already twisting in her stomach, she came to a halt at the bench outside the shop, glaring disdainfully at the brown and black yapping excuse for a dog at her feet.

'Fat lot of good you were,' she told the animal.

The dog barked in response, probably letting Jessica know that she hadn't drenched herself in glory, either.

Jessica took a few deep breaths, trying to regain a degree of composure, grateful there was no one other than the dog to witness her embarrassment. It was the fag packet that had done it. That, and the cobbles. And the cocktails.

She turned and walked back to the house, trying to picture the woman's face. She'd seen it clearly at the community centre, but that was a vague memory now. Skinny, blonde, hoody: it wasn't much to go on. She wondered if the woman had been watching Bex, the house, or Jessica herself. Jessica had spent the past few days visiting a string of local crooks; was she something to do with them?

She returned to the house where Bex was yawning her way down the stairs. She was never more of a teenager than first thing in the morning: pale skin, sweaters, pyjama bottoms and a general sense that any time before ten in the morning was an ungodly hour to be up.

Bex mumbled something that sounded like 'bleugh' as she leant against the banister.

'Coffee?'

Bex peered up through half-closed sleepy eyelids. 'That'd be epic.'

Jessica took a step towards the kitchen, then turned

back. 'Do you remember a blonde woman in a hoody at the community centre yesterday?'

Bex scratched her head. 'Vaguely . . . it was the first time I'd seen her. She left early.'

'I think I just saw her outside watching the house.'

'Huh?'

'I know – I was wondering if you knew her?'

Bex shook her head. 'I saw someone outside the other day.'

'A blonde woman?'

Bex held her palms up. 'Maybe . . . it was someone in a dark hoody. I was in the living room and spotted them walking past at least half-a-dozen times. It was weird, because it's been warm out, but they were dressed for winter.'

Or keeping their face covered.

Bex continued: 'When I went out, they were across the road, sitting on the wall. I thought they might be lost, but as soon as I opened the door, they ran for it. It was a bit weird but I've not seen them since and I forgot about it.' She twisted her eyebrow piercing. 'Is there a problem?'

Jessica shook her head. 'Nah – there's all sorts who live around here.'

Jessica wanted two things from a hairdresser. The first was obvious: a haircut. The second was far harder to find: complete serenity. She didn't want to witter on about where she might or might not be going on holiday that year, let alone listen to someone banging on about whatever had happened on *Corrie* the previous night. Or the latest pile of shite on the telly with 'celebrity' in the title. Assessing a TV show wasn't that hard: if it had the word 'celebrity' associated with it in any way, it was *definitely* rubbish.

Hair 'n' Dipity was perfect. Its owner was a sour-faced Serbian woman, Nataliya, who was the height of efficiency. In-pay-out: no mucking about. She was pretty good with a pair of scissors, too. Almost too good. There was nothing official but the rumours went that she was a widow who'd used the insurance money from her husband's death to buy the shop. Jessica had no problems imagining that her creative scissoring had been put to good use upon her other half.

When Jessica entered the shop, Nataliya was already at work on another customer. She peered at Jessica over her glasses, holding the scissors out to one side.

'I don't mind waiting,' Jessica said.

'For what?'

'I have an appointment . . .'

'Daniel, yes?'

'Right.'

Nataliya used the scissors to point, probably not trying to be threatening but certainly managing it. 'You cancelled.'

'When?'

'You called an hour ago.'

'*I* called? I only live round the corner – plus I don't want to cancel.'

Nataliya shrugged. 'You cancel, you don't cancel. Make up your mind.'

'Who called? Was it a man's voice?' Jessica was thinking Archie. He'd disappeared pretty sharpish with Paige the previous night. This was easily the type of thing he might do for a joke.

'Pfft. I know the difference between a man's voice and a woman's. She was, how you say . . . common. Like you.'

Charming. Customer service Nataliya-style.

Carol Ficus lived on a dodgy estate a shortish walk from Longsight Police Station, close to the unmarked border with Moss Side. To call her flat grotty made it sound cleaner than it was. She lived in a pebble-dashed, whitewashed block, which had a mushy mound of dog waste at the bottom of the concrete stairs. Without needing to move towards the lifts, Jessica spotted two used condoms, a crumpled packet of cigarettes with Eastern European scrawl on the front, a shopping basket, and scattered pages from an *FHM* magazine. Lovely.

Jessica stepped around the welcoming gifts, making an effort not to touch the handrail as she edged carefully up the stairs. Everything was a potential health hazard. Even though it was warm, there were half-a-dozen drips coming from various corners of the stairwell, leaving a succession of pools along the steps. Heading upstairs was like taking part in *Total Wipeout* but worse.

Halfway up was a tiled walkway, dimpled windows high on the wall, out of reach. Below, MSYD gang tags were graffitied along white breezeblocks, short for either 'Moss Side Young Defenders' or 'Moss Side Young Dipshits', depending on who was asked. By the time any of them got to court and gormlessly confirmed their names, no one was in doubt about which it was.

Jessica emerged into a concrete hallway with a row of five mustard yellow doors on either side. There was more graffiti on the far wall, plus the ashen part-burnt remains of what looked like an Argos catalogue in the middle of the floor. She knocked on Carol's door, getting an instant: 'All right, keep yer knickers on, gimme a minute.'

Soon after, the door swung open, revealing a woman in a pink tracksuit, dark hair tied into a tall ponytail. 'Who are you?' she snapped, looking Jessica up and down.

'I'm Detective Insp—' The door started to slam as Jessica lunged forward and wedged her foot in the gap. 'Ow!' she screeched.

'Git yer foot out of my door.'

'I just want a word.'

'I can give you two.'

Carol was behind the door, continuing to shove it into the instep of Jessica's trainer. Jessica couldn't see anything other than a grubby once-cream wall, though she could hear a television in the background.

'Is that Theo?' Jessica asked.

The pressure from the door eased slightly. 'What's it to you?'

'I'm the one who got him away when his dad was holding a pair of scissors against his neck.'

Jessica gasped as the gap between the door and the frame widened. Carol tugged it open and stood scowling at her. 'So it *is* true? I thought those social service pricks were having me on.'

'We went to arrest Eric but he wouldn't put Theo down.'

'Then one of you lot shot him.'

'In the shoulder – Theo was never in danger.'

Carol glared at her, top lip snarled, before her face fell. 'You should probably come in.'

Jessica clicked the door closed behind her, wondering how long it would take Izzy to pay up.

If Theo recognised Jessica, then he didn't let on. He was sitting on the living-room floor, using his savage little teeth to bite into a Lego Darth Vader. Carol made them cups of tea and then joined Jessica in the living room, relaxing into an armchair that had yellow foam spilling from the side. She'd clearly made the best of what she had, decorating the sparsely furnished room with a host of crayon drawings, each with an endearingly wonderful 'tHeO' stencilled into the corners. Animals seemed to be his thing, with giraffes, elephants and lions lining up outside a white block that was probably this flat. Theo was lost in his own world, ignoring them as he hummed to himself and played with the Lego.

'I always knew Eric would end up doing something stupid,' Carol said.

'Why didn't you tell that to our officer earlier in the week?'

She threw an arm in the air, raising her voice. 'I was battling to get Theo back from social services and your lot weren't helping. I kept telling your woman I'd talk once it was all sorted but she wasn't 'aving it. The only reason Theo was with his dad in the first place was because the court told me to. If it was down to me, Eric wouldn't be allowed to own a dog, let alone look after Theo.' Carol gazed adoringly at her son, her face softening. 'How long's he gonna get?'

'Eric? Assuming he's found guilty, probably a few years.'

Carol glanced towards Theo, lowering her voice slightly. 'Chuffin' brilliant. They can chuck away the key for all I care.' She glanced up, catching Jessica's gaze before rolling up her sleeve to reveal a V-shaped brown scar in her skin. She stretched out her forearm, making sure Jessica could see it clearly. 'He did that with an iron when I got home late from the supermarket one time. Told me I was 'is and that if he ever caught me with another bloke, he'd kill the pair of us.'

Carol rolled down her sleeve, before tugging down the waistband of her tracksuit bottoms, revealing three raised circular marks on her skin. 'He came in pissed one night while I was asleep, reckoned I was on 'is side of the bed, so he pinned me down and dug his fag into me.'

Jessica swore under her breath, unable to stop herself.

'Yeah, you're telling me,' Carol replied, straightening her clothes. 'The sooner he goes down, the better.'

'Did you ever report him?'

Carol snorted, staring at Jessica as if she had two heads. 'When I was living out Stockport, I reported my ex for smacking me about with a belt. What did you lot do? Nothing.' There was little Jessica could say, which Carol clearly sensed. 'I'm with a proper bloke now, anyway.' Her voice raised a few octaves as she peered to Theo. 'He loves you, little man, don't he?'

Theo didn't appear to notice he was being talked to, continuing to play with his Lego. It looked as if he was making a windmill, though there were wheels at the bottom and he was making engine noises. A windmill with wheels . . . he was a genius engineer in the making. One with vicious teeth.

'How long ago did you break up with Eric?' Jessica asked.

Carol snorted again. 'Break up? He fu—' She stopped herself, glancing at Theo. 'He chuffed off with some other woman.'

'Is he still with her?'

'Don't reckon. She was some Romanian or Hungarian type. Nicked his money then went off home – bloody hilarious.'

'He was short of money?'

Carol threw her head back, braying like an excited horse. 'He never paid me a penny of maintenance, despite what the court said – yet the minute I stopped Theo visiting him at the weekend, they had me up in front of the judge to explain myself.' Another glance at Theo, protecting his delicate ears. 'Chuffin' joke if you ask me.'

'If Eric came into money, where do you reckon he'd spend it?'

'Bookies.'

'Anywhere else?'

'I s'pose he might've paid off some of the money he owes.'

'To whom?'

Carol shrugged. 'Everyone – he owes me hundreds without even touching the child maintenance he hasn't paid. He's borrowed off his friends, his family, everyone. Then there's his gambling debts.'

23

Jessica knew that letting a teenager take control of the music would be a mistake. Instead of its usual mix of Brit-pop and rock, the stereo system in her house was being subjected to what could only be described as giant tortuous bag of shite. It started with some sort of electro-pop, before blending into a tweeny whiner carping on about a boy who'd left her. Jessica knew neither the singer, nor the song – but she was definitely on the side of the boy.

'I hope you realise this is a one-off,' Jessica said, leaning over to speak into Bex's ear.

The newly turned eighteen-year-old grinned at her. 'You should come and dance.'

'I'd rather cut off both my legs.'

Bex sniggered, mouthing a 'thank you' and twisting back towards her friends, who were dancing/having fits at the far end of the living room. Jessica gave her a wave and then headed through the kitchen into the back garden.

As eighteenth birthday parties went, it was relatively serene: crisps, dip, mini sausages, sausage rolls, some Indian goujon things, pizza, wedges – everything Bex had asked for. Jessica was half-hoping she wanted jelly and ice cream, if only for an excuse to get tucked in herself, but, alas, no. There was a cake bought from a bakery Fat Pat had recommended, plus half-a-dozen crates of various bottled lagers.

Aside from the dodgy music, it was all going well. Bex had invited seven or eight people she knew from college, while, largely to make up the numbers, Jessica had asked Archie, Izzy and Rowlands over for a few beers.

The four of them sat on the patio at the back of the house, leaving the kids to themselves.

'Aren't you worried they're going to trash the house?' Izzy asked, sipping from a bottle of Corona and peering nervously towards the house.

'There's only a few of them – that's why I asked you round.'

'Yeah but you hear about this type of thing all the time – one minute it's half-a-dozen teenagers, the next it's on Facebook and three thousand people turn up.' Izzy giggled tipsily, a day of chasing after her daughter and husband in the sun giving way to a deliciously warm evening. She hiccupped and slumped lower in her chair. Two nights on the razz were too much for her.

'How'd you persuade Mal to let you out two nights in a row?' Jessica asked.

Izzy winked. 'I made certain promises.'

'Eeew . . . there's always someone who has to drag down the conversation.'

Izzy hiccupped a second time. 'She's luuuuvvvverly.'

'Who is?'

'Bex.'

Jessica nodded, a strange swell of pride creeping into a smile. 'I know.'

Archie raised an empty bottle. 'Anyone?'

Jessica, Rowlands and Izzy shook their heads, Izzy adding a hiccup for good measure.

'Don't say I didn't ask.'

Archie disappeared into the house, heading into the living room, where Jessica could see him through the window. He was weaving between the dancing teenagers, wiggling his arse towards a red-headed girl who, surprisingly, didn't seem to mind.

'There's no way you should let him loose in a room of young girls,' Rowlands said, giggling too.

'All right, Romeo. Where did you end up last night?'

'A gentleman never tells.'

'Why are you keeping quiet then?'

Rowlands blew a raspberry at her, leaving Jessica to wonder if she was the only sober adult at the party. Well, *actual* adult. Bex and her friends were technically adults, but still . . .

Jessica sat up a little straighter, trying not to make it seem like she was watching Archie that closely, even though he was now in the middle of the dancing girls, arms in the air, belting out whatever Eurocrap was currently playing. 'Iz, did Katy seem a little familiar to you last night?'

Izzy hiccupped and giggled at the same time. 'There was *something* about her.'

'What?' Rowlands said, peering between them.

'I dunno. Did she use the toilet a lot?'

Izzy spluttered a spray of lager into the nearby rose bush. Rowlands's eyes narrowed. 'You're just jealous,' he said.

'Yeah, that's it,' Izzy replied.

Jessica raised herself higher, trying to get a better view

through the living-room window. 'Oh, for . . .' She was instantly on her feet, telling them she'd be right back, before heading through the back door into the house. Bex was in the corner of the living room, while Archie had one arm leant against the wall next to her trying to make himself seem taller. His free hand was holding a bottle of Peroni, frosty condensation dripping onto the floor. Bex burst out laughing at something he'd said.

As Jessica approached, she only heard the tail-end of the conversation but it was enough. '. . . so how many piercings have you got?' Archie asked.

Jessica cut him off with a 'Never you mind,' smiling at Bex, then turning to Archie. 'Can I borrow you for a minute?'

Bex left them in the corner, returning to her friends as Jessica lowered her voice to a growl. 'What did I tell you about flirting with teenagers?'

Archie held his arms up defensively. 'She asked me how I knew you, then asked what I was drinking!'

'So you thought you'd ask about her piercings?'

'I told her I liked the eyebrow one.' His spun to look at the group of dancing teens, then turned back to Jessica. 'Are you jealous?'

'Oh, piss off, Arch – just stop flirting with kids.'

He started to say something, then stopped himself, taking a breath instead, lowering his voice. Over his shoulder, Jessica could see Bex peering sideways at them. Izzy and Rowlands had come inside too, hunting through the boxes of beer, though both were watching Jessica and Archie.

Archie spoke quietly, his lips barely moving. 'You've still

not told me if you want to do something when my parents come down for the football.'

Jessica replied while still watching Izzy, Rowlands and Bex across the room. Her lips remained together, as if they were each practising ventriloquism. 'We're not going out, Arch. I'm engaged.' Her gaze flicked to the photograph underneath the television of her and Adam in a city-centre pub that had been taken not too long after they got back together. He had his arm around her, grinning lovingly; Jessica was rolling her eyes, trying to hide from the picture-taker. It summed up the pair of them.

'But—'

'But nothing, Arch.'

'We've been together for months.' He cursed as his phone started to ring, glancing at the screen and rejecting the call.

Jessica finally turned to face him, consciously standing taller so that he was shorter than her. 'That's just a bit of fun,' she said.

He stared at her defiantly. 'Fine.'

'Fine.'

Archie skirted away without another word, grabbing a second beer and then stomping into the garden. Jessica was alone in the corner, catching Bex's eye for long enough to realise that the girl had seen everything. The cat wasn't just out of the bag, it was doing photoshoots for *Pets Weekly*.

Izzy shrugged away Rowlands and crossed the room, handing Jessica a Tuborg. 'All right?' she asked, voice low, hiccups gone.

'I probably could've made it a little less obvious.'

Izzy pulled Jessica onto the sofa, resting her head on her friend's shoulder. 'I've drunk too much,' she said.

'Quitter.'

Izzy giggled. 'You should've introduced us to Bex earlier.'

Jessica sighed. 'I didn't know how people would take it. It's a bit awkward, we're not related but she lives in my house. I don't know how to explain it.'

'We're your mates, aren't we?'

'I sometimes wonder if all this happened because I wanted to make myself feel better.'

'You're allowed to help people without feeling guilty about it.'

Another sigh: 'I know . . . I just . . . I really care about her.' They went quiet for a moment as Bex supped on a Diet Pepsi, nudging one of her mates with an elbow and dragging them onto the makeshift dance floor. 'I've told her she can stay as long as she wants but then I wonder if I'm only doing that because I want a reason to come home. Is she here for her benefit or mine?'

'It's not something you need to think about. She was homeless when you invited her in, right?'

'Yeah.'

Izzy lifted her head from Jessica's shoulder, cricking her neck. 'So why can't it just be a good deed? Her life is surely better since she got a roof over her head and a college to go to? If you end up feeling some satisfaction because of that, then so what?'

Jessica took a sip of the beer. 'How was Blackpool?' she asked.

'Busy. How was Eric Maudsley's other half?'

'Delighted he's off to the nick, plus very forthcoming. She reckons he's got debts with an Oldham casino.'

'Hyde's?'

'It's the only one. I spoke to Topper but we've already gone through Maudsley's bank accounts and there's no sign of payments to a casino. We've only got Carol's word to go on and don't particularly want to ask the Hydes for their accounts, especially with the funeral on Monday. Still, it's a link.'

'What sort of link?' Izzy asked. 'Maudsley owed money to the Hydes, so he broke Owen Priestley out of a prison van to clear his debts? I get that part, but who killed Priestley?'

'It could be the other way around – Maudsley was angry at the Hydes because he owed them money, so this was payback. Either way, I have no idea. It's all unofficial, just something to bear in mind.' Jessica stood, offering a hand to help Izzy stand. 'Now, do you fancy joining me in the garden? I'm not sure I can take much more of this music.'

Aside from the odd spillage, the party went off as well as Jessica could have hoped. No trashed house, no teenagers crying in the corner because some unnamed lad had been caught copping off with some 'bitch' who was supposed to be a friend, just one happy eighteen-year-old, who'd had the first proper birthday celebration she could remember.

Bex and her friends were heading into town to finish off the evening; Rowlands had nicked off, muttering something about 'meeting Katy'; while Archie had dozed off on the sofa and was snoring like a goat with a sinus infection. Izzy helped Jessica clear away some of the bottles and then said she had to go when the waiting taxi beeped its horn.

Light was just about clinging on as the dusky remains of the day left an orange haze burning from the horizon. Izzy gave Jessica a hiccuppy hug, then headed along the path to the waiting cab. Jessica watched her, grateful that somebody seemed to understand her. There was rarely a time when Izzy didn't know the right thing to say. She was completely wasted on the police force, where the politics would surely drag her down sooner or later.

As the taxi pulled away, Jessica leant against the doorframe, peering across the road, feeling the gentle chill across her bare arms. She was tired but knew she wouldn't be able to sleep yet. She was about to turn and go inside when there was a crack of dry wood. Jessica stepped away from the door, staring into the deepest shadows across the road, where she thought she saw the outline of a figure silhouetted under the gently swaying branches of Mr Green's always-overgrown oak tree. She moved onto the pavement, squinting and shifting from side to side, trying to decide if it was a person, or a twisted piece of tree trunk.

'I can see you,' Jessica called.

The figure didn't move, which was only an issue if it *was* a figure. If it was a tree trunk, then fair enough.

Jessica stepped onto the road and crossed it slowly, still trying to get a better angle on the thick shadows that were coating the area around the tree opposite. She was about to step onto the pavement on the other side of the road when there was a loud *bang*. Jessica turned to see her front door slammed shut, realising with a sinking feeling that her key was in the kitchen and the catch was set to lock automatically. Behind, there was a scuff and a rustle, with Jessica turning in time to see a hooded shape racing towards the nearby alley, not bothering to look backwards. Was it the blonde woman from before? The figure seemed taller, with narrower hips. More . . . male? More like the person Bex might have seen watching the house?

She turned from one problem to the other, knowing she was never going to catch the escaping figure – male or female. Instead, she was left wondering how she was going to wake Archie from his drunken, snoring slumber and get him to open the door.

24

Jessica woke alone in her own bed, sunlight creeping through the curtains as Sunday decided she'd slept for long enough. She yawned and stretched, swallowing the bitter morning-after taste of lager. Ick.

After hauling herself out of bed, Jessica crossed to the window, yawning, gazing out to the street below looking for anything untoward, but not seeing anyone, hooded woman or otherwise. She brushed her teeth, yawned, peered around Bex's bedroom door to see the teenager fast asleep on her bed, yawned, and then headed downstairs, still yawning.

Archie was topless on the sofa, lying on his front, chest puffing him up and down as he slept. Jessica sat on the arm of the sofa, pulling the dressing gown tighter around herself, fighting back another yawn.

'Arch . . .'

He grunted but didn't move, so Jessica rocked his shoulder gently.

'Arch.'

His voice was a low grumble. 'What?'

'It's morning.'

'What time?'

'Just before nine.'

'Ugh.'

'Do you want something to eat?'

Archie rolled onto his back, eyelids fluttering open, grin sliding across his face. 'I thought you'd never ask.'

'Bacon butty?'

'You got brown sauce?'

'Obviously.'

'My hero.' He yawned, which set Jessica off.

When she'd finished, she placed a hand on his shoulder, unable to look him in the eye. 'I'm sorry,' she whispered.

He shuffled until he was sitting. 'What for?'

'I thought you were okay with . . . us.'

'No worries, it's all sweet.'

He wasn't very good at putting a brave face on it. Jessica wondered if she should say something else but found herself staring at the photograph of her and Adam. They were interrupted by her ringing phone: Izzy.

'Why are you up so early?' Jessica said, by way of greeting.

'I've got a three-year-old who thinks wake-up time is seven at the latest.'

'Good point. What's up?'

'Is Archie with you?'

Jessica's gaze shot to Archie, then away again. 'Archie? I've not seen him since he went home in a taxi last night.'

Archie perked up, stretching his shoulders and mouthing 'Who is it?'

'That post on the Internet's still saying that boxing match is tonight,' Izzy replied. 'We've got a venue just outside the city. Can you get hold of him and ask if he's heard anything?'

'I'll try calling him and come back to you.' Jessica hung

up and then asked Archie if he could get onto his friends while she cooked.

He puffed out a loud breath, still stretching. 'I'll see if anyone's up.' Jessica only heard the start of his conversation as she headed to the kitchen but it was more than enough for her to know she didn't want to eavesdrop. 'Marty, y'big gay. How's tricks?'

By the time she returned to the living room, brown-sauce-drenched bacon butty in hand, Archie was still going strong: 'Yeah, well, you tell Ollie I don't care what slag he pulled last night, I want to know if he's heard anything.' A pause, then a bellow of laughter. 'Aye, sounds about right. Didn't Davey give her one last Christmas? I heard she loves it there.' He started cackling again, before realising Jessica was watching. 'Right, I've gotta go – but call me if you hear anything. I'll see you at five-a-side.' He hung up and then took the plate from Jessica. The butty was halfway towards his mouth when he realised she was still watching. 'What?'

She shook her head. 'Is that how you talk to all your mates?'

He shrugged. 'Depends on the mate. If you want to know about bare-knuckle boxing matches, that's what you get.' He took a big bite, sending an oozing dollop of sauce onto the plate and sighing with pleasure. '*That* is perfection,' he said.

'What did your mates say?'

'It ain't happening tonight.'

'Izzy says they've got a venue.'

He shook his head. 'If she wants me to head out there

with her, then fair enough – but someone's taking the piss.'
He licked his lips. 'Now, if you'll excuse me, I need a poo.'

It had taken Jessica, Archie and Izzy almost an hour to get out of the city, following Izzy's disjointed directions along a series of country lanes until they found a line of cars parked in the verges. Small groups of people were traipsing along the edge of the narrow road, dressed as if they were ready for a music festival, not a trip to an underground boxing match. There were girls in short dresses and wellies; lads in combat shorts, open-necked shirts, and vests. If fists and blood were going to be flying, they really weren't dressed for it.

Jessica, Archie and Izzy parked and followed the others along the lane in the dimming sunlight, passing through a wide metal gate into a field. The week of summer had left the grass yellow and straw-like, a path of trampled, flattened turf leading towards a barn on the far side.

Izzy had told them to 'dress normally' in order to fit in, so Jessica was in jeans and a jacket, while Archie was at his chav-tastic best, jeans tucked into Rockports, collar up, hair recently re-greased, ready for a ruck.

'This really doesn't seem like a boxing match,' Jessica whispered.

'I told you, it's not,' Archie replied.

Izzy remained quiet, not wanting to be wrong, though the sinking feeling must be growing within her: they'd not seen anyone over the age of thirty.

'Where did you get the info?' Jessica asked.

'We've been following Internet discussions all week.

There's a team with the Met who deal with this sort of stuff, so we've been liaising with them.'

'There's your problem,' Archie said. 'The Met. Soft southern twats. Too busy quaffing champagne and eating canapés to know what's going on in front of them. These fighters aren't idiots – they're hardly going to stick a place and time on an open forum.'

'It wasn't an open forum – the Met gave us a password and a list of code words.'

'Then this lot know the Met are onto them and they've planted the info.' Archie nodded to the barn. 'This is one big setup. They're hoping to draw us in to create a big stink, then, while we're mucking about here, the fight will be going on somewhere else.'

'Now?' Izzy said.

'I doubt it – there'll be spotters here looking out for police, wondering who's taken the bait, then the fight will be on in a few days or so and the same people will be keeping an eye out there. You've not got a radio, have you?'

'Just my phone,' Izzy replied.

'How many uniforms have you got on standby?' Archie added.

'Two dozen.'

'They're going to have a quiet night. Unless there's a big-time crack den in there, you want everyone to hold back, pretend we haven't noticed.'

'But they're going to see us,' Izzy said.

'Yeah . . . stick with me.'

Archie puffed his chest out and upped his pace, marching towards the barn. As they got nearer, the music became louder, strobing pillars of light flashing through the windows. *Doof-doof-doof-doof*. Two big bald men in suits were on the door, frisking the line of people waiting to enter. The girl in the short dress and wellies did a spin and they waved her through, but the lad in combat shorts had to turn out his pockets. Jessica and Izzy hung back slightly, letting Archie take the lead as he strutted ahead with a flick of his head. 'A'ight, lads. How much?'

The doorman's gaze flashed to Jessica and Izzy, then back to Archie. 'They w'you?'

Archie winked. 'Aye, pal.'

'Tenner each.'

Archie made the transaction with a handshake, then held his arms out wide as the other man in a suit frisked him. Jessica and Izzy got off lightly, each having their pockets patted but, aside from a phone and wallet, they were clear.

As soon as Jessica passed through the corrugated metal door, the noise hit her: a thunderous bass that made the ground tremble, so loud that it felt like the walls were going to collapse. Before she knew it was happening, a girl just inside the door grabbed Jessica's hand and pressed a stamp onto the back of it. The impression left a clear image glowing in the dark: a hand with a raised middle finger. Archie and Izzy turned their hands around to show identical marks.

Each step felt painful, the thudding *thump-thump-thump* growing louder until they emerged into the main open area of the barn. Izzy's information hadn't simply missed the target; it had shot over the top, wiping out half-a-dozen bystanders in an act of appalling collateral damage. It wasn't a bare-knuckle boxing match, it was a rave. Around the edge of the barn was a series of raised platforms, barely clothed women gyrating into poles as groups of lads gawped beneath. At the far end, two men were standing behind DJ decks, bobbing their heads in time to the deafening chorus of dance music, while, in front, a wave of people had their hands in the air, glow-stick bracelets illuminated in the flashing lights. Next to the door they'd entered through were five bikini-wearing girls behind a row of plastic milk crates, which served as a bar. Behind the girls were stacks of bottles and cans, a scrawled sign reading: *EVERYTHING = £5*.

Archie leant in, tugging on Jessica's sleeve until she and Izzy were close enough for him to be heard over the music. 'I hope you've brought cash,' he said.

Jessica shrugged. 'I've got about a tenner.'

Izzy sighed: 'I've got fifty quid.'

Archie held out a hand, pooling their cash into his pocket. 'I don't reckon the guv will let us put this through on expenses.' He nodded up towards an alcove built into the wall near the closest pole-dancer. Jessica hadn't seen it at first but there were two men inside, each gazing towards the floor, scanning from side to side. 'There are two on the other side as well,' Archie added. 'Spotters, looking for anything weird.'

'We could just call it in,' Izzy said.

He squinted and shrugged. 'If you want – but that's what they're after. They want to know police are watching that forum. This is your test. What's the best that can happen?

We arrest a few ravers, maybe get the odd kid with a few Es in his pocket? They don't care because none of the people you're interested in will be here.'

'What do you suggest?' Izzy asked.

He winked. 'What do you think? Drink, dance and don't act like a copper.'

Izzy turned to Jessica, the highest-ranking officer on site. Her call. Archie's head was beginning to bob like a nodding dog in the bag of a car; Izzy – for once – looked out of her depth.

Jessica turned to the makeshift bar. 'Well, if it's a fiver a drink, I'm at least getting something good.'

25

The organ music wasn't helping Jessica's throbbing head-ache. Three nights on the booze was too much for someone in their thirties. Drinking was a young person's game and, while Izzy had the excuse of driving, Archie had insisted he and Jessica throw themselves into the role of excited party-goers. They'd got out of the barn at half-one in the morning, trailing back to the car amid a series of yawns and attempts to appear inconspicuous. Perhaps against her better judge-ment, Jessica was confident Archie knew more than either of them about the situation. Underground boxing, nods, winks and cash-filled handshakes were his thing – though that was little consolation for Izzy, who was embarrassed at dragging them out to a rave when she was supposed to be trying to stop an unlicensed, illegal boxing match.

Not that any of that mattered, because the only thing GMP's high-ups were bothered about was Lisa Hyde's funeral going off without a hitch. If anyone asked, the murder investigation was ongoing, they were following up promising leads and were confident of a result, blah-di-blah-di-blah. In actuality, no one had a sodding clue what had happened to Owen Priestley or Lisa Hyde. There were hardly any leads to start with, plus minimal forensics. It seemed likely that it was part of a move by a 'business rival', which explained the professionalism, and they were still on tenterhooks, hoping there was no retribution, no war. For now, all the police could do was offer a presence at the funeral, sending out a message that *they* knew what was going on behind the scenes, even if they didn't.

Jessica was in a regular black suit, with a dark blouse, waiting on the path leading to the church as the organ music continued to pound her disjointed senses. It wasn't raining but the sunshine of the previous week had gone, leaving an overcast wash of grey and a warm breeze in its place. The grounds of the church were slightly tatty, an overgrown patchwork of grass snaking across the pathways, ready to consume its prey.

Richard, Richie and Natalie Hyde were at the entrance to the church, heads bowed, shaking hands with the people attending, which provided a strange dichotomy in which everyone was acting tactfully, even though Jessica knew most of the people couldn't stand one another. Not only that, chances were that one of those attending had arranged the murders. She watched Christian Fraser, Thomas Braithwaite and Carter each shake hands with the Hyde trio, offering brief words of condolence, before stepping into the church.

The church grounds were flanked by long rows of leafy hedges, with uniformed officers positioned intermittently around the rim, though Jessica wondered who was being protected from whom. Was the enemy within the church, or without?

Her head bowed, Jessica joined the back of the line, as Topper had told her she should. They were the token police attendees, and trooped along until they reached the trio of

Hydes, with Natalie and Richard shaking hands, accepting the muttered condolence. Richie simply glared at Jessica, daring her to say something untoward. Her head was far too throbby for any of that.

After Jessica and Topper had found a spot towards the back of the pews, Richard, Richie and Natalie Hyde entered, walking from the back of the church and taking their places in the front row. The floor was stone, loud and echoing, with ancient pillars, walls and stained glass creating a heightened sense of melancholy. Jessica had been to funerals before, including her own father's in a place similar to this, but there was a different feeling about this. The rows of wooden benches were packed with mourners, yet Jessica got the sense that very few people actually knew Lisa Hyde. People were here for status, wanting to appear as if they were standing shoulder to shoulder with the Hydes, without actually knowing the person who'd died. As well as the faces Jessica recognised, there were more than a hundred she didn't: normal-looking, well-dressed business owners and associates who, perhaps, didn't realise the true nature of the Hydes' enterprises.

At her father's funeral, there'd been tears throughout, not only Jessica's, but from the people who really knew him. He had run the post office in a small village, a central figure, on first-name terms with everyone. Here, there was no crying, just mournful, predictable stares towards the priest amid a wave of sitting and standing that greeted various hymns and readings. It left Jessica with no sense of who Lisa Hyde was. Neither of the dead woman's children spoke in testimony to the type of mother she was, and all Richard

Hyde contributed was a passage from the Bible, before concluding with 'I love you'. It felt mechanical, though that wasn't necessarily surprising. If the Hydes had built a reputation on fear, they could hardly expect warmth in return. If Lisa Hyde's own children had nothing positive to say, then who else would speak for her? Richard Hyde had to keep a brave face. He was surrounded by rivals, each looking for a sign of weakness that he couldn't risk showing. Besides, if one of them *was* responsible for the killing, he wouldn't want to give them the satisfaction of knowing how hurt he was. It was a bizarre circus of respect where these men turned up to witness each other's mourning, all fully aware that none of them could have cared less.

As the priest spoke, Jessica kept an eye on Richard Hyde, who was sandwiched between his children. He was staring past the altar towards the enormous stained-glass image of Jesus's birth at the front of the church, where a large wooden cross hung from the roof. He was holding hands with Natalie, who leant forward and whispered something in his ear. He sat tall throughout, not daring to let the mask slip. Collectively, the message was going out: the Hydes were dealing with what had happened and the empire wasn't crumbling.

The soulless display continued as everyone headed outside after the service, moving from the rear of the church into the graveyard. Nearly everyone was already through the gates when Jessica noticed Natalie and Richie Hyde were by themselves. She turned in time to see Richard clambering into a shiny black Jaguar at the front of the church, head bowed, desperate to get away. She didn't blame him.

*

After the farce of the funeral, the hellos and goodbyes, the nods and apologetic glances, Jessica and Topper returned to the station for a debrief from Serious Crime. They had photographs of the funeral attendees, saying it was the biggest gathering of professional criminals they'd seen in years. No one cared. The police had watched it all happen, not intervening, because, on paper at least, none of them were crooks. When Jessica finally got out of meetings, briefings, a working lunch, debriefings, and more meetings, it was already past the end of her shift. Another day wasted. If they spent as much time doing as they did talking, things might actually get solved.

Jessica had not had time to do anything about Annie, nor hunt through *The Big Book of Bastardly Shites*, © Greater Manchester Police, to see if she could spot the blonde hoody-wearing woman who seemed to be watching her or Bex.

She would have got as much done if she'd spent the day in bed.

After the trudgery of driving across the city, Jessica parked outside her house, fumbled in the back seat for her bag and, eventually, keys, then made her way to the front door. Click, clunk and she was in, met by a scrabbling sound from upstairs and a scraping of a stool from beyond the door ahead.

'Bex?'

Jessica moved through to the kitchen, stopping in the doorway, confused as she was met by the hoody woman with dirty blonde hair, sitting calmly next to the counter, sipping a cup of tea.

26

'Who are you?' Jessica asked.

The woman panicked, eyes darting both ways as she coughed an unintelligible reply, before pointing to the hallway behind Jessica. Bex was emerging from the stairs, notebook and pen in hand.

'Oh, hi,' Bex said. 'I didn't hear you come in.'

Jessica glanced between Bex and the newcomer. 'What's going on?'

Bex handed the book and pen to the other woman, turning back to Jessica. 'Just . . . trust me.'

Jessica wanted to object, to say that she'd seen the stranger spying on them, but Bex sounded so reassuring, so . . . adult, that she said nothing.

The woman looked up at Jessica, making squirrelly quick scrawls with her hand before thrusting the pad back to Bex and standing abruptly, knocking the counter and spilling the remains of her tea. 'Sorry, sorry . . .'

Bex pressed past her, dabbing the area with a tea towel. 'It's fine. Are you sure you don't want to stay for anything else?'

'No, no, no,' she glanced quickly at Jessica, 'time to go.' She touched Bex's arm. 'Will you . . . ?'

Bex shook her head, blinking rapidly, definitely upset. 'I don't know.'

'Okay . . .'

Bex showed the woman to the front door and let her out, shutting it and then leaning against the inside, closing her eyes and taking a deep breath. From nowhere, tears were pouring down her face and she was gasping for air. Jessica couldn't do much other than hold her, rubbing the young woman's back and stroking her hair. In the near nine months Bex had been living with her, Jessica had rarely seen her upset at all, let alone to the point of tears. At first, there'd been only the street-girl exterior, which had slowly given way to a calmer, truer personality. Being homeless and having to look after herself had left Bex toughened and world-weary beyond her age, emotion something that didn't come easily. Now, she was crying so violently that her entire body was shaking as she tried to gasp sentences that were barely formed. At first, Jessica could make out only the word 'sorry' but then, slowly, as Bex managed to calm down and sat on the bottom step, hugging her knees into herself, there was one more, something that made even Jessica shiver.

'Mum.'

Bex settled on the sofa, fingers linked around a mug of steaming hot chocolate, shortbread biscuits at the ready. It wasn't quite time for ice cream but it wasn't far off.

'Sorry,' she whispered.

'You really don't have to be. If I apologised every time I had a meltdown, I'd end up tattooing "sorry" on my fore-head . . . not that I meant—'

Bex gasped a smile, the tears almost gone but not quite.

'It's okay, I know what you meant . . . at least we know who was watching the house.'

'Is that who you saw?'

Bex shrugged. 'I suppose. I forgot to ask. Anyway, she knocked on the door – I guess she was waiting for me to be alone.'

'Why?'

'She used to live next door when I was a kid – Mrs Bryant. I didn't recognise her till she said the name, then it all came back. She had a son named Jamie, who I used to play with on the balcony outside our flat.' She scratched her head. 'It was so long ago.'

'This woman – Mrs Bryant – she knew you, though?'

'She'd been to the community centre to pick her mum up one time and, somehow, recognised me. She still knows my mum and said something like, "Oh, I saw your Rebecca the other day", without realising we're not in contact.' Bex took a sip of her drink and bite of her biscuit. 'She said my mum would like to see me if I'd like to see her . . .'

Bex had been just fourteen when she'd left home, preferring to sleep rough than deal with the string of men her mother was bringing into their lives. She'd spent more than two years on the street until picking Jessica's pocket and, eventually, moving in.

Jessica had a hand on Bex's knee. 'What are you thinking?'

Bex shrugged. 'Mrs Bryant says Mum's clean. She's living in sheltered housing where they have to take fortnightly drug tests. If they fail, they lose their flat. She's been looking for me for a while.'

'That sounds good.'

Another shrug. 'When I was seven, I went to school and had to go home ill because she'd accidentally mixed a line of coke into the sandwiches she made. I was throwing up for two days and she'd yell upstairs, telling me to shut up because she was trying to watch the telly. When I was twelve, she was seeing this bloke, Colin – Uncle Col. She'd get me to dress up in short skirts, make-up, all that, then sit on his lap. He'd bounce me up and down and, well . . . he was excited by it. She'd laugh and then drag him upstairs, leaving me in front of the telly by myself. When I was fourteen, the night before I left, I woke up in the middle of the night to find her boyfriend, Stu, standing at the bottom of my bed with his pants round his ankles. When I screamed at him, Mum came in and told me off for waking her up.'

Bex gazed unflinchingly at the wall, almost reciting lines from a play, as if the incidents had happened to someone else. She was biting her tongue piercing, twiddling her eyebrow bar.

'I don't know what to do,' she whispered.

Jessica put an arm around her, cuddling the young woman onto her shoulder. 'It's only you who can decide.'

'What would you do?'

Jessica took a moment to think. 'It'd be really unfair for me to say. I'd love to tell you I know what you're going through, but I don't. Hardly anyone would.'

'If I visit her, will you come with me?'

Jessica's fingers tightened on Bex's shoulder, sensing the sobs about to begin again. 'Of course.'

27

Something that Izzy had said the previous week had been bugging Jessica ever since. If someone wanted Owen Priestley dead, why go to the trouble of breaking him out of prison? Jessica had answered that the killing was more public, but it was so risky, so reliant on Irfan and Eric not messing up, that it would have been significantly easier to have had him attacked in prison. As Izzy had pointed out, Priestley had slashed a fellow inmate with a knife, so weapons weren't impossible to come by.

With Lisa Hyde's funeral over and things seemingly back to a normal routine, Jessica had a word with DCI Topper and then drove to Liverpool Prison in the Walton area of the city. It was a little down the road from Aintree Racecourse, across the road from a cemetery and with a park on one side, a Catholic primary school on the other. A hospital was around the corner, making it feel strangely like part of the community.

Jessica had visited more prisons than she cared to remember, big and small, hosting all categories of prisoner. It was never a fulfilling experience, even at those with a greater focus on rehabilitation. Part of that was down to the onerous procedures to get inside. It was necessary, of course, but she had to sign in, was searched twice, had her phone confiscated, and was then marched by a pair of guards through a series of empty, ominously echoing hallways until they reached an interview room. Jessica wasn't there for anything official, with no need to record or document the interview. She was there for a chat, though the prison authorities were taking no chances.

Dean Lypski was led into the room by a pair of guards, who handcuffed him to a thick metal bolt in the centre of a solid table that was welded to the floor. One of the guards asked Jessica if she was okay, and then told her they'd be outside if she needed anything, making a point of watching Lypski as he said it.

As the door clanged closed, Jessica shuddered with a needless sense of feeling trapped. Lypski saw it, smiling and licking his lips as he gazed at her like she was a delicious meal. Aside from one thing, he was remarkably unremarkable: five eight or nine, normal build, with a tight buzz cut. What set him apart was the diagonal scar running from his left ear to the right of his chin. It was where Owen Priestley had left a permanent mark.

Lypski spoke with a strong Eastern European accent, though his understanding of English seemed to be perfect. 'You here for Priestley, no?'

'Something like that.'

Lypski had two missing teeth on his top row and each time he breathed in, there was a low whistling. He'd been sent to prison after a vicious, unprovoked attack in the centre of Manchester in which he'd kicked a stranger in the head so hard that the victim had been left in a wheelchair, permanently brain-damaged.

'You should bring champagne – we have party!' Lypski said.

Jessica pointed a thumb towards the door, remaining deadpan, wanting him to talk, even though he repulsed her. 'I had balloons, streamers, fizzy wine, pigs in blankets – the lot. They confiscated it at the gate.'

Lypski eyed her for a moment then roared with laughter, stretching back in the chair as far as he could manage with his hands manacled to the table. 'You funny,' he said.

She nodded at the scar on his face. 'Want to tell me about it?'

He continued giggling for a few moments and then his features hardened. 'Why?'

'Because I'm asking.'

'It no matter now.'

'It might to me.'

The handcuffs clinked against the metal bolt as he tried to lift his hands. 'It get me out early, no?'

Jessica shook her head. 'Not a chance.'

He eyed her for a few moments, licking his lips. 'You English? Scottish? Irish?'

'Do I sound Scottish or Irish?'

He shrugged. 'You all sound same . . . except Welsh. They gay.' He sniggered at his own remark.

'I'm English.'

'You used to rule the world, now look at you.'

Jessica held her hands out. 'What do you want me to say?'

'You smoke?'

'No.'

'Drink?'

'Sometimes.'

'You like Polish?'

'I've never really thought about it. If people are nice to me, I'm nice to them.'

Lypski bobbed his head from side to side. 'I like you.'

'So you can tell me what happened to your face.'

He sucked in his cheeks, the peppering of stubble a dark black. 'Priestley and me had, how you say, a swapping of opinions.' Lypski threw his head back and roared once again, sending a trail of spit onto the table, landing narrowly in front of Jessica. He didn't seem to notice, continuing to howl with amusement for at least a minute until he eventually calmed himself. 'Priestley piss people off, want to take over prison, think he own everyone.'

'You tried to show him he didn't?'

His head bounced from side to side again, like a bobble-head toy. 'Not just me. He all talk without knife.'

'Where did he get the blade from?'

'You tell me.'

'I don't know.'

'I not know either. I have . . . suspicion.'

'Want to tell me?'

He smiled, showing off his teeth again: 'No.'

'What *can* you tell me?'

Lypski's lips pressed closed again, eyes darting across her. He wasn't an intimidating presence as such but Jessica didn't like the way he was looking at her, like a child with a present to unwrap on Christmas morning. If they were in a pub on the outside, she'd be trying to avoid him, putting other people between them.

'Priestley say he set up.'

Jessica waited to see if Lypski would elaborate. He seemed happy to toy with her. 'For the off-licence robbery?' she asked.

'He say he no do it. Say no even there.'

'Doesn't everyone in here say it wasn't them?'

Lypski winked. 'Yeah, but he mean it.'

'The police found his blood at the scene. The shop owner testified against him.'

He shrugged. 'You see on TV?'

She presumed he meant CCTV: 'I don't think so.'

'Anyone else see?'

'I'm not sure.'

Lypski laughed gently. 'Me no think you real police lady.' Jessica bristled as he threw his head back once again, braying with amusement.

She waited for him to settle, but the smile was now a permanent feature. 'What else can you tell me?' she asked.

'What you want know?'

'If Priestley wasn't in the off-licence to commit that robbery, then why didn't he tell the police what he was doing?'

Another shrug, though the smile was uninterrupted. 'He say he with someone.'

'Who?'

'Dunno. Why you no ask him?'

Another burst of cackling laughter so intense that Lypski had tears streaming down his face. Jessica was glad she hadn't been the arresting officer when he'd first been brought in – the interview would've gone on for hours if he found everything this funny. He'd probably spontaneously combust if he went to an actual comedy gig.

Jessica pointed to his face again. 'There must be a reason why he chose to slash you with the knife. There are hundreds of people here, I'm thinking he pissed off more than a few inmates.'

Lypski thrust his crotch in the air – quite the achievement as he was bolted to the table. He licked his top lip slowly, making sure Jessica was watching. 'Maybe he have thing for me? He fancy a bit of Pole, no?'

'Is that the reason?'

'You fancy a bit of Pole?'

Jessica stared at him, not amused. 'You're not my type.'

Lypski frowned, seemingly offended. 'Who your type?'

'Men who aren't in prison and don't kick other people in the head.'

He glared for a moment and then threw his head back in laughter again. Lypski wasn't simply a vicious thug, he was charmless and annoying. More tears streamed from his eyes, the handcuffs clinking into the bolt, before he leant forward and dried them.

'What wrong with head kicks? You kick in head, they no get up.'

Jessica felt a tingle along her arms, the hairs rising, goosebumps prickling. He was trying to wind her up. 'Why did Priestley attack you?'

'He no like my jokes. How 'bout you? Knock knock.'

'I'm not playing.'

The smile started to spread again, his filthy teeth so

disgusting that Jessica couldn't stop looking at them. 'No play, no answer. Knock knock.'

Jessica said nothing, breathing in and out, once, twice, wondering if it was worth it . . . 'Who's there?'

'Polish burglar. Ha!' Lypski sent another spray of spit across the table, the handcuffs rattling back and forth as he struggled to control himself amid the hilarity. Jessica was unmoved, staring across the table at him. He peered up at her. 'You get, no? 'Cos Polish burglar so stupid. One more, no? Why no Polish woman use vibrator?'

'I don't care.'

''Cos keep breaking teeth! Hahahahahaha!'

Jessica didn't laugh and was moments away from calling for the guards to return Lypski to his cell, or, hopefully, hole. It was only when she scraped her chair backwards that he lunged forward, not getting far, though the laughter ended immediately. 'Hey, you go?'

'I'm not in the mood for jokes.'

'We have talk here. You talk, I talk.'

'Why did Priestley slash you?'

Lypski retook his seat as Jessica slotted hers back into place. He glanced towards the doorway and back again, showing for the first time that he didn't want to be returned to his cell. Jessica suspected she was the first woman he'd been alone with in a while. He wanted to draw it out, not have the encounter cut short.

'Priestley no like my old boss,' he said.

'Who's that?'

His eyes narrowed. 'Where you from?'

'You wouldn't know it.'

'Round here?'

'Nope.'

'You, how my mum say . . .' The handcuffs clinked again as he clicked his fingers. 'You wedding woman.'

'How do you mean?'

He was still clicking his fingers, searching for the words. 'I have wedding woman to marry, then, how you say, women for sex. You no sex woman, you wedding.'

Jessica's stony gaze didn't slip.

'You no like compliment?' he said, head tilted playfully.

'*That* was a compliment?'

'Yeah, me say you no just for fuck, you good for baby, too.'

He didn't know how close he was to pressing her buttons, how she longed to reach across the table, punch him in the face and keep punching until she was dragged off. He knew that she needed him, that she wouldn't be back. All she had to do was remain calm for a while longer and he'd eventually give up the information. 'Who's your old boss?' she said, sternly.

He nodded. 'You take off jacket, no?'

'No.'

'Undo some button? Show some titty?'

'Who's your old boss?'

'You no know him.'

'Try me.'

'You show titty, I give name.'

'How about you tell me the name and I don't break your nose?'

Lypski wailed with laughter again as Jessica cursed

herself. This wasn't her any longer. Adam had changed who she was: she was calmer, more considered. She didn't have to prove herself, didn't have to throw herself into everything. She could feel the fury boiling, her breathing becoming heavier. The old her returning.

'Who's your old boss?' she repeated calmly, though Lypski was ignoring her, laughing so hard, he had almost fallen off his stool.

'Sod this.'

Jessica slid her chair back with a resounding scrape and stepped towards the door. She was touching the handle when Lypski finally answered: 'Hey, you want name, no?'

'I'm not messing around any more. Tell me who your old boss is, or I'm off.'

There was a short pause as Lypski's eyes narrowed. He wasn't laughing any longer. 'He called Carter.'

Jessica stared at him, looking for a hint of a lie but Lypski's face was as straight as it was ugly. '*Carter?*' she said.

'You know him?'

'He runs Casino 101.'

Lypski nodded, twisting his hands to point at his face. 'You *do* know. Priestley no like Carter, so he do this. Say he do to me 'cos he can't do to Carter.'

Jessica remained standing, running through the scenario. Priestley worked for Hyde, who was a major rival to Carter and, formerly, Harry Irwell. He insisted he'd been set up for the robbery that had seen him sent to prison, and took it out on one of Carter's employees. So was Carter the person who'd arranged the break-out in order to take revenge? Was he making a move on the Hydes? He was certainly on the Serious Crime Division's list of suspects.

'What else do you know about Carter?' Jessica asked.

The smile slipped across Lypski's face again. 'You sit, no? We have, how you say, chit and chat?'

Thirty minutes later, Jessica walked back to the main reception area of the prison, utterly exhausted. Lypski would push his luck further and further and then, just as she was ready to walk, he'd drop the tiniest of morsels. He'd not known much but had said that Carter was obsessed with getting back at the Hydes, that he blamed Richard Hyde in particular for the death of his mentor, Harry Irwell. It was largely what the SCD had hinted at – one of the names on their list would make a move on another and then wait for the retribution. In this case, Hyde somehow had Irwell killed, so Carter was taking revenge. Whether any of that could be proved was another matter entirely.

Jessica retrieved her phone, signed out, and turned the device on as she headed back to her car. She was in the driver's seat, key in hand, when the phone started to tinkle and flash like a Christmas tree in Debenhams. One missed call, two, three. By the time it had sorted itself out, Jessica had thirteen missed calls, all from Izzy, Topper, or the station. She called Izzy, who answered on the first ring.

'Are you still at the prison?' Izzy asked, out of breath.

'Just leaving.'

'Good – it's all kicked off here. Richie Hyde is dead.'

28

Jessica parked her car at the end of a row of marked police vehicles in front of Deansgate train station. She didn't need to worry about knowing where to go because she followed the trail of officers, the drips of spilled tea on the pavement, and the smell of bacon sandwiches. It was lunchtime and the Greater Manchester Police weren't going to let something like a dead body get in the way of filling their bellies.

DCI Topper was waiting for her close to the locks, where the tram lines, train tracks, canal, road and row of bars all met. He was sitting on a low wall facing a white Scene of Crime tent, sipping from a polystyrene cup.

'Where'd you get that?' Jessica asked.

'Soon as we set up, some bloke in a burger van pulled up. He must've raked it in.'

She nodded at the tent. 'What's it like in there?'

'Not much to see. Richie Hyde went out drinking after his mum's funeral and never made it home. They reckon he was killed at three or four in the morning – we'll know for sure in a day or two.'

'How'd he die?'

'Looks like he was beaten to death. His wallet and driving licence were still in his pocket, which is the only reason we know it's him.'

'Not just a robbery then?'

'If it was, they forgot the robbing part. Superintendent Jenkinson has already spoken to Richard Hyde, who's going to formally identify the body at some point this afternoon.'

Jessica waited as Topper sipped his tea. The white investigation tent was set up close to a large green wheelie bin at the edge of a narrow alley running along the back of the train station. Overhead a train screeched past, making the entire area shudder like in a low-level earthquake.

Jessica waited until the noise had passed. 'Who found the body?' she asked.

'A cleaner from the train station. Poor sod was dragging a couple of bin bags back here when he practically tripped over it. There's a bloody trail of footprints from where the cleaner panicked and ran back inside.'

'I bet Scene of Crime loved that.'

'You bet wrong.'

Jessica took a seat on the wall next to Topper. For a moment, they said nothing, listening to the buzz of the city. 'Was Richie drinking by himself?' she asked.

'As far as we can tell. It's a bit sketchy but updates are coming in all the time. He was still in a full suit from the funeral, so people noticed him, plus all of the bars around here have CCTV. Managers and owners are gradually opening up – give it a couple of hours and we'll know exactly where he went . . . well, until he ended up here.' He took another sip. 'How was our Polish friend?'

'Utterly delightful – one of Carter's men, so he says.'

'As in Carter from the SCD's list?'

Jessica nodded. 'Exactly. Priestley told people inside that he'd been set up for the robbery that got him put away.

Lypski reckons the reason Priestley slashed him is an extension of the battle going on out here – the Hydes versus everyone else. Carter apparently thinks the Hydes were responsible for killing his old boss, Harry Irwell. It could be simple revenge.'

'Maybe – this is being escalated, though. The super's getting more hands-on.'

'"*Escalated*"? What does that even mean?'

Topper smiled. 'Police-speak. There's little point in me even attempting to run things because of how high this all goes. We're being left to float.'

'I don't get what you mean.'

Topper didn't sound as if he knew himself. 'This is now about containment, if it wasn't already. They want people like you and me to be free to visit Hyde and the rest.'

'That's what I've already been doing.'

'I know – which is why Jenkinson's going to be based in Longsight for a while. You keep doing what you're doing and he'll take care of what is now a triple murder investigation.'

'He's actually taking work off us?'

'I know – things must really be bad.'

'Basically, they're admitting these are professional jobs and no one has a clue.'

He smirked. 'Perhaps.' Topper's phone started to buzz and he answered with a series of 'yes', 'no' and 'okay' responses. When he hung up, he pointed towards the row of bars. 'One of the managers over there remembers chucking Richie out at three in the morning – it's the latest time we've got him definitely still alive. I've got to hang around here for a bit, so if you want to go say hello . . .'

Deansgate was a road that stretched for a mile from Manchester Cathedral and the shopping area of the city at one end to Bridgewater Canal, the train station, and the Locks at the other. It frequently caused confusion to people unfamiliar with the place, who'd heard the shops were around Deansgate, only to get off at the train station with the exact same name to find a busy road junction and some advertising billboards.

Too many Deansgates.

Deansgate Locks added another level of misunderstanding, with around a dozen bars, restaurants and a comedy club sitting on the edge of the canal, underneath the railway arches across the road from the station. Whenever a train or tram passed, the entire area juddered as if it was being shelled.

It was particularly unhelpful when emergency calls came through to say something had happened on Deansgate, with police cars and ambulances trawling up and down the busy road, trying to figure out which end. Jessica often wondered why whoever ran the city didn't go the whole hog and rename everything Deansgate – they were halfway there in any case.

She crossed the road from the train station, wondering where the burger van had disappeared to. It was nowhere in sight and the faint smell of bacon and brown sauce had set her stomach grumbling.

Aside from skiving uniformed police officers, locals trying

to figure out what was going on, and a handful of confused Japanese tourists most likely wondering why they'd got off at the wrong end of Deansgate, the only person Jessica spotted was a man in skinny jeans and a T-shirt, dragging circular tables out of Bar X onto the path at the edge of the Locks. He was stubbly with swooshy dark hair, younger than her, and attractive in an annoying way because he knew it too. The type that went for eyebrow tints and would buy himself pec implants for Christmas. He offered his hand – 'The name's Pete' – talking to her side on, face half in shadow as if he was posing for a catalogue. He perched on the edge of a table, leaving Jessica to stand.

'I gather you just called us?' Jessica said.

'One of the other bar owners reckoned you'd found a body of a bloke in a suit and I had a few problems with a guy like that last night.'

Jessica fumbled through the folder Topper had given her, finding an image of Richie Hyde. As she held it up, Pete started to nod.

'That's the guy,' he said.

'You sure?'

His eyes met hers, lips creeping into something that wasn't quite a smile. Perhaps fifteen per cent grin, eighty-five per cent smug. 'I never forget a face.' Ugh. 'Richie-something,' he added.

'How do you know that?'

Pete nodded towards the bar with the tiniest inflection of his head. He wouldn't want to get a hair out of place. 'He came in at about half one or so. It's just starting to wind down then, with the groups leaving and going home. He was by himself and got a beer, then slumped on the sofa next to the front door. One of my staff overheard him abusing one of the girls on the way out.'

'What was he doing?'

'Calling her names. She was wearing a short dress and he had a few suggestions about what might be underneath. I didn't hear it but I can get you the details of someone who did.'

'That'd be good.'

'I was behind the bar helping out, so didn't know about that until later. The first time I noticed him properly was when he came to get another drink. He was falling all over the bar, slurring his words. He couldn't even say "Stella", he was asking for "Senna". I told him he'd had enough and he started shouting about his mum.'

'What about her?'

'I thought it was funny at first, grown man crying for his mum, then I realised he was saying she was dead and he'd been at her funeral. His exact words were, "If I can't get pissed after my mum's funeral, when can I get pissed" . . . well, they weren't his *exact* words, there were a few more effs.'

'What did you do?'

Pete flicked his hair, though it was so stiff with hairspray that it barely moved. 'We were getting ready to close, so it was around twenty to three, quarter to, something like that. I was saying I'd help him get a taxi but he started shouting, saying everyone was out to get him, that his sister was a bitch . . . it was hard to make much of it out.'

'Did you get him out in the end?'

'I had to get two of the security lads, partly because I thought he might get violent but also because he could barely stand. He was stumbling from side to side, bouncing off the bar stools.'

'Where did you last see him?'

Pete gazed along the length of the Locks, pointing towards the end, where they joined the road that led to the train station. 'Around there. I told him there were taxis by the station that'd take him home and thought that's where he was going. He was shouting "Don't you know who I am?" but I didn't have a clue. No one knew who he was. Just some drunken bloke.'

'Was he with anyone?'

'Nope, there was hardly anyone around at that time. We were clearing up, getting ready to close. I assumed he was going to get a cab.'

'Would anyone else have seen him leaving?'

'Most of my staff, perhaps a couple of the other security lads at the other bars? I got the impression he'd been in and out of places all day long. I can get you some contact details if you want, though most of them will be getting to work in the next few hours anyway.'

Jessica thanked him for his time and then sauntered back to Topper, thinking it would be the easiest of easy sells when they told the PCs they were looking for volunteers to hang around the bars of Deansgate Locks all evening.

29

It took less than an hour to get the name of a taxi driver who'd seen Richie Hyde. The man's account was consistent with everything else Jessica had been told. The driver had been parked close to the train station when Richie had fallen into the side of the car face-first with a solid *thump*. The driver had tried to help him up but received a barrage of abuse for his troubles, before Richie had vomited over the taxi's wheels. Unsurprisingly, the driver declined the fare and the last he'd seen of Richie was the youngest Hyde stumbling around the side of the train station, using the wall to hold himself up. That was a few metres from where his body had been dumped. The driver hadn't seen anyone nearby, in fact he hadn't seen anyone at all. After half an hour without a fare, he'd given up and gone home for the night.

Some poor sod had been dispatched to test the wheel rims for traces of vomit, which would allow them to confirm at least part of the driver's story. Yuck.

Richie had been spotted on all sorts of CCTV systems. In one sequence, he was leering at girls in a pub, in a second, he was abusing different young women in another. From what they could make out, he'd left his mother's funeral, got a taxi from Oldham to Manchester city centre, and then spent the best part of twelve hours lurching from bar to bar, drinking himself into a stupor, while simultaneously being turned down by most of the female population of England. It was what Archie might have called 'a good night', though it hadn't ended so well for Richie.

Predictably, the one thing they didn't have on camera was anything to do with Richie's demise. No one had been spotted following him, let alone beating him up. The train station closed at midnight, meaning its security cameras showed long periods of empty corridors and unoccupied platforms. Richie Hyde had walked around the corner from the taxi rank and then turned up beaten to death in a nearby alley six or seven hours later.

Two Hydes and a close friend down, two Hydes to go.

It was a balmy, warm evening in the grounds of Richard Hyde's house, though the collective mood, unsurprisingly, wasn't matching the weather. There were three marked police vehicles outside the main gates, plus Jessica's and two more unmarked cars. Natalie Hyde and her father were both at home, the casino left in the hands of others, as a succession of officers with ever-increasing ranks sought to assure them that the police were doing all they could to find out who was targeting the family. To an untrained eye, it looked like a strange garden party, with lots of people in suits milling around the perfect lawn, chatting calmly. It was the body language that gave everyone away, with flappier arms than usual revealing a sense of pervading fear, more on the side of the police than either of the Hydes.

As the other officers did the talking, Jessica watched.

Richard Hyde seemed to be in shock – he'd not long identified the body of a second family member and now he was being talked at by a list of people wanting to tell him he was safe. She couldn't figure out if he was nodding because he was taking them at their word, or because he didn't know what else to do. His eyes were blank as he stared from person to person, not saying much.

Natalie Hyde was almost ignored in the attention being lavished on her father. She was wearing tight jeans and a loose shirt, out of a suit for the first time that Jessica had seen. It completely changed the way she looked, no longer the tough businesswoman with a steely exterior, now an attractive, attentive woman absorbing everything around her. She could blend in anywhere like this, a social chameleon.

Jessica crossed the lawn, unnoticed among the chattering, worrying men in suits, and sat next to Natalie at a small round metal table.

'Are you okay?' Jessica asked.

Natalie didn't look at her but she snorted, unamused. 'What do you think?'

'I meant with all of this.'

Another snort. 'A bunch of scared men talking in clichés, making promises they can't keep.'

Which, in one sentence, summed up exactly what Jessica thought.

'Do you know who did this?' Jessica asked.

There was a long pause, the silence eclipsed by the chattering male voices. Blah-di-blah-di-blah. So many words, so little knowledge. Superintendent Jenkinson was whispering to Topper as one of the assistant chief constables took his turn in trying to reassure Richard Hyde that the triple murder investigation wasn't a dud. Hyde must've known it was bullshit. He might have kept his hands clean over successive years but he knew a professional hit when he saw one. He knew the point was that no evidence was left. His family was being exterminated.

Natalie knew too: 'You don't have a clue, do you?'

'I wouldn't put it like that.'

'So who did this?'

'We have a list of suspects.'

'Shall I name them? Nelson Carter, Christian Fraser, Thomas Braithwaite. Not them directly, obviously. People who work for them. Do you want me to go on, or can you be honest and admit you haven't got a scrap of evidence that points to any of them?'

'I'll be honest if you can be honest.'

'Go on.'

'If you're naming those three, how about you give us a reason, a motive why they'd be coming for you? Something specific.' Jessica nodded at the crowd of people in front of them. 'This is one big farce. My lot know who your father is, they suspect the things he's done, yet they're talking to him like they're trying to schmooze a business lunch on expenses. The reason we have no evidence is because it's one giant charade – everyone wants to pretend we're dealing with legitimate businesses but people are dying. If you don't give us a reason for who might be coming after you – a real reason – then what do you expect?'

245

Natalie was quiet for a few moments and then she shuffled in her seat, turning to face Jessica. 'Y'know what? You're absolutely right – you have no right being here, there's no point. It's a family matter we have to deal with.'

'I told you before, there's not going to be a war.'

'Wake up – it's already started. What are you going to do to stop it?'

'How do you know Eric Maudsley?'

The question took Natalie so by surprise that she reeled back in her seat, blinking rapidly. 'Who?'

'He owes money to your casino. How can that happen?'

'Um . . . sometimes we give credit. It depends on individual circumstances. If a person has won a substantial amount, they might choose not to withdraw the money and keep going instead, so we'd give a little leeway.'

'What happens when they can't pay?'

'We get it back through direct debits, or, occasionally, debt-collecting agencies. It almost never comes to that and really isn't a problem. It's a tiny part of the business.'

'If it's a tiny part, then you'd know the names of the people who owe you.'

'Not necessarily . . .'

'So tell me about Eric Maudsley.'

'I don't know the name.'

'Sure?'

They stared at one another but Jessica couldn't tell if Natalie was telling the truth. If she wasn't, she was a good liar, not a flicker of movement among her features. 'I can look it up for you.'

Jessica smiled sweetly. 'No need. We already know the details.'

It was a half-truth, with Jessica hoping for a reaction. She got none.

Jessica's shift had long since finished when she found herself in an upstairs office at the police's main Newton Heath headquarters, the lone woman among Superintendent Jenkinson, two assistant chief constables whose names she couldn't remember, Assistant Chief Constable Aylesbury, DCI Topper and Josh from Serious Crime. There was a resigned atmosphere until one of the assistant chiefs passed around a bottle of Scotch and told everyone they could get taxis home on expenses. It was the most generosity she'd seen from upper management since the time she'd followed one of them to the tea machine and they'd accidentally forgotten to pick up their change.

She'd still not had time to look into Annie, the woman who'd stolen money from her next-door neighbour.

'There's going to be a press conference tomorrow,' Aylesbury said, his apparent solution to everything. Jessica didn't know why she was there. He took a swig from a glass generously filled with Scotch. Rustling up the bottle was one thing but the appearance of the glasses meant they were probably having much more fun at headquarters than anyone was willing to let on. 'We're going to appeal for calm,' he added.

Jessica wasn't drinking; she wanted to go home and be done with it all.

Josh had the same weary expression that she did, catching her eye and offering a small shrug, the look of a man who'd spent too much time in meetings over the past few days. Someone said his name, so he turned away from her, back into professional mode. 'There's still nothing official to indicate this is a gang war,' he said.

Topper interrupted, passing on the information Jessica had found at the prison, which brought a few guffaws and more clinking of glasses. It wasn't just Scotch, there was ice too. There must be a hidden bar somewhere.

Everyone turned to Josh, who was absorbing the information. 'Carter was already on the suspect list, precisely because of this sort of thing. We hadn't made the connection from Priestley to Lypski within the prison but there was no particular reason for us to do so. It wouldn't surprise me if Carter's behind this but he is traditionally more hands-on than some of the others – he worked as Harry Irwell's right-hand man and is used to getting his hands dirty. We've not been able to pin anything on him. As far as we can tell, he draws a salary from Casino 101 and meets once a month with Irwell's widow, Barbara. We still think it's a front for laundering but it's difficult to get into the accounts and the business has definitely been scaled back since Irwell overdosed.'

One of the nameless assistant chiefs was filling his glass for a second time. 'We should talk to him again.'

Aylesbury's gaze flickered to Jessica and away towards Josh. 'What do you think?'

Josh shrugged. 'Like before, Serious Crime can't officially be involved. We're putting together a laundering case, so it's down to you.'

The first time Jessica was officially acknowledged was also the time she was officially stitched up.

Aylesbury turned back to her. 'What do you say, Inspector?'

What could she say? No? As if.

'Is there any point in me constantly talking to someone like Carter?'

She was met by a sea of nodding faces. Aylesbury spoke for the group, rim of the glass pressed to his lip: 'Good point – we'll send you in with surveillance.'

Anything that meant he didn't have to get his hands dirty.

30

It was almost dark by the time Jessica got home but Bex was still up, legs curled under her on the living-room sofa, drinking a can of pop and watching cartoons. She looked tired herself, skin paler than usual, hair unwashed.

'Long day?' Bex asked.

'Ridiculous.'

'Are you going to bed?'

Jessica sat next to her on the sofa, not needing to be a mind reader to know what Bex was really asking. The curtains were still open, allowing the greying wash to seep through the window, dousing the living room in semi-darkness. 'What's going on?' she asked.

'I want my life to be sorted one way or the other before my course starts in September . . .'

'That sounds sensible.'

'. . . but I still don't know if that means I should see my mum.'

Bex reached for Jessica, resting on her shoulder. For a few minutes, the only sound came from the television.

'I can't tell you what to do,' Jessica said. She put an arm around the other woman and then turned towards the window, where someone was pacing past, momentarily casting a shadow.

'I can't decide by myself,' Bex said. 'I want everything to

be fine, but . . . there's so much bad stuff there. Things have been going all right and I don't want to be that fourteen-year-old kid again.'

'You've never met my mum, have you?' Jessica said.

'No, I think she was round a few times while I was out.'

'She's in a residential home a few miles away. I visit when I can but, God, she's annoying.' Jessica laughed softly, not really meaning it. 'My dad died two-and-a-half years ago and she was left alone. She got a bit of money from the life insurance, but that's not the type of thing you want to talk about. I'm their only child and she didn't want to stay in the village I come from by herself, so she was looking for somewhere down here. I half-thought she wanted us to move in together, but I ended up helping her get the spot in the home.'

'Is it an old people's home?'

'Sort of, the youngest person's probably fifty-odd but they're pretty much all fit and able-bodied. They're more active than I am, but I still feel guilty about leaving her there.'

'Isn't she happy?'

'I think so but that doesn't stop me feeling guilty that I basically left her there.'

Bex said nothing for a moment as someone else strode past the window, hands in pockets. They were wearing a dark top with the hood up. Was it the same person from a few moments before?

'It sounds like it was your mum's choice too,' Bex said.

'If you listen to her, she's practically running the place but we've always had an awkward relationship. I was always a daddy's girl, wanting to chase after him and get muddy. Mum wanted to stay at home, or close to the car. She was always safety first. I thought, sod that, let's try something and see what happens. We're opposites.'

'What's wrong with that?'

'Nothing, I suppose. The truth is, she had to end up somewhere like that, or we would've sent each other crazy. If she'd found a place by herself, she'd have been over here all the time: cleaning up, wanting to cook, going on about my weight or my friends. She'd have a field day if she knew who you were and that I'd invited you to stay.'

Bex twiddled her eyebrow bar. 'Sorry . . .'

'I didn't mean it like that, but that's how different we are. It's why I can't give you the advice you want. The stories you tell about your mum aren't things I can relate to. When I was nine years old, we went to the village's summer fete. I'd spotted this bloke juggling with fire and thought it'd be fun to learn.'

'You were nine?'

'Exactly – I just thought, "Fire, ooh, that's interesting", and off I went. I couldn't even juggle, let alone with fire. I ended up in this area at the back of a massive tent where everyone assumed I was meant to be there, like I was the daughter of one of the other entertainers. I was pestering this guy to teach me how to juggle and, the next thing I know, there's a voice on the tannoy giving my description and asking if anyone's seen me. This guy looks me up and down and says, "Isn't that you?" I remember thinking, "Oh, yeah, I wonder what's wrong?" He took me to the lost property counter and it was only then I realised over an hour had passed. My mum was half-upset, half-angry, saying I shouldn't wander off. She didn't stop crying for ages. My dad was there, hands in pockets, shaking his head as if he didn't know what all the fuss was about.'

'Did you used to wander off a lot?'

Jessica coughed a snigger. 'Some would say I've never really stopped.'

Bex sat up, laughing at first, before her face sank. 'I can't remember anything good that happened to me when I was nine. There were needles in the bathroom and different men in and out of our flat.'

'It's your choice,' Jessica said.

'When your mum was angry at you for running off, what did you feel?'

Jessica didn't need time to think, it was a long time ago but as fresh in her mind as if it had been that day. 'I was sorry I'd upset her. It wasn't nice to see her crying.'

Bex nodded slowly, clinking her tongue piercing into her teeth. 'That's how I want to feel.'

'Upset?'

'At the moment, when I think of her, I don't feel anything. I'm not even angry, she's just someone who was once there, a person who's nothing to do with me. If I see her now, even once, maybe I'll know if she means anything to me?'

'If that's how you feel.'

'Will you come with me tomorrow? The note says she's free every morning, all I have to do is call.'

'I'll be there.'

'What about your work?'

Jessica shrugged: the Hydes, Carter, Niall O'Brien and everyone else could wait. 'Some things are more important.'

She stood, crossing to the window to close the curtains, noticing someone in a dark hoody hurrying along, glancing quickly towards the house and then continuing past.

31

Bex's mother lived in a block of flats not far from Hyde Road, close to the greyhound and speedway stadium. Away from the main road, a pair of white buildings faced each other, two storeys high, a communal lawn in between. At either end were signs saying it was a drug- and alcohol-free zone, listing the names of the groups and charities who were sponsoring the project.

Bex had come to Jessica with the clothes she was wearing and an almost empty bag. Over the following months, she'd found things in charity shops, as well as reappropriating a few things that Jessica never wore. Probably because Bex had never had any as a child, she hated spending money, preferring to save what little she had just in case. She was wearing tight jeans and a leather jacket, both bought from charity shops, and seemed nervous, constantly fiddling with her piercings as Jessica tried to reassure her.

Bex nodded to a flat on the upper tier. 'It's that one.'

The area felt deserted, the gentle hum of traffic conspicuous simply because everything else was so quiet. Across the two blocks, there were thirty-two flats, each spick and span, except for a black bin bag sitting next to one of the doors on ground level. The tips of a pair of trainers were sticking through a hole, with a tatty denim jacket laid on top. Presumably a bag of unwanted clothes.

Bex led the way up a set of stairs until they were on the balcony. They passed one flat, two, Bex's pace slowing as they neared the centre of the row.

'I'm here,' Jessica said softly.

Bex edged towards the middle until she was standing in front of a white double-glazed door. Aside from the number, there were no distinctive markings, nothing visible through the rippled window next to it that might give an indication of the person inside. Bex lifted a hand, forming a fist and resting her knuckles against the plastic. She took a breath, two, and then knocked loudly.

As soon as the door was opened, Jessica saw the resemblance. There were no piercings but Bex's mother had the same long, straight black hair, narrow face and rounded dome of a nose.

'Rebecca . . .'

Even their voices were similar, local but husky, though Bex's mother's tone was harsher, the years of abuse having worn away at her throat and nasal passage. The woman turned to Jessica. 'I'm Helena,' she said.

'Jess.'

Helena opened her arms for a hug but Bex didn't move, leaving an awkward gap until the older woman dropped her arms to her side. 'Do you, er, want to come in?'

Bex nodded, so the three of them headed through the door, directly into a living room. There was a red carpet and clean brown walls, clear of photos or pictures, with a pair of almost empty pine cabinets squeezed either side of a sofa. It felt soulless, as if the flat was there to be passed from person to person, more like a hotel room than a place to live. The only indication of any personality was a pair of fluorescent yellow and white running trainers underneath a radiator.

Helena walked to one end of the room, then turned and started back again, unsure what to do with herself. She was as thin as Bex, bony pointed elbows sticking out through a tight training top. From the leggings and sweaty, tugged-back ponytail, it looked like she'd been running.

'Do either of you want a drink?' Helena asked. 'I've got juice, water, Coke, tea, the usual.'

Bex waited for Jessica to sit on the sofa then sat next to her, leaving the armchair free, ensuring there was no room for her mother to get anywhere near her.

'I'm fine,' Bex said.

Her mother hovered close to the door that led into the kitchen, bobbing uncomfortably from one foot to the other. 'I'll, er, brew up anyway.' She turned to Jessica. 'Do you want a tea? Coffee?'

'Tea, milk, no sugar.'

'Okay.'

Helena disappeared through the door, leaving it open, the sound of clattering cupboards and running taps drifting into the living room.

Bex had her arms crossed, breathing slowly and deliberately.

'Are you okay?' Jessica whispered.

'I wish she didn't look like me.'

'*You* look like you.'

'How do you mean?'

'We wear the scars of who we are. There might be a physical resemblance but that doesn't mean you look the

257

same. You're someone with a life ahead of her, someone with hope.'

'You don't think Helena is?'

She didn't say 'Mum', not now they'd met again. When she'd used the word at Jessica's house, it was more of an idea, now Helena was a real person.

'Maybe,' Jessica replied. 'I've been around addicts in various states for years. If you ask me, she looks like somebody who's recovering – you look like somebody already recovered. You're someone who knows what she wants from life, she's still trying to figure that out.'

'Is that why she wanted to see me?'

'Perhaps, or maybe it's because you're still her daughter.'

Helena re-entered the living room, handing a mug to Jessica and then sitting in the armchair, nervously gazing at her daughter. 'Thanks for coming,' she said.

Bex nodded but didn't speak, the pair sizing each other up, unsure what to say.

'What's it like living here?' Jessica asked, trying to break the impasse.

Helena nodded enthusiastically, speaking too quickly. 'It's quiet – everyone gets a one-year lease as long as they stick to the rules. The people who run it come into the flat once a month to make sure you're looking after it, plus you get tested every couple of weeks to make sure you're not back on the booze or the pills.'

'I was more worried about the needles.'

Bex stared at her mother defiantly and Helena couldn't maintain eye contact. She looked away, nodding slowly. 'I know . . .'

'Do you get help with anything else?' Jessica asked.

Helena spoke slowly, not wanting to trip herself up again. 'Not really. If you can't get a job yourself, the housing company have things that people can do – cleaning, cooking, that sort of thing. That helps you build a CV before you can sort your own thing.'

'Does everyone get on with each other?'

'Mostly. There are a few niggles – there's this brown woman downstairs who stinks the place out when she's cooking but what can you do? It's all right apart from that.'

Brown woman? Jessica had heard far worse and it wasn't the time to challenge Bex's mother, but it wasn't the best choice of words.

Helena waited for Bex to peer up from the spot on the wall at which she'd been staring. 'The people who run the project make you sign a contract,' she said. 'You're not allowed to drink or take drugs. You can't make loads of noise or create a disturbance. When the year is up, everyone should hopefully have a job and be clean.'

'Okay . . .'

'Fiona downstairs only has a couple of weeks left. She's got a decent job in the city and is making money for herself. She's clearing out her clothes because she's ready to start again. That'll be me in a few months.'

Bex didn't want to engage. 'Why are you telling me?'

Helena's bottom lip pouted out. 'I dunno . . . I figured you might want to know.' She stopped to sip her tea, then added: 'How have you been?'

Jessica knew what was going to happen a moment before it did. Bex's leg started to twitch and then she lunged forward, finger wagging. 'How have I been? How do you think? I was fourteen – fourteen! Do you even know I turned eighteen on Saturday?'

'I—'

'Course you didn't, why would you? It was only my birthday. How many have you missed? There's no point in counting because it's not as if you were worried when I lived with you. I was *fourteen* and you let your boyfriend come into my room and watch me sleep while touching himself. When I called for you, you told me off for waking you up.'

'Did he—?'

'What? Touch me? No he didn't but you should've asked that then, not now.'

'I'm sorry, I—'

'*Sorry?* Do you think that makes up for it?'

'Of course not.'

'Do you even know what I've had to do for the past three years?'

Helena shook her head, gulping back tears.

'I lived on the streets as a fourteen-year-old. I slept in parks, bushes, doorways, alleys. I used to know which day the bin men came to various parts of the city because that meant there'd be a night, perhaps two, where I could find a wheelie bin that was empty. It might have stunk a bit, but at least there was a roof. I'd hang around the back of McDonald's, KFC and Burger King, waiting until they threw the food out. I ate out of bins. I had to teach myself how to nick wallets, so I could find a few quid to get into the hostel for a shower and a bed. I had to keep a knife on me, sleep with it, walk around with it, in case anyone tried to rob me.' She waited for her mother to stare into her eyes, then added, 'Or rape me.'

Helena gulped. 'I'm sorry, I—'

'You're not allowed to be sorry.' Bex waited until her mother had completely lost it, head in her hands, tears pooling through her fingers onto the floor, then she repeated herself with even more venom than before. 'You're not allowed to be sorry.'

Bex re-crossed her arms, leaning back into the sofa, watching. Jessica didn't dare say anything. She felt as if she was intruding by being there, that this was a moment that should have been shared solely between mother and daughter. Bex was trembling, goosebumps peppering the back of her hand.

'Do you want to go?' Jessica whispered, quietly enough that only Bex could hear.

Bex shook her head, staring at her mother. Eventually, Helena looked up, cheeks red, eyes puffy. 'I don't know what you want me to say.'

'I could've gone to prison. I got caught nicking and had to keep a knife. It was Jess who saved me. I've got a life now: I've been to college and I'm going again so I can be full-time. I've got friends, I'm somewhere safe.' She touched Jessica's arm. 'I've got someone who cares for me.'

There was a silence, eventually broken by Helena. 'Oh.'

Bex sat back defiantly, still trembling, waiting for someone – Jessica – to put an arm around her, and then adding, 'I want to go.'

32

Jessica drove Bex home, ignoring the buzzing phone in her pocket. The journey was silent, aside from Bex's solemn sniffing and nose-blowing. At the house, she insisted she'd be fine by herself, practically forcing Jessica back out of the door. Bex said she might call some of her friends to see what they were up to, though it was clear she wanted to be by herself. Jessica didn't blame her. She'd seen anger in Bex before: the spitting, defensive fury of self-preservation, but it had been in hibernation for the past few months. If Jessica had been thinking, she would have predicted that the memories of being fourteen and vulnerable would make Bex blow, but perhaps it was something that had to happen anyway. Some things couldn't be apologised for, couldn't be taken back. When they walked out, Helena said she was free every morning if Bex did want to meet again but that was where it had been left.

Still ignoring her phone, Jessica drove across the city, following her own handwritten directions, which was always a mistake. She got lost twice around Moston and was almost on the motorway when she realised she'd missed her turn. Jessica eventually found the place she was looking for, a lone shop on the edge of a housing estate. The One2One off-licence was the place Owen Priestley had robbed, before battering its owner into intensive care. Jessica had only read about it in the files but the store was bigger than she'd thought, not just a place selling booze, but a mini super-market. There were posters in the window advertising two-for-one mini rolls (yum), half-price cornflakes (meh), five Crunchies for a pound (legendary), a third off Ben and Jerry's (heroic), two-for-one frozen curries (hmm) and twenty toilet rolls for the price of twelve (understandable, given the offer on curries).

It looked as if it had been recently refurbished, with gleaming red and green signs running across the top and brightly painted matching gutters and window frames. As Jessica entered, the alarm nee-narred, with an Asian man behind the counter peering up from his newspaper and nodding to her.

Jessica approached, offering her ID. 'Do you own this place?' she asked.

He examined her picture carefully and then handed it back. 'My brother and I do. Can I help you?'

'I'm looking for Rohit Bose.'

The man shook his head. 'Rohit? He's long gone. We bought this place from him.'

'When?'

'A year ago, something like that.'

'Where did he go?'

'Back to India, I think. It was quite sudden – we got a great deal.'

Jessica was parked in the **EMERGENCY ONLY: DO NOT STOP HERE** bay outside Longsight Police Station. DCI Topper peered through the passenger's side window of her car, nodding at the carrier bag on the floor. 'What are they?'

'Crunchies.'

'How many did you buy?'

'A bunch – for God's sake, don't tell Pat.'

Topper leant in closer to the footwell, smiling. 'I can be bought.'

Jessica scowled, reaching into the bag of sixty-five Crunchies – thirteen quid well spent – and handing him a bar of chocolate. 'I'm reporting this to internal investigations for bribery. They'll have you.'

He winked. 'You do that. Are you all set with surveillance?'

'I'm off to the casino now but I wanted to grab you before. I've been to the off-licence that Owen Priestley robbed.'

'Why?'

'Priestley told the other inmates he was innocent but his blood was found at the scene and the owner he supposedly beat up – a bloke named Rohit – identified him.'

'Has he changed his story?'

'Better – he's gone back to India. No one's heard anything from him in almost a year. The guy who owns the shop now says Rohit left in a rush and that he didn't even bother haggling over the price. His exact words were: "I think he won the lottery".'

Topper had the Crunchie unwrapped and was nibbling from the top. 'Why would he think that?'

'Because Rohit didn't care about the money from the

sale of the shop. He was happy to take anything, he just wanted to leave the country. If he was paid to stitch up Priestley, he was getting away with the money. If he didn't, he was escaping before Priestley arranged payback.'

Topper's eyes narrowed as he took it in. If that was right, there was every chance that Priestley had been sent down for something he didn't do, only to be broken out and killed. Someone *really* had it in for him.

'I'll tell that lot upstairs,' Topper said, rolling his eyes.

'You're sick of them too?'

He winked. 'Your words, not mine, Inspector. Now, if you'll excuse me, I've got a meeting to get to.'

By the time the chief surveillance engineer had stopped feeling up her chest, apologising as he did so, Jessica felt as if she'd just spent a sweaty night in the old student's union. She was in the back of an unmarked dark van parked around the corner from Casino 101. A cliché on wheels.

'Say something,' the engineer said, putting on a set of headphones.

'Stop touching my tits.'

The man blushed, turning away sheepishly. 'I said I was sorry. It was an accident.'

'I'm winding you up.'

Jessica was trying not to giggle at the bright redness of the man's face. In his defence, she had told him to clip the microphone onto her bra because his pointy 'try it there' instructions were more annoying than a minor bit of inno-cent groping.

She turned to Josh, who was the third person in the van,

sitting with a laptop on his knee. 'You can stop laughing, too,' she said.

'I'm not laughing, I'm observing.'

'I thought Serious Crime didn't want to be involved with this?'

He grinned. 'Serious Crime don't want to *appear* to be involved with this.'

'I don't get the difference.'

'You know who Al Capone is, right?'

'The bloke who runs the pizza shop at the bottom of my road?' She tilted her head. 'Of course I bloody know.'

'Do you know what the US authorities finally nicked him for?'

'Cow-tipping?'

'Tax evasion. Their priority was to get him off the streets, anything would do – but they were only going to get one shot at it. You can't keep arresting people this big over and over because they're too rich, their lawyers too good. If it gets in the media that we've arrested Christian Fraser in association with a murder, then he gets bail and the charges are dropped through lack of evidence, that sticks. Say we nick him again: drugs, laundering, girls, whatever, if it's not completely watertight, he's back on the streets again. He might skip bail and hide out in South America or, worse, when we nick him for something we really do have proof of, it's too late. His lawyer's in front of a judge, pointing to all these arrests and reports, saying there's no way his client can get a fair trial. They'll argue that the police have it in for their client, that the evidence is tainted and untrustworthy. If we're going to take down people like Fraser,

Carter, Braithwaite, Hyde, or anyone else, it's got to be incontrovertible – and we only get one shot. That's why it's got to be CID sorting this out, not Serious Crime.'

'Because all I'm doing is asking questions about events that are unrelated, not arresting and not accusing.'

A nod: 'Precisely.'

'And if I balls something up, it doesn't come back to whatever you're working on.'

'You're smarter than you look.'

'Oi – just for that, you're not getting a Crunchie.'

Carter was sitting in the same office as the first time Jessica had met him. She'd declined to shake his hand, still feeling the slight click of her bones from the last time he'd crushed her fingers. The office seemed as if it had been built for someone else, dark red walls and a dark wood décor too upmarket for a man of Carter's *talents*. There was a bar at one end, with Carter sitting behind a large circular table at the other. The upper parts of the walls were covered with maps of Manchester, plus a floorplan of the casino. He was by himself, no lawyer, no one to hide behind.

'I'm not sure I understand why you're here,' Carter said.

'I'd like to know where you were between the hours of two and four the morning before last.'

'The night Richie Hyde was killed?'

'If you like.'

'Am I under suspicion?'

'Not particularly.'

'So why ask?'

'A natural curiosity – I've been walking up and down

Deansgate asking strangers where they were. After hearing three or four hundred alibis, I figured I should probably concentrate on the people who actually knew Richie.'

'This isn't police harassment, then?'

'Maybe I fancy you and can't stay away?'

Carter couldn't stop himself smiling, if only at her gall. 'I can give you alibis for each of the recent deaths. Would you like the name of the girl I was with? Phone number? Measurements? Tit size?'

'You can keep that to yourself but I am interested in how much of your own dirty work you do.'

The smile remained. 'There's an agency that does the cleaning around here, then there are bar staff, people who run the tables. You can't have the person at the top doing all of that, can you?'

'I was thinking more about some of the other things that an organisation might need doing.'

'Would you like to be specific?'

It was Jessica's turn to offer an uneasy smile. Like the senior officers when they were talking to Richard Hyde, she could only dance around the truth.

That wasn't enough for Carter: 'If you've got something to say, Inspector, then say it.'

Jessica waited, knowing Josh and the surveillance engineer would be listening, that the recording would be relayed back to the more senior officers at some point. They wanted her to stay on message, to tread carefully for all the reasons Josh had explained.

On the other hand, sod it.

Jessica took a breath: 'I'm saying that there was a long-running dispute between the Hyde family and the Irwells. When Harry Irwell – your mentor – died from an overdose, you blamed the Hydes. You arranged for Priestley to be framed for something he didn't do, but that wasn't enough, you wanted to wipe them out completely.'

There was a pause, in which Jessica knew Josh would be scratching his head, wishing he hadn't heard what he just had. She might have to give him a Crunchie after all.

Carter's gaze didn't shift from her, but then, out of nowhere, he was laughing. He was so big that it seemed utterly unnatural. She could picture him pulling someone's fingernails out with a set of pliers, yet, even though he was laughing in front of her, it still didn't seem believable.

'Bloody hell,' he said. 'I thought you were gonna go all round the 'ouses, feed me a bunch of shite. I didn't think you'd just come out with it.' He nodded. 'Respect to ya.'

It felt like they were moments away from fist-bumping.

'So?' Jessica said.

'You can think what you want – but I didn't get Priestley sent down. If that's all you're bothered about, you should look closer to home.' His eyes narrowed, daring her to ask the follow-up. Suddenly, Jessica felt nervous, her mouth dry. This wasn't what she'd expected.

'You're saying someone in the police set him up?'

Carter continued smiling. 'You tell me – but if you're coming here with that, you must be desperate. The usual method is to come up with something I *have* done, then try to prove that, rather than make up something I haven't.'

Time for a change of tack. She'd already crossed the line

by such a distance that it was no longer a line, merely a speck in the deepest distance.

'What are you going to do if Richard Hyde comes for you?'

The smile evaporated in an instant as Carter leant forward, brow furrowing. 'I've been waiting for someone to come after me for the past twenty-odd years and it's not happened yet.'

'It happened to Harry Irwell – on your watch. It's happening to Richard Hyde right now. Everyone has an expiry date.'

He nodded, eyes boring through her, leaving Jessica fighting an imaginary chill. She thought of the figure she'd spotted outside her house. A coincidence, or had one of these men sent someone to scare her? Perhaps her bravado had gone too far, giving way to paranoia? She'd definitely seen Mrs Bryant watching her house – and she'd been there to speak to Bex. Was the rest a figment of her imagination?

Carter didn't give her time to think too much, his voice firm, decision final: 'I think it's time you pissed off.'

Jessica parked back at Longsight, feeling as if she'd already done a day's work. Josh hadn't been too annoyed by what she'd said, nothing that a Crunchie couldn't fix. The panic was over the implication that someone within the police had arranged for Priestley to be framed. It would have been a touchy subject anyway but, on the back of the Pratley report into the conduct of Greater Manchester Police, it was potential dynamite. The chances of Carter elaborating were zero, so it was up to other people above her to decide what they wanted to do.

Fat Pat was licking his pudgy fingers behind reception as Jessica entered the station. She might have felt sorry for him being constantly teased by everyone if it wasn't for the fact that he was so oblivious to it and that he gave as good as he got – better, in fact. Izzy might be the purveyor of serious news around the station, but Pat knew where the metaphorical bodies were buried. Perhaps the actual ones, too. Quite how her relationship with Archie had been kept from Pat, Jessica didn't know.

He waved an arm at her, trying to get her attention.

'You could just say my name,' Jessica scolded.

'Got something 'tween my teeth.'

'I don't respond to flaps.'

He lowered his voice to a whisper, peering over his shoulder conspiratorially. 'I've heard you've got a supplier for cheap Crunchies.'

'It's not crack, for Christ's sake, it's chocolate – and you can buy a Crunchie from the vending machine in the canteen.'

'Yeah, but they cost 75p there. How much can you get 'em for?'

'I'm not having this conversation, Pat.'

'Spoilsport – you just want to keep your dealer to yourself.'

Jessica laughed in his face. 'You're right, I do. He only sells to people he knows anyway, you need to text a password to his mobile, then he'll give you a time and place.'

'Really?'

'Of course not really. I think too many trips to Gregg's have tipped you over the edge.'

'It's not my fault, I have a medical condition. I need to eat. HR have it on file – ask them.'

'I've really got more important things to do.'

'How about you give me your dealer's details and I'll tell you who the delectable DC Evesham's taken a shine to.'

Jessica opened her mouth to say 'no' but the word wouldn't form. Her sensible, adult, detective inspector head said she couldn't care less about gossip. The rest of her desperately wanted to know with whom the new constable had been spotted flirting. The only reason her workmates stayed sane was the constant chinwagging about one another.

'I can get five Crunchies for a quid,' Jessica said.

Pat looked like he was going to pop with excitement, his cheeks puffing as if he was swallowing a pair of golf balls. 'A quid?! You can barely get five Freddos for that nowadays.'

'You first,' Jessica said.

'Fine.' Pat glanced over his shoulder again, though the reception area was still empty. 'You didn't hear it from me but she had lunch with a certain Detective Constable Archie Davey. They went to the Wounded Duck. I heard there was a significant amount of arm-touching and, though I've only got it from one source, she was spotted smiling when she got back here.'

Jessica stared at him, shaking her head. 'You're such a dick.'

'What?'

'She was spotted smiling? What does that mean?'

'What do you think it means? She was loving it. She

couldn't get enough.' He stuck his palm out, patting his fingers as if asking for money. 'Right, who's your supplier?'

'The One2One minimart out Moston way. They've got loads and they're doing two-for-one on mini rolls too.'

He rubbed his hands together gleefully. 'You should've called in!'

'I was kinda busy doing real work.'

'Haven't you heard?'

'Heard what?'

'Someone doing the DNA testing has dropped a bollock. According to them, Richie Hyde's DNA matches two people already in the database.'

'What do you mean?'

'Dunno – I'm only telling you what I heard. They reckon he's got a half-brother and half-sister that no one's ever heard of.'

33

Jessica hated trains. It wasn't simply the cramped conditions and lack of seats; the fact that they stopped at every sodding station; the stupid woman shoving the cart up and down, trying to sell a coffee for eight quid; or the bloke with three – *three* – massive suitcases he was trying to balance; above all of that, it was the pricks in suits on their phones.

'Hello? Yeah, sorry, I'm on a train, so it keeps cutting— Hello? Hello? Yeah, right, sorry, I lost you for a moment there. I'm working from the Liverpool office today but Karen said the posters aren't ready . . . Hello? Right, yeah, I don't know what's going on? I called the printers yesterday and they assured me it'd all be sorted? . . . Exactly, and when's the delivery due? . . . That's what I heard, I mean I can't do everything. What are they even doing in Wolverhampton? Hello? Hello?'

The morning after her talk with Pat, Jessica and Archie were both standing on a train heading to Liverpool, stuck listening to the endless conversation about marketing materials and the printers' delivery. If the first thing she had to do when she got up was have a phone call about printers, Jessica would've ended it long before now. Not only was this arsehole's job so boring that suicide was the preferred option, he was seemingly determined to drive everyone else in the carriage to top themselves too. Archie practically had steam coming from his ears, eyeballing the back of the man's head so intensely that, seemingly through telepathy, the man on the phone turned around to see Archie's ferocious stare.

'Can I help you?' he asked, oblivious to the simmering tension around him.

'You could hang up the phone.'

The man peered around the windows. 'There's no sign to say this is a quiet carriage.'

Archie spoke through gritted teeth. 'There's also no sign to say you can't punch people repeatedly in the head, but no one's doing that. Yet.'

The man hung up.

Their train eventually arrived at Liverpool Lime Street forty minutes late. Archie was sniffing the air as they walked through the main doors, pulling a face.

'What are you doing?' Jessica asked.

'Bit Scouse for my liking.'

'Don't start this again – it was bad enough when we went to London and you spent the whole day moaning about southerners.'

'What?'

'Manchester is not the centre of the universe and, even if it was, we're only thirty miles down the road.'

Archie nodded towards a man walking down the street, wearing a Liverpool football shirt. 'Look at the state of that,' he sneered.

'I knew I should've left you at the station – Franks needs someone to help him with paperwork.'

'You wouldn't.'

'I will if you don't stop whingeing.'

Jessica checked the address on her phone, using the maps app to figure out where they were. 'This way,' she said, 'there should be a hospital down here, then we're on the next street past.'

'You've not properly told me what we're doing here.'

'That's because we were on a crowded train.' Jessica stopped, waiting to cross the road. 'Richie Hyde had never been arrested, so his DNA wasn't in the national database. He was spotted by a taxi driver on the night he died and was sick all over the taxi's wheels. Because it was the last time Richie was seen, we had to get the testers in to make sure it was definitely him. Anyway, someone must've put a bit of money their way because they tested it super-quickly. When they analysed it, they concluded the vomit belonged to Richie, but they also found a partial match to two people already in the database.'

The lights changed and they crossed to the other side of the road, still following the directions on Jessica's phone.

'So two people related to Richie have been arrested before?'

'Exactly, one half-brother from Liverpool, one half-sister from Southampton, neither of whom we knew about.'

Archie sounded confused. 'Does that mean Richard Hyde's the father of all three?'

'That's a bit awkward – Richard Hyde's DNA isn't in the database. He was done for drink-driving but too long ago for anything to be on record. He's not been arrested since, so unless he chooses to give us a sample, we won't know.'

'Could it be the mother they share in common?'

'Nope – it's a paternal match. The three of them have the same dad.' Jessica continued walking, remembering how Adam had described DNA testing and blood types to her too many years ago to think about. He was the scientist, the one who was able to explain things properly. It was through a situation a little like this that she'd met him in the first place.

'I heard you had a fun lunch yesterday,' Jessica said.

Archie paused momentarily, falling a step behind her. 'It was only lunch. You can't do anything at work without people sticking their noses in.'

'It *is* a police station, that's pretty much what people's jobs are.'

'Ruth only wanted someone to talk to.'

'Ruth, is it?'

'I—'

'It's fine, I just thought you might've said something.'

Archie puffed out a breath. 'Must've slipped my mind.'

Isaac Foster looked nothing like Richie Hyde. He had blue eyes compared to Richie's brown, with fairer hair and a stockier build. Isaac was twenty-four, fourteen months younger than his half-brother, but, while Richie had a rich father and had grown up abroad, Isaac was pure Scouse and worked in a Burger King. He was wearing the dark blue polo shirt with logo and red trim as he welcomed Jessica and Archie into his house. Archie took an instant dislike to the Everton scarves pinned to the walls but managed to keep his mouth shut.

Isaac was nervous, standing next to the dining table and biting his nails. 'The woman on the phone said this was something to do with the fight,' he said.

'Fight?' Jessica replied.

'That's why they swabbed my mouth last year. I wasn't even involved, I swear, I know what they said in court but I was trying to get away. I was the one who got hit.'

Jessica held her hands up, trying to calm him. 'We're not here because you're in trouble.'

'Oh . . .'

'There's not an easy way to tell you this but you might want to sit down.'

Isaac lowered himself slowly into a chair, eyes widening. 'It's not Mum, is it . . . ?'

'This might sound strange, Isaac, but we think you might have a half-brother. Possibly a half-sister too.'

A pause. 'Oh.'

'Is this something anyone's ever told you?'

Isaac shook his head slowly, confused. 'I'm an only child, but . . . you're saying I've got a brother and sister?'

'Maybe. If it's all right with you, we'd like someone else to come out and re-swab your mouth. It's only so that we can re-check everything.'

'Okay . . . but I still don't really understand how.'

'This is also an awkward question, but things have moved really quickly. We've been able to contact you, obviously, but it's unclear if either of your parents is alive . . .'

Isaac stood, suddenly perky. 'They live out back.'

'"Out back"?'

'Two streets away. I can walk you round if you want? If

278

we go now, we'll catch Dad before he nicks off down the legion. It's a pound a pint before six.'

'Right . . .'

Jessica gave Archie a shrug as Isaac bounded from the room, grabbing a hoody and leading the way out of the house, through a pair of alleys until they emerged onto a street with long rows of red-brick terraced houses so similar to where they'd just been that it was as if they hadn't moved at all. Jessica didn't want to get too deeply into thoughts about why someone would leave home, only to move two streets away into an almost identical house. She figured that was what therapy was for.

On first impressions, Rhys and Nicole Foster *did* look like their son. That was until Jessica had spent a minute or two with them. She felt bad for thinking it but the three of them were all overweight, which clouded her initial judgement. The more she looked at them, the more she concluded that Isaac didn't look much like either of his parents. His father had darker, more olive, skin with black hair; his mother was covered in freckles and had dark eyes. Not that any of that particularly mattered. There were lots of kids who looked nothing like their mum and dad.

Isaac's parents were both in their late fifties and either unemployed or prematurely retired, depending upon a person's viewpoint. It was an awkward matter to discuss, so Jessica approached it with the same brutal honesty she'd used with Isaac. As the three Fosters sat in a semicircle on the sofa and armchair, Jessica told them that Isaac *might* have a pair of half-siblings and, if he did, it was the father's genes that were shared.

Rhys turned to Nicole, who stared back at him. They both seemed bemused. 'Don't look at me,' she said. 'You know how hard it was having Isaac.'

'How do you mean?' Jessica asked.

'It took me a while to get pregnant. At first, we thought I couldn't have children and then it just happened.' She squeezed her husband's hand.

'I'm not trying to accuse anyone here,' Jessica said. 'I realise this is difficult and there's still a chance it could be a giant mix-up. Unfortunately, the results of this relate to something we're investigating in Manchester at the moment. No one here is implicated and I can't give too many details but, if you'd be so kind to oblige, it would be really helpful if you'd allow me to arrange for someone to swab your mouths. We'll be able to give you results in a day or two that should give you answers to everything.'

Rhys didn't seem convinced. 'How do you mean, answers?'

'For one, they'll tell Isaac if he does have a brother and sister. If so, they'll be able to give some indication of who the father is.'

'*I'm* his father.'

'I realise that.'

'And I've not touched another woman for nearly thirty years.'

He didn't seem angry, more joking – as if this was one giant mix-up they'd all be laughing about one day.

'Me neither,' Nicole added, taking her husband's hand. 'Well, another man, I mean.'

'I'm not arguing with any of that,' Jessica said. 'I'm really not – but something's not right here.'

'With what?' Rhys said.

'I'd like to say there's been an error with the DNA that was held after your son's conviction,' both of Isaac's parents shot him a dirty look, 'but I can't tell you anything for sure without the swabs.'

Three faces frowned at her, for which Jessica didn't blame them. She'd expected more anger, wishing there was an easier way to ask the question, a method which didn't involve suspicion of infidelity, but there was only this. Nicole stood quickly, asking them to wait as she hurried to a cabinet at the back of the room and started fussing. She returned with a square piece of paper, thrusting it into Jessica's hand. It was a birth certificate – Isaac Hayes Foster. Either or both of Rhys and Nicole were soul music fans, with their names etched on the bottom, though that in itself proved little.

'I'm really not doubting you,' Jessica said, handing the paper back. 'It's probably a mix-up but I can't say for certain without the tests. The labs are going to rush it through if you agree – it'll should take around two days.'

Jessica and Archie were on their way back to the train station, her walking deliberately quickly because she knew he'd have to quick-step to keep up.

'Well, *that* was awkward,' Archie said, arms swinging crazily as he attempted to match her pace.

'No one was trying to hide anything – Rhys is certain he's Isaac's dad and I believe him when he says he's not fathered any other kids. She's being honest too. They're going to be devastated if the test suggests otherwise.'

'If they're both telling the truth, then how can Isaac and Richie Hyde be half-brothers?'

'I really don't know – let's wait for the results. The potential half-sister in Southampton is being tested too. It's probably one big cock-up and we've overreacted. It wouldn't be the first time somebody's mucked up.'

'What if they *are* all related? How does that affect the fact the Hydes are being targeted?'

'I don't know that either, Arch.'

Jessica upped her pace further, hoping it would keep him quiet. She checked her phone as she walked – no calls, thankfully, but there was a text message from Bex: **Hey. Been thnkin – gonna c helena again 2moro morn. Dint quite work last tim. X**

Jessica sent her a message back: **Want company?**

Her phone fizzed almost straight away: **Not this tim. Gotta do by self ;) Thx tho. X.**

Jessica left it at that.

34

The following morning, Jessica drove to Richard Hyde's house, her thoughts with Bex, not the dwindling family of apparent crooks, of whom she was thoroughly sick. It was Friday, with Natalie nowhere in sight, though Richard was dressed down in loose chinos and a golf jumper. He pottered around his enormous bright white kitchen, making coffee as Jessica sat on a high stool, watching and waiting for him to settle. Hyde was muttering under his breath, asking where the milk was, then answering himself. He seemed like a bumbling old man, not the fearsome figure Serious Crime had painted. The deaths had unsurprisingly hit him hard, leaving Jessica unsure if it was worth talking to him at all, especially as the DNA results were at least a day away.

'Sugar?' he barked.

'No.'

'How many?'

'I said I didn't want any.'

He tugged on his jumper, then stuck a finger in his ear. 'Oh . . . milk?'

'Just a splash.'

Preferably not poured using the finger that had just been in his ear.

Hyde finally stopped moving around the kitchen, settling on a stool next to Jessica, though he couldn't sit still.

He started with the tiptoes of each foot touching the floor, then lifted his legs up, then dropped them again, all the while fidgeting and twitching. He seemed broken.

'Are you sure you're all right to talk?' Jessica asked.

'Talk, talk, talk, talk, talk. All I do is talk.'

'We could do this another time.'

'I've got to get to the casino, so out with it.'

He sounded like her primary school headmaster.

'Do you have any other children, Mr Hyde?'

Hyde eyed her like she was stupid. 'Natalie.'

'Other than her.'

'Of course not.'

'Is there any chance you could have a son in Liverpool, or a daughter in Southampton?'

'Absolutely none.'

'When we found Richie's body, we DNA-tested it as we were trying to work out his final movements. We discovered that there are two other people in the database who are related to him.'

He was now fixed on her: 'Two?'

'There could actually be more – those are the pair who are in the DNA database for whatever reason. If there are two half-siblings *on* our system, it's statistically likely there are others who aren't.'

It took him a moment to take it in. 'I don't understand what you're saying.'

'It could be a mistake but I've spoken to the labs this morning and it's looking increasingly likely that it isn't – because it wouldn't be one error, it'd be a series. We'll have final confirmation soon, but your son, Richie, almost certainly has at least one half-brother and one half-sister.'

Hyde was unmoved, staring at her, impossible to read. Was he surprised? Confused? The fidgeting had stopped but that had been replaced by a statue-like stillness. 'But it could be a mistake . . . ?' he stammered.

'It wouldn't just be *one* mistake, it'd be two or three. It's possible but unlikely. That leaves an obvious question – are they your children?'

'I . . . who are these other people? These other kids?'

'I can't tell you that but, for instance, the young man in Liverpool is fourteen months younger than Richie.'

'The same mother?'

'No, they have the same dad.'

'I don't understand.'

'Neither do I – but you must see why this matters. If someone is targeting you and your family, these other people could be in danger. We're testing the fathers from Liverpool and Southampton to see, but—'

He stood, jabbing a finger towards her, small smile appearing. 'Aaah, I get it. Absolutely not. Is that what this is all about? One big con? These so-called other children don't exist, do they?' He tapped a finger into his temple. 'You're trying to get in here, because you want me to agree to giving you a sample.'

'I can assure you that's not the reason.'

'You've spent all these years trying to pin something – anything – on me, but I know the law. If you want to take my DNA or fingerprints, you need a reason to arrest me. You can't just steal things I've touched because it doesn't count in court, you need my permission – and you're not having it. My daughter runs a legitimate business and I'm retired.'

'That's not what this is about.'

'Yeah, yeah, I'm sure it's not. What's next? Are you going to get these mythical children to appear on my doorstep and call me Daddy? You wait until all this has happened and then try to take advantage?'

'Mr Hyde, that's really not—'

He pointed at the door. 'Out. You tell your bosses it's not worked. They thought they could soften me up the other night and then send in a girl to do their dirty work. Next time you want to talk to me, you come through my solicitor.'

Jessica was off the stool, coffee untouched as she tried to backpedal away from Hyde. For the first time, she could see everything that Josh had been trying to tell her. Hyde wasn't a harmless old man, there was fury in his eyes; he'd transformed into a ferocious, spitting, imposing presence. Jessica felt a twinge of fear, knowing she was by herself. It wasn't his size or the way his finger was pointing, but the depth of his anger. She could hear it in his voice, see it in the way he was snarling. Anything felt possible.

'You think you're clever, do you?' he said.

Jessica was into the hallway, almost running for the front door.

'Think you're smarter than me?'

'No.'

She was trying to open the front door but there was a

catch and it was stuck. Hyde wasn't reaching to open it, he was looming over her, seeming taller in his rage.

'Think you can take advantage after everything that's happened? Try to play me as a mug?'

His face was inches from hers. He smelled of shaving cream and she could see the bulging whites of his eyes.

Jessica's voice was a whisper, with her unable to muster any strength. 'Let me out . . .' For more than a week, she'd thought this entire case was about a bunch of bullies going after one another; now it felt real. She could sense all the lives that had been touched by – massacred by – the men she'd been in the midst of. Winding up Carter suddenly didn't seem like a good idea. What had she been thinking?

'Do you know who I am?' he said.

'I know.'

'Yet you still come to me with this story, wanting to kick a man when he's down.'

'It's the truth.'

'What you're saying is impossible.'

'I thought that too but it's not.'

Hyde lunged forward and, for a fraction of a second, Jessica thought he was going to punch her. Instead, he reached to the side of her head, clicking something on the front door and then levering down the handle.

'Tell your bosses that you failed – and don't come back here without a warrant.'

Jessica crouched under his arm and hurried from the house, along the driveway, through the gates to her car. She sat for a few minutes catching her breath and replaying the events. She hadn't thought Hyde would take the knowledge of potential other children well, but she hadn't expected such fury. The assumption at the station was that Hyde *was* the father of the others, that he was a powerful man who'd got around in more ways than one. Is that why he'd been so angry, that now Natalie would know? Or that his other bastard children would be in danger?

Eventually, Jessica took out her phone and called DC Rowlands, asking if he fancied staying up late over the weekend.

35

Jessica hadn't actually expected confirmed DNA results within the day – it wasn't CSI: Manchester and the science geeks most likely had *Doctor Who* box sets to wade through – but it would have been nice. Nothing came through, meaning the Fosters in Liverpool would have to spend another day worrying over the outcome.

She decided not to tell Topper or anyone else about Richard Hyde's sudden ferocity. The more she thought about it, the more Jessica convinced herself it wasn't as bad as she'd first thought. She'd been too quick to hurry into the hall and then got herself trapped by the front door.

Because of everything else she was working on, the trio of murders were being checked over by a wider team of people overseen by Superintendent Jenkinson. Jessica skimmed through the daily reports anyway, looking to see if there was anything she didn't already know about. There wasn't.

After spending so much time away from the station through the week, there was paperwork galore to wade through, forms to sign, letters to open, emails to delete, people to ignore. Plus, she got dragged into the daily brief/debrief from Serious Crime. Much tea was drunk, much shite was talked, very little was done.

Jessica found a few minutes to search for the e-fit of

Annie among their catalogue of crooks, remembering her promise to Alf and Nerys that she'd find the person who robbed them. She should have palmed it off onto a constable to deal with, someone who had more time, but the case had already been bodged once. Not that she was doing a better job of it.

Annie sounded local and knew the area on which she was preying, so there was little point in searching too widely around the rest of the country. Of the few potential facial matches Jessica did find, almost all were instantly shot down because the people had either moved away or were in prison. There were a couple of names who could be 'Annie' but the women didn't look *that* similar and Jessica knew she was more hopeful than confident. Thoroughly exhausted, she asked Izzy if she could find a competent constable to make a few inquiries, doubting it would come to much. At least she was doing something.

Jessica hadn't wanted to call or message Bex through the day, not wanting it to seem like she was prying. It had been in the back of her mind throughout, wondering how Bex and her mother had got on when it had been just them.

Bex was sitting at the dining table when Jessica arrived home, typing on the laptop that Jessica had more or less given her. She rarely used it herself. Bex seemed content, in one piece with no puffy eyes or hints of upset.

'Everything all right?' Jessica asked.

Bex nodded, closing the lid of the laptop, ready to talk. 'I didn't want to disturb you at work.'

'How was your morning?'

'Confusing.'

'How so?'

'It felt different . . . I wasn't angry today.'

'Perhaps you'd said everything you had to?'

Bex nodded, crossing the room and sitting on the sofa, next to Jessica. 'We just talked, not about the past, about now. I told her about being part-time at college and that I'm starting properly in September, she told me about the agency job she's got. She works one till five on weekdays doing data input at the university. She got into the agency herself because, otherwise, the people who run the housing project put you into manual work, cleaning and so on. She didn't want to do that, but it feels weird that she did it for herself.'

There was something she wasn't saying but Jessica didn't want to push too much.

'You got on then?'

'I suppose. I didn't shout this time. It felt . . . normal. Two people having a cup of tea.'

'That's good?'

Jessica phrased it as a question because Bex didn't sound so sure.

Bex looked away. 'She asked me something . . .'

'Okay.'

'She'll be moving out of the sheltered housing at the end of the summer and will need a new place. When I told her about going to college in September, she asked if I wanted to find somewhere with her. She wants to start again in all ways. She said we could rent and then, if it doesn't work, we're not stuck.'

'Oh . . .'

Jessica didn't know what to say. It felt as if she'd been punched in the stomach, winded. She tried to breathe but it hurt. She'd lived alone before and enjoyed it, but things had changed – she'd changed. The idea of being by herself in this big house full of memories left her worried in a way she hadn't felt in a long while. She needed people around her.

'I didn't give her an answer,' Bex added quickly.

'It's okay – you need to do what's right for you.'

'I don't know what's right for me.' Bex took a breath, turning back. 'Jess . . . ?'

'What?'

'It wouldn't mean I appreciate what you've done for me any less.'

Jessica nodded, resting a hand on Bex's shoulder, wanting to hug her but wondering if it would feel weird. 'I know – I just want you to be happy.'

Bex continued what she was working on through the evening as Jessica ate off her lap and watched television, or, more to the point, she had the television on. She wasn't taking anything in. She didn't want to live by herself but, at the same time, this was the place she owned with Adam. What she *really* wanted was him back. She wanted Adam out of the coma, at home, the way things used to be.

Izzy had said that Jessica was never one to stay still. She hadn't been talking about houses or places to live, she'd meant in life. Jessica always had something going on, good or bad. If Bex left, Jessica would feel for the first time in a long while that she'd stalled, that she was trapped.

Her phone rang at a few minutes after seven – Archie. Jessica thought about ignoring it, not in the mood for him wondering if she 'wanted to do something'. It was how he always phrased it, but the implication was obvious. She answered anyway, in the mood for an argument.

'I'm busy, Arch,' she said.

'I need your help.'

For the first time ever, he sounded like he meant it.

'Are you in trouble?'

'Not at the moment but you've got to come now.'

Jessica parked her car close to the same verge as when she, Archie and Izzy had inadvertently ended up at a rave less than a week previously. It was a very different atmosphere this time. Rather than the dancing teenagers, there were big men and a handful of bigger women traipsing along the edge of the road, then into the field and walking towards the distant barn.

As they crossed into the field, Archie stretched and took Jessica's hand. 'What are you doing?' she asked.

'Trust me – we want to fit in.'

Jessica let his fingers slide into hers, slowing her pace slightly so he didn't have to hurry. 'How do you know the fight's definitely tonight?' she asked, keeping her voice low.

'One of my mates, don't worry.'

'Why didn't you tell Iz – or anyone else?'

'Iz has been stressed all week because her last tip was wrong. She doesn't want to muck up again.' Archie used his free hand to indicate the groups of people ahead of them – almost entirely men, wearing jeans and big arse-kicking boots. The few women who were there looked as if they could dish out a bigger hiding than the blokes: tree-trunk arms, enormous chests, the type who enjoyed watching two men beating each other senseless. 'It's not really her scene,' Archie concluded.

'Is it mine?'

His fingers squeezed hers. 'That's not what I said. Anyway, I didn't want to make a fuss in case my tip was wrong.'

'Why don't you call it in now?'

'Because these people aren't stupid. Whatever's going on in the barn at the moment will be the warm-up. If anyone important's going to be here, we're going to have to sit tight.'

It was annoying that he was right but Jessica was more worried by his greasy, sweaty palm – despite the local lad bravado, he was nervous too.

The queue to get into the barn was far longer than it had been for the rave, with almost no noise coming from the inside. There were no strobing lights and if it hadn't been for the rows of parked cars on the roads that lined the field, no one would have known anything untoward was going on. Jessica tried not to spend too much time gazing around, not wanting to attract attention, but there were at least ten men for every woman, probably more. Archie kept hold of her hand but, as the sun dipped beneath the trees, casting a dark orange glow, he started to become edgier, moving from foot to foot and peering around the people in front of them towards the entrance.

The reason for the delay became clear as they got closer.

There were four men on the door – each huge, wearing jeans, plaid shirts and vests, arms covered with tattoos and scars. They called forward two people at a time, frisked them, and checked their pockets, then sent them inside.

The only exception Jessica saw was the couple three ahead of them – two women, both enormous, wearing tube tops too small for their chest size. The four doormen didn't even ask them to empty their pockets, let alone frisk the women, before sending them inside.

Soon, Archie and Jessica were waved forward by the biggest of the four. He had a pointy grey and black beard, bushy grey eyebrows and a ponytail down his back. Greedy eyes settled on Jessica before he turned to Archie.

'What's the word, bro?'

'Indigo.'

Ponytail nodded and Archie took the hint, emptying the wallet and phone from his pocket. The guard flicked through the wallet, checking through the various flaps and removing two twenty-pound notes before handing it back with the phone. Jessica wasn't sure but it didn't look like Archie's regular phone; it seemed older with buttons instead of the touchscreen.

'Turn it off,' the man said.

'Now?'

'Before you go in – you can keep it with you but anyone caught using a phone inside, well . . .'

Archie pressed and held the button on top of his phone as one of the other men stepped forward, running his hands along Archie's arms, then up and down his legs. One of the other guards stepped forward but Ponytail waved him away.

'You,' he said, nodding at Jessica. She handed him her phone, the only thing she'd brought aside from a few folded-up ten-pound notes. He flipped the phone around in his hand and then passed it back. Jessica turned it off and took a step towards the door. Ponytail reached forward, grabbing her wrist. 'Where are you going?'

'Inside.'

'Not yet, hold your arms out.'

'You let those other women in.'

He winked. 'You ain't other women.'

Jessica held her arms out, crucifixion-style.

'Open your legs.'

'Are you joking?'

'Open 'em, or piss off.'

Jessica did as she was told, taking the star jump position: arms wide, legs apart. Ponytail stood behind her, running his hand slowly along her left arm, then her right. She could feel his beard tickling the back of her neck, his breath creeping along her hairline. As the next two men in line moved forward to be checked by the rest of the guards, Ponytail remained focused on her. His hands stroked her back, before reaching around and touching her tummy. She winced, shivering, as they flitted across her breasts before he was cupping them both, squeezing gently at first before firmly pinching her nipples.

'You're certainly packing something,' he said.

Jessica's eyes had been closed but she felt a flash of movement, looking up to see Archie in front of her, fists balled at his side. She shook her head the tiniest of amounts but Ponytail had removed his hands.

'You all right there, tough guy?' he said to Archie.

Jessica stared into Archie's eyes, seeing the fury in him, but begging him not to do anything. There were four guards, almost certainly more inside too. There was no police backup, just them. It wasn't the time.

'Just anxious to get inside,' Archie replied, voice quivering just enough to keep Jessica on edge.

Ponytail purred his reply. 'Not much longer, bro.'

She felt him drop behind her, gripping her ankle and running his hand up the length of her leg, passing her knee, stroking her inside thigh and then, horrifically, sickeningly, pressing the side of his index finger into the space between her legs and rubbing back and forth. Jessica bit her bottom lip, knees wobbling. She felt sick.

Ponytail finally stepped away. 'You're clear. Have fun and keep those phones off.'

It was a good job Archie took her hand because, without him, Jessica felt like she might fall. She felt weak, used. The next thing she knew, they were inside. There was no thumping music, just the grunts and cheers of men crowding a boxing ring in the centre of the barn. Archie kept hold of her hand, leading her along the back of the crowd until they were in a dark corner.

He let go of her hand, resting it across her back: 'You okay?'

'Yeah.'

'He—'

'I know, Arch. We can't do much about it now. Let's just get this over with – I hope you've got a plan of how you're going to call it in.' She was struggling to hold it together,

297

not wanting Archie to see how affected she was. Jessica nodded up to the viewing platforms they'd spotted during the rave. There were four spotters watching the action, or, more likely, watching the crowd.

'I'll sort something,' he said.

'How did you know the password?'

'My mate.' He took her hand, stepping towards the ring. 'Come on, let's not get noticed.'

It wasn't long before the first fight started, though it couldn't really be classed as a contest. It was a brutal one-sided beating, one big guy with frying-pan hands pounding someone half his size until there was so much blood that a man, loosely on hand as a referee, stepped in. There were no gloves, no headguards, no pads in the corner. Nobody seemed to be keeping time, with no distinctions for rounds or time-outs. It was a street fight confined to a ring, with little concern for either of the competitors' well-being.

As the loser was carried away on a stretcher, disappearing towards the back of the barn into an area behind a set of wooden panels, Archie leant in to whisper in Jessica's ear: 'That was a family dispute.'

'What?'

'The warm-up act – the only rules are no biting or gouging. It will have settled some argument between families.'

The winner was parading around the four corners, arms aloft. When he reached the one closest to them, a huge woman – probably his mother – heaved herself up onto the side of the ring and hugged him. She stepped away with smears of blood across her front, getting a series of cheers for the effort.

When the winner finally left, four young men leapt into the ring, scrubbing the worst of the blood away as part of the crowd disappeared towards one of the two bars that were selling cans.

'We can't let this go on,' Jessica whispered. 'Someone could get killed.'

'There's no one here yet, no promoter, no champion. These are kids having a Friday night out. Wait until the men in suits turn up.'

'Men in suits?'

'You'll see.'

The second fight wasn't as brutal, and there were at least rounds, if not gloves. Jessica didn't want to watch but also didn't want to be picked out by one of the spotters as someone who didn't want to be there. That's exactly what they'd be looking for.

After three rounds, one of the fighters hit the canvas and the referee counted to ten. The loser was on his feet a few seconds later, shaking his head and then hugging the bloke who'd just battered him. They left together, patting each other on the back.

The barn had been filling up slowly over the course of the first two fights but there was a definite change of atmosphere through the third battle. Bigger men were entering, more women too: slim with long hair – far too tarted up to be spending a Friday evening in a barn. They were escorted to the front, standing on the side of the ring opposite Jessica and Archie. As the fight continued, a series of big men continued squeezing in and out of the crowd, carrying chairs as they arranged a front row. The women sat but there were half-a-dozen empty seats.

The third fight ended in the second round with a vicious knockout that made Jessica wince. A spray of blood flew over the top rope, splattering the people in front of them to a loud cheer. The beaten man was counted out at ten but wouldn't have got up if the referee had counted to fifty. He was carried out on a stretcher – the victor taking one of the corners.

'Here we go,' Archie whispered.

A path had cleared through the crowd opposite, half-a-dozen burly minders making space for a man in a suit and long coat to walk through. He was stopping to point and say hello to the people at the fringes of the crowd, like a movie star on a stroll down the red carpet.

'Who's that?' Jessica asked.

'He'll be the promoter but I have no idea who he actually is. I guarantee our pals at the Met will know him.'

'How do you promote something like this?'

'Someone's got to arrange for the guards at the front and sort out the venue. That twenty quid a person to get in will be going somewhere and I doubt the fighters are getting much.'

The promoter gave a small wave to the crowd, before taking a seat next to the underdressed young women. His knuckles were adorned with chunky gold rings, with more jewellery around his wrists and neck. If he were tossed in the canal, he'd sink straight to the bottom. The other free seats were taken by the men who'd cleared space for him.

Jessica could sense Archie's arm twitching next to her.

She started to turn, spotting his hands in the pockets of his jacket, but he hissed 'No' fiercely enough to make her face the front.

'What are you doing?'

'Nothing.'

There was a delay as the ring was completely cleaned and cleared, not that it mattered with the amount of booze being consumed. At least twenty minutes passed until everything was ready, by which time the canvas of the ring was almost the dusty grey it had started.

None of the other fights had been introduced but now there was a man in the ring, tall and thin, also in a suit. He had a slight Irish twang as he flapped his arms, whipping the crowd into a frenzy. The challenger was announced first – 'Harrison "Born To Be" King'. He was short and bald with a hairy chest and thick, muscled arms, like a little tank. As he came through the crowd, people started booing, the volume increasing until it became cheers. Jessica had to stand on tiptoes to see what was happening. Harrison King was in a shoving match with someone from the crowd as the big men from the front row rushed backwards, trying to stop the fight before *the* fight.

The tension was almost unbearable by the time King reached the ring, raising his arms and goading the crowd. It felt like something bad was going to happen, that if King triumphed, he wouldn't get out in one piece.

Liam 'Nine Fingers' Flanagan was announced to enormous cheers, having no such trouble in getting to the ring. He was tall, ginger and ripped, muscles so taut it looked like his limbs could explode at any moment. The promoter was standing, clapping enthusiastically, as the announcer went through his shtick: weights, heights, measurements. Despite the names, King was Scottish, Flanagan English, which explained the welcomes. As Izzy had said, they were fighting for the British middleweight title, though Jessica doubted this was anything official. She could see the gap in Flanagan's left hand, where he was missing his ring finger.

Each fighter was sent to a corner as the shiny gold belt was raised and shown to all four sides of the arena. Official or not, it felt as real as anything Jessica had seen. The crowd was an overfilled, overheated pressure cooker, ready to pop.

Jessica leant backwards, whispering into Archie's ear. 'What do we do?'

'Just wait.'

'We've got to leave and call in.'

'Trust me.'

Archie's fingers interlocked with hers again and, instinctively, she had faith in him.

Someone had found a bell and with a *ding-ding-ding* and a mighty cheer, they were under way. The two men circled each other, shuffling and dancing until King landed the first blow with a vicious right hand. Flanagan's head snapped sideways to a loud *ooh* from the crowd, but he ducked away, smiling at the man who'd almost taken his head off. They continued to trade flurries but nothing too serious. As the round progressed, Archie edged through the crowd, looping the pair of them in a semicircle until they were on the side closest to the exit. Jessica followed his lead, unsure what was going on.

By the time the bell sounded to signal the end of the

first round, there was clear disappointment among the crowd. The two competitors returned to their respective corners for a drink and rub from the towel.

'Arch . . .'

Jessica didn't get a chance to say anything else because a man's voice bellowed from the doorway. Two words that started a rush of movement: 'Old Bill!'

Archie didn't wait for Jessica, turning and barrelling for the door. She didn't need an invitation, running as fast as she could to follow him. Behind, there were screams and the sound of hundreds of people racing to the exits. Archie got there just behind the first dozen people. Flashing blue lights were streaming into the field through the open gates, with a sound of a helicopter *chikka-chikka-chikkering* nearby. There were figures silhouetted in the distance, uniformed police officers running towards the barn, but Archie didn't run towards them. Jessica had never seen him move so fast: he had his head down, target in his sights.

As Ponytail dashed for the hedgerow, Archie crunched into him from behind, tackling him to the floor. They scuffed along the dried grass for a metre or two but Archie was up quickest, lunging across and straddling Ponytail's chest.

Wham!

Archie's first punch sent a flail of spit and blood hurtling from the other man's face. No warnings, no arguments, no explanation.

Wham! Wham! Wham! Wham!

Archie kept punching until Jessica dragged him off. Five punches, six, seven, eight. Ponytail's head crunched onto the ground with each blow, eyes rolling into his head as the blows continued to come. Around them, people were running in all directions, heading for the hedges and trees as the police cordon closed. The helicopter appeared over the treeline, dousing the area in a bright white light and suddenly it was like the middle of the day. There were a hundred stab-vest-wearing officers rushing the scene, truncheons in hand.

Ponytail was a bloody mess on the floor, blood spattered around the crown of his head, his nose a pulpy mass of flesh. Archie wiped his hand on the grass and then turned to Jessica. For a moment, he wasn't the police officer she knew, he was the street kid who'd grown up on a tough estate.

He spat a thick wad onto the ground, chest heaving with exertion. 'Let's go,' he said.

36

Jessica sat in her office trying to work but unable to focus on her screen. The words were mangling into a mixed jumble of letters that made no sense. Her report about the previous night was going to take some time to write up – and, yet again, she was working on a bloody sunny Saturday. Topper had a secretary to write things up for him, she was stuck typing herself.

Izzy was supping a coffee. 'Have I ever told you how much I love Archie?'

'I've heard you calling him a dickhead before.'

'Really?'

'Numerous times.'

'Yeah, well, I owe him one after last night. Not only did we arrest a whole bunch of people, it was me he contacted. He could've called it in himself and taken the glory. Someone from the Met was singing our praises earlier – apparently they've been looking to pin something on that promoter guy for years.'

'How *did* he contact you? I was there and he didn't take his mobile phone out.'

Izzy laughed. 'Well, I say "contact" but it's a bloody good job I'm used to getting dodgy texts from Mal. He might be my husband but his thumbs are too big and his phone buttons are too small. His texts are like trying to decipher the Enigma code.'

She passed her phone to Jessica, showing her a text message from Archie: 'Box mow ta born.'

'What does that mean?'

'Boxing now at barn – compared to some of Mal's messages, it's perfectly legible.'

'He must've texted you while the phone was still in his pocket. I thought he was playing with himself.'

Izzy laughed but Jessica didn't. She wasn't ready to call Archie a hero after what he'd done to Ponytail.

'What's the damage?' Jessica asked.

'One guy in intensive care but it doesn't look like it was any of our lot, thank God. You never know when they start handing out truncheons. We think he got in a fight with one of the other people at the boxing and came off worse. One of the boxers is in a bad way but refusing to speak. There are a couple of others with bumps and bruises but no complaints of brutality. One of the uniforms tripped and twisted his ankle, so he'll probably be on the sick for the next three months, but that's the lot. It couldn't have gone much better.'

'It might have been better if Arch had called you before we went in there.'

Izzy shrugged. 'Is that what you're going to write?'

'Course not.'

'If he'd called earlier, we'd have gone earlier – we'd have never got the big boys. As it is, we've got all sorts of charges to lay. It's going to be a fun weekend. Nine Fingers wasn't happy – he kept saying someone nicked his belt.'

There was a knock on the door, and then Archie appeared. 'A'ight?'

Izzy leapt to her feet, kissing him on the forehead and offering him her seat. 'I didn't get a proper chance to say thanks earlier.'

He waved a hand. 'Don't worry 'bout it. One of my mates were bound to come through at some point.'

Izzy looked between Archie and Jessica, the tension obvious. 'I'll leave you to it,' she said, picking up her coffee and closing the door behind her.

Neither of them spoke for a while, Jessica continuing to type until Archie broke the silence. 'You 'kay?'

She spun to face him. 'What do you think? I'm not saying thank you for beating a bloke into intensive care, if that's what you're asking.'

He stared at his feet. 'I'm not.'

'We spend our careers trying to stop that kind of violence. I've sat through briefing after briefing about Hyde, Carter, Fraser and everyone else where Serious Crime talk us through what they're supposed to be into.'

'I didn't plan it . . .'

'Yes you did – the minute the call came that the police had arrived, you ran straight for him.'

'He touched—'

'I know what he did, Arch – it was me he did it to, remember? That's why we have laws. We could've nicked him and both given statements.'

Archie shrugged as his phone started to ring. He peered at the screen and then pressed the reject button. 'Is that what you wanted?' he asked. 'File the paperwork and see it crawl through the courts?'

Jessica stared at him then turned away, back to her screen. She said nothing for a while, knowing she should disapprove. When the reply eventually came, it was barely a whisper. 'You should've hit him harder.'

There was a much longer silence this time. Jessica had done worse but it still felt wrong. It was another line crossed, something that couldn't be taken back. Even when Ponytail got out of intensive care, he wouldn't know who'd hit him. They'd get away with it, but to what end? How many lines could be crossed before it permanently changed a person?

There was a popping sound and a new email dropped into Jessica's inbox. She skimmed it, utterly unsurprised by its contents.

'Guess what?' she said, spinning in her seat.

'What?'

'The labs say Rhys Foster *isn't* Isaac's father. It's the same deal in Southampton – neither of their fathers are their own.'

'Does that mean Richard Hyde is the dad to both?'

'Not necessarily. *Richie* Hyde and these two all share a father but we don't have *Richard* Hyde's DNA on record. There's no match in the database to anyone else, either.'

'So there are two people who don't know who their dad is?'

'Right . . . and Nicole Foster has a bit of explaining to do to her husband.'

'We could ask her if she knows Richard Hyde.'

Jessica shook her head. 'It's not really any of our business. She already told us Isaac was her husband's son, I can't see her changing her mind.'

'It sounds like Richard Hyde's got a whole bunch of kids around the country . . .'

'Probably – but there's only one way to find out.'

37

It was the end of another long day, except that it wasn't even the end. Jessica rolled the driver's seat back in the car, stretching until her joints clicked and succumbing to a yawn so big it left tears streaming down her face.

'*That* is one of the worst things I've ever seen,' Rowlands said. He was in the passenger seat, pulling a face.

'Sod off.'

'No, seriously, I've seen murder scenes, people who've been bottled, but nothing like that. I thought your jaw was going to separate – and your shoulder sounded like a gun going off.'

'I've had a few long days.'

'So why are we here?'

The neon lights were blinking at the front of Hyde's casino, sending a cascade of yellow, purple, red and blue across the tarmac. They were parked towards the back, shielded in the shadows.

'Because I'm an idiot,' Jessica replied.

'If you're waiting for me to argue . . .'

Jessica let herself yawn again. 'I'm not.'

'I heard about the boxing thing last night. What was it like?'

'Chaos – Archie seemed at home. I got the feeling it wasn't the first time he'd been to something like that.'

'You can take the kid off the street, you can't get the street out of the kid.'

It didn't sound like he was having a dig.

'We could do with more Archies and fewer people with too many letters before their name. It's ridiculous the number of briefings the guv's been stuck in all week. It's not his fault, but it's no wonder nothing's getting done. Christ knows what Jenkinson's up to – all I do know is that there's no one in the frame for murdering Priestley and the two Hydes. They're still banging on about Carter but it's not him.'

'You don't reckon?'

'No, he's taking the piss out of us. We've spent so long focusing on that list of names Serious Crime gave us that no one's considered anything else.'

'Like what?'

'I don't know.' She sniggered. 'You know me, all criticism, no answers.'

Rowlands laughed. 'Why'd you ask me to come out here with you?'

'Because I wanted to spend the evening with someone I like, plus I've got something to tell you.'

'Oh . . . ?'

'It's about that girl from the bar – Katherine. Did you go home with her?'

'Well, er—'

'I don't want details, I was wondering if you're seeing her again.'

'Um . . .'

An obvious yes.

'Did she tell you her last name?'

Rowlands scratched his head. 'I guess not. We've only been out twice. It's not come up.' Jessica saw the panic flicker in his eyes. 'Oh, no . . . she said it in passing, I didn't even clock it . . . it's not . . .'

'I thought it couldn't be because you work right next to Franks and he'd have photos of his family on his desk.'

Rowlands's head was in his hands as he shook it from side to side. 'Franks only keeps pictures of himself. We all take the piss.'

'I know – I went to have a look. I felt dirty just by being in his corner. There are seven different photos around his desk and monitor – all of himself.'

'There's another as his screensaver too. It's creepy. I think he keeps photos of himself in his wallet too. He's a psycho.'

'I've got some really bad news.'

Rowlands lifted his head. 'Don't say it, there's no way she can come from him.'

'I spoke to one of the girls in HR. She gave me the usual bollocks about everyone's file being private but I had a carrier bag full of Crunchies.'

'No . . .'

'Detective Inspector Franks has one daughter, named Katherine.'

'But she's funny . . .'

'I'm sure she is.'

'She's good-looking . . .'

'I noticed.'

'She's normal!'

'I'll take your word for it.'

'How can she be his daughter? She must be adopted, or fostered.' He clicked his fingers. 'Franks is a child-snatcher! He must've stolen her at a young age and brought her up as his own.'

'I think we've got enough paternity tests happening at the moment.'

Rowlands looked haunted, as if Santa had come down the chimney and made off with all his presents. 'Funtime's never once mentioned a daughter.'

'He's a dick.'

'She knows I'm a copper but she never mentioned her dad was one.'

'She probably thinks he's a dick.'

'We went to the cinema and had a meal. It was really fun. We're going out again on Monday night.' Rowlands rubbed his head, closing his eyes, before they shot open again. 'Fat Pat doesn't know, does he?'

'Not from me. If he did, everyone would know.'

'This is, like, the worst thing ever.'

'Well . . .'

Rowlands suddenly reached out, touching her arm. 'Sorry, I didn't mean that. Christ, what you've been through, what an idiot. Sorry.'

Jessica shook him off. 'It's fine.'

'I'm going to have to break up with her.'

'I thought you said she was funny and good-looking? You can't dump her because of who her dad is.'

Rowlands squeezed the bridge of his nose. 'I should text her.'

'You're not dumping her by text.'

'Every time I look her in the face, I'm going to see Wanky Frankie.'

'Tough, you're still not dumping her by text – you shouldn't dump her at all. Sleep on it and see how you feel tomorrow. Just because Funtime's a toilet-sniffer, it shouldn't stop you from being happy.'

'That's almost profound.'

Jessica stretched again, feeling her shoulders pop. Rowlands *was* right – it was bloody loud. She was so distracted by the creaky nature of her body that Jessica almost missed the shadowy figure exiting the back of the casino, heading towards the shiny black Jaguar.

'Dave.'

'What?'

'We're up.'

Rowlands tried to lean forward, succeeding only in bumping his head on the roof. Jessica eased her door open as quietly as she could, stepping carefully out of the car.

The figure hadn't quite made it to the vehicle and was using a gatepost to hold himself up. Jessica stuck to the shadows, edging closer, recognising the figure she knew would be there: Richard Hyde. He was fumbling in his pockets, making a scratching sound, before he uttered a triumphant 'a-ha!' He set off towards the car, not quite staggering but not completely upright, either. There was a plip and a set of flashing lights as the car unlocked.

Hyde had one hand on the door when Jessica stepped out from the shadows behind him.

'Richard Hyde . . .'

He jumped, spinning to face her. Rowlands was by her side, the pair of them advancing together.

'. . . you're under arrest on suspicion of attempting to drive with excess alcohol—' He tried to interrupt but Jessica continued speaking as Rowlands handcuffed him. 'You do not have to say anything; however, it may harm your defence if you do not mention, when questioned, something which you later rely on in court. Anything you do say may be given in evidence.'

His words were slightly slurred: 'Are you joking?'

'Let's see, shall we?'

38

Jessica waited in her office, knowing what was coming. She'd had two nights with little sleep and could really have done with a day out of the station. Superintendent Jenkinson and DCI Topper were in the office upstairs, doing whatever it was they did. Meet, probably, that's all they ever did: meeting after meeting.

When she'd arrived, Jessica had thought she might get through a bit of outstanding work but she wasn't in the mood. The only thing she achieved was checking her emails to find a note from one of the constables saying that neither of the potential facial matches were 'Annie'. Jessica knew she should crack on and try to find out who'd robbed her next-door neighbour but she couldn't get motivated for any of it when she knew what would be coming any time . . . now.

There was a knock on her office door: nice and polite, a good start, which wouldn't last for long.

'Come in.'

The agents of doom entered: Superintendent Jenkinson and DCI Topper, faces grim, set against horrific Sunday-wear: chinos and shit jumpers. What was it with men once they hit fifty? All the clothes they'd spent their lives wearing were bundled up and discarded, replaced by a look that made it clear they'd given up. Nothing said coffin-dodging quite like chinos with a jumper.

Topper perched on the edge of the free desk, Jenkinson taking the chair. The superintendent had the air about him that this was too big a space for one person and that it could be converted into some sort of office for half-a-dozen constables. He could sod right off.

'Lovely day, isn't it?' Jessica said.

In the time since he'd been promoted, Jessica wasn't sure DSI Jenkinson had ever had a direct conversation with her. That didn't stop him pointing a finger, thumping the side of his hand into his free palm. 'What on earth did you think you were doing?'

'When?'

'You know when.'

'I was off-duty but still doing my job, Sir. I've done a lot of that recently.'

'Really?'

'*Really* – do you want me to log it all as overtime?'

Jenkinson was nodding slowly, the bollocking not going as he'd expected. He was obviously used to arse-kissing apologies but then he'd not been at Longsight for too long.

'*Attempting* to drink and drive,' he said. '*Attempting?* Do you know how many people would be arrested for that if the law was interpreted as literally as you've taken it?'

Jessica held his gaze. 'Have you actually read the law?'

'That's not the—'

'It *is* the point, Sir. I've read the law.' She patted the paper on the desk in front of her. 'I've got it right here – endorsement code DR10, the wording is clear. "It is an offence for a person to drive or attempt to drive a motor vehicle on a road or other public place with excess alcohol". Under guidance, it says: "Attempting to drive can include any effort to use a vehicle regardless of whether it is successful".' She looked up. 'I don't see what the problem is.'

Jenkinson pounded his fist on the free desk, speaking through gritted teeth. 'The *problem* is that, as you were told, Serious Crime are building separate cases—'

'So we ignore the law? Richard Hyde was attempting to drive while intoxicated.'

'That's not what he says.'

'Who cares what he says? Everyone says it wasn't them – if that's the basis for arresting people, we'd never bring anyone in.'

'He says he unlocked the car and was waiting for his daughter to drive him home.'

'Was he over the limit?' Jessica asked.

'That's not the—'

Jessica turned to Topper. 'Was he?'

There was a moment of impasse, Jessica defiant, Jenkinson unwilling to bend. If she wanted to defend the superintendent – which she didn't – he'd probably had it in the neck himself. Hyde was fuming even before he was left in a cell overnight. By the time his solicitor arrived in the morning, he'd have been apoplectic. Hyde's solicitor would have caused such a fuss that the assistant chief constables would have been involved. Someone at the Serious Crime Division would have had a thing or two to say as well. Jessica was lucky she wasn't on her way to professional standards, not that it couldn't still happen.

'He was twice the legal limit,' Topper said.

'There you go then,' Jessica replied.

Jenkinson wasn't having it: 'He *wasn't* trying to drive.'

'You weren't there. It looked like it to me.'

'How did you know he spent time outside waiting for his daughter to drive him home?'

Jessica shrugged. 'I didn't.'

'Did he tell you on one of the occasions you spoke to him?'

'Not to my recollection,' Jessica replied.

'You know what Hyde's solicitor is going to say?'

'Something about his hourly rate?'

Jenkinson huffed: 'Don't get smart.'

Jessica shut her mouth, knowing she was pushing her luck. The destructive streak that she'd almost shaken off had returned. If Adam wasn't waking up and Bex was moving out, then who cared?

'What's his solicitor going to say?' she asked, trying to remove the annoyance from her voice.

'That you were following him, targeting him. If not, what were you doing in a car park in the early hours of a Sunday morning?'

She shrugged. 'I've got a gambling problem, I didn't realise they were closing for the night.'

Jenkinson pounded his fist into the desk again, furious. 'You're lucky you're not suspended.'

Jessica said nothing, maintaining his stare until he eventually turned, standing and sending a pile of folders flying. He didn't bother to pick them up, stepping over the paper and card and storming out of her office door, slamming it behind him. Jessica could feel Topper watching her but spun back to face her monitor anyway.

'What?' she asked, her back to him.

'You do know who you've just been rude to?' Topper said.

'I've been rude to bigger and more important people than him.'

Topper sniggered, perhaps without meaning to, then he sounded serious again. 'He's right, you could've been suspended.'

'No I couldn't. What do you think would've happened if I'd ended up in tribunal, gave my account of things and that law was read out? I'd wind up with reinstatement and a nice payoff. There was another constable there, remember, he'll back everything I've told you.'

'Both got gambling addictions, have you?'

'Whatever – Hyde was attempting to drive and I arrested him. If his solicitor's got a problem, then tough shite. Read him the law, then tell him his client was twice the legal limit. If he wants to call it wrongful arrest, then let him try.'

Topper paused, waiting for the anger to dissipate. 'Believe it or not, that's exactly what Superintendent Jenkinson did before coming in here. He bailed Hyde, then sent the pair of them packing.'

Jessica spun round. 'Oh.'

'Exactly. You should probably apologise.'

'Yeah . . .'

Topper stood, taking a step towards the door. She might have been mistaken, but Jessica was pretty sure he winked at her. 'I suppose it's a coincidence that we're legally allowed to take DNA samples from anyone we arrest.'

'Really?' Jessica replied. 'I'd not even thought of that . . .'

39

Another week, another Hyde funeral – this time on a Tuesday. It was as if the previous eight days had never passed – everyone was in the same position at the same church, doing the same thing, except Richie Hyde was now in the casket, rather than waiting in line. Jessica was standing on the path watching the same collection of people pass through the church doors, offering their condolences to Richard and Natalie Hyde. As the Hydes stared daggers at her, Jessica thought that it had been quite the two weeks. She'd managed to piss off pretty much every crime boss in the city, plus Superintendent Jenkinson and the Serious Crime Division. Even by her standards, it was a monumental effort. Who was left? The Lord Mayor? The Home Secretary?

Her invitation to enter the church ceremony was presumably lost in the post, so Jessica remained outside, Topper and Jenkinson representing the police in paying respects they surely didn't mean. If anything, there were more officers than the previous week, clad in thick chest padding, patrolling the perimeter of the church, whispering into radios. Jessica wasn't entirely sure why she was there, other than punishment, or keeping up appearances. She was left sitting in one of the marked police cars, fiddling with her phone as the ceremony continued.

Forty minutes later, everyone started to emerge, so Jessica got out of the car, watching from the furthest edge of the path closest to the road. For once, she was trying to stay out of trouble.

Richard and Natalie Hyde emerged from the church, heads bowed, shaking hands and saying their thank yous to the people who'd come. Jessica tried to stay out of sight, waiting for Topper and Jenkinson to return so they could get going. They were there to provide a presence and send a message, not be in the way.

Jessica was leaning against one of the stone gateposts, lost in her thoughts, when she heard the footsteps. Richard Hyde was almost upon her, Topper racing after him in a failed attempt to catch up. Hyde was in a smart suit, his shiny shoes clip-clopping across the path. He was sprightly for his age.

Jessica had both her hands up defensively. 'I'm not looking for trouble.'

Hyde stopped a metre from her, staring but not with the same viciousness as when they were at his house. 'I just want a word.'

Topper arrived moments later, out of breath, shirt untucked and looking scruffy. He might be trim but didn't seem much of an athlete as he tried to step between them, arms outstretched. 'This really isn't the place,' he gasped.

'I'd like a private word with your inspector,' Hyde told him. 'Nothing untoward, no problem, no solicitors, just a chat.'

Topper turned to her. 'Jess?'

She nodded towards a spot on the pavement, away from

the graveyard but in sight of the church. She said nothing as Hyde followed a few steps behind until she stopped. Over his shoulder, Jessica could see Topper and Jenkinson standing together, watching them nervously, probably expecting the worst.

Jessica spoke first: 'If you're after an apology . . .'

'On the contrary, I underestimated your deviousness.'

'Cheers.'

'What were the results?'

Jessica glanced towards Jenkinson and Topper, remembering the conversation they'd had earlier when the DNA results had arrived back. Richard Hyde was now a part of the National DNA Database, whether he liked it or not. Unsurprisingly, they'd not been able to pin any unsolved crimes on him, but, as a consequence, they did know the paternity results. Neither Jenkinson nor Topper had specifically told her *not* to give the results away . . .

'Are you telling me you don't know?' Jessica asked.

Hyde seemed nervous, tapping his foot anxiously. 'I wouldn't be asking.'

'Are you sure you want to know?'

'Again, *I wouldn't be asking* . . .'

'I want you to tell me there'll be no repercussions.'

Hyde glanced sideways towards the crowd still emerging from the church. His rivals were all there, watching the private conversation from a distance, wondering what it was about. Natalie would be there too, wondering what Jessica was up to.

He snapped his reply: 'Fine.'

'Tell me properly.'

Hyde stared into her eyes. 'There will be no comebacks, no repercussions. You are completely, one hundred per cent off-limits. Happy?'

'Delighted . . . what's happening with the drink-driving charge?'

He shook his head. 'Seriously?'

'I wouldn't be asking . . .'

He sighed. 'My solicitor was all set to get the lot of you into court and shout the place down, but it's not going to happen.'

'Why?'

'I don't want the trial. I'm going to plead guilty in absence.'

'Really?'

He shrugged. 'My solicitor read me the law, saying he had a few ideas of various precedents that've been set. The problem is, if you take it to the letter, I'd probably be found guilty anyway. It's your word against mine, but the breath-alyser result will go in your favour. If I plead guilty, no one will notice. I have people who drive for me, so I'll take the ban and fine, no harm done. If it goes to trial, it'll be in all the papers. You played your hand and won.'

Jessica bit her lip, not wanting to seem cocky or sarcastic, even by accident. It was a big moment and Hyde was going to get his answers in a public place, with all the people he didn't like watching from afar. It wasn't the time to be a smart-arse. 'Richie wasn't your son,' Jessica said.

Hyde put his hands in his trouser pockets, wanting to appear casual. He took a deep breath and started to nod.

'It's definite – Richie and the other two we know about all share the same father,' Jessica added.

'And you know who . . . ?'

'No, why would we?'

Hyde seemed momentarily surprised, unable to stop his eyebrows rising before he caught himself. It was most likely shock. He had just found out his dead son wasn't his own. He'd lost his wife, one of his best friends. Aside from his daughter, he didn't have a lot left. When he spoke again, he sounded shattered. 'I just . . . I don't know how it works. I'm not sure what to say. Lisa, she . . .'

'I'm sorry you had to find out this way.'

'No . . . I know, it's just we tried long and hard for a second child after Nat. I wanted a boy, not realising that Nat would be the most capable child I could've hoped for. We didn't always get on because Nat took over the business and Richie thought it should've been him . . . I thought he was my little miracle and now . . .' He blinked, realising where he was, the moment of honesty gone. 'I should get back.'

40

For the first time she could remember, Jessica had made an effort to tidy her office. The scattering of paper balls around the bin had been put *in* the bin, her desk had been cleared to the point that she could see the wood, and everything on the spare desk had been lumped into boxes, ready for someone else to sort. She'd even found a two-pound coin in the process. Bonus!

Now she was playing the waiting game . . . or she was until her phone rang unexpectedly. 'Well, well, well . . . look who it is,' she said. 'This is quite the blast from the past.'

Jessica hadn't spoken to Garry Ashford all year. He was a journalist who'd helped her a few times in the past, most recently on the case that might or might not have led to her car blowing up with Adam inside. It wasn't that they'd fallen out, more that Jessica didn't want to deal with his natural suspicion about what had happened to Adam. It was bad enough reconciling with Rowlands. They both must have their fears of something deeper. For now, she'd do what she always did with Garry: annoy him.

'Jessica, hi—'

'How's the engagement going? Has she come to her senses yet?'

There was a sigh: 'If by "senses", you're asking if we're

both really looking forward to the wedding, then yes . . . anyway, I'm calling to give you a heads-up.'

'What's going on?'

'Niall O'Brien.'

'Oh, for—'

'He's called us ten times today and about a dozen times yesterday. He says people are breaking into his house but nobody at your end's doing anything. Sounds like a bit of a nutter to me but there's a story there.'

'He's not a nutter, Garry, he's just an old bloke. We've been to his house and checked for fingerprints and the like but there's no sign anyone's broken into his house – ever – let alone the times he's saying. He says nothing's been stolen but that someone's done his washing-up, or drunk his milk . . . so to speak.'

A hint of a snigger: 'He told me they'd opened his mail.'

Jessica pinched the bridge of her nose. 'There's not much I can tell you, definitely not on the record. You'll have to talk to the press office if you're doing something. We've done everything we're supposed to – more, in fact. I've been out there twice.'

Garry sighed, which reflected her thoughts. 'We're not writing about him as such, more about the stalled development for the park and new houses. He'll be a part of it though – that's what I was tipping you off about.'

'Are you naming me?'

'Not specifically but there'll be something about the police in there.'

'Wonderful . . . y'know, if this goes badly, I'll sneak out there myself in the middle of the night, just to see if he's locked his back door. If it's open then I'll go in and give him a piece of my mind.'

'You're not going to do that, are you?'

Garry was winning the sigh-off, though Jessica threw in another one, trying to keep up: 'No . . . it's just been a long week.'

'Good – he was telling me something about shooting the next person to break in.'

'Please tell me that's not true.'

'I think he was joking.'

'I bloody hope so. Look, I've got to go – but thanks for the tip.'

Out of everything that could go wrong, the one thing GMP's upper management feared the most was bad press coverage. Niall O'Brien's 'case' – if it could be called that – had Jessica's name all over it.

DCI Topper took Jessica by surprise when he finally turned up in her office forty-five minutes later than he'd said he'd be there. She was sure he was greyer than he had been a few weeks before, the strains of the job taking their toll.

He was checking his watch as he closed the door behind him. 'I've not got long.'

'Aren't you going to say "wow", or something similar?' Jessica replied.

'Why?'

'I cleaned.'

Topper perched himself on the corner of the spare desk, peering around the room. 'It looks like someone's emptied a skip in here.'

'Oi!'

'It really does.'

'It's clean compared to this morning.'

Topper ran a hand through his hair. 'I guess that's not saying much. Anyway, I'm at the point where I can't believe your previous chief inspector lasted as long as he did. What was it? Four years?'

'Something like that.'

'What can I help you with?' Topper asked.

'Richard Hyde.'

Topper shook his head. 'Serious Crime aren't going to let you within a mile of him.'

Jessica had expected that reply. 'They've been wanting to get him in the DNA Database for years – I did them a favour.'

'Let's not go over that again. You know why they're annoyed – if he ends up in court for something, his lawyer will argue previous harassment.'

'They won't because he's going to plead guilty for attempting to drink-drive.'

'Who says?'

'He did.'

Topper's eyes narrowed. 'I have no idea how you get away with what you do.'

'Talent.'

He rolled his eyes. 'Serious Crime are still not going to let you anywhere near him. What are you after?'

'I want to know who Richie Hyde's father is. Isaac Foster's too.'

Topper turned as if to leave. 'It's none of our business –

330

we're not some chat show doing paternity tests. What crime are you investigating?'

'*We're* investigating a triple murder.'

He spun back. 'So tell me how it matters – for one, you have *no idea* who Richie's father might be. You can't ask every male in the country to be DNA tested.'

'It matters because everything to do with the Hydes, Carter, Fraser and the rest is to do with relationships and rivalries. It's the centre of everything we do, regardless of the crime.'

'I get that.'

'It's about maths too: two people unknown to each other, who share a father, are in our database. Then there's Richie Hyde.'

'I'm not sure what you're trying to say. Crime runs through all sorts of families.'

Jessica was struggling to explain herself. 'There's Richie Hyde here, Isaac Foster in Liverpool and some girl in Southampton. These three don't know each other. We can argue about nature and nurture, say they inherited this sort of thing from their shared father, or whatever, but that doesn't make sense.'

'Why not?'

'Because if there are three people with the same father, why wouldn't there be more? Say you're the dad—'

'I'm not.'

'Say you are. You have three kids who *all* end up coming to the attention of the police – a one hundred per cent hit rate.'

'Right.'

'How many families do we know where there's a one hundred per cent rate like that? With the worst of families, the ones who are always in trouble, even then there's always one person who we never catch. A brother or sister, uncle or aunt who don't get into the same hassle as the rest.'

If there was a lightbulb over Topper's head, it couldn't have pinged any brighter than the way his eyes lit up. 'There are probably more people with the same father . . .' he said.

'Exactly – we have no idea who killed the two Hydes and Priestley, let alone why. We need to find the father, because we need to know if there are any other children. Any of them could be doing this, or, at the very least, know something about it.'

'*Maths?*' Topper smiled. 'Have you ever used maths as an argument for something before?'

'At the bar when I'm counting my change.'

He nodded, unsurprised. 'This is probably why you get away with the amount you do.'

'There's something else . . . the Fosters from Liverpool used to live in Manchester, but our family in Southampton didn't. Do we really believe that those women and Lisa Hyde had an affair with the same man? With the ages of the kids, they'd have had to all be sleeping with the same man more or less at the same time.'

'We're not a chat show, Jess.'

'In Liverpool, when she and her husband were talking about having children, Nicole Foster said, "You know how hard it was having Isaac". She said she'd had problems conceiving but then it happened. When I was talking to Richard Hyde, he called Richie his "little miracle".'

There was a pause until Topper realised what she was saying: 'They both had fertility treatment?'

Jessica spun her monitor around, showing him the Wikipedia entry for IVF: 'Exactly.'

'Did Richard Hyde mention anything about that?'

'No, which is something I don't understand. He wanted to know if Richie was his son. If he and his wife had been for fertility treatment, he'd know. I don't know enough about this stuff.'

'Could she have had treatment without him?'

'Maybe – I don't know if you can do that. The Fosters are the really confusing ones. We were questioning who Isaac's father was. If they'd had fertility treatment, they'd have made that clear. They'd have said that Rhys was definitely the dad because she was artificially inseminated.'

'So you've shot down your own argument . . . ?'

'Maybe. I want to speak to the Fosters to ask if they had treatment. They didn't say so specifically, just that it was hard having Isaac. If they did, they might have the name of the doctor. If not, I'd have to go through the NHS Trust – which would take ages. That's assuming it is NHS, it could've been private.'

'You haven't got ages.'

'How long?'

'The rest of today.'

'Are you joking?'

Topper shook his head. 'The super's packing up and taking his investigation with him. There's only so long we can keep going over the same things. Take Lisa Hyde – we've got her on traffic camera leaving the airport, we've got her joining the motorway, and then she disappears. We don't know at which junction she got off, nor where she went. The next time the car's spotted, it's abandoned in Eccles; the next time she's seen, she's floating in the canal. The only witnesses who came forward weren't witnesses at all – they saw different cars that were similar, and so on. We got ballistics for the bullet she was shot with – but knowing the type of pistol she was killed with doesn't mean that much when it's so common. I could go on but you've been in the same briefings I have. It's the same story for Priestley and Richie Hyde. This was never something we were going to solve by the usual methods.'

'Which is why you should give me time.'

Another head-shake. 'The decision's been made – they're going to run things from headquarters.' He pointed towards her phone. 'If you really think knowing the father or finding any other children is going to help, then you'd best get on with it.'

41

Nicole Foster sounded exhausted when she answered her phone. Jessica was at her desk, panicking over what Topper had said. She knew she should visit the Fosters in person but there wasn't time. A phone call was so impersonal. Jessica re-introduced herself, receiving a sighed 'oh . . . you'. If she had actually gone there, the door might have been closed in her face.

'Have you got a few minutes free?' Jessica asked.

Nicole sounded more weary than angry. 'Haven't you done enough?'

'I'm really sorry for everything that's happened. I wish there was a better way for this to have come out.'

There was another sigh. 'Rhys is off down the Legion, like usual. I don't blame him, he feels like he's had his life taken away. Isaac hasn't been round in the past two days and I don't know what I'm supposed to do. Neither of them believes me. Isaac keeps asking who his father is but what can I say? I was with no one but my husband when Isaac was conceived. It doesn't make sense. If it was something I could understand, I'd be angry but all I can do is look at the piece of paper they sent us. All anyone will tell me is that the test is ninety-nine point nine nine per cent accurate. I guess I'm the point zero one.'

It felt as if Nicole had been waiting to release those

feelings ever since she'd found out. She sounded lonely. 'This is going to sound a bit odd,' Jessica replied, 'but you said something that stuck with me when I met you. You told Rhys that he knew how hard it was having Isaac. What did you mean?'

There was a pause, then a cough. 'It's such a long time ago . . . there was a long while where we didn't know if I could have children.' Jessica shuddered. She knew those feelings. 'We tried for a while before we got married but it still wasn't happening. We tried to get the NHS to look into IVF but it was harder then and they wouldn't pay for it. We managed to save some money and did it ourselves.'

Jessica didn't understand: 'If Isaac's a test-tube baby, how can his father not be Rhys?'

'That's not how he was conceived. We went to this clinic in Manchester for fertility treatment. It takes about four or five weeks. Do you know how it works?'

'Only a little.'

'Most of it is taking drugs. They fill you full of stuff that makes you produce more eggs, then you get hormone injections every day. The side-effects were awful – I couldn't keep food down most of the time and, even when I could, I felt sick all the time. After ten days or so, they take out some eggs and try to fertilise them. A day later, they see if it's worked. If so, they put them back inside you a couple of days after. That whole thing takes under a week, then you're pregnant or not.'

'You've made it sound really simple.'

Nicole blew out loudly. 'I wish – we went through the information so many times that it's hard to forget. The first treatment didn't take but we had enough money to try one more time. Even if we'd had the money, I don't think my body could have taken any more after that. Some people don't get any side-effects but they were worse for me second time round. I remember one day where I couldn't get out of bed. I went through the whole lot again, praying it was going to work. Then we went to see the doctor and he did his tests and said he was sorry but it hadn't taken.'

Nicole sounded so sad that Jessica found it impossible not to be drawn into the story. A horrible, creeping suspicion was beginning to grip her, something that had been tickling the back of her mind ever since Richard Hyde told her that Richie was his 'miracle'.

'We went home that night and were devastated,' Nicole continued. 'We talked about things like adoption but it was never really serious. I think we were trying to come up with anything to console ourselves as we were so disappointed. Two weeks later, I was pregnant.'

There was a moment of silence. The story had ended so abruptly that Jessica wondered if she'd missed something. 'Sorry . . . you were pregnant?'

'I know, that's what we were like. One day it looked like I'd never have children; then, suddenly, I was pregnant with Isaac.'

'What happened?'

'The doctor told us that the fertility drugs can kick-start things down there. It's rare and not usually that quick, but not unheard of. I suppose he was our little miracle.'

That word again.

'There was only a week to ten-day window,' Nicole said.

'That's when Isaac was conceived. It wasn't with the test tube, it was naturally – I wasn't with anyone other than Rhys, so how can Isaac not be his?'

Jessica wished she had an answer. Perhaps she would in time – by the end of the day if she was going to stay out of trouble. First she needed a crucial piece of information.

'Can you remember the name of the doctor?'

Nicole didn't hesitate: 'Of course – I saw him so many times, he was like family. He retired a few years ago and we went to a party in Manchester. There were hundreds of us.'

It had been fifteen days since Owen Priestley was broken out of the prison van, fifteen days in which they'd chased in circles. After all that time, Jessica was left with barely a few hours until DSI Jenkinson took his ball and sodded off home. After speaking to Nicole Foster and hearing a similar story from the family in Southampton, Jessica had managed to persuade Topper to let her snag Izzy for the rest of the day.

Jessica was in her car, driving the forty miles to Chester in order to visit Dr Matthew Layton. While she'd been arranging the details, Izzy had been looking into Layton's background. Ideally, they would have been able to go through everything before sorting out the visit, but with time short, Izzy was skimming the printouts as Jessica drove. She'd decided that Tuesday afternoons were ideal for motorway driving. There were few cars, hardly anyone to annoy her. Even the lorry drivers were sticking to the inside lane, a rare occurrence seeing as they usually seemed to enjoy overtaking each other by travelling at the exact same speed over the course of ten miles.

Izzy was flicking through the pages. 'How's Niall O'Brien?' she asked.

'Still refusing to move out of his house, still leaving me messages. I'm not sure what to do. His son's staying over but that's not slowed things. He insists someone's coming into his house but there's nothing – literally nothing – that supports that.'

'Have you got to visit him again?'

'Maybe . . . I keep putting it off. There's too much else going on.'

'Hmmm . . .' Izzy plucked off the top page, changing the subject. 'It sounds like Dr Layton was quite famous in his day.'

'Can doctors be famous?'

'Not red-carpet well-known but he got around. He was one of those experts that the papers and the TV news always drag out when the story's too complicated for them to understand. He's quoted all over the place talking about fertility.' She held a page up for Jessica to glance at. 'Bit of a silver fox.'

'If you say so.'

'He's in his seventies now – there was a piece in the *Herald* when he retired ten years ago. They reckon he helped more than a thousand women conceive.'

'I don't think I could ever trust a man who knows more about wombs and cervixes than I do. It's too weird.'

Izzy was skimming through one of the articles. 'It says he was a pioneer in the north west, one of the first to run what they call "an affordable private clinic for fertility treatment".'

'That sounds like a press release if ever I heard one.'

'Probably – but didn't you say the couple from Southampton came up to Manchester for treatment because of the cost? Layton would've attracted people from all around the country.' She continued hunting through the pages. 'Blah, blah, blah . . . lifelong bachelor . . . blah, blah, blah . . . writing papers up until a couple of years ago . . . most of this stuff is quite dull. He was a doctor – what were you hoping to hear?'

Jessica didn't turn her gaze from the road. 'Unfortunately, I think I've already heard it.'

Dr Layton's cottage was a few miles outside Chester, away from busy roads, sitting on the border between Wales and England. It was utterly beautiful, hard to tell if it had been built hundreds of years previously and restored, or if it had been custom-built. There was a thatched roof and thick dark slats, with everything decked out like a small medieval pub. The backdrop was a vast breadth of fields and trees, the smell of recently cut grass drifting on the warm, gentle breeze as a tractor blazed across a velvety field on a bank in the distance. The type of place in which to retire and reflect on a life well spent.

The front door was opened by Layton's carer, a woman in her thirties, wearing a white apron and slightly out of breath. She checked her watch. 'I told you it was cutting it fine, even if you came straight here.'

'I promise we won't take long,' Jessica replied.

The carer was annoyed. 'I know you won't – he's not been out of bed for two days. You did hear me when I told you he has cancer.'

'I heard but I still need to ask him a question.'

'You can ask all you want but if he doesn't answer – or can't – you'll have to leave. I don't care if you are the police. I'm trusted to look after him and that doesn't involve upsetting his routine.'

Jessica didn't argue, following the woman through a low hallway into what would have once been the living room. One half still was, with a television, sofa and armchair, but the other had been converted into a makeshift bedroom. There was a double bed pushed against a wall next to a pair of machines with dials on the front. Jessica didn't know what they did but there was also a stand holding a bag of transparent liquid and a tube hooping down under the bedcovers.

'Dr Layton . . .' The carer was at his side speaking softly but not touching him. '. . . those people are here to see you.'

The bedcovers were tucked tightly, wedging the doctor underneath. He was turned to one side, skin grey, cheekbones sharp, almost skeletal as if there wasn't enough skin to stretch across the shape of his face. He had some small patchy tufts of grey hair but was mostly bald. He looked as ill as anyone Jessica had ever met.

The carer helped him to roll over in order to see Jessica and Izzy, then fussed around him, puffing up a pillow and pressing the palm of her hand to his forehead.

'Would you like some water?' she asked.

Layton tried to shake his head but could barely manage to move. His breaths were shallow and scratchy.

'Can I get you anything else?' she added.

Another shake.

The carer frowned at Jessica. 'I'll be back in five minutes.' She stood still and then re-emphasised the point. '*Five* minutes.'

'Okay.'

When the door was closed, Layton started shuffling, gasping and kicking until he'd loosened the covers. He pressed back onto his pillow, exhausted.

Jessica was wary of the time but didn't want to speak too quickly because she wasn't convinced he could follow her. 'Dr Layton, I'm investigating something in Manchester which has led me to you. I've got a few instances of twenty-somethings sharing the same father, who is unknown to them. None of them knows each other but they share one thing in common – their mothers were treated by you.'

His head dipped up and down slowly, barely moving.

'Is there anything you can think of to explain that?'

Layton's mouth opened and closed like a goldfish.

'These families are real people, desperate for answers.'

He was fighting the covers again, managing to snake a frail arm out of the side of the bed towards her.

'Do you want something?' Jessica asked. 'Water?'

His reply was croaky and painful, though the minuscule hint of a smile told Jessica all she needed to know about the devil lying in front of her. 'I knew you'd come one day . . .'

42

By the time Jessica called Topper and told him what she'd discovered, any thought of DSI Jenkinson shifting the investigation to headquarters had been forgotten. The triple murder was almost a side issue, with a crime far more serious to unravel. Someone would need to speak to Richard Hyde but it would be days before anyone knew what to tell him. Jessica had her own ideas.

She arrived home a little before seven, conscious of how important the evening was to Bex, perhaps her as well. The house smelled of the greatest thing known to mankind. If stores wanted to entice people in, they should forget the aroma of freshly baked bread and go for gravy. Bex was in the kitchen, crouched in front of the oven, trying to peer through the grease-coated door.

'How do people get all this stuff ready at the same time?' she asked.

'You're really asking the wrong person.'

Bex opened the oven, wafting the intoxicating smell of roast potatoes across the kitchen. Jessica's mouth started to water. She'd had an awful day but this wasn't a bad way to finish it. Bex closed the door and fiddled with the cooker dial.

'I thought you were going to be late,' she said.

'I know how important tonight is to you.'

Bex didn't reply, turning back to the stove and stirring the delicately bubbling pan of vegetables.

Helena arrived a little after half seven, out of breath and muttering about the buses. Jessica found herself wanting to dislike Bex's mother for reasons she knew were entirely self-ish. She didn't want Bex to leave and return to the person who'd put her through so much.

As well as cooking, Bex had cleaned the living room and laid the table. Shortly after Helena arrived, the three of them were sitting down to eat a monstrous roast meal. It would have been quite an effort for a Sunday lunchtime, let alone a warm Tuesday evening. Bex had made enough for seven or eight people, with platefuls of roast and new potatoes, carrots, beans, Yorkshire puddings, beef, parsnips and a jug – an actual jug! – of steaming, thick gravy. For the first few minutes, none of them spoke, focusing on the food instead. Jessica couldn't remember the last time she'd eaten so well. For Bex herself, this would have been enough to feed her for a week when she lived on the streets.

Eventually their bellies began to fill – well, Jessica and Helena's, Bex had no such trouble, continuing to eat and eat.

Helena was staring around the living room, momentarily gazing at the photo of Jessica and Adam before moving on. 'This is a nice place.'

'Thank you,' Jessica replied.

She nodded at the photo. 'Is he . . . ?'

'It's complicated. He's not around at the moment.'

'Okay . . .'

Helena peered from Jessica to Bex and back again. 'Do you have any children?'

'Just me.'

'And you're a police officer. I suppose that means you have odd hours . . . ?'

'Sometimes. I make it work.'

'Mum . . .'

Bex cut across them both with a single word. Jessica had interviewed enough people to know when someone was getting at her. Helena wasn't as skilled as the many who'd tried in the past. She was looking for holes in the relationship Jessica had with Bex, wanting to point out how valid she was as an alternative. Bex was clever enough to see it too. She continued chewing, drawing the attention of the two older women, making them wait until she was ready.

Jessica felt as if she was waiting at the back of a courtroom having given evidence. Even when things were tough, she could cope when she was able to influence the outcome. Being in court was the worst: you'd be as honest as you could and stand firm, even when the defence solicitor did all he could to call you a liar without actually using the word. When the magistrates or jury left to reach a decision, it felt like they were casting a verdict on you as a person. Were you believable? Likeable? A nice person? It didn't matter how many times you had been in court, there was always a horrifying sense of nerves. Were the magistrates or jury looking at you? The victim? The accused? Heads, you're decent; tails, you're a dick.

It was nothing to do with the food but Jessica's stomach

was gurgling, butterflies bursting from their cocoons and having a ruck.

Bex licked her lips and clicked her tongue piercing against her teeth. She was focusing on her mother, voice husky and nervous. 'I'm going to stay here, Mum.' Almost instantly she turned to Jessica. 'If that's all right with you?'

'Of course.'

Helena's chin plopped to her chest. 'Oh.'

'It's not you, Mum, it's me. Life's stable here and that's what I need. I'm going to start my course in September and see how it goes. I might hate it, I could drop out after a few months and want to try something else. I'll see how it goes.

'Right.'

'Mum.'

Helena didn't look up. 'What?'

Bex waited, firmly in control. Jessica wondered when she'd made the decision. She herself was so conflicted, thankful that Bex was staying but guilty at the same time. She was an adult, supposedly mature, yet she was clinging onto relief that an eighteen-year-old had chosen her. It felt pathetic. Whether or not she liked it, Helena *was* Bex's mother. She shouldn't feel such pleasure.

Bex's mother eventually peered up, making eye contact.

'I still want you in my life,' Bex said, 'but I can't forget everything that happened . . . not yet.'

'Okay.'

'Are you all right?' Bex added.

Helena shrugged, gazing back at her plate, like a petulant child. Jessica didn't exactly blame her. She'd have had her heart set on getting away from the housing project, into her own place with her daughter at her side. Now, she'd have to come up with something else. For a horrifying moment, Jessica thought either Bex or Helena was going to ask if they could *both* stay. Jessica's mind raced, trying to think of reasons why that couldn't happen, something other than the truth that she didn't want it.

The suggestion never came.

Bex continued eating, the scraping of her knife and fork the only sound until she put them down and said she was going to the toilet. Her footsteps echoed up the stairs, leaving Jessica and Helena alone. Jessica had felt more comfortable sitting opposite any of the crime bosses than next to Bex's mother.

Helena's voice was low enough that no one could overhear. 'I guess you win.'

'I didn't realise it was a competition.'

'She's *my* daughter.'

A long list of critical replies flitted through Jessica's thoughts – *'Then why didn't you act like it?'*, *'You could've fooled me'*, *'Is that how a mother treats a daughter?'* She batted them away, not wanting to argue.

'I've never tried to say she isn't.'

'Then why don't you tell her to leave?' Helena nodded at the photo of Jessica and Adam. 'You have someone.'

'Bex isn't a possession, she's—'

'Her name's Rebecca. *I* named her.'

'She's eighteen and can make her own decisions. I never asked her to stay, I just said that she could. It won't be long and she'll be off doing her own thing; travelling, going to university, meeting a boy or girl who she likes.'

'She's not a lezzer.' Helena's eyes arrowed in on Jessica, seeing something that wasn't there. 'Is that why—?'

'Of course not.'

Helena used her fingers to pick up the mushy remains of a potato, blobs of gravy dribbling onto the plate. 'Blood will always win out. There's nothing like a bond between a parent and child.' She chewed the potato and swallowed. 'Well, what've you got to say?'

'I . . . I'm not sure. I was thinking.'

'About what?'

'Maybe you're right? Blood's won out.'

'What are you talking about? She picked you.'

'I didn't mean Bex.'

Helena was silenced by the flushing toilet and Bex's descending footsteps. The teenager re-entered the living room, smiling at them both, hands on hips. 'Now, seeing as I cooked, I was hoping you'd both do the washing up . . .'

Jessica and Bex's mother were finally united by a collective sigh that made Bex giggle. She turned to her mum: 'If you want a rest first, I can show you some photos of my birthday party . . . ?'

Helena smiled, genuinely as far as Jessica could tell. It felt like their whispered argument was more disappointment on Helena's behalf than anything particularly vicious.

Bex took out her phone, pressing the button on top and then flipping it around. 'Aah . . . battery needs charging.' She turned to Jessica. 'Are there some on your phone?'

'Yeah, though I've probably got more of the food than I have the people.'

Jessica shifted her plate to the side and put her phone on

the table, flicking through the photographs one by one for Helena to see. Bex talked her mum through the names of her friends as Jessica thumbed across the touchscreen. She continued scrolling until moving one photo too far, settling on the e-fit of the woman who'd robbed her next-door neighbour. It was only on there because she'd shown it to Nerys.

'Oops,' Jessica said, scrolling back quickly.

'Go back,' Helena said.

'You shouldn't really have seen that.'

'Why have you got a picture of Fiona on your phone?'

Jessica zoomed back to the e-fit of the woman she knew as Annie. 'You know this person?'

'It's Fiona from downstairs. I told you – she only has a couple of weeks before she moves into her own place. She's making decent money working the city – that's why she's been clearing out her clothes.'

Jessica remembered the overflowing bag when she and Bex had first visited Helena. If Annie was Fiona, then the 'decent money' the woman was making belonged to other people. It was no wonder she was giving away her old clothes if she had enough to afford new ones. Jessica put her phone away, telling Bex and Helena she'd do the washing up – but then she had a few calls to make.

43

It took three days for Jessica and her team to collate the rest of the information they'd been looking for. Despite DCI Topper claiming the Serious Crime Division would never let her anywhere near Richard Hyde, they were willing to do just that. She was the one who'd figured it out, after all. The surveillance engineer managed to wire her up without any accidental groping and off she went into Hyde's casino a little after ten on Friday morning. He'd picked the time and place.

Hyde opened the door, letting Jessica through the front entrance. He peered past her towards her parked car, unable to see, but probably suspecting, the unmarked van parked a short distance across the retail park. He might be many things but stupid wasn't one of them.

Jessica expected there to be an army of staff cleaning, polishing and readying the casino for opening but the main gambling floor was eerily quiet. The lights of the fruit machines twinkled, sparkled and rippled in silent rainbow waves of colour.

Hyde was wearing a suit that was smart but crumpled, as if he'd slept in it. His hair was ruffled and there was a sprinkling of stubble across his face. He was striding quickly as Jessica hurried to keep up.

'Is Natalie around?' she asked.

'It's just us. Did you want her?'

'I was more interested in you.'

Hyde continued until he was behind the bar. He plucked two heavy glasses from under the counter and placed them on the surface with a heavy thud.

'What are you drinking?' he asked.

'I'm on shift.'

'If you want to talk, then you're going to drink.'

'Whatever you're having.'

Hyde skimmed his gaze across the rack of spirits before reaching to the back and pulling out a bottle of brown liquid. He read the label, then moved back to the counter. 'Single malt, eighteen years.'

'Okay.'

He poured two generous measures and passed her one, raising his glass. 'To the end.'

'Is it?' Jessica asked.

'You tell me.'

'Do you know the name Dr Matthew Layton?'

Hyde took a sip, nodding for Jessica to do the same. 'Enlighten me.'

'He's a fertility doctor who ran a private clinic in Manchester.'

Hyde nodded slowly. 'I don't remember the name, but there was a small hospital . . .'

Jessica took a tiny mouthful of the whisky but it didn't burn like many she'd tried. She still shouldn't be drinking, though. 'I hope you can understand why this has taken time, but Dr Layton impregnated at least fourteen women with his own sperm instead of that of his clients. We might never know the full details but he preyed on certain types of women, primarily those whose first attempt at IVF didn't work. We've found thirteen former patients of his, all of whom were told their second attempt had also failed, only for them to become pregnant within weeks, sometimes days. Each time, Dr Layton told them that fertility drugs can spur the reproductive system into action, which it can, except that wasn't true in their cases. Each woman thought it was a pure conception with their partner, when it was Layton himself who'd fertilised their eggs.'

There was a small nod. 'You changed the number: fourteen women, then thirteen former patients . . . ?'

'That's because we can't speak to the fourteenth . . .'

The glass was beginning to shake in Hyde's hand. He tried to take a sip but the whisky ended up dribbling along his chin. He put it down and then, from nowhere, burst into tears. It was uncomfortable enough when anyone was crying, let alone when it was an older man barely metres away from a long row of blinking slot machines. Jessica didn't feel sorry for him, not after everything she was certain he'd done. Hyde squeezed the bridge of his nose, trying to make his emotions go away, but his entire body was heaving.

'That's why Richie wasn't mine . . .'

'Yes.'

Hyde's croaky gasps were hard to make out: 'Lisa . . .' Jessica waited, unsure what to say. 'Why would he tell them they weren't pregnant?' Hyde added.

'Dr Layton isn't speaking. He can't. We're assuming he told the women that because there would be fewer questions. If someone had a son who looked nothing like them who came via IVF treatment, they might query it. With a natural conception – especially for a "miracle baby" – most parents would be blinded.'

Hyde peered up at her, puffy red eyes blazing. 'What do you mean, he can't speak?'

'Dr Layton has cancer and around three months to live, perhaps not even that. There's no point in prosecuting him because he'd be lucky to make the referral hearing, let alone the court case.'

'So he gets away with it?'

Jessica had had this conversation with too many people already, those who rightly wanted justice and were never going to get it.

'I'm sorry.'

This time, she did mean it.

Hyde downed the rest of his drink and reached for the bottle. He threw away the top and swigged deeply. Jessica could sense the surveillance team listening, knowing this was the moment. Hyde was already damned but would he damn himself?

'When did you find out your wife was having an affair with Owen Priestley?'

Jessica left the question hanging, waiting for an angry reaction. She got nothing as Hyde took another mouthful from the bottle.

When it was clear he wasn't going to answer, Jessica continued: 'Priestley told everyone in prison that he didn't rob the off-licence or beat up its owner, even though his blood was at the scene and the victim identified him. I can't say either way but the owner has disappeared and when I asked Nelson Carter about it, he told me to look closer to home. I thought he meant the police but he was telling me to look closer to *Priestley's* home – at the person who'd employed him for twenty-odd years.'

Hyde put down the bottle, his face still blotched by the tears that had now gone. His eyes were red, almost closed.

'When he was inside, Priestley told people he was with someone on the night of the off-licence robbery,' Jessica continued. 'The obvious question is why he didn't tell that to the police. Of course, if it *was* a person he shouldn't have been with, he'd have to choose between prison, or telling the truth. Priestley knew he'd been set up but thought it was Carter. He ended up slashing someone in prison because they worked for Carter, not knowing that *he* should've looked closer to home for who set him up.'

Hyde shrugged, defeated. 'Does it matter now?'

'It matters because that's why all this has happened. This move on your family, this gang war, it was all a smoke-screen.' No reply. 'Why didn't you leave Priestley in prison? Why break him out just to kill him?'

Hyde had the bottle to his lips. 'I was on holiday.'

'We both know your tendrils stretch a lot further than that. Of course you were on holiday – that's why you went, because it was a great alibi. When Priestley was broken out, the first name that came up was yours. But Eric Maudsley owed this place money. Someone told him that'd all be for-gotten if he could do one simple job. All he needed was a mate. He might be useless but at least he'd keep his mouth shut and that was the most important thing.'

Hyde might not be much of a talker but give him a bottle of whisky and he was quite the listener.

'When did you come to the conclusion that Richie wasn't your son?' Jessica asked.

Hyde nodded at her glass. 'You drinking that?'

'No.'

He snatched it away, downing it in one. 'You tell me.'

'If only we'd checked two weeks ago, we might've avoided some of this but there was no reason to do so. I think what really sent you wild, the thing that made you decide that leaving Priestley in prison wasn't enough, was when your wife started to visit him. Her name's there in the records – Lisa Hyde. You knew they were seeing one another, which is why you arranged for Priestley to be set up. But it kept niggling at the back of your mind that the affair might have been going on for a lot longer. You told me you wanted a son but Richie was a disappointment to you. He had none of Natalie's drive or ability. He didn't seem much like you.'

'He *wasn't* much like me.'

'When you approached me outside the church after Richie's funeral, you thought we were closer to you than we actually were. Priestley had been in the DNA Database for a while and you expected me to say that *he* was Richie's father. When I told you we didn't know, it changed everything. You were confused – I saw it in your face but misread it at the time. You thought there must've been a mistake, but, when it was clear there wasn't, that's when you realised the only mistake was yours.'

'*Mistake . . .*'

'How much of it was down to Natalie?'

Hyde had slumped onto his elbows but he jolted away from the bar. 'This is *nothing* to do with my daughter.'

'It's everything to do with her unless you tell me differently.'

'Leave my daughter out of this.'

'We've got three murders to investigate and a motive for both you and her. If that means we have to dig and dig into the pair of you, then we will.'

'Not my daughter.'

'It's your choice.'

Hyde seized the bottle again, peering at the murky, sloshing liquid and then putting it down again. 'Are they listening?'

Jessica shrugged. 'You tell me.'

He nodded, knowing it was over regardless of what happened. He'd lost one of his most-trusted workers, his wife and the boy he'd raised as his son. He wasn't going to let Natalie go too.

'It's nothing to do with Nat,' he insisted.

'So tell me.'

Hyde gulped, speaking slowly, choosing his words. 'A couple of years ago, a dear friend of mine died. I grew up with Harry Irwell and we ended up going our separate ways, each running different businesses, employing different people. It was all a bit of fun, until it wasn't. I sent my children abroad to keep them safe from him. They returned as he died and it was then I started to think about retiring. Richie was never going to be up to it but Nat . . . she might be a woman but she's as capable as any man I've worked with. With me starting to scale back how much I did, I ended up at home, pottering around, playing golf and getting old. I started clearing out all our old things and found a letter from Owen to Lisa, written twenty-five years ago. There was nothing explicit but there didn't need to be, it was there in the way he phrased things.'

'What then?'

'The timing was all there, so I had a private DNA test done. I sent off some of my hairs with some of Richie's. It took about two weeks and then they told me: not my son.'

It was largely as Jessica had thought. 'I'll need details – specifics of what was done to Priestley, Lisa and Richie.'

He shrugged. 'I'll tell you what you want.'

Jessica was about to arrest him formally when she had a thought. She cupped her palm across the microphone clipped to her bra and lowered her voice. 'When did you start having me followed?'

Hyde stared at her, before he shook his head. 'Do you really think I'd worry about following people?'

Jessica let go of her top, releasing the microphone, realising he was right. People like Hyde didn't bother watching people, they acted. She wondered if the person in the dark hood was her mind playing tricks. Loads of people wore dark clothes, even in summer. The street on which she lived wasn't exactly heaving with people, but it wasn't quiet either. After everything that had happened to Adam, it was a wonder that paranoia had taken this long to set in.

Hyde was standing, peering back towards the drinks cabinet. 'There's just one more thing I'd like to do before we go.'

'What?'

He started fussing through the bottles behind the bar again.

Jessica knew her colleagues would be moving outside. There'd be a marked car outside the main doors, plus more officers just in case. Jessica doubted they'd be needed: Hyde had lost everything but his daughter and would do anything to make sure she was unaffected.

'What are you looking for?' Jessica asked.

Hyde ignored her, running his hand underneath the counter until she heard Velcro snapping. She saw it happening almost in slow motion, the holster being unhooked and the pistol in Hyde's hand. It was metallic and dark, with a thick handle that fitted perfectly in his hand. Jessica put her hands up instinctively but Hyde wasn't interested in her, using the barrel to scratch his chest.

Time sped up as he stared at her, eyes glazed, unfocused. 'I'm not going to prison.'

44

The tea machine in the canteen of Longsight Police Station had a strop on. It was probably the years of abuse over the state of its drinks. If it had feelings, which was admittedly doubtful, all the hurtful remarks had to be grating on it. The physical abuse probably wasn't helping, either.

Jessica thumped a palm into the reject button. 'It's stolen my money.'

Thump, thump, thump.

She turned to Rowlands, who was sitting at a nearby table, smiling a bit too smugly for her liking. 'This thing owes me 40p.'

'It's been doing that all day. I think someone's coming to fix it. Someone should probably put a sign up.'

'Why didn't you say something?'

He shrugged. 'I thought it'd be funny.'

Jessica slumped into the seat opposite. 'That's 40p you owe me.'

'It is not.'

'I suppose you've got enough on your plate . . .'

Rowlands smiled wearily. 'I didn't dump Katy. We went out the other night and I got the conversation around to her family. We couldn't keep going out without telling her dad, so I said we should do it.'

'How did Franks take it?'

'He went off on one, saying he'd singled me out to work with him, that he was passing on his years of experience and expertise in order to help me progress, and that he couldn't believe this was how I was repaying him.'

Jessica struggled not to laugh. '*Expertise?* At what? Hanging around toilets?'

'I know. There wasn't much he could say – but he's not happy.'

'If you're really lucky, he'll palm you off onto someone with half a brain.'

'I doubt it, he'll keep me around to torment me.'

Jessica nodded. 'Probably – I would.'

She felt restless, needing something to fiddle with. The tea might be awful but the machine at least provided cups that were easy to tear to shreds and create spinning plastic helicopters.

Rowlands was loosening his tie: 'We're up to five people robbed by Fiona Grant, all over sixty and living alone. Most are smaller amounts of money but she stole at least eight thousand in total. Hopefully more people will come forward when they read about her being in court.'

'I should've left it with you in the first place.'

He shrugged. 'She was only found by accident.'

'If it wasn't for accidents and stupid people, we'd never solve anything.'

He laughed. 'Speak for yourself.'

The main door banged as a pair of constables headed towards the counter, smiling and chatting. Jessica watched them, remembering when she was their age, wondering if this was what she wanted from life. In many ways, she still wasn't sure, but being here with her friends was all she knew. The job had made her who she was – good and bad – but it could take it away, too.

'Is there any news on . . . ?'

Rowlands didn't need to finish the question because Jessica knew who he was talking about.

'Adam's in the same place he has been for months. Not getting better, not getting worse. He's just there.'

Jessica didn't know what else to say. She'd crafted two worlds, one in which she could go about her daily life, the other where it was just her and Adam. If she were to face the horror of what had happened to him, she'd never leave the hospital.

Déjà vu.

Topper appeared in the doorway, hand on hip, smiling thinly, knowing Jessica would rather stay where she was.

Jessica stood, ready to go. 'Thanks.'

'For what?' Rowlands asked.

'Not being a dick.'

Roll up, roll up: the Press Pad was all set for the show. Microphones were pointed; cameras angled; journalists bored, wondering when the fun would start. The front of the room was decorated with a white piece of card covered with the GMP logo. A desk was set up in front with four seats, each fronted by copperplate name cards. An investigation was never complete until the press conference. There was no point in solving stuff if the Chief Constable or one of the assistants couldn't turn up at the end, looking serious with a row of medals pinned to his lapel.

Topper ushered Jessica into a storage room along the corridor. Buckets and mops were packed towards the back, with the toxic whiff of cleaning fluid working its magic on her sinuses.

'I wanted to make sure you're going to be all right in there,' Topper said.

'Is Pomeroy here?'

'Yes, it was felt this needed the gravitas of the Chief Constable.' Jessica's expression must've told the story because Topper asked what he never had before: 'What happened between you?'

'You wouldn't believe me if I told you.'

He stared at her for a moment, before nodding acceptingly and heading back into the corridor. Someone in a plaid jacket she didn't recognise was hurrying into the Pad but the hall was otherwise empty. A low chatter was spilling from the media room, anticipating confirmation of what they'd already been told: Richard Hyde had killed Priestley, his wife and his son, consumed by jealousy and rage over a child that, ultimately, came from Dr Matthew Layton. Two huge stories were colliding in a flurry of front pages. Only Natalie Hyde was left, sitting atop a crumbling empire, her family wiped out. Jessica had the feeling that the young woman would find a way to thrive.

Topper nodded at a closed door. 'Rosie's in there waiting for us.'

Jessica shook her head. 'I don't think I can face her. She's crazy. She's supposed to do our PR but she keeps saying how she can get me extras work on *Corrie* if I fancy it.'

Topper smiled: 'Do you?'

Jessica's reply would have been short and direct but she didn't get a chance to deliver it as the door was flung open. Chief Constable Graham Pomeroy emerged, a behemoth of a man, chins wobbling, belt fighting the laws of physics to cling on for dear life. Superintendent Jenkinson was behind him, tarted up, ready for the cameras. Pomeroy shook hands with Topper, muttering congratulations before turning to Jessica. She'd refused his handshake in the past and he didn't bother trying again.

'Inspector.'

'Sir.'

She wondered what else he might say but Rosie bundled her way out of the side room, tripping over a cable and sending a noxious guff of flowery perfume towards them.

'Jessica's not been feeling well,' Topper said. 'I think it's best if she sits the conference out.'

Pomeroy and Jenkinson stared at her, each probably relieved that she wouldn't get the opportunity to say something stupid. Jessica was fine with it, wanting neither to be front and centre, nor to share the same space as Pomeroy.

Rosie ushered Topper, Jenkinson and Pomeroy towards the door to the Press Pad, where the volume of the chattering media dropped to an expectant whisper. Jessica slipped in behind Rosie unseen, sidling close to a cameraman where she had a view of the entire room. At the front desk, Rosie was removing the name card bearing Jessica's name, with Topper rearranging the chairs to make it seem as if they had only ever intended for there to be three officers answering questions. Journalists were placing their phones and dictaphones on the desk, then taking their seats. Pomeroy was in the centre, ready to bathe in the glory he wasn't due.

Phwooosh.

There was a pop as the bright white lights at the back of the room were turned on, dousing the three officers in an instant paleness. Topper and Jenkinson were blinking rapidly but Pomeroy's eyes were wide, staring towards the far end of the room. Neither Topper nor Jenkinson noticed what was happening between them but Jessica knew. Pomeroy started patting his left arm, then clasped for his tie. As he gasped for air, the front row of journalists realised something was wrong. There was a camera flash and then Jenkinson's chair went spinning into the GMP backdrop as he stood too quickly, calling 'ambulance'.

Everyone stood, trying to get a view in order to work out what was going on. As they surged forward, Jessica slipped into the corridor, hands in her pockets, phone firmly untouched. If Pomeroy wanted an ambulance, he could call for it himself. She hoped it drove carefully.

45

Spencer O'Brien opened the front door and sat on the step waiting and watching as the spinning blue lights filled the hallway. Someone had sent an ambulance anyway, though the paramedics wouldn't have much to do. People in uniform had already gone upstairs to speak to Spencer's father, though what could be said? He might be in his seventies, he might be a war veteran, but he'd set a trap and killed a police officer. They might never know if anyone had ever been breaking in. Perhaps he'd been leaving the door open the entire time, or maybe it was all in his head. For now, Spencer could only assume that DI Daniel had been round the back of the house, spotted the back door open, and then come in to see if anything was going on.

A red Corsa careered between two of the marked police cars that were scattered across the main road and screeched to a halt. A woman climbed out of the driver's seat, not turning the engine off as she dashed towards the house. She was wearing pyjamas with a teddy-bear pattern, wrapped in a dressing gown. Behind her a man with curly hair trailed. Spencer recognised them both . . . except that it couldn't be true. She stopped in the doorway, peering down at him.

Spencer tried to say something, but could only manage a croaked: 'It's you, but . . .'

She pressed past him, heading towards the kitchen, the curly haired man behind her. Spencer followed, the kitchen crowded with officers, paramedics, the two newcomers and himself all crammed into a small place, trying not to corrupt the scene.

One of the uniformed officers held his arms wide. 'Scene of Crime are on the way. Everyone should clear out.' The woman peered around him, so he stepped in front of her. 'Sorry, who are you?'

She pushed him away. 'I'm DI Daniel.'

The officer turned towards the body on the floor, the ID card bearing Jessica's name facing up: '*You're* DI Daniel? So who's that?'

Jessica turned to the man she'd arrived with. 'Well, Arch – I hope you've got an explanation because I bloody haven't.'

46

Archie turned in a circle as a series of camera flashes lit up the room like a low-rent fireworks display. 'I didn't know . . .'

They both realised the subsequent investigation was going to reveal their relationship, though that was the least of their problems. First of all, they had to deal with Paige Pearson. After identifying the woman's body and leaving the O'Brien house, the tactical entry squad had helped them blast their way into her flat underneath Archie's. The living room was covered with photographs of Archie, many snapped from Paige's window with him in the car park outside the building. He was smiling in some, talking on his phone in others, scratching his balls in at least three, and generally coming and going. Interspersed with the pictures of him on his own were others of him with Jessica.

This was really not good. They'd not done anything wrong and there were no rules specifically banning officers from having relationships with one another. It happened all the time, plus they weren't *really* in a relationship . . . they just 'spent time' together away from work.

Paige clearly hadn't seen it that way. In her bedroom, there was a photograph of herself, next to a photograph of Jessica. The picture of Paige was marked with narrow red lines around her hair and the word *BLONDE* at the top.

Archie sat on the bed, staring at the photographs. 'I didn't know she was like this.'

'Did you sleep with her?' Jessica closed the door, leaving the other officers banging around in the rest of the house. 'Arch.'

'What?'

'Did you sleep with her?'

'Once or twice . . . before you.'

She slapped his arm. 'For Christ's sake, I'm not asking for me. What did you do? Dump her?'

'No, I thought it was a bit of fun. I didn't realise she was . . .' He threw his hands up.

'Don't you dare call her a nutter.'

'She was in the Duck and we had a drink. She asked about going out some time but I said I was seeing someone.'

'Did you tell her about Hair 'n' Dipity?'

'Huh?'

'When we were out, I told you I was getting my hair sorted – did you tell her?'

'I don't know . . . I found the name funny. I might've done.'

Jessica pointed at the pictures. 'She got *her* hair done to seem more blonde, like me. Then when you told her about the shop I was going to, she phoned up pretending to be me and cancelled it. She was trying to look like me.'

'How do you mean?'

'You saw her fake ID. It had my name on it with a picture of her.'

'But why was she at the O'Brien's house?'

'No idea.'

Archie suddenly sat up straighter, delving into his pocket. 'She's been calling me ever since I saw her in the pub. I just ignore the calls. Hang on.' He held the phone to his ear and then placed it on the bed, hitting the speakerphone button.

A woman's robotic voice echoed around the room: 'You have one new message.'

Archie pressed a button and then another female voice sounded: 'Oh, hey, Arch. It's me again . . . erm, Paige from downstairs. I guess you're not answering your phone. I was hoping we could do something together again. I had a great time in that Duck place, hope you did too . . . er . . .' She sighed. 'Look, I saw that thing in the *Herald* about that bloke whose house keeps getting broken into. I know you like other police people, so I was thinking maybe I could go and talk to them, something like that. Perhaps even go one night to see if there's anyone hanging around . . . maybe tonight.' There was a muffled scrabbling sound. 'How does that sound? Is tonight all right for you? If you get this, perhaps meet me there? We can do one of those whatchamacallits . . . stake-outs. Anyway, hope to hear from you. Love you, babes.'

Archie had his head in his hands. 'Oh, shite . . .'

47

Jessica tried to push her key into her front door but it wasn't having it. She twisted, poked and prodded, before trying the handle.

It was already unlocked.

Bex's keys jangled against the inside of the double-glazed door as Jessica closed it behind her. The house smelled vaguely of burning, as if someone had charred a few toast slices a few hours previously.

'Bex?'

There was no answer, so Jessica headed into the kitchen. There was a red light on top of the electric cooker, a trickle of smoke wafting airily from the pan on the stove. Jessica switched the cooker off, peering into the pan to see a crusty lump of baked beans welded to the bottom, the juice completely evaporated. The cooker dial had been on low, so the beans must have been simmering for a while. Two slices of uncooked bread were poking out from the toaster.

'Bex?'

Still no answer.

Jessica was really hoping to see her friend after such a long day. As it stood, neither she nor Archie were in trouble – they'd done nothing wrong – but it looked very bad. She really needed someone with whom to share some wine, have a gossip and watch dreadful TV.

Jessica went upstairs, glancing through the open door into the empty bathroom and then knocking on Bex's bedroom door. There was no reply, so she headed inside. Bex's room was as tidy as always. There was a row of textbooks on the shelf above the bed, with pairs of trainers and shoes neatly lined up against the wall. The wardrobe doors were open, revealing a rack of clothes, but no Bex. Jessica made to leave before turning back to the shoes. There were two pairs of trainers, some low heels donated by Jessica, and slippers. As far as she knew, they were all the shoes Bex owned.

Jessica took out her phone and called Bex's number, only to hear a pop song bursting from somewhere downstairs. She followed the noise, heading into the living room to find Bex's phone lit up and vibrating on the sofa. Jessica hung up and picked up Bex's phone. There was a lock to which she didn't know the password, but nothing on the screen other than the missed call from her.

She turned in a circle, listening to the silence. What could have happened that made Bex leave the house without her shoes or phone, leaving the cooker turned on? She'd never done any of those things before, let alone all three in one go.

Jessica headed back through the front door, stepping over the low wall that separated her house from Alf's.

He smiled as he answered the door: 'I've been meaning to knock on your door to say thank you for catching that woman, Fiona or Anne, whatever she was called.'

'I was only doing my job.'

'At least she won't be able to do it to anyone else.'

'Have you seen Bex today?'

Alf shook his head. 'Don't think so.'

Jessica didn't want to be rude, allowing Alf to make small talk before she finally got away. Back in the house, she checked for messages on the house phone, though there were none.

Something felt wrong, not just the fact that Bex wasn't there, but because of the events of the past few weeks: the return of Bex's mother, the death of Paige, and – possibly – someone else entirely watching the house.

Jessica peered through the window towards the empty back yard, then returned to the kitchen. Pinned to the fridge with magnets was the word 'Helena' and a number. Jessica called it, waiting. One ring, two rings. Three.

'Hello?'

'Helena, this is Jess.'

'Oh . . .'

'Have you heard from Bex today?'

'No . . . is everything okay?'

She sounded worried, the way a mother should. Jessica wondered if she should be truthful and tell Helena how concerned she was – but it felt silly. Bex was eighteen, an adult. If she had gone out with her friends without saying anything, then that was up to her, even if she had left the cooker on and disappeared without her phone or keys, and with no shoes.

Jessica muttered a quick 'it's fine', before making her excuses and hanging up. She scraped the saucepan's crispy remains into the bin and left it to soak in the sink before returning to the living room. She switched on the television and eased onto the sofa, waiting for Bex to come through the front door, full of apologies, acting like the teenager she was. She had to be okay . . . didn't she?

AFTERWORD

I seem to keep ending these books on cliffhangers . . .

For those wondering, many of the characters who appear here also show up in one of my other books, *Down Among the Dead Men*. It's a prequel of sorts, where you find out what really happened between the Hyde and Irwell families.

Nothing but Trouble wasn't my original title for this book. My first draft was called *The Death of Jessica Daniel*, which was probably a bit *too* naughty, although it amused me then and now. Hope you don't mind my little bit of deception.

Thanks to my agent, Nicola, plus the crew at Pan. There's Tom, the other Tom, Alex, Susan and Trisha.

This series is now eleven books old. In literary terms, that's sixty years old . . . or perhaps I'm thinking of dog years. It's certainly a lot of words in the life of Jessica Daniel and, now I've got her death out of the way, I can get on with even more stories about her.

Above all, thanks to you for reading and for sticking with the series. There's more to come.

Cheers,

Kerry Wilkinson

Interview with Jessica Daniel

My first impression of Detective Inspector Jessica Daniel is that she seems a very angry individual. There's a bluster of straightened browny-blonde hair, and an open tone of something close to hostility.

'There,' she says, lumping a wad of papers onto the coffee table between us.

She's ten minutes late for our interview and this is the first word she says. It's not usually how a subject would introduce themselves. I'm not even sure she's the person to whom I'm supposed to be speaking. This could be one big case of mistaken identity.

'Sorry . . . ?' I reply limply. If I'm honest, I'm slightly intimidated. I'm sitting by myself in a quiet cafe, sipping from a sweetened cup of tea. The woman towering over me is sagging from what I imagine to be a series of long days. It looks like she's battled through a torrential downpour, which, given the Manchester weather, she probably has. Then she breaks into a smile and straightens her suit jacket. When she grins, it's not even really with her lips. There's a slight upturn, but it's all with her eyes. A defiant streak of mystery and mischief.

'That's what the media department gave me,' she adds. 'A list of things not to say, key messages I'm supposed to get across. I think they want me to give you a foot rub or something. Get you on board.'

I glance down at the top sheet of paper she's plonked on the table and there it is:

> *Mention the community outreach programme*
> *Do not swear*
> *Remind reporter that knife crime is down by 61%*
> *Try to use the word 'us' instead of 'the police'*
> *Use reporter's name frequently (Her name is LUCY)*

The list goes on.

'You can have that if you like,' DI Daniel adds. 'Save me carrying it around. Oh, and by the way, knife crime is down by sixty-one per cent. If you could write that, someone owes me a Kit Kat.'

She smiles once more and then nods at my half-empty cup of tea. 'The shortbread whirls are amazing. You want one? It's not quite up there with a chocolate Hobnob, but it's on the way.'

I tell her I'm fine and then she's off. It's hard to stop watching her as she approaches the counter. The barista is drawn to her, two magnets connecting, and then it's all complaints about the weather and traffic, a joke about the menu. It's effortless and then she's back with me talking about how she's suspicious of anyone who drinks tea without milk. She bought me a short-bread whirl anyway. A 'peace offering' for her lateness.

It's a good fifteen minutes of back and forth before she blinks up at me through those greeny-blue eyes and remembers why she's here.

'Careers,' she says. 'You write about careers.'

'For the *Saturday* magazine,' I tell her. Then: 'What qualities would you say are required of someone who wants to be a police officer?'

It's a standard question. A bit boring, if I'm honest. It's the first serious grilling in our conversation and she takes a moment to think as she sips from her tea and glances up at the ceiling.

Then the smile is back. 'A love of paperwork,' she says. 'You've got to be in to lots of meetings as well, plus you have to learn another language. This sort of corporate double-speak where you can waffle on for ten minutes and not really say anything. It's a real skill. You need a meeting face, too.' She looks at me, neither smiling nor scowling, gaze fixed as she nods.

'"Yes, guv",' she deadpans. '"Amazing idea that, guv. Good thinking. I'd have never come up with that."'

She pauses, features softening. 'You're not going to print that, are you?'

I say I can leave it out if she wants. It's her interview. She pauses to think, but I'm not sure she's really considering it. 'Nah, leave it in,' she replies. 'Just bang on about the community outreach programme as well, and it'll all even out.'

I laugh. It's hard not to because it's so rare to be told the truth. Everyone, understandably, wants to talk up the better parts of their jobs. Outrageous hours become 'a committed environment'; low pay is 'an opportunity for advancement'. These are the lies we tell ourselves and yet I get the sense that DI Daniel has no such delusions about who she is and what she does.

'It's the people,' she says quietly, taking me by surprise. For the first time in our conversation she's not looking directly at me. She's staring off towards the counter, perhaps a little embarrassed at her own sudden gravity.

'You have to care about other people.'

There's a moment between us that's hard to write about.

A second or two of understanding. At its core, journalism is about people, too; it's about telling the stories of others.

'How do you cope?' I ask. It's an odd question, I know. I'm not even sure where it comes from. It wasn't what she said, it was the way she said it. Among the jokes and sideways glances, away from the asides about milk and the weather, there's a glimmer of vulnerability.

There's no smile this time. No smirking or joking. 'I guess you figure it out,' she says. 'It's nice when someone says "thank you".'

I ask her what she means and her forehead ripples with a frown. 'You say "thank you" for everything, don't you? Hold a door open for someone and it's "thanks". Let someone in at a junction and you get a thank-you wave. Sometimes people don't even realise how nice it is to hear that. When you've interviewed a load of people, searched through hours of CCTV, matched everything against each other, put the case together, gone to court and got a conviction . . . when you've done all that and someone says "thank you", when they *really* mean it because you've had a positive effect on their lives . . .'

She tails off, perhaps catching herself in this newfound seriousness because her eyes twinkle again.

'Well, yeah,' she adds. 'That's all right. Not a patch on a packet of choccie biscuits, though, is it? By the way, *Lucy*, did I mention that knife crime is down by sixty-one per cent?'

SOMETHING WICKED

Kerry Wilkinson

*There's nothing worse than watching your child
walk out the front door, never to return . . .*

Nicholas Carr disappeared on his eighteenth birthday and the world has moved on. His girlfriend is off at university, his friends now have jobs and the police are busy dealing with the usual gallery of thieves and drunks.

But his father, Richard, can't forget the three fingers the police dug up from a sodden Manchester wood. What happened to Nicholas on the night he disappeared, and why did he never return home?

A private investigator is Richard's last hope – but Andrew Hunter has his own problems. There's something about his assistant that isn't quite right. Jenny's brilliant but reckless, and he can't figure out what she gets from working for him. By the time he discovers who's a danger and who's not, it might all be too late . . .

SOMETHING HIDDEN

Kerry Wilkinson

The second book featuring private investigator
Andrew Hunter

Everyone hates Fiona Methodist.

Her war veteran father shot a young couple in broad daylight before killing himself. The engaged pair had witnessed a robbery and were due to give evidence but, with all three now dead, no one knows the true motive.

For Fiona, it's destroyed her life. It's not just those who whisper behind her back or the friends who pretend she doesn't exist; it's the landlords who spot her name and say no, the job agencies who can't find her work.

But Fiona knows her dad didn't do it. He couldn't have – he's her father and he wouldn't do that . . . would he?

Private investigator Andrew Hunter takes pity on the girl and, even with stolen bengal cats to find, plus an ex-wife who's not quite so 'ex', he can't escape the creeping feeling that Fiona might be right after all.

DOWN AMONG THE DEAD MEN

Kerry Wilkinson

Money can't buy everything . . .

Jason Green's life is changed for good after he is saved from a mugging by crime boss Harry Irwell. From there, he is drawn into Manchester's underworld, where stomping into a newsagents and smashing the place up is as normal as making a cup of tea.

But Jason isn't a casual thug. Fast cars and flash clothes don't appeal – he's biding his time and saving his money, waiting for the perfect moment to make a move.

That is until a woman walks into his life offering one thing that money can't buy – salvation.

OUT NOW

FOR RICHER, FOR POORER

Kerry Wilkinson

Jessica Daniel – Book 10

Three houses have been burgled in five weeks. The robbers break in through the back, disable any contact with the outside world, and then ransack everything – before distributing the stolen cash to local charities.

It might be robbing from the rich to give to the poor, but Detective Inspector Jessica Daniel is not happy. The new DCI has a whiteboard with far too many crimes on the 'unsolved' side and he wants the burglars found.

Doesn't he know Jessica has enough on her plate? There's a lottery winner who's gone bankrupt; the homeless teenager she's taken in; a botched drugs raid; a trip to London with DC Archie Davey – and a man-mountain Serbian with a missing wife who's been pimping out young women.

All the while, someone's watching from the wings and waiting for Jessica to mess up. Officers are being pensioned off and booted out, and a certain DI Daniel is firmly in their sights.

NOTHING BUT TROUBLE

Kerry Wilkinson has been busy since turning thirty.

His first Jessica Daniel novel, *Locked In*, was a number one ebook bestseller, while the series as a whole has sold one million copies.

He has written a fantasy-adventure trilogy for young adults, a second crime series featuring private investigator Andrew Hunter, plus the standalone thrillers *Down Among the Dead Men* and *No Place Like Home*.

Originally from the county of Somerset, Kerry has spent far too long living in the north of England, picking up words like 'barm' and 'ginnel'.

When he's short of ideas, he rides his bike or bakes cakes. When he's not, he writes it all down.

For more information about Kerry and his books visit:

www.kerrywilkinson.com or www.panmacmillan.com

www.twitter.com/kerrywk

www.facebook.com/JessicaDanielBooks

Or you can email Kerry at kerrywilkinson@live.com

extracts reading groups
competitions books new
discounts extracts extracts
competitions extracts discounts
books new events
events extracts books reading groups
extracts new titles reading groups reading groups
interviews extracts new
books events extracts events books
discounts interviews new
new books events books extracts
events new events
discounts extracts discounts books

www.panmacmillan.com

extracts events reading groups
competitions books extracts new books